MILLION
ARE A GIRL'S BEST FRIEND

MILLIONAIRES ARE A GIRL'S BEST FRIEND

LOUISE BRODERICK

Published 2018
By Lavender and White Publishing,
Cornwall,
England.
Email info@lavenderandwhite.co.uk

LOUISE BRODERICK 2018

The moral right of the author has been asserted.
Typesetting, layout and design Lavender and White Publishing.

A huge vote of thanks to superb artist Tony O'Connor of White Tree Studio for allowing me to use some of his amazing paintings for my book covers. More of Tony's equestrian and animal paintings can be found on his website www.whitetreestudio.ie

www.lavenderandwhite.co.uk

Contents

MILLIONAIRES – ARE A GIRL'S BEST FRIEND

CHAPTER ONE

The worst thing of all was that Rory laughed. And it wasn't as if it was a sympathetic oh-what-a-dreadful-thing-to-happen kind of embarrassed chuckle. No - this was a full-blown what-a-fool-you-have-made-of-yourself kind of guffaw.

At first Stella hadn't realised that there was anything wrong.

"This is my horse," Rory had announced proudly as an enormous prancing mass of muscle and flailing hooves was led across the parade ring towards them, "and my trainer, Henry Murphy," he said, shaking hands with the tall man who had walked across the damp turf to join them.

Stella had done a double take. Henry was gorgeous. Stella dragged her eyes away from him to look at the nondescript looking owners and trainers who were standing in the parade ring. Then she chanced a look back at him. Yes. He was defiantly gorgeous.

"Move Out looks very well," Rory yelled above the roar of the spectators watching the races as the horse halted beside them.

Move Out's black coat shone was damp with sweat, his small white teeth champed frenziedly at his bit sending showers of foam into the air as he tossed his elegant head, while his sour looking girl groom, red-faced from exertion, clung to his bridle, her knuckles white with the effort.

Henry grinned, gazing lovingly at the horse. "He should do well in this next r......".

And that was when Stella realised that something was wrong. Amid the cacophony of noise from the racecourse there was a stunned silence from the group surrounding them.

And everyone was staring at her.

Stella felt a cold shiver of horror run down her spine, sending icy tendrils over her limbs, as if a bucket of cold water had been thrown over her. She gazed at the wide-eyed, shocked expressions of those surrounding them.

And that was when Rory started to laugh.

Stella looked down at the beautiful cream jacket that she had brought especially for the day. A huge blob of dirty greenish brown foam from the horse's mouth had landed on the front of her jacket, and had dripped slowly downwards leaving a stain in its wake while small splatters of foam covered one arm. Slowly Stella raised her head and looked with intense hatred at the man who had ruined her first date with Rory. Henry's face was filled with concern, but in his eyes she read……. something……. Amusement no doubt Stella decided.

"Excuse me, I need to go to the ladies to get cleaned up," Stella whispered tearfully before turning away and walking with as much dignity as she could muster across the seemingly endless stretch of grass of the parade ring. The amused and cruel sounding laughter of those who had witnessed her embarrassment rang in her ears.

The racehorses were being led around the concrete path that circled the parade ring intense looking grooms clung to their bridles as their nervous charges pranced in anticipation of the coming race. The exit from the parade ring was barred by the horses, Stella waited fretfully, aware of the curious stares of the spectators.

An enormous grey horse, scared by a sudden gust of autumn wind that lifted his brightly coloured rug jumped sideways towards Stella. Panic stricken she darted out of the way of his flailing hooves and enormous grey body, feeling her high heels sinking into the damp grass, slowing her down. She crashed into an elderly horse faced woman who tutted as Stella stammered an apology and then seeing a gap in the line of horses made a dash for the edge of the ring.

Stella ducked under the white guard rail at the edge of the parade ring, the line of spectators who had been leaning on the rail moved out of the way. She was aware of their looks of amusement and sympathy as they noticed her ruined jacket and painfully aware of her face, burning crimson with embarrassment and disappointment.

Only pride kept her from crying out as she walked through the racecourse towards a sign for the toilets positioned high above the racecourse with an arrow pointing to a dingy looking red brick building.

After what felt like an eternity she reached the open door of the ladies toilet and plunged thankfully inside into the dim, tiled interior that reeked of disinfectant and cheap air freshener. Two smartly dressed ladies, preening themselves in front of a smeared mirror, glanced at her through the reflection as Stella went inside. Stella saw one nudge the other and look at her with a grimace of distaste, she looked away quickly as Stella met her glance with cold, angry eyes.

"Come on Maeve," said one of the women, gathering up her handbag from beside the washbasin and flashing Stella a sympathetic smile before she sashayed out of the toilets. Her companion, dabbing hard at a blob of mascara that had smeared beneath her eyelids was slower to move. She glanced at Stella as she turned and saw the stained jacket, so transfixed as she walked away that she missed the turn for the exit and lurched straight into the wall.

Stella was too busy looking in the mirror herself to laugh at the other woman's misfortune. She stopped dead, frozen in horror, staring at her reflection in the mirror. Bitter tears of disappointment trickled unchecked down her cheeks, smudging her mascara and leaving a dark trail through the foundation that she had so carefully applied that morning. The smeared, pitted glass could not disguise the dreadful mess the horse had made of her jacket.

The jacket that she had chosen so carefully for this so, so special occasion. The day that she had so, so looked forward to.

Stella had wanted Rory even before she had met him.

Her boss, Kevin O'Mara had ordered a brainstorming session for a special valentine's edition of the magazine that she worked for, 'MiMi'. He wanted to do a special feature on Ireland's most eligible bachelors and chicks-about-town. Eligible spinsters he had decided was really not the kind of word that should be used to be described the unmarried, wealthy female readership of the magazine.

And so, all of the editorial staff had found themselves sitting around the vast expanse of the boardroom table early one Monday morning, sipping strong black coffee, nibbling croissants and nursing hangovers while they racked their brains for names of wealthy singletons of a certain age.

Kevin had suggested Rory McFadden. Born into a wealthy landowning family he had made millions running his own property development company. Sorcha, Stella's stroppy assistant had found a photograph of Rory, in an old copy of Hello magazine. He made an imposing figure, lolling against the bonnet of his sports car. Perfect, Stella had decided, looking at the photograph as Sorcha handed it around. He was just the kind of man that she wanted to marry.

None of the other eligible bachelors interested her, they were all either too young, too old, or too involved. Either that or the other members of staff on the magazine had dreadful tales about their sexual preferences or debauched styles of living.

And that wasn't what she wanted. No, when a girl got to be twenty six she was looking to settle down. To get married, have a few children, live the kind of existence that Stella constantly read about in her glossy magazines.

Securing an invitation to meet Rory had not been easy. It just wasn't possible to go into Kevin's office and lean across the desk and demand to be introduced to him. "By the way Boss, I would like to marry Rory McFadden. I think that he is just the kind of man that I have had on my wish list for all of these years." No. it all took time. Had to be done slowly, subtly, with patience and planning.

And then finally her chance came.

The guest list for an art gallery opening landed on her desk.

"Organise a photographer for this can you, I want to cover it for the social diary," Kevin had said as he hurried past.

Stella propped the list against her in-tray to remind her to make the call and then a name leapt off the page at her. Rory McFadden! Her big chance.

She went along to the gallery opening to 'help' the photographer and within half an hour of walking through the doors had managed to get herself introduced to Rory.

He had been just what she had hoped for. Tall – ish, thankfully she wasn't wearing her high heels – and rather than drop dead gorgeous, he was a majestic figure, immaculately and expensively dressed. (Stella knew all about these things).

By the end of the evening she had secured herself an invitation to the races to watch one of his horses running. That was the first hurdle over.

Now all she had to do was to get Rory to fall in love with her – and hopefully fall in love with him in the process. First step, knock him dead with her beauty, charm and wit on their first date. Well she had done that all right. Her new cream suit had cost a week's wages, the handbag and shoes had cost a similar amount. She had never paid so much before at the hairdressers, but it had been worth every penny when she saw the glorious golden blonde colour and the sleek stylish cut that flattered her high cheekbones.

Rory's mouth had dropped open when he had picked Stella up before the races. "You look fantastic," he had grinned, opening the passenger door of his new Mercedes for her to get in.

Stella had settled herself into the seat with a smile of satisfaction, all of the trouble and expense she had gone to for this first date had been worth it.

And now it was all ruined. Ruined because bloody Henry bloody Murphy couldn't control a bloody horse.

Rory had laughed at her. He obviously thought that she was an idiot, not knowing enough about horses to stay well out of their way.

She had made a total fool of herself; her much dreamed of fledgling relationship with Rory was over before it had even had the chance to begin.

A noise made her start and turn. "Erm….." Rory stood uncertainly in the doorway, holding out the long black coat that he had been wearing, "not sure if I should come into the ladies toilet, but I thought that you might need this," he said earnestly, shoving the coat in Stella's direction. "It will probably be enormous on you, but it will hide the worst of the stain on your jacket."

Stella looked at him gratefully, hoping that she had properly repaired the damage to her makeup. She took the coat. "Thank you."

"Right then," Rory said, backing rapidly out of the toilets as if he expected to be yelled at by some prudish old lady.

Stella put on the coat and checked her reflection in the mirror. The coat was enormous, but once she had turned up the collar and rolled up the sleeves it looked quite stylish, the great dark swathes of fabric making her look delicate and waif-like. Then dabbing a small smear of mascara from the corner of one eye she turned away and taking a deep breath went back outside into the bustle of the race meeting.

Rory obviously cared enough to come and find her and help with her dreadful predicament, perhaps the date wasn't going to be such a disaster after all.

Rory was back in the parade ring, with Henry when Stella returned. The horse was saddled and being led around by his groom.

Stella glared at the enormous black horse which was still tossing its head and dancing as if the ground were red hot beneath its delicate hooves. How anyone could actually like those bloody minded creatures was beyond her.

Henry smiled sympathetically as she went towards them, but Stella ignored him completely and flashed a wide smile at Rory. "My coat suits you," Rory beamed holding her by the shoulders at arm's length to study her. "Now Henry, look after Stella while I go and put my bets on. And try not to let another horse damage her!"

"He'll have to be quick," mused Henry watching Rory sprint lightly across the parade ring, "the horses will be going out onto the course in a few minutes."

Stella stared fixedly at the horses, anything to avoid having anything to do with Henry. He really was the most annoying man that she had ever met; her fingers itched to slap his cheek to remove his inane grin. He seemed to think that the whole incident was highly amusing.

"Are you ok?" Henry asked coming to stand right beside Stella.

Stella wanted to punch him. "Well obviously bloody not," she said tightly. "Your horse has just ruined my jacket."

"It's only a few speckles of horse spit," Henry gave a barely disguised snort of laughter, which, seeing the look of anger on Stella's face he rapidly turned into cough, "I could hardly stop the horse tossing his head, could I?" he said, sarcastically, tilting his head to one side, to look at her quizzically.

Stella met his eyes for the first time and felt her stomach lurch uncomfortably. Henry had gorgeous eyes, deep green, surrounded by the longest thickest lashes that she had ever seen.

She looked away abruptly. "I thought that you were his trainer. You can't do a very good job if you can't even teach him to stand still."

This time Henry didn't even bother to disguise his howl of laughter, "I train him to race not to stand to attention. He's a racehorse not some circus performer!"

"So," Henry said smoothly, a short time later, as they stood in the Owners and Trainers bar toasting Move Out's brilliant win, "am I still a bad trainer?"

Stella shrugged and took a long swig of her champagne, "I neither know or care," she said airily, moving across the bar towards Rory who was drinking his champagne out of the enormous cut glass vase that he had been awarded as the winning owner of the horse that won the race. "I just hope that I never have to see you or that bloody horse again."

"I'm sure that you will see plenty of me, if you carry on seeing Rory," Henry grinned, fixing his beautiful eyes on her.

"Not if I can help it," Stella snapped back, dragging her own eyes reluctantly away from Henry's.

She turned away, quickly before her eyes, which seemed to be acting as if they had a life of their own, made contact with Henry's again. She reached Rory who merrily offered her a swig of champagne out of the cut glass vase. "You've brought me luck today," Rory grinned enthusiastically as he put his arm around her shoulder. "I've really enjoyed having you with me. And I'm sure that your jacket will clean up," he said moving his black coat aside to look at the stain on her jacket with a grimace of concern.

Stella pulled the coat shut again quickly; she didn't want reminding about Henry and the bloody horse. "Will you come out with me again?" asked Rory, with a smile as she handed the champagne back to him, raising his eyebrows quizzically.

Stella felt her heart leap with delight; the day hadn't been a disaster. Rory was going to take her out again. And this time there would be no mistakes. No horses to ruin everything.

"I'd love to," Stella nodded gratefully.

"Great," Rory said, giving her arm a playful squeeze. "We'll go for some lunch on Sunday and then we can drive over to Henry's to look at a horse he thinks I should buy."

CHAPTER TWO

Gingerly Amber turned the door handle and crept stealthily into the bedroom her bare feet padding lightly on the carpet. Then taking a deep breath she snapped on the switch flooding the room with light. She expelled the breath, feeling her heart pounding against her ribcage.

This was ridiculous. Stella was out for the evening. It wasn't as if she was going to come back and find Amber rifling through her wardrobe to find a dress to go out in. Was it? And if she did – then it wasn't likely that she would be very upset. Well.........not very. It wasn't as if Amber made a habit of going through her flatmate's belongings, but this was an emergency.

If only her credit card hadn't been rejected while standing at the checkout of a really trendy shop with half of Dublin standing in the queue behind her gawping and sniggering at her embarrassment.

The shop assistant had lovingly folded up the wispy-slip-of-a-dress, its dark satin fabric shimmering in the shop lights and the tiny embroidered flowers with the tiny dots of shining beads glittering and winking at Amber with delight at being taken out of the shop on an adventure.

She had swiped Amber's credit card through the machine and then stood drumming her long red talons on the counter as the machine remained silent. Amber glared at the machine, willing it to spew out the payment slip, but nothing happened.

Finally the assistant shifted her position; sighing as if the weight of the world were on her shoulders and peering smugly at the card tapped the number into the machine, her long nails clattering on the keyboard. Then finally the machine whirred into life. The assistant raised her eyebrows and pulled a wry face at Amber.

"Rejected," she had snapped, almost throwing the card back at Amber and, lips pursed with annoyance, snatched the gorgeous dress back out of its bag and threw it onto a rail behind her.

Amber could almost hear the dress scream in protest. How it had really wanted to belong to her. How she had needed that dress. How could her card be rejected? There must be some mistake. Amber was sure that she had sent in a payment to reduce the balance on her credit card. But maybe she had used it to buy that gorgeous pair of shoes last week? And hadn't there been a letter about a cheque and insufficient funds?

As quickly as the thoughts came into her head Amber forgot them.

The bank manager certainly was no friend of hers. Life seemed to be a constant battle to afford the things that she really had to have. A constant juggle of credit card against pay cheque, with the pay cheque usually losing out.

There was nothing in her wardrobe at the flat that warranted being suitable for such an auspicious date. And so she had been forced into the raid on Stella's wardrobe.

It wasn't every day that Amber was asked out by a gorgeous super-cool guy. Usually it was ugly dorks with spots and nerdy haircuts. For some reason Amber seemed to attract them like a magnet.

But this guy was different. This was the guy in the pub casually playing pool, that all of the girls from the hotel who Amber worked with had surreptitiously been looking at. Watching the way he ran his hand through a lock of hair that kept flopping over this forehead and the tight curve of his bottom as he leant across the table to make a shot at the pool ball.

All of the girls from work had been watching him, even those who were old enough to know better, or who had men of their own waiting at home.

Miraculously though, it was Amber that he winked at when he looked up and saw all of the girls drooling over him. When he finally drained his pint and headed to the bar it was Amber that he grinned at.

Amber had felt her mouth drop open as one of the girls nudged her in the ribs and hissed, "he fancies you." No one that gorgeous ever fancied her. He had a nice haircut and not a spot in sight.

The girls parted, like the Red Sea, as he walked towards Amber.

They stood, staring enviously, as he boldly walked straight up to Amber and asked her what she wanted to drink. When she opened her mouth, nothing came out and she stood for what seemed like minutes dumbstruck, until Jules, one of her colleagues said loudly, "red wine. She drinks red wine."

"Thanks, girls," he spoke dismissively and as if obeying an unheard command they all backed away from the bar leaving Amber standing alone with him.

A glass of red wine appeared on the bar beside her. "Thank you" Amber managed to speak, but her voice came out like a strangled squawk.

Over his shoulder she was aware of the stares of naked envy from the other girls. She picked up the glass watching as some of the dark liquid slopped over the side as her hand trembled. She cursed herself for acting like a silly nervous teenager overawed by the presence of such raw testosterone.

"I'm Luke," said Mr Raw Testosterone, clinking his glass against hers.

"Amber," she replied, taking a long swig of her drink to steady her nerves. Even his name was cool, why couldn't he have had a nerdy name? Anything to make him seem ordinary.

Once she was halfway down her drink Amber began to relax, Luke was nice, really nice. He made her laugh, she glowed beneath the full spotlight of his very impressive charm. He made her feel as if she were the only woman in the room.

And then far too quickly he was telling her that he had to go, he and his friends were meeting people in another pub. It was someone's birthday, he was terribly disappointed when he had just met her. He would have loved to have stayed with her all night. There was a strong emphasis on 'all night'. He would meet her in the pub on Saturday night and they would have more time to get to know each other. They exchanged phone numbers and then he was gone, leaving Amber feeling breathless and bewildered.

And it was all because of Luke she was having to do the raid on Stella's wardrobe. That and a credit card which wouldn't come out to play.

Stella's room was immaculate. Her double bed was covered in a cream duvet, with a bright rose coloured satin throw tastefully arranged over the end, which coordinated with the silky cushions that she had arranged around the curve of the pillow.

Yet it was a room devoid of personality, too tidy. No photographs littered the bedside table which was artfully arranged with a vase of roses and a few books. There was nothing to tell anyone of the person who spent their time in the room, like an expensive hotel room.

Amber opened the wardrobe. Stella's clothes were arranged in regimented rows, skirts at one end, then blouses, dresses and finally coats. Beneath the clothes, Stella's shoes stood in regimented lines, with a row of handbags beside them.

Amber ran her hand along the rail of clothes, looking at the expensive labels. Stella was going to have to find herself a wealthy husband to support her in the manner that she obviously wanted to become accustomed to.

Slowly Amber shifted through the line of dresses until she found the one that she had wanted.

It was gorgeous, bright red and clingy in a tasteful kind of way. Stella didn't do tarty. This dress showed off the body's curves without flaunting them.

Gingerly Amber took the dress of the rail, feeling like a thief. Stella would probably kill her if she knew what she was doing. But this really was an emergency.

She pulled the dress off its hanger and held it against her body, savouring the luxurious feel of the fabric. She looked in the full length mirror that hung on the wall beside the wardrobe. The dress looked gorgeous, the red colour highlighted her dark colouring.

It was perfect. She took the dress and shot out of the room before she lost her courage and put the dress back.

Amber felt gorgeous as she emerged from a taxi outside the pub. All her preparations for the evening had gone perfectly. Even her hair had co-operated and now hung in soft waves around her face, unlike the wiry frizz that it seemed to prefer.

Beneath her best black coat, the red dress looked perfect, Amber had finally gone for broke and borrowed Stella's black killer-heels to go with the dress. In for a penny, in for a pound, she might as well be hung for a sheep as a lamb, she supposed.

Besides which she would have the dress and shoes back in the wardrobe before Stella got back.

Amber glanced at her watch; she was a few minutes late. It was good not to appear too eager.

She crossed the pavement and went around the corner to the front of the pub, feeling her heart sink as she saw the entrance to the pub was Luke-less.

Relief that he wasn't there, pacing impatiently, waiting for her, mingled with a nagging concern that maybe he had changed his mind. Feeling terribly conspicuous she walked to the pub door and stood beside it.

From across the street someone wolf whistled, she looked up expectantly, hoping it would be Luke, dashing towards her, but only a group of young lads clustered on the street corner opposite, laughing and giggling.

A man came around the corner; Amber felt her heart lurch with excitement which rapidly cooled to bitter disappointment. It wasn't Luke.

"All on your own darlin?" he slurred drunkenly, leaning too close to her and giving her the full benefit of his whiskey laden breath.

"No," she snarled, glaring at the man, who thought better of chatting her up and lurched into the pub. Where could Luke be? He had been so definite about their arrangement to meet here.

Amber checked her telephone, maybe he had called and she hadn't heard the phone ring. The smiley face on the phone grinned inanely at her. No missed calls.

Maybe Luke was waiting inside, she thought, hopefully. Amber shoved her telephone back into her bag and pulled open the pub door. Taking a deep breath she plunged into the mass of people who crowded in the bar, conscious of the fact that everyone seemed to be turning to look at her, sure that they all knew that she was on her own and looking for someone.

"Lost your boyfriend?" some wit yelled from across the bar. Amber smiled tightly. Where the hell was Luke? She moved through the pub, trying to ignore the nasty little voice inside her that laughed over the hum of conversation. 'You've been stood up again!'

Amber scanned the crowded bar, it was hard to see over the tall heads of the men, everyone was so much taller than she was. It was painfully obvious though that Luke was not there. He had stood her up. Built her up with all the bull-shit chat up line, all the mega-watt attention and then just not turned up.

"Look where you're goi.......ng!" Amber, her head turned to look around the bar, walked straight into the protruding beer belly of an enormous man.

Icy cold beer from one of the glasses he was carrying at head height cascaded down her front.

Amber jumped back, gasping as the icy liquid poured over her coat and soaked through the front of the dress

"Stupid cow!" the man growled, looking in annoyance at the half empty beer glass. Amber turned and fled, her killer heels skidding on the soaking floor.

Outside a couple were just getting out of a taxi, barging past the man who was paying the driver, Amber darted into the back seat, biting her lip to stop herself crying.

She gave the driver the address and sat back feeling the beer, sticky against her skin, clinging to the fabric of the ruined dress. She watched the darkened streets slide by as the driver crossed the city, couples out walking, enjoying the night – together, while she headed home – alone. As always.

How could she have been so stupid as to expect him to turn up. He had just been messing with her. But she had believed him. She had really thought he had wanted to see her again. How the girls at work would laugh when she told them that she had been stood up.

The driver drew to a stop outside the apartment block. Amber looked up at the darkened windows.

Stella wasn't home, that was something. Numbly she paid the driver and walked slowly up the stone steps to the front door. How different this evening should have been. She had thought that now she would be laughing somewhere with Luke, bathing in the spotlight of his megawatt charm.

Amber let herself into the apartment that she had shared with Stella for the past two years. She pulled off Stella's shoes and in a sudden burst of temper, threw them across the room; they hit the wall and then lay abandoned in a heap on the carpet.

Grim realisation of her situation slowly seeped over Amber. Not only had she been stood up, but she had ruined Stella's dress in the process. Hardly daring to look she stood in front of the living room mirror and pulled off her coat. A dark wet line marred the immaculate fabric of the dress from top to bottom.

"Oh shit!" Amber growled between clenched teeth. Why did everything always go wrong for her?

She went into the chaos that was her own room and unearthed her nightdress and a dressing gown from beneath the pile of clothes she had tried on earlier in the evening before the raid on Stella's wardrobe.

She took off the dress, the drying fabric sticking to her skin leaving a damp, itchy line on her flesh. Maybe the beer would sponge out of the dress, then she could get it back in Stella's wardrobe and she would never know, Amber thought, hopefully.

How could she have been so stupid as to borrow the bloody dress in the first place. She should have realised that Luke was not going to turn up. It was all too good to be true.

She fetched a hanger and put the dress on it, ran warm water from the tap into the washbasin and began to dab ineffectively at the stain with a sponge. The water spread further across the fabric, making it worse than before. She was going to have to hide the dress, bring it to the dry cleaners and then get it back into Stella's wardrobe. Somehow.

Amber stifled a sob. Crying was not going to change anything. She shouldn't have been so stupid in the first place.

Above the noise of the water running came the shrill note of the telephone ringing. Amber threw the sponge into the washbasin and ran into the living room. Luke was ringing to apologise for standing her up. Something had delayed him. He really did want to see her. Cursing her fumbling fingers Amber rummaged in her handbag, desperately searching for the mobile phone. Finally she found it, dragged it out and pressed the receive button.

"Hello," Amber spoke into the receiver.

"Amber. Sweetheart!" her Mother's voice drilled into Amber's ear. Amber's heart sank. After the night that she had just had the last thing that she wanted to hear was her mother. Mrs-You-Should.

She could picture her mother, sitting in the immaculate house, immaculately dressed as always, her beautifully manicured nails holding the telephone, not quite up to her face in case the receiver smudged her makeup, or pushed her hairstyle out of place.

"Hello Mother," Amber forced herself to sound bright.

"Darling, I have wonderful news about Ruby!" Amber felt her heart sink further. Ruby, her dreadful older sister. A twenty eight year old version of her mother. Miss-Can-Do-No-Wrong.

"Oh?"

"Darling! Ruby's getting married!!" her mother's voice was full of excitement.

Amber closed her eyes in disbelief. Damn Ruby. Ruby was her Pearl Casey's favourite daughter, she could do nothing wrong in their mother's eyes, a perfect childhood, a glowing career as a top flight solicitor and now a perfect marriage to a perfect man.

CHAPTER THREE

The odour of 'Lavender Garden at Midnight' gradually covered the all-pervading odour of stale beer. Stella gave the spray can a final squirt up into the air and shut the bathroom door. It was strange that the whole flat and especially the bathroom absolutely stank like a pub bar.

As soon as Amber had gone out to work, Stella had gone around with the air freshener to get rid of the smell. She had also checked all of the rooms and cupboards to see if Amber had been sick somewhere or if there was some drunken man secreted in one of the rooms. But there was nothing.

It was all very strange, especially when Amber had told her, very sincerely when she had come about the advert for a roommate that she very rarely drank.

Stella had been a bit sceptical then, but Amber had been the best choice out of some very dodgy applicants wanting to share the apartment with her.

The choice had been limited to a rather large woman who kept sniffing into a grubby handkerchief as she explained that her husband had just moved his much younger mistress into the house and that she didn't want to do her washing as well as his and a waif like hippy with rings everywhere and hair that looked as if it hadn't been washed or combed since she was about ten years old.

Amber at least had looked fairly normal.

Except for today when she had gone out at the crack of dawn clutching a bag and mumbling something about dry cleaning.

That had been strange in itself, as she had never known Amber to take anything to the dry cleaners before and as far as Stella knew, there wouldn't be a dry cleaner open anywhere on a Sunday.

And Stella was often in the dry cleaners, so she should know.

The apartment was immaculate when Amber returned.

Stella had spent the morning in a frenzy of cleaning; she was such a bundle of nerves thinking about her lunch date with Rory. She couldn't afford for anything to go wrong this time.

Amber stomped miserably back into the apartment a few hours later, clutching the newspaper and a huge box from the cake shop which she dumped on the table.

"Comfort eating," she explained, tearing at the string that tied the box closed. She finally succeeded in getting the box open and shoved the cakes onto a plate.

"Would you like one?" she asked, shoving the box under Stella's nose.

"Erm. Thanks," said Stella looking at the cakes as if she thought that they were going to bite her. Stella worked very hard to keep her slender figure.

"Why are you comfort eating?" Stella asked, longing to sink her teeth into one of those spongy cream oozing creations.

Amber slumped down on the sofa and took a huge bite out of one of her cakes.

"I got stood up," she sighed miserably.

"What? By Mr Testosterone himself?" Stella winced as a blob of cream slid out of the cake that Amber was eating and landed perilously near the edge of her plate. She fought the urge to leap up and get a cloth to give to Amber in case the cream slid off her plate and landed on her expensive sofa.

"I waited for ages outside the pub and then I went in to see if he was there………" Amber's voice trailed off to a whisper as she miserably remembered the previous evening.

She didn't dare mention the accident with the dress.

Even if she pretended that it had been one of her own dresses Stella would have wanted to help sort it out and then it would have all come out about borrowing her dress and that was the last thing that Amber wanted.

"And he didn't even call to say he wasn't coming?"

Amber bit into her cake and chewed it hard, concentrating on the taste of the cake rather than letting herself remember the awful evening.

"I did get a call," Amber took the cake out of her mouth and ran her finger along one edge of it and slurped the whipped cream into her mouth from her finger, "but that was from my mum wanting to say that my darling sister is getting married."

Stella who had just taken a small bite of her own cake almost choked. Sometimes Amber really annoyed her. She just let herself be pushed into the shadow of her successful older sister.

Ruby was the complete opposite of Amber, extremely beautiful, annoyingly organised and efficient. She worked for one of Dublin's top law firms as a solicitor. Amber was chaotic, disorganised, un-ambitious and twice as nice as Ruby.

"Bloody Ruby," sighed Amber. "She always does better than me. Better looking, better job. Now she is going to have the perfect marriage to the perfect man."

Stella ran her finger around the edge of her cake and scooped the cream into her mouth. She wished she could protect Amber from the hurt she was feeling.

"How am I ever going to get married, I can't even find a boyfriend?" Amber wailed, mournfully.

Stella sucked the end of one of her fingers and picked the cake crumbs up off her plate, licking the crumbs off her finger. If only Amber could decide what kind of man she wanted and wait until he came along, rather than just being grateful for any man.

Stella had a master plan, she was very selective about the type of man she had anything to do with. To get anywhere with her they had to be obviously wealthy, unmarried with a good job and good prospects. There was no point in messing around with anything less. She was not going to marry just for love and end up living from hand to mouth. Like her mother had done. Stella was never going to fall for anyone unsuitable.

"Henry," Stella spoke without being aware that his name had slipped from her lips. Just the thought of unsuitable men had brought him clearly to mind.

"What?" Amber frowned quizzically over the top of her cream sponge.

"Nothing," Stella sighed curling her lip in annoyance at the very thought of Henry. She pictured her ruined jacket, hanging forlornly over the back of a chair in her bedroom. She must take it to the dry cleaners to see if they could do anything to remove the stain. And then she pictured Henry, his gorgeous eyes dancing with amusement, and that lovely, lovely smile. Her stomach fluttered suddenly with butterflies. It must have been annoyance at how he could have ruined her beloved jacket so carelessly, rather than the thought of his cute eyes that had given her the butterflies. It was annoyance. Nothing else.

"You said Henry," Amber persisted.

"Oh he sprang to mind when we were talking about unsuitable men," Stella said airily, getting quickly up from the sofa and putting her empty plate on the table, hoping that Amber wouldn't notice the flush that was darkening her cheeks. "He ruined my jacket."

"Not personally he didn't," muttered Amber. "It was his horse."

"I hope that the dry cleaners can get the stain off," sulked Stella, petulantly, wondering why Amber suddenly looked flushed herself.

"Surely he's not that bad?" Amber finished the last cake and dabbed at the remaining crumbs with a fingertip.

"Well, he…………." Stella fought to think of a word to describe Henry. How could she explain how awful he was? How much he had irritated her and yet how attractive she had found him.

Amber let out a snort of laughter, "I think that you rather fancy him,"

"Most definitely not," Stella said huffily, "I've got Rory now. He's perfect for me."

"Really?" asked Amber, with more than a hint of sarcasm in her voice.

Stella got up and fetched her coat. Rory would be here any minute. She would never be stood up. She wished that she could go and stand outside and wait for his arrival, she couldn't stand listening to Amber a moment longer. How dare she suggest that she fancied Henry. Nothing could be further from the truth. He was the most annoying man she had ever met. She breathed a sigh of relief when she saw Rory's car glide graciously down the street. "See you later," she dashed out of the apartment and down the stairs.

Then reaching the entrance hall, she waited. It wouldn't do to appear to be too eager. She would keep Rory waiting, just for a few moments, before she pulled open the front door and walked slowly down the steps to the waiting car.

"You look great," Rory said, as Stella settled herself into the leather front seat of the car.

"And that colour won't show up any horse spit," he joked. Stella forced herself to smile and laughed airily.

"Lunch first I think and then we'll head off to the stables. I want to take a look at a horse Henry thinks I should buy." Rory accelerated away, oblivious to the other drivers who courteously pulled into the side to let him down the narrow street.

"How many horses do you have?" Stella asked when they were finally settled into a corner table of the restaurant.

"Four," Rory replied, not bothering to look at her over the top of the wine list.

"Are they flat horses or jumpers?" Stella persisted, eager to show off her new found knowledge about racehorses.

She had spent the last few days reading the racing section of every newspaper that she could get her hands on in order to have something to discuss with Rory to make him think she was interested in his hobby.

"Chasers," Rory snapped his fingers at the waitress. "A bottle of number twenty seven," he yelled across the crowded restaurant. The flustered looking waitress glanced in his direction and muttered under her breath.

"I prefer chasing to anything," Stella told him, at least she knew the difference between flat racing, hurdles and chases.

"I like to do a bit of chasing myself," Rory shoved his hot and clammy hand on her leg beneath the table and ran it up her thigh.

Stella smiled gratefully when the waitress arrived a moment later and put the bottle of wine and two glasses down on the table. Rory reluctantly withdrew his hand and grasped the wine glass and gulped down some of the dark red liquid that the waitress poured for him.

Stella felt her eyes widen in disbelief as Rory suddenly began to churn the wine around in his mouth making a noise like a washing machine that was about to explode. "That will do, I suppose," he declared, swallowing the wine. The waitress looked as if she would love to hit him over the head with the bottle.

An hour later Rory had drunk most of the bottle of wine and eaten the most enormous meal that Stella had ever seen. "One hundred and thirty seven euros and seventy five cents," said the waitress coming to the table with the bill.

"Right then, let's go and take a look at this horse," he said, counting out a handful of change to make the seventy five cents.

"Thanks, call again," snapped the waitress, wryly looking at the tip-less payment.

Thornhill Stables, Henry's home was a mile off the main road, down a rutted track. Stella grimaced when she saw the ramshackle sprawl of grey stone buildings.

Rory drove beneath a soaring arch into the stable yard, parked his car on a stretch of weed encrusted concrete and got out.

Stella felt her cheeks darken as Henry appeared from a cottage at the far end of the yard that looked as if it would fall down if a puff of wind blew.

"Nice jacket!" Henry grinned as Stella eased herself gingerly out of the car, looking tentatively at the ground in case she trod in the end product of racehorse.

"Thank you," she smiled, tightly. The joke about her jacket was going to run and run. She risked a glance at Henry and then looked away quickly as she saw his eyes on hers.

"Let's have a look at this horse then!" Rory slammed the car door loudly, making Stella fear for the safety of the buildings.

Stella followed the men as they walked across the yard. What a dreadfully run down place this was.

The buildings formed a square around a tangle of grass in the centre. Three of the sides of the square were taken up with stables, doors with chipped and peeling paint hung drunkenly from broken hinges. Only a few shut properly and those had elegant horse's heads looking out of them.

Above the stable yard the slate roof sagged dangerously in the middle and there were gaping holes where the slates were missing and the bare wood of the trusses showed through.

Henry must be absolutely penniless thought Stella as she followed Rory into the dim interior of one of the buildings. Inside the old building retained its once beautiful features, the cobbled floor was immaculately swept and the wood panelling around the stable was freshly painted.

"This is Monday Man," said Henry proudly, sweeping the rug off an enormous grey horse. "I think that he would be perfect for you Rory. This horse could win you the Galway Plate."

"Let me show you my own Grand National horse, The Entertainer " Henry said, once Rory had finished writing what Stella thought was an alarmingly large cheque for Monday Man. Henry led the way across the yard to another stable. Inside stood a tall, scrawny looking horse, with ears that even Stella could see would have looked more suitable on a donkey.

"He's not done much yet," Henry said proudly patting the horse's skinny neck, "but I think he will do very well eventually."

"My new horse looks a good one, but Henry's one, the Entertainer looks pretty useless," Rory said scathingly as he turned his car off the rutted driveway onto the main road. The engine roared into life as he shoved his foot hard on the accelerator.

Stella grinned as the thrust from the car pushed her back into the leather seat.

"Look. Down there. Thornhill House," Rory swerved the car to the wrong side of the road, bumped up onto the grass verge and jerked to a halt.

Stella looked in the direction he was pointing. There, peering through a gap in the trees across fields and parkland she saw a sprawling old mansion, standing proudly amidst gardens that were a riot of autumn colour. The enormous house was built of old stone, faded to a myriad shades of grey beneath a dark slate roof. A long driveway wound through trees and shrubs to the front of the house.

Stella gave a gasp of pure delight. "Oh, Rory," she breathed. "What a gorgeous house."

"Yes," Rory replied with a snort, "Henry rather thinks so too."

CHAPTER FOUR

"Just look at this!" exclaimed Stella, startling Amber who was painting her toe nails on the sofa while watching a video of her favourite movie, 'Love Actually'.

Amber paused the movie and got regretfully off the sofa. What did Stella want her to look at that could possibly more important than admiring Hugh Grant's dance scene?

Across the room Stella was removing the plastic wrapping from the cream jacket that she had just fetched back from the dry cleaners. Amber walked slowly across the room, severely hampered by the wedges of cotton wool that she had stuffed between her toes to keep them apart while she painted them ruby red. Heaven knows why, it wasn't as if anyone was going to see them, but somehow watching a 'happy-ever-after-movie gave her the hope that just maybe someone soon would be looking at her toes, and hopefully the rest of her body, so it paid to be prepared.

Stella of course had proper separators for when she painted her toe nails, but then someone was looking at her toes, or presumably soon would. Even if it was Rory, the arrogant jerk she had come home with last weekend.

Amber shoved her way past carrier bags bearing the names of some pretty exclusive dress shops, fighting the urge to drop a sly kick at some of the bags. She did not dare even venture into 'Chez Penney's', let alone 'Chez Vogue', the snooty shop girls in there would be able to tell at twenty paces that Amber's credit card was dead on its feet.

Stella pulled off the remaining plastic wrapper protecting the jacket and laid it reverently on the table. "Look at that," she whispered, shaking her head in disbelief at the immaculate expanse of cream fabric.

Amber looked. The jacket, that, the last time she had seen it, had been liberally splattered in greenish brown splodges, was now pristine again. Amber looked enviously at the obviously expensive and very beautifully cut jacket. "Well, at least you will be able to forgive Henry now," she mocked lightly, jealously making her feel malicious.

"Henry!" spat Stella, viciously, "I'll forgive him when hell freezes over."

Amber stifled a smile, me think she doth protest too much, she mused, slowly waddling back to the sofa to continue painting her nails.

"Funny thing," Stella said, sliding the plastic back over the jacket, "I saw a red dress, just like mine in the dry cleaners."

Amber swallowed hard and was very glad that her back was to Stella, so that she couldn't see the hot flush that was spreading rapidly up from her neck. "Oh?" Amber gulped.

"The girl in the Tamara Pierce shop where I bought it, told me the dress was unique. Only one like it had been made." Stella was saying, Amber could hear her heading towards her bedroom.

At any moment she would go into the bedroom and find that her dress was missing and then she would know that Amber had 'borrowed' it – and probably ruined it. The woman in the dry cleaners was very doubtful that the beer stains would come out without leaving a permanent mark.

Amber stole a glance over her shoulder, Stella had gone into her bedroom and laid the jacket on the bed, "I'll have it out with the girl in Tamara Pierce the next time I go in there."

"Yes, you should," Amber fought to keep the panic out of her voice, Stella was going to open the wardrobe and start looking for her red dress, with her organised wardrobe it wouldn't take her long to discover the dress was missing. And she would be so angry.

The wardrobe door creaked open, Amber's neck began to ache with keeping it craned at such an odd angle and with the tension that she could feel tightening every muscle in her body.

"I'll just put this jacket away and then find my dress, I want to see if it really is the same as the one in the dry cleaners," Stella was saying, her voice muffled by the wardrobe door.

"I've got to go out!" Amber yelled, leaping off the sofa, scattering the wedges of cotton wool in all directions in her panic to get out of the apartment before Stella discovered her dress was missing. Amber had meant to get it back from the dry cleaners, but somehow she had managed to forget it.

"Where are you going?" Stella's head appeared around the wardrobe door.

"Oh, I forgot my Mum is expecting me at lunch time!" Amber lied.

"That's lovely, have a great time," Stella said enthusiastically.

Amber smiled wryly, "Mum just wants to discuss the colour scheme for the wedding of the century." She pulled on her socks over the tacky nail varnish, feeling the woollen fabric sticking to the ruby red paint. She had ruined her toe nails in her panic. She shoved her feet into her shoes and grabbed her jacket from her bedroom.

"See you later," Stella had settled herself down on the sofa rewound the film and opened a glossy looking homes and gardens magazine, "I'm going to start planning for the future," she mused dreamily.

Amber walked along the pavement already strewn with damp rust coloured leaves, blown by the autumn gales.

A few dates with Rory and Stella was already re-decorating a country estate and planning a menu for dinner for twenty. Amber scuffed through a pile of damp leaves. Stella seemed to think love should come on demand, something that you order, like a pizza. 'I'd like a handsome rich man with a swanky car on the side please. Deliver to Stella O'Rorke immediately.' She was determined the only person she was going to marry had to be wealthy. But love didn't come like that. Nothing could determine who you fell in love with. It all had to do with chemistry. Fate. It was written in the stars. Then when you fell in love you went through life together, taking whatever came at you, like a team. You couldn't just decide you would only fall in love with someone who had a certain bank balance, or who lived in a certain neighbourhood, or who did a certain job. Love was something no one had any control over. If love was something you could control then she wouldn't be walking miserably through the streets alone on a Saturday morning.

A couple walked towards Amber, heads together, sharing their own secret world. Amber sighed as they passed her. If love was something that could be controlled she would have someone with her, someone who would love and cherish her forever. But it wasn't something controllable. Love was wild and unruly. That was why she kept falling for utter, utter, absolute bastards who kept breaking her heart.

If Stella was attracted to rich men, then Amber was very definitely attracted to scum-bags. And they never usually had fat wallets either. A pretty face and charm in buckets and the morals of an alley cat was the type of man Amber was usually attracted to.

She passed a shop window and glanced at her reflection, there was nothing unusual about her, she was pretty, but not in an exceptional way, her mass of dark wavy hair, now beginning to frizz with the damp air, was definitely a good feature. There was nothing about her that said 'I'm a sucker for a bastard. Come and hurt me.'

Amber reached the bus stop and ducked into the shelter, out of the wind. A tall, good looking guy grinned in greeting.

"Cold out there," he shivered dramatically. Amber nodded and then ignored him. Too good looking. He was bound to be a bastard of the first degree.

Surreptitiously she reached into her handbag and pulled out her purse, it felt worryingly light, she jingled it hopefully. Unless some miracle had happened and fresh air had been turned into money she was virtually penniless. Shit.

She rummaged in the zipper pockets of her hand bag, fumbling into the furthest recesses, looking for loose change that might have been abandoned there. Amongst screwed up bus tickets and sticky sweet wrappers she found enough change for a return bus ticket, provided the driver didn't check the one cent coins too hard.

She hadn't dared visit the hole in the wall. Her card would have melted if she had put it into the machine.

Thank goodness money was deducted from her wages as soon as they were paid into the bank for the rent on the apartment. And she had to give money to Stella as soon as she was paid for food for the month, otherwise she would never be able to eat. The money would just go....... And it would never be any good trying to borrow some from her mother. She would only get a lecture about the vast amounts of money Ruby was earning and what a wonderful pension scheme she had.

The bus arrived. The tall man stood back with a courteous smile to let her on first, Amber stuck her nose in the air and ignored him. Creep needn't think he could get around her that way. She plonked herself down on a seat and watched the cityscape slide by the window until it was her stop.

The Swiftbrook Estate was a prim and gentile cluster of houses grouped around an immaculate stretch of manicured grass and young oak trees. Even the trees stood in regimented lines.

As Amber opened the garden gate the familiar sinking feeling settled uncomfortably into the pit of her stomach. She walked slowly up the path, past orderly lines of prim looking flowers towards the featureless two story red brick house where she had grown up.

As she neared the house Amber shot a furtive glance at the net curtains that swathed each of the windows. There was no sign of her mother peering out to watch her approach.

Then grinning maliciously Amber walked boldly across the lawn instead of following the path around the edge of the garden.

As a child putting a foot on the pristine grass of the manicured front lawn was close to being considered a mortal sin. The back lawn was for playing on. The front lawn had to be kept immaculate so it could be admired by all who saw it.

Amber studied her reflection in the brightly polished brass door bell, puffing out her cheeks to make the distorted image even funnier. The door swung open. "Amber! darling!" Her mother always spoke in exclamations.

Pearl Casey took Amber's arm and pulled her into a hallway that smelt of furniture polish and lavender scented candles. Pearl cast an inquisitive eye hastily down the length of the street, hastily rubbing Amber's finger print from the pristine shine of the doorbell.

"That colour doesn't suit you at all!" Pearl said, shaking her head so that her tightly permed curls bobbed busily.

"Hello mother," Amber wrinkled her nose behind her mother's broad back as she led the way into the lounge. Amber knew she looked washed out in the pale blue tee-shirt. "Mammy!" demanded a voice that set Amber's teeth on edge. "Where can I find a vase? I want to arrange the flowers I brought for you." Ruby, Patron saint of high achieving daughters, nemesis of under achieving sisters.

Amber dragged herself unwillingly into the sitting room. There, amongst the claustrophobic clutter of china ornaments and over stuffed velour furniture sat Ruby, like some huge pink praying mantis waiting to devour Amber.

"Hello Amber," Ruby's tone was smug. "How are things? Job? Boyfriend?"

"Great thanks," Amber said through gritted teeth, clinging to her temper, Ruby knew exactly how to needle her. "Where's Dad?" Amber glanced around the room, desperate to escape from Ruby and her mother.

"Daddy's in the garden," Ruby said dismissively, before launching into another jibe guaranteed to irritate Amber. "Are you still seeing that man with the long hair, the one who wants to be a rock star?"

"What man with the long hair....?" Her mother's voice trailed after Amber as she bolted through the sitting room, into the gleaming kitchen, gasping at the over whelming smell of disinfectant and polish and then out into the pristine back garden.

Amber fled down the garden path. Spending an afternoon with Ruby and her mother had to be a far worse punishment than staying at the apartment and telling Stella she had ruined her favourite dress.

The garden was deserted. Amber burst into the wooden shed that was tucked neatly into the far corner of the garden, almost hidden from view behind a screen of sweet smelling rambling roses.

Her father, startled by her sudden entrance hastily shoved the newspaper he had been reading behind the plants he was pretending to replant in plastic flower pots. "Amber," Jack Casey breathed a sigh of relief, unfolding his crumpled paper, "I thought that you were your mother. Or Ruby."

"Which is worse?" Amber kissed her father's cheek as he shrugged, guiltily trying to ignore her question, loyalty preventing him from ever saying anything derogative about his bossy wife or eldest daughter.

"There is great excitement about this wedding," Amber's father continued, pulling a wooden stool from beneath his work bench and gesturing at her to sit down.

"Of course it will all have to be just perfect," Amber sighed, wryly, crumbling a fist full of damp peat between her fingers.

"How could it be any other way," her father raised his eyes in the direction of the shed roof, puffing out his cheeks in a sigh. "Thank God they aren't expecting me to pay for it," he grinned, "Ruby and her fiancée are going to pay for it all themselves. Suits me to leave them to it. I can save my money to pay for your wedding."

Amber grinned back at him enjoying the closeness of being a co-conspirator with her father. "You will probably have a long wait. My love life is desperate."

"Mine too."

Then as if he were afraid of having said too much he heaved himself wearily to his feet. "Come on, we had better go inside."

"I was just about to telephone the Guards and report you both missing!" Pearl disguised her jibe as a joke. They had obviously been caught enjoying their time out of the house.

"Daddy, do hurry up, I want to talk to you about the wedding," Ruby's shrill tones echoed around the kitchen.

"Just coming," Jack answered wearily, running his hands quickly under the hot water tap.

"That is the tea towel! The hand towel is hanging in its proper place," snapped Pearl, as he rubbed his hands dry. Wearily Jack put the tea towel down and headed in the direction of the lounge.

As a child Amber had wondered why her father did not stand up to his bossy, bad tempered wife, but now she knew it was easier for him just to agree with her.

"Oh Daddy, do sit down," said Ruby, impatiently as Amber followed her father into the lounge. Amber sat down beside her father.

"Mummy!" roared Ruby.

"Just tidying up after your father!" Pearl Casey hurried into the room and perched herself on the arm of the sofa.

Ruby eased herself up to the edge of the armchair and looked at the expectant faces. "This is going to be the wedding of the year," she nodded smugly, "Roderick has booked the Park Hotel for the reception and we are getting married in a tiny church in a lovely village in Wicklow."

"What's wrong with our own church?" said her father. Amber could hear the resignation in his voice.

"This church is perfect for my wedding," Ruby answered dismissively. "And my Roderick likes everything to be perfect."

Jack Casey sank further back into his armchair, his expression filled with hurt.

Amber fought the urge to make vomiting noises, "Roderick sounds like he is really something," she said, wishing that she could think of some quick put down to prick Ruby's bubble of self-importance, but it was not worth it. Ruby was so thick skinned sarcastic comments just bounced off her.

"He is incredible," Ruby smiled smugly. "Good looking, wealthy, very successful."

"Lovely," Amber said, wearily, Ruby always got the best out of life, while for Amber everything was a constant struggle from disaster to disaster.

"You can see for yourself," Ruby continued regally, "Roderick's brother, Ernest, is coming back to Ireland from Milan for Christmas. You could come out with us, make up a foursome."

"Great," Amber heard herself saying eagerly, delighted that Ruby considered her worthy of being introduced to her fiancée and his exotic sounding brother. Maybe her engagement had brought out a streak of kindness in Ruby. Maybe finally they were going to be friends.

CHAPTER FIVE

Driving out to Henry's ramshackle racing stables again really was a sign of how far she was prepared to go to show Rory what a wonderful girlfriend she was.

Just to have to go near Henry again, let alone set foot in that dreadful place was beyond the call of duty for any prospective wife.

It was lovely to go out with Rory again; he seemed to have become really fond of her, really quickly. Since their first couple of dates he had telephoned once or twice every day wondering where she was and what she was doing.

It was lovely to have such a devoted boyfriend; he made her feel really protected and cherished.

Stella wished though, that Rory had another interest rather than his bloody racehorses. It was too much really, having to stand in cold miserable race courses watching his horses hurtle around a muddy track. Since the incident that had almost ruined her jacket she had made sure that she had stayed well away from any of the horses.

And she certainly didn't want to spend any time near to Henry; it was strange though, considering how much he annoyed her and how much she was sure she hated him, how often her thoughts strayed to him.

She would often find herself prickling with annoyance at the thought of how his eyes danced with amusement when they saw her.

It certainly wasn't Stella's idea of fun, to head out to the racing stables on a miserable cold winter afternoon, but if that was what Rory wanted, then she would go along with him.

At least she could enjoy sitting in his lovely car, luxuriating against the squashy leather seats and watching the envious glances of the passers-by as they glided along the road.

Now though Stella sat up, peering hard through the bare winter branches. They were near the racing stables. Soon she would be able to get a glimpse of the beautiful Thornhill House. As she glimpsed the grey stone house far away from the road, something rust coloured caught her eye, a slight movement at the side of the road amongst the foliage.

"Rory, stop!" she yelled, putting a hand on Rory's arm.

"What on earth's the matter?" Rory snapped impatiently stepping hard on the brakes to bring the powerful car to a halt.

"There was something just back there, an injured cat or fox or something," Stella reached for the door handle.

"Oh for heaven's sake," sighed Rory, peevishly. "Can't you just leave it." But Stella was already out of the car and jogging back up the road as fast as she could in her high heels.

Then yards from the car she began to slow her pace, maybe she had imagined something on the side of the road. It was probably just a piece of cloth, or some rubbish.

She looked out through the trees to Thornhill House, what a wonderful place to live. Maybe Rory could buy something like that when they were married. She was sure that he was fond enough of her to want to marry her, not now though, maybe in a years' time, when she had proved to him what a suitable wife she would be.

Then she saw what had caught her eye in the first place. Lying on the side of the road, was a small, rust coloured terrier puppy.

The little puppy raised its head when it saw Stella and the very end of its tail thumped faintly against the damp earth.

"Oh you poor little thing," Stella winced in sympathy as she crouched beside the little form.

Growing up in the West of Ireland countryside had made her used to dealing with injured animals. The kitchen at home had been constantly full of rescued animals and birds she and her siblings found in the fields or on the beaches and brought home to nurse back to health, sometimes successfully, although often the creatures, weak and terrified when they were found, died in spite of their ministrations.

She ran a gentle hand over the puppy's harsh coat. There were no obvious signs of injury, the pup had probably just been abandoned and had been wandering for days until it had collapsed through exhaustion and hunger.

"You poor little thing," she slipped her jumper over her head and lifted the puppy into the warm fabric and then stood up,

"What is it?" Rory said peevishly, he had parked the car and walked back up the road to her.

"A puppy, I think he's been abandoned," Stella moved her jumper away from the pup to show it to Rory, who made an impatient tutting noise.

"Leave the bloody thing here, it will probably die anyway," he said with a trace of sullenness in his voice.

"Rory, I can't, that would be cruel," Stella smiled warmly at him, trying to melt his coldness. She had to bring the puppy with her and help it.

"I think you are bloody mad," he snapped sulkily and spun around on his heel and marched back to the car, his shoulders hunched petulantly.

Stella followed him; she couldn't just abandon the pup at the side of the road. Surely Rory could see that. Rory slammed the car door and then turned to Stella as she cradled the puppy on her lap. "Well it's a cute little thing, I hope that it lives. The rescue centre will be able to find a good home for it."

Stella shot a quizzical look at him. At least he had accepted she had to bring the puppy now, but she certainly could not imagine taking it to the dog pound. The last thing that she had ever wanted was another dog, there had been enough of them when she was growing up, but now…..

A few moments later Rory turned off the main road and the car bumped down the long track to Thornhill Stables.

"What have you got there?" Henry asked, coming across the yard to greet them.

"A puppy, I found it on the road, it's sick," Stella said, showing Henry the contents of her bundle.

"We'll take it inside, it will be warm by the Aga and I'll get it some milk," Henry said, gently rubbing the top of the puppy's head. "He's like a little teddy bear."

Henry led the way across the yard to the cottage. Rory followed for a few strides and then turned and walked towards the stables.

"Rory?" Stella asked quizzically but Rory had already gone. The front door of the cottage was warped and Henry had to shove his shoulder against it to push it open, it shrieked in protest as the wood caught on the worn sandstone floor.

"Come in," Henry led the way along a short sandstone corridor lined with photographs of him and horses at various race meetings.

At the end of the corridor was a cavernous kitchen, dominated by a large cream coloured Aga and an enormous pine table, one leg of which Stella noticed was held up with a pile of books. Quickly he poured some milk into a cup and shoved it into the microwave, seconds later the milk was tepid and he spooned a few spoons of it into the puppy's mouth. He dragged a towel off the drying rail above the Aga and gently wrapped the puppy in it and handed Stella her jumper back.

"Now, leave him by the Aga and we'll see if he's any better in a while." Henry said taking the pup off her and laying it gently beside the warmth of the Aga. Stella began to put her jumper back on, but as she lifted it over her head the musty doggy smell made her wrinkle her nose in distaste.

"I don't think I need this on," Stella bundled the jumper under her arm and giving the puppy's head a gentle rub, followed Henry outside.

"I've come to look at my horse, Lover Boy working, not tend to some bloody puppy," snapped Rory, sulkily, stomping across the straw strewn yard towards them.

"Right then," Henry said, in a voice that could have been used to pacify a sulking toddler. "Jimmy!!" he yelled for the stable lad to come and saddle Rory's horse and bring it up onto the gallops. "Do you want to walk to the gallops or do you want to come in my jeep?" Henry asked as the horse was led out into the yard.

"Walk," Rory said, shortly and began to head off across the yard to the field behind the stables that Henry used as a gallop. Stella jogged to catch up with Rory and shoved her arm in his.

"Oh, you've torn yourself away from the mutt have you," Rory hissed, nastily.

Stella bit her lip, surely Rory wasn't sulking because of the puppy.

He hurried across the grass, paying no heed to the fact that she had to jog to keep up with him, her heels sinking into the soft grass making it hard to walk. Then he stood, impassive as the horse galloped around the field.

"He's magnificent," Stella breathed, caught all of a sudden by the bug that afflicts thousands with a love for the horse.

Lover Boy powered along the field, following a high stone wall, behind which she could see the grey stone of the gorgeous Thornhill House, beautiful even from this different angle. From here she could see the side of the house, with its sloping roof and tall windows.

"Magnificent," Henry agreed, coming to stand beside her. Stella wasn't sure if he was talking about Lover Boy or the house.

"That's enough," Rory growled and turning on his heel, headed back to the yard. "Come on we're going."

"I'll just get the puppy," Stella hurried to the cottage before Rory had the chance to leave. It was warm inside the kitchen; the puppy was curled beside the Aga, still wrapped in his towel. He was sleeping and whimpered and stirred in his sleep as she picked him up.

"Keep the towel," Henry said, appearing in the doorway. "You had better go. Rory wants to go now." He moved out of the doorway to let her pass. "And when Rory wants something he usually gets it," Henry said so quietly that Stella wondered if she had really heard him speak.

Stella ran out into the yard. Rory had already turned the car around and was revving the engine.

"Don't let that fucking dog pee on my seat," he snapped without taking his eyes from the windscreen.

"He's wrapped in a towel that Henry gave me," Stella told him, adjusting the puppy on her lap.

"Nice of him," snarled Rory shoving the car into gear and lurching out of the yard. Stella stared miserably out of the window, watching the countryside slide by as the car hurtled back towards the city. What on earth was the matter with Rory she wondered, was he really angry that she had picked up the dog?

"I'm sorry for picking up this dog," she stammered, wanting to put right the dreadful atmosphere that existed in the car.

"I don't give a damn about the dog," he said tightly.

Stella sighed, what on earth had gone wrong with the day. Rory had been so nice up until today. Why had he changed so suddenly?

The countryside changed abruptly as the fields gave way to the urban sprawl of the city. Rory slowed the car as the traffic built up. Stella longed to be home, to get out of the car and try to talk to Rory properly to see what was wrong with him.

At least Amber was out for the day and so they could have the apartment to themselves to try to put this dreadful atmosphere right.

At last they arrived outside the apartment and sat in dreadful silence as the final notes of the car engine died away.

"Do you want to come in?" Stella asked.

Rory shrugged. "I suppose so," he sighed, as if she had asked him an almighty favour.

Stella could have wept with relief, at least he wasn't going to drive off in temper and her never know what was the matter. At least he was going to come inside and she would be able to put the dreadful wrong behind them. Whatever it was that had upset him, she would make it right. The last thing that she wanted was to lose Rory.

Stella led the way into the apartment, the puppy cradled in her arms. She gently laid him, still wrapped in the towel in a corner of the living room, beside the radiator. She wished with all of her heart that she had never seen the damn thing. Whatever had happened, the puppy was the start of everything going wrong with the day.

Rory prowled around the apartment, his face tight, lips white where he pressed them into a taut line.

"Coffee?" Stella asked, trying to ignore the obvious anger in him. Maybe if she pretended everything was normal then he might forget his temper and everything would be ok again.

"No."

"Are you alright?" it was patently obvious that he wasn't. In fact far from alright.

"Why did you come back with me?" he snapped suddenly.

"What?" What on earth was Rory on about, she wondered, feeling a cold panic sinking into the pit of her stomach. Rory was very angry. At her. Their relationship was in grave danger; she had to put things right between them. Had to.

"Well it was obvious to me that you wanted to be with Henry. You couldn't wait to get into that cottage with him."

"Rory, I went in to keep the puppy warm and to get some milk for it."

"I won't be made a fool of while you play around with Henry. I can see how he looks at you."

"I'm not interested in Henry, far from it!" Stella exploded, filled with self-righteous indignation. "I can't stand the sight of Henry."

"It doesn't look like that to me," Rory growled. "And don't start crying, you won't get around me like that."

Stella stifled a sob of frustration. How could she make Rory see that she wasn't interested in Henry?

"Rory, honestly I'm not interested in Henry. I'm sorry if you thought that. Look I won't even talk to him in the future if you are worried."

Rory glared at her for a moment and then sank tiredly down on the sofa. "It's just that you are so attractive. All the men want to be with you. I can see them looking at you. They look like hungry dogs looking at a bone."

"I can't help how they look at me," Stella scowled, "I'm not interested in them. Only you."

Rory held out his hand and Stella grabbed it, thankfully, "It's just that I care about you so much," he said, clutching her hand. Stella felt the tension slide out of her body, the crisis was over.

CHAPTER SIX

Stella glanced at her watch and gave a groan of frustration. Time was getting short and she still hadn't decided what to wear to go out with Rory.

Behind her the bed was littered with outfits she had discarded. The knot of tension in her stomach gripped tighter. Going out for an evening did not usually cause such chaos and confusion, but this date was very important.

Thankfully, Stella had mused, when she had come into her bedroom to get ready, their fledgling relationship had survived The First Row. Hopefully there would not be any others. But it was blatantly obvious that she was going to have to be careful not to make Rory jealous again, which made choosing an outfit rather difficult. She wanted to wear something elegant, but not too plain, feminine without being sexy. But sexy enough for him to fancy her.

Rory's reaction to Henry helping her with the puppy had made her feel very wary. The last thing that she needed tonight was for him to start to feel jealous if a waiter started to peer down her chest if she wore a top that was too revealing.

The pile of clothes on the bed grew steadily higher and she grew steadily more flustered.

"Maybe….." she wondered out loud, reaching into the wardrobe and pulling out The Red Dress.

Since she had seen what looked like an identical red dress in the dry cleaners Stella had rather gone off her much loved dress. What was the good of paying a fortune for a dress and then having someone else walking around in one exactly the same?

She really must have words with the girl who had sold her the dress. But for the moment this was an outfit crisis. She slid off her dressing gown, yet again, and pulled the dress over her head. The red dress was perfect, elegant, yet sexy, yet demure.

"So. What do you think?" Stella asked, closing her bedroom door on the chaos that littered the bed. She would deal with all the mess when she got home.

Amber sat on the floor in front of the gas fire, cradling the puppy in her arms like a baby.

"Yep, lovely," Amber glanced quickly in Stella's direction, with something that looked strangely like panic in her eyes, before turning her attention to the puppy again.

"Thanks for your vote of confidence," muttered Stella crossly, twisting her arm around to her neck as something prickled her. She had needed Amber to tell her she looked nice, but she was too busy with the puppy.

Since the puppy had appeared Amber had spent every moment cuddling and playing with it.

Stella's grasping fingers found what had been prickling her – a laundry ticket, pinned into the label at the back of the dress. That was odd; she must have forgotten to remove it the last time the dress was cleaned. Deftly she unpinned the label and shoved it into the bin. Now that really was odd. An enormous piece of clear plastic wrapper had been shoved into the bin. Like the stuff they used to wrap dry cleaning.

Amber was too grungy to use the dry cleaners very often; maybe living with Stella was finally smartening her up.

"Did you get some dry cleaning done?" Stella shoved the label into the bin. "Erm…yes," Amber's voice rose fractionally higher.

"Ahh," Stella replied. Amber was obviously too embarrassed to admit that she was finally cleaning up her act.

A car horn blared loudly outside.

"I think your date has arrived," Amber said, holding up the puppy and waving its paw in Stella's direction. "Can't he be bothered getting out of his car and walking all the way up here to fetch you?" she asked, her voice tinged with sarcasm.

Stella clamped her lips together, unable to think of a smart reply.

"Don't wait up, I may be late," she told Amber pulling a black jacket on over the red dress.

"You hope!" retorted Amber. "This puppy is just like a teddy bear, how about we call him Teddy?" she asked, following Stella to the door with the puppy draped over her shoulder.

"I like that," Stella smiled, rubbing the puppy's soft fur.

Rory sat in his flashy sports car, revving the engine. "Come on, I've got a table booked for eight thirty," he told Stella, impatiently, as she got into the car, barely glancing in her direction.

He shoved his foot on the accelerator and powered the car away from the pavement before she had even shut the door properly. Stella hutched her dress down and fastened the seatbelt,

"Where are we eating?" she asked, glancing out of the windows and seeing the envious gazes of people on the pavements as the flashy car whisked by.

"Farley's, it's a new restaurant. Very exclusive." Rory said, honking his horn aggressively at a car in front of him, which was slow to pull away from a set of traffic lights.

A short time later Rory turned the car off the main road onto a sleek tarmac drive that ran through a broad avenue of trees.

"Hmmm, nice job they've made of converting the farm buildings," Rory guided the car into a space between a Rolls Royce and a Ferrari, he nodded approvingly, gazing out of the car windscreen at the old stone buildings. Bright lights set into the grass at the edge of the car park shone upwards, making the stone shine a burnished gold in the yellow glow. Inside, through enormous arched windows, Stella could see the restaurant was full of people.

"This was a derelict farm a year ago," Rory told her, as they walked across the car park towards the restaurant. "Some friends of mine have converted the buildings into a restaurant and some rather exclusive art galleries and shops." He opened the door and marched in.

"There's Kian O'Sullivan," Rory strode across the crowded restaurant; Stella just grabbed the door and pushed it open before it banged shut behind him. "Kian, wonderful to see you!" Rory pumped the hand of a large red faced man who was sitting at a table in the centre of the restaurant, surrounded by a hoard of very young looking girls. "The place looks fantastic!"

Stella crossed the restaurant in his wake and then stood uncertainly on the edge of the conversation.

Kian glanced at her briefly and the girls by his side glared at her and then deciding that she was of no consequence went back to their giggling conversation.

"This is Stella," Rory introduced her finally, and then continued his conversation with Kian.

A flustered looking waiter bustled through the crowded restaurant. "Your table is ready, Sir," he told Rory, guiding them across the room to a window table. He pulled out the seat for Stella to sit down and made a huge show of arranging the napkin on her lap.

Stella looked nervously at the huge array of cutlery and glasses crammed onto the table. It would be awful if she used the wrong knife, just when she was trying to impress Rory.

"The guinea fowl is supposed to be rather nice," Rory said, as another waiter handed them menus.

Halfway through the meal Stella began to relax. Rory, after downing half a bottle of red wine, was in fine form. She glanced around the room. The restaurant was gorgeous, all wooden floors and bare stone walls set off with beautiful, opulent furniture which formed the perfect back drop for the obviously wealthy crowd that had gathered there to eat.

This, she decided, was really the way to live, mingling with wealthy people, in the finest restaurants, with an expensive car sitting outside in the car park for the trip home. The waiter had just cleared their dinner plates away when suddenly there was a shriek of recognition from across the room.

"Rory!" yelled three, high pitched and very posh voices. Stella looked across the room to see three scantily clad girls in various shades of blonde descending rapidly on them.

With barely a glance in her direction the three girls launched themselves at Rory, covering him in kisses before dragging vacant chairs from adjoining tables and plonking themselves close to him.

"This is Tiger, Olympia and Noki," Rory introduced the three, "Stella, a friend of mine." He told the girls as they looked at Stella, with disinterested eyes.

Once she had been dismissed as a mere friend the three girls, assuming that she wasn't worth bothering with turned their attention to Rory, swigging wine out of his glass and chattering loudly, all flirting outrageously with him, completely ignoring Stella.

Stella took a long swig of her red wine, downing half of the glass as if it were lemonade on a hot summer's day; she couldn't bear the three young women. How dare they muscle in on her date and completely monopolise Rory's attention?

"Rory, I think I need to get home," Stella said quickly when there was a momentary lapse in the clamour of conversation.

"Oh," said the dark blonde, who Stella guessed was called Noki, she looked across the table at Stella as if she had announced that she was going to dance naked on the table. "Isn't it a bit early?" the middle blonde scowled at Rory.

"I have to get up early for work," snapped Stella, the girls were really getting on her nerves; she just wished that they would clear off and leave her with Rory, they were ruining her evening.

"Work?" said pale blonde, as if she had never heard the word before. "Oh, how awful."

"Ring me darling, won't you?" The pale blonde smacked a lingering kiss on Rory's lips and shooting Stella a triumphant look led the way back across the restaurant with the other blondes trailing regretfully in her wake. Rory let out an audible sigh of regret as he watched the girls sashay their way through the tables.

"Lovely girls," he breathed, turning his attention slowly back to Stella. "Better get the worker home then."

Stella stalked out of the restaurant; the blondes had ruined her evening. She had hoped for once she would have been able to sit and talk to Rory away from those awful racehorses of his, without the distraction of the race course. Her first real chance to show him what a lovely person she was and how he would be foolish not to consider her as a future wife.

"Nice restaurant," Rory commented, as he gunned the car engine into life.

"Yes," Stella snapped, shortly, she just wanted to go home to cool off the ferocious temper that was boiling within her.

"Didn't you enjoy yourself?" asked Rory, when she had sat silently for some time. "Yes, but…." She stopped lamely, before bravely ploughing on, "those girls….chatting you up…all over you.."

Rory let out a guffaw of laughter. "They are just friends."

"Yes, but, they were so obviously chatting you up."

Rory signed. "Look if you don't like me having friends then there's no point in continuing with this. Is there?"

Stella was silent, listening to the purr of the car engine, watching the array of lights on the dashboard, seeing a man nudging his companion to look as the car glided by.

In the semi darkness she looked at Rory, with his expensive clothes, his gold watch glinting in the light from lamp posts. She didn't want to give this up.

"I'm sorry," she whispered quietly.

"That's better," Rory ran a hot hand up the length of her thigh. "Now. Do you fancy coming back to my place for a nightcap?"

Stella woke with a jolt. Bright light flooded into the bedroom, streaming in through the open curtains.

"Oh my God!" she gasped, shoving back the bed clothes. She was going to be late for work.

"What the hell!" roared Rory, as a blast of cold air hit his warm skin.

Shit, shit, shit. How could she have been so stupid as to oversleep, Stella lurched across the bedroom, still half asleep, to find her clothes. Damn, she couldn't go into work wearing her red dress. That would be just too obvious. Everyone would know that she hadn't been home all night. Stella pulled on her underwear and slid the red dress over her head,

"Where are you going?" Rory propped himself up on one arm and grinned at her wolfishly, as she fastened her shoes.

"I must get home; I've got to change and shower and get to work. I am going to be so late!" Stella said, anxiously.

"Oh for heaven's sake, relax," Rory yawned. "Ring up and tell them you aren't coming in." he picked up his mobile phone from the bedside table and held it out to her.

Stella shook her head. "I can't, I need to get to work, they are relying on me."

Rory slammed the phone back down peevishly. "What's so fucking important at work? Why are you in such a hurry to get there? You must be shagging the boss or something."

"No! Of course not!" Stella retorted. How could Rory say such a thing? She just needed to get to work, she had a responsible job.

She had taken a long time to climb up the ladder at work, she was damned if she was going to let them down on a whim.

"Must be. Otherwise why wouldn't you want to spend the day here with me," Rory turned away and pulled the bed clothes up around his neck, his whole body rigid with tension.

"I can't just take days off just like that," Stella whispered, tears threatening to spill down her cheeks. How could Rory make accusations like that? She loved her job and certainly wasn't in love with her boss like he was implying. Nothing could have been further from the truth. Kevin O'Mara her boss was a horrible creep, but Stella did enjoy every bit of her job.

"You could if you cared anything for me," Rory said in a wheedling little voice. "You must have someone else. Go on. Go off to your boss."

Stella crossed the room and sat on the edge of the bed and gingerly touched Rory's shoulder, he shrugged off her hand with a vicious jerk.

"There's nothing between me and my boss," she said, quietly, bewildered by the sudden twist in his mood. "Please believe me."

Rory was silent. Stella put her hand slowly back onto his shoulder, with a sigh of frustration and looked around the gorgeous room. This was the kind of place that she would love to live in.

She had adored Rory's apartment from the moment she had walked in the previous evening. Every inch of the apartment had a deliciously expensive air about it, from the acres of pale carpet, to the opulent furniture and bright modern paintings that adorned the walls.

And now she would never be able to spend time here. Rory was dismissing her as curtly as a waiter who had given bad service. Just because he had suddenly assumed that she was having an affair with her boss. The injustice of it rankled terribly.

"Stay if you want to," said Rory, sullenly, breaking the tense silence. "Ring up and say you aren't coming and then get back into bed."

He was giving her a reprieve. Stella snatched up the mobile phone and began to punch in her work number.

CHAPTER SEVEN

Amber shook her head slowly in disbelief. "So you just telephoned work and said that you were sick?" She glared across the room at Stella who pushed her hair behind her ears and then shrugged in a helpless gesture before hesitantly saying, "yes."

"And your Boss believed you?" Amber finished mopping up the puddle of puppy wee Teddy, had just done. Sshe got to her feet, tucking the small rust coloured puppy under her arm. Teddy wriggled furiously, his short legs working in an effort to free himself from her grasp. Amber crouched down and let the puppy go. He scampered away with his curious uncoordinated gait, growling furiously at a rubber ball the girls had brought him to play with.

"He must have known you were lying, you have never had a day off sick. Ever!"

"I know," Stella tapped Teddy's rubber ball with the toe of her kitten heeled mules, sending it rolling across the carpet. The puppy dashed after it, small black tipped ears flapping.

"But Rory........" her words ground to a halt. She sighed trying to gather her thoughts and frame the words to explain she had not gone to work because Rory had accused her of having an affair and because she had been feeble enough to let him manipulate her into staying with him for the day.

It had been a nice day. They had spent the morning lolling around his apartment, and then had lunch in a lovely restaurant and in the afternoon he had taken her shopping. She had come home with carrier bags filled with expensive underwear and clothes. But the trip had been spoilt by the nagging sensation of guilt that she had let them down at work.

She loved her job and had spent years working her way up from humble Girl Friday to Editor of the beauty page, at MiMi Magazine. And she had done that by making herself indispensable to everyone – and never missing a day's work.

"Bloody Hell!" Amber crawled across the floor to retrieve the ball from Teddy's needle sharp tiny teeth.

"Was he so wonderful that you couldn't tear yourself away?" she sat on her heels and grinned at Stella.

"Not exactly," Stella answered, wryly. "He did not want me to go."

The pup, tiring of playing with the ball, capered across the room and began to gnaw at the heels of Stella's shoes.

She reached down and pulled him onto her lap, tilting her face down so that Amber would not be able to read her expression, as she recalled Rory's hasty and very inadequate lovemaking – if it could be called that. Climbing on top of her and banging away for a few moments hardly warranted the grand title of lovemaking.

Amber gave a snort of annoyance.

"But surely you couldn't miss work just because he wanted you to stay with him. You have responsibilities."

"He accused me of having an affair with my boss."

This time the snort was one of amusement that turned rapidly to amazement as the impact of Stella's words sank in.

"What?!" Amber spat, incredulously.

"His apartment was gorgeous," Stella changed the subject abruptly; she did not want to discuss the pathetic way she had let Rory manipulate her.

Amber watched her friend as a myriad of emotions flickered across her beautiful face.

Stella jumped to her feet, wanting to stop the discussion. "I think that we need puppy food. Do you want to come? We could get a drink on the way back."

Then seeing the startled look of horror on Amber's face and realising that yet again she had no money, Stella added, "my treat."

They walked to the shop brought the dog food and then went to a pub crowded with early evening drinkers relaxing before making the journey home.

Amber took her wine glass from Stella with a guilty smile, this month the repayments on her credit card bills had taken most of her spare salary. The repayment had hardly made a dent in the balance figure.

Amber slowly sipped the dark liquid and then almost choked as a familiar face caught her eye. Amber looked, transfixed over Stella's left shoulder, unable to hear the words she was saying, she was just aware of her mouth opening and closing while all the time Luke was coming towards them, a huge grin splitting his face.

"Hey......Babe," Luke struggled to think of her name and failed. He squeezed past Stella and enfolded Amber in a bear hug. He smelt of beer and smoke.

"Where were you the other night?" Amber yelped, and saw Stella raise her eyes skywards. Ok so it was completely un-cool to be so naked in her demanding to know why she had been stood up. Of course she should have immediately apologised for standing him up, make him feel that she didn't give a damn about him.

Amber could almost hear Stella lecturing her about how to make a man weak with desire. But how could she talk? Ms Stand-By-Your-Man-And-Don't-Go-To-Work-Just-Cus-He-Say's-So.

"Oh!" groaned Mr Super Cool, slapping a long fingered hand to his forehead, "I had some urgent business I had to sort out – and I hadn't got your phone number with me. I felt terrible letting you down like that."

Amber caught Stella's eye and ignored the glare of disbelief she was giving her. Ok so it did sound a feeble excuse. But it might be true. And he really had the nicest smile.

"Let me make it up to you. Please come out with me tonight." He fixed his beautiful brown eyes on her, reminding her of Teddy when he was hungry or wanted playing with.

"Ok," she said shooting a defiant glance at Stella, who shook her head imperceptibly in disbelief.

"He's really nice, don't you think?" Amber swung the shopping bag gaily as they walked home.

"He's a total slimeball," declared Stella tonelessly.

"He said that he couldn't get hold of me to tell me that he wasn't coming," she replied huffily. Amber stopped swinging the bag and walked silently beside Stella.

"That's total rubbish, the oldest line in the book."

"Well I believe him," Amber snapped, clamping her mouth shut into a tight line. Sometimes she really hated Stella, she was such a know it all. She was hardly any great expert on how to deal with men. Look at the jerk she had landed herself with. Just because he was rich.

"What shall I wear? Amber asked, desperate to break the uncomfortable silence that had fallen between them.

"I don't know," Stella replied, shortly. Then softening to one of her favourite subjects – clothes, she added, "how about that nice pink top with your black trousers?"

Teddy began to yap loudly as Stella put the key in the lock.

"He's going to be a good guard dog," grinned Amber, she pushed open the door, abandoned the bag of dog food down on the kitchen worktop and headed into her bedroom to see what she could find to wear.

Stella followed Amber into her bedroom, if she was going to make a fool of herself over some cold hearted lying cheat then she might as well make sure that Amber looked nice doing it.

Amber wrenched open the wardrobe door and sighed. Every inch of space was crammed with the results of her shopping forays, and yet there still wasn't anything to wear. None of the clothes she bought ever went with anything else. And something that had looked like a bargain in the shop had become rather less so when she got it home and realised that it really didn't suit her or go with anything else in the wardrobe.

"What about this?" Stella reached into the mass of colour and texture and pulled out a tee-shirt. Amber saw a look of distaste flicker over her face before she managed to assume a polite expression. "Perhaps not," she folded the hideous creation solicitously before shoving it back.

Amber felt the familiar knot of tension grip her stomach as it always did when she was faced with the decision of what to wear for an important date. If only Stella had gone out, Amber could have raided her wardrobe. Again.

47

"Maybe we should have a look what's in my wardrobe." Stella shut Amber's wardrobe door and headed into her own room with Amber trotting thankfully behind her. "Here," she flung open the door and immediately pulled out a beige dress.

Amber took the dress and held it up against her and gazed in the mirror. The long, plain dress had tiny buttons all the way down the front and a pretty scooped neck. It looked gorgeous against her dark colouring, highlighting her dark hair and green eyes.

"You may as well look pretty while you make a fool of yourself." Stella said, tightly.

A short time later Amber had showered, blow dried her hair and even found enough change in a side pocket of a discarded handbag for a taxi to the pub to meet Luke.

As the taxi got closer to the pub Amber clamped her knees tightly together to stop them quivering. This was ridiculous, she was behaving like a schoolgirl on a first date. Just because Luke was gorgeous she had gone to pieces. She must keep control of her feelings; maybe he wouldn't turn up again and then she would have to go home looking like a total idiot and Stella would take great pleasure in saying 'I told you so.'

Then, as the taxi swooped around the corner Amber's heart lurched in her chest. He was there. Luke was actually standing outside the pub waiting for her!

Amber fumbled in her purse for the money to pay for the taxi and then succeeded in dropping the small change that she had so carefully counted out all over the front seat of the cab.

"Oh, go on," snapped the taxi driver, impatiently, lurching to a stop outside the pub. He shook his head, wryly as Amber fumbled with the door handle and then half fell out of the cab in her haste.

"You look great," Luke planted a kiss on her cheek and grinned disarmingly. Amber fought the urge to stand on the pavement and gaze at him with her mouth open in sheer wonderment. "Come on, let's get a drink. I think I've got a lot of making up to do for letting you down the other evening."

"Ok," Amber wished that she could think of something witty to say as he took her arm and guided her into the pub. Or actually, just anything to say at all.

"Red wine isn't it?" Luke shoved his way to the bar. The barmaid almost fell over her high heels in her rush to get to him. "What can I get you, Luke?" she breathed, Amber saw her face fall as she saw that Luke was with someone. A grin of triumph split her face, this trophy man, who everyone seemed to fancy was actually with her!

"We'll sit over here," Luke handed Amber a glass of wine and led the way across the bar, to a crowded table. "Shove over Max," Luke perched on the edge of the bench seat and shoved the lads who were at the table over to make room for him and Amber. "These are the Party Boys," Luke grinned, naming all of the lads who were at the table, then chinking his glass against Amber's he said, "drink up now and we'll have a grand time."

Amber made her way slowly back to the table after yet another trip to the Ladies. "Shorry," she slurred, cannoning off a man who was standing at the bar. Three glasses of wine was one too many.

"Got another red wine for you!" Luke roared, pushing the tall glass across the table towards her. Amber felt her stomach heave at the thought of the dark liquid.

She shouldn't have drunk so much, but nerves and the sheer delight at having hooked such a prize as Luke had made her gulp the first few glasses as if they were lemonade.

And now she was paying the price.

Luke's friends had gone. Amber could not remember them leaving.

Luke put his arm around her. Amber struggled to focus as his face moved closer and closer. And then his lips closed onto hers, she felt herself turn to liquid inside, he was soooooooooo delicious, she wanted to stay kissing him forever.

A taxi took them to a party, Amber was aware of thumping music, and Luke kissing her in the most delicious way, slowly, his lips soft, pliable against hers, his hands roving over her body, awakening sensations that made her shiver with longing.

"Do you want to come upstairs?" he whispered, his voice hoarse in her ear, she felt her hair move as he breathed against her skin. She nodded, enthralled. This gorgeous man, who everyone had fancied, actually wanted her.

Luke took Amber's hand and led her upstairs past couples entwined together and two girls by the front door who were arguing, shrieking at each other in high pitched voices.

Amber heard herself giggling as Luke threw a man, who had been

49

sprawled fully clothed on the bed, out of the bedroom and locked the door.

Luke lay her down.

Amber gave a sigh of infinite pleasure as he undid the buttons on Stella's dress and finally moved his warm hands over her body.

Afterwards she felt more sober, the vigorous exercise working the alcohol out of her system. She lay in Luke's arms and grinned with sheer delight.

This was truly wonderful, she was very lucky to have such a lovely man who so obviously wanted her so much.

Stella had been wrong about him.

"Come on, Babe, I'll get you a taxi," Luke rolled out of bed and started to pull on his jeans. Amber slid reluctantly out of the warmth of the bed and began to button Stella's dress. Damn, some of the buttons were missing; she did not remember losing them, although there was a vague and uncomfortable memory of Luke pulling at the buttons in frustration when he could not undo them fast enough in his haste to get her undressed.

Luke punched some numbers on his mobile and ordered a taxi.

"It will be about ten minutes, I'll get you a coffee," he told her, snapping off the phone.

"When will I see you again?" Amber asked, sipping the bitter coffee. Stella would be horrified if she could see how un-cool Amber was being. Never be too eager, she would say, scornfully. But Amber could not bear the thought of not knowing when she would see Luke again. He must have just forgotten to make another date or to take her phone number, he must have been just about to do it when she asked.

"I'm not sure, I'm a bit busy for the next week.............or so, but I'll see you around I'm sure," Amber stared hard at the dregs of her coffee. He was giving her the brush off.

Stella had been right all along. He was worse than even Stella had thought. He had taken her out and she had let him use her for sex. What a cheap fool she had been to fall for him.

Luke pulled back the curtains and peered along the darkened street. "Here's the taxi." He walked her outside, gave the taxi driver money and told him to take Amber home. Then dropping a perfunctory kiss on her cheek he went back inside the house without a backwards glance.

Amber sat in the back of the taxi and gazed numbly at the houses, they passed, all in darkness, the orange street lights casting an eerie glow over the gardens.

"Night love," the driver said cheerily, as he dropped her off at the entrance to the apartment. Amber let herself in, barely aware of Teddy, scrabbling against her legs with his sharp claws, desperate for attention. How could she have been such a fool? Getting drunk and being used for sex.

"Had a good time?" Stella emerged from her bedroom.

"No!" gasped Amber, clamping her hand to her mouth and dashing to the toilet where she was violently sick.

CHAPTER EIGHT

"Glad that you were feeling well enough to come back to work for the Christmas Party," Kevin O'Mara, her boss whispered silkily in her ear.

Stella smiled tightly, she had not seen Kevin slinking up beside her.

She had spent the whole evening avoiding him, remembering the sarcastic tirade that he had subjected her to when she had returned to work after Rory had persuaded her to take the day off.

Kevin took a long swig of his drink, Stella suspected that the tumbler full of pale liquid was virtually all whiskey. "I hope that you will be well enough after Christmas to work on the special spring fashion edition," Kevin glared at her, his pale green eyes filled with malice. "Your wonderful assistant, Sorcha did a brilliant job while you were off."

Kevin brushed back a lock of long curly hair off his forehead with plump fingers, the unspoken threat was clear in his words. If Stella was not going to be at work then Sorcha was going to take over from her. Simple as that.

Stella nodded, glad that the boardroom was in virtual darkness and so Kevin would not be able to see the blush she was sure was staining her cheeks. She could not blame him for making the threat. She held a responsible position in the magazine and knew she had let him down badly when she had taken the day off. She knew she should have been firmer with Rory, but she had not been able to stand up to him.

The threat from Rory was as clear as it now was from Kevin. She had to be the perfect girlfriend to Rory, pander to his every whim, otherwise she would lose him.

Stella loved her job, and she loved Rory, for all his jealous tantrums, she was sure that he loved her. And he was everything that she had ever wanted. Stella was determined not to let him go. She was tired of looking for the right man, one with wealth, looks and power. And now that she had found him, Stella was not going to give him up.

People were starting to drift away from the party, Kevin, having made his point, waltzed away to stand at the door, taking up a position where he could kiss everyone goodnight. Stella collected her coat and headed home.

She wished that Rory had agreed to come, she would have enjoyed showing him off to everyone, but he had business to attend to.

Stella let herself into the darkened apartment, in the pale orange light from the gas fire Stella could see Amber sprawled on the sofa, nursing Teddy across her chest like a baby. Stella snapped on the light, Amber rummaged in her jeans pocket for a tissue and wiped her eyes, surreptitiously.

"Had a nice time?" Amber asked, her voice was thick with tears.

"What's the matter?" Stella ignored her question. Amber hoisted Teddy onto her knees and rubbed his head.

Stella would have been furious at Amber for letting herself get in such a mess with her life. Everything was awful, and then to cap it all, she had gone for a drink with the girls from work tonight and had seen Luke and his mates in the pub, sniggering at her, he must have told them all about how he had got her drunk and taken her to bed.

"Will you be ok while I've gone to Rory's over Christmas?" shouted Stella through her open bedroom door as she began to take off her makeup. There was another line at the corner of her eyes that had not been there before, she was sure of it.

Stella leant further towards her magnifying mirror. She had to settle down, get married, before it was too late, once her looks had gone no one would want her.

"I'll be back just after New Year," she added, wishing that Christmas were over. She felt so guilty all the time. She even felt guilty about leaving Amber to care for Teddy, although she did not seem to mind, she had virtually taken over the little dog anyway. But she felt worse about not going home for Christmas.

When Rory had asked her a few days previously what she was going to do for Christmas she had told him she usually made the interminable journey home to Mayo until the New Year.

"Oh, you don't want to go all that way surely," he had grumbled. "Stay with me instead." And so she had readily agreed.

It was nice to have the excuse not to make the interminable drive across the country to Mayo. Nice to know that she would be spending Christmas in a gorgeous luxury apartment, with a charming, handsome man, instead of in the noisy chaotic cottage where she had grown up.

It had been hard to explain to her mother that she could not come this year. The disappointment was clear in her voice as she told Stella that she hoped that she would come and visit them soon and that she would miss her.

Stella had put down the phone with a heavy heart, she hated how relieved she felt, now that she was not going back home.

"Sound's like your lord and master is here," Amber said, peering out of the window as Rory honked his horn aggressively to announce his arrival. Stella hastily grabbed the bags that she had lined up by the door and then seeing Amber's crestfallen face, dropped the bags and crossed the room to enfold her in a bear hug. "I'll see you soon, have a great time."

Amber wrenched her face into a smile. "You too."

Amber watched Stella hurry across the pavement in her impossibly high heels. She looked so happy, delighted that her life was going so well. Amber puffed out her cheeks and sighed bitterly, everything was going so well for Stella. And Ruby. While for Amber it was a constant battle from one mess to another. Amber slumped down on the sofa and buried her head in her hands. How could she have been such a fool? Yet again.

She had only wanted to buy Christmas presents for everyone. If only she had not taken an extra-long lunch hour, if only she had never gone into town...... Festive garlands hung across the streets and tinsel and bright lights glittered in the shop windows.

Amber had felt the familiar tension gripping her stomach.

Christmas was coming rapidly and she had no money to buy gifts for anyone, and they would all be expecting her to produce goodies for them. Her credit cards were at the limit, and this month's salary had all been magically transferred by the bank into Stella's account to pay for the rent on the flat and her contribution towards the food and utilities. She had enough left for bus fares and maybe a night out, but that was all. Wearily she mooched down the street, gazing bleakly at the shop windows, crammed with inviting goodies all screeching 'Buy Me'.

Amber wandered into one of the big shops and was immediately warmed by a blast of hot air from the blowers in the doorway.

She undid her coat, and drifted slowly down the aisle, letting the piped music wash over her, lulling her into a delicious sense of relaxation.

At every side of the aisle, shoppers heaved overflowing trolleys and hauled bulging shopping bags through the shop floor, jostling with each other to grab overpriced and over packaged boxes of toiletries as if they would never be available again.

If only Christmas was another month later, her bank balance would surely be a little bit healthier by then and she would be able to afford to buy presents.

And then Amber saw the answer to her problems. Over by the Customer Service desk a huge sign, with flashing lights attracted her attention. 'Buy Now. Pay nothing until February. Instant Credit.' The answer to all of her problems. Amber hurried across the crowded store, elbowing blank eyed shoppers out of the way in her haste to get to the desk.

An hour later she was cramming heavy shopping bags into her locker at work, with a sinking heart.

It had all been so easy. She merely had to fill in a form, answer a few questions about her income and where she lived.

The Customer Services Assistant had keyed her answers into a computer, her long red talons flying over the keys and a few moments later a plastic card had been handed across the desk into Amber's clammy hand. And then, short of breath and flushed with excitement Amber had begun a trolley dash around the store, shoving expensive goodies into the most co-operative trolley that she had ever pushed. The trolley seemed to guide her, as if by its own vocation towards the beauty counter, where her arms, weak with relief at having so much money, hauled gorgeous cellophane wrapped creations into its shiny wire recesses. And then the trolley set off across the store to the men's department, bypassing the cheap clothes until it came to rest beside the gorgeous cashmere sweaters that seemed to melt into her fingers as Amber hauled them off the shelves and threw them gaily in amongst her other treasures. With a final flourish, the trolley whisked her back across the store to the ladies department, where a whisper thin silk and lace wrap that would look gorgeous on Stella, flew from the rail and nestled in amongst the cashmere sweaters.

Even visiting the checkout was like magic, a grinning assistant skimmed her card through a machine and reverently packaged her goodies slipping the till receipt into one of the bags and handing Amber a slip to sign. Gaily she signed her name beneath the rather large bill, adding a flourishing swirl of delight to the end of her signature. And then she was outside, fingers clamped around the string handles of her bags, feeling the cold air seeping into her bones again as the full horror of what she had just done washed over her.

Amber wiped her eyes with the back of her hand. What the hell had she done? How could she have been such an idiot to get into yet more debt? She could have just got small inexpensive presents for everyone. No one would never have noticed. Or cared. Instead she had gone completely over the top, buying presents as if she were using toy money. Now it would take forever to pay off the balance on the store card. Shit. Shit.

Teddy shoved his nose against Amber's leg, pleading to be picked up to be cuddled.

Miserably Amber picked him up and pulled him towards her. If only she were a puppy dog, with nothing to worry about.

The back seat of Rory's sports car was filled with interesting looking beautifully wrapped presents; Stella put her bags in and settled herself into the passenger seat. She was going to really enjoy this Christmas.

"Have you got a tree?" Stella breathed excitedly as Rory opened the door to his apartment.

"Nah," Rory shook his head. "They make too much mess." He stood aside to let Stella in, struggling beneath the weight of her bags.

A wave of disappointment washed over Stella, surprising her with its force.

Christmas trees were untidy, but Christmas was not Christmas without a tree, gently dropping needles all over the floor and crammed with an odd selection of mis-matched decorations, like the one that would be no doubt taking up a huge part of the cramped lounge at her parent's house.

"Don't put those bags on the work top." Rory frowned as Stella heaved her bags onto the black granite, "I don't want anything to scratch the surface. It cost me a fortune" Rory said peevishly, eyeing her bags suspiciously.

Later they went out for dinner and then returned to the immaculate, silent apartment.

Usually at this time, Stella thought, with a tinge of regret, she would be rolling out of Eagan's Bar with her brothers and sister, holding onto each other for support as they began the long walk home along the road that wound beside the seashore, singing carols as loudly as they could to drown out the noise of the sea hitting the rocks. But this was nicer, she told herself firmly, going to bed with her handsome, wealthy lover, in his beautiful apartment.

This was everything that she could possibly wish for.

She woke before dawn, accustomed to early starts and lay in the vast bed, watching the orange glow of the city slowly change to a murky grey as Christmas morning began.

In Mayo they were probably just having the first power cut of the day as all the children in the West of Ireland turned on their new electrical presents and the antiquated system faltered under the strain.

"How about making me some tea?" Rory opened his eyes and grinned at her, running his hand gently over her stomach and sliding it slowly downwards. "Tea, first!" he whipped the bedclothes back off her warm body.

Laughing Stella grabbed his cashmere sweater and pulled it over her nightdress and padded, barefoot to the kitchen. She returned a few minutes later with the tea, laid the china mugs on the bedside table and slid back under the covers.

"You're freezing," Rory groaned, rolling on top of her to warm her with his body. "I bet that will be your best Christmas present ever," he grinned after a few moments of frenzied pumping. He eased himself out of her and fell back onto his pillow, a sheen of sweat on his face. He wiped away the beads of moisture that had collected in the dark haze of stubble above his top lip.

"Definitely," lied Stella, good grief, she thought picking up her tea mug; the liquid had barely had time to cool down. Sex was definitely not Rory's strong point. At least he was nice to make up for his failings in the bed department, most of the time anyway.

"What time shall we go to Mass?" Stella asked, putting down her empty mug. "Mass?" Rory chortled with amusement. "You don't really want to go there do you?" Stella's heart sank, no Christmas tree and no Mass, "No, I suppose not."

Rory slid out of bed. "Come on, I want to open my presents!" he pulled on a silk dressing gown and shoved his feet into leather slippers and padded into the lounge.

Stella shoved the cashmere sweater over her head again and followed him. The presents, stacked up on the long dining table, looked oddly out of place in the tidy apartment, there should have been tinsel and lights and Christmas cards lying scattered around.

In Mayo the lounge floor would have been covered in discarded wrapping paper, while her mother went around frenziedly gathering up bits large enough to salvage for next year.

"These are yours," Rory said, grandly, pulling out one of the dining room chairs for Stella to sit down and pushing a stack of beautifully wrapped parcels in front of her. "And these must be mine," he grinned, wrapping his arms around the parcels Stella had wrapped for him and dragging them towards himself.

Feeling very self-conscious, Stella unwrapped her presents as Rory watched her. In Mayo everyone opened their presents at the same time, in a chaos of exclamations of delight and groans of disgust.

"Oh this is lovely," Stella unwrapped a red nylon baby doll nightdress with tiny knickers to match. She fingered the fluffy trim around the open crotch of the knickers and cringed inwardly. Surely Rory did not expect her to wear them!

A short time later she had accumulated a pile of revoltingly repulsive underwear and a blouse that looked as if it had been made for someone's maiden aunt who was six sizes bigger than she was.

Amber had got her a gorgeous silk dressing gown, Stella fingered the luxurious fabric lovingly, this really was gorgeous. She pulled off Rory's sweater and slid into the whisper thin dressing gown. This must have cost a fortune. What had Amber been thinking of? Saving so hard to buy such an expensive present. A bottle of bubble bath would have been fine; Stella thought guiltily of the small handbag that she had brought Amber.

Rory began to open his presents, pulling open the expensive gift wrap that she had chosen so carefully.

"Very nice," he said, finally, once he had unwrapped a sizable pile of beautiful cotton shirts and a very expensive leather wallet. "Thank you very much." He lifted one of the shirts. "Did you keep the receipts for these; I might change some of them?"

Stella pursed her lips together. "Yes of course."

Hurt settled like a cloak around her shoulders.

Rory had brought her the most awful presents, things that she would never wear, and that he would know that she would never wear, if he had paid any heed to her on the numerous dates that they had. She felt as if he had no idea about her at all. And then wanting to change the presents that she had so lovingly chosen for him that was so hurtful.

Rory scooped up his presents and wandered back to the bedroom with them. Stella followed and shoved hers into one of her bags, with a sigh.

Men were just so stupid; they never had any concept of what a woman liked. Next year she would have to go with Rory to make sure they both got something that they liked. For now at least she would make the most of being in this lovely apartment, with Rory. Maybe next year she would be married to him, maybe thinking about a family.

That evening they curled up on the leather sofa, Stella her earlier hurt pushed firmly to the back of her mind, rested her head on Rory's shoulder as they watched age old films and worked their way steadily down a bottle of red wine.

"I was just thinking," Rory said, suddenly, flicking off the television as the adverts came on. "We get on really well, don't we?"

"Yes," Stella began to unbutton Rory's shirt, perhaps now if they went to bed, he might manage to last a bit longer than this morning.

"Why don't you stay here with me? You could look after me, keep the apartment nice. Give up that bloody silly job of yours."

CHAPTER NINE

Mark Hardcastle really had to be the world's worst boss, thought Amber as she aimed a frustrated kick at the metal door of her locker. The slimy bastard had taken great pleasure in telling her that she could not have any time off at Christmas. "This is A Restaurant Amber," he had told her about five minutes after Amber had asked him for a night off work. In reality it probably was not five minutes at all, but it felt like that as he glared at her, his round moon face growing more incredulous by the second as if Amber had asked him for the keys to his dark blue Porsche, not just a few hours off. Amber had swallowed hard, her cheeks burning crimson.

"We are here to provide a service," his voice rose higher. "We have to work when everyone else is on holiday!" Mark flung out his arms, punctuating his cries with expansive gestures.

"Right, yeah, sorry," Amber backed away, afraid that at any moment Mark was going to start flinging dinner plates at her. "So that's a no then?" she added, in a last ditch attempt at defiance.

Mark's pale eyes bulged from deep within the folds of his chubby cheeks. "Exactly," he snarled, turning on his heel and stalking down the restaurant.

Amber wrenched open her locker door and tugged her frilly white apron off its hanger. Mark Hardcastle was a dreadful man to work for. He was a ferocious bully who seemed to take great delight in terrorising and undermining his staff.

Amber pulled the apron on over her head, smoothing the white bib over her chest and tying the frilly straps into a bow around her waist.

Mark had really enjoyed refusing her request to have the evening off work. Amber looked longingly at the back door of the restaurant, how she longed to tear off her apron and march out and never come back. But what then? Yet again she would be out of work, with no references and no money.

If only she had realised years ago why Sister Joyce had told all of her pupils how important it was to work hard and get good qualifications.

Ruby had paid attention to her words and had studied endlessly, but Amber, realising that she could not compete with her bright older sister had deliberately rebelled against her education, bunking off school, flunking her exams. And now she was paying the price. Stuck in a dead end job with the boss from hell.

Taking a deep breath Amber put on her brightest smile and strode brightly out into the restaurant, determined not to show Mark that he had wound her up. If he would not give her the time off then Amber was going to make the best of the situation. She would do a great job and earn loads of tips, then she would be able to pay off a load of money on her debts.

Amber had been looking forward to meeting Roderick, Ruby's fiancée. And his brother Ernest. She had already been imagining herself and Ruby miraculously becoming friends, falling in love with Ernest, (anything was possible in dreams, even falling in love with someone called Ernest). Maybe they would have a double wedding. Ruby would understand how hard it was for Amber to get time off work. She would arrange the night out for another time.

Amber had already decided how she was going to explain to Ruby that she could not get the time off work. Somehow her words had made it sound as if she were a far more crucial part of the restaurant than actually just being a mere waitress.

It had all sounded so easy as she had walked home, especially after finishing up half a bottle of red wine that one of the customers had left. But then she had not expected Ruby to telephone to make the arrangements very early in the morning, when Amber was half asleep, and half crippled with a brain numbing hangover.

For a moment she had been dreaming that the ringing noise was the bell from the kitchen that the chef rang to announce that the dish was ready.

Then Amber had lurched into wakefulness, grabbing blindly at her mobile telephone, knocking it to the ground and fumbling wildly for it amongst the chaos of mugs and abandoned clothes. "'Lo," her mouth had felt as if her tongue had been wallpapered to the roof of her mouth.

"Amber, I'm sorry did I wake you?" Ruby's incredulous tones bored into Amber's ear, as if she were surprised to find anyone at eight thirty in the morning that had not done at least two hours in the gym and had already been at work for an hour.

"No, course not," Amber struggled to make her tongue function.

"Are you still ok for our night out just after Christmas? We did agree on the twenty eighth of December if you remember."

"Um, er, um, yeah." A myriad of thoughts shunted together in Amber's befuddled brain. She had to work on the twenty eighth of December.

That bastard Mark Hardcastle would not give her the time off. Ruby would really enjoy knowing that Amber could not even get a day off work. 'Well, what do you expect – working in these dead end jobs?' "The twenty eighth, of course, I'm looking forward to it." Amber winced as the words tumbled out of her mouth.

She groaned as Ruby severed the connection. What had she done now? Mark had already said that she could not have the night off. Shit. Shit. Now she would have to ring in and pretend that she was sick. Then she would spend the whole night dreading that someone would recognise her and tell Mark.

Amber coughed weakly into a tissue and ran her hand distractedly over her forehead as if to wipe a film of sweat away. If she was going to have a night off sick then she had better at least have the appearance of being ill.

Worrying about telling Mark that she was not coming in, was actually beginning to make her feel really ill.

"Don't bloody cough near my customers," Mark snapped, petulantly, glaring in Amber's direction. "I can't help it," Amber pretended to sniff, "I feel terrible."

"Tough," Mark growled, narrowing his piggy eyes as he stared at Amber. "You can do your shift in the kitchen; you can do the washing up." He steered Amber towards the vast aluminium sink overflowing with dishes of burnt pasta sauce and enormous saucepans. "Maria, grab an apron, you are waiting tables tonight," Mark yelled in the direction of the plump Italian woman who normally washed the dishes. Maria grinned as she grabbed one of the white frilly aprons and tied it around her vast middle. Being a waitress for the night was infinitely better than standing over a pile of dirty dishes and steaming, greasy water.

"Fuck," Amber muttered through gritted teeth, she had been hoping that Mark would take sympathy on her and send her home.

The long shift felt as if it would never end. Mark was so mean that he was determined to keep the restaurant open as long as possible to get the most work out of his staff and the most money out of his customers.

"How much longer?" Amber pleaded to Jules, one of the waitresses, as she brought in yet another pile of plates to stack on the huge pile that was crammed onto the draining board beside Amber. "He has to let us go home sometime," moaned Jules, gently moving a stray strand of Amber's sweat slicked hair from her forehead.

It was Christmas morning before the restaurant finally closed. "Fuck that bastard," complained Jules as Mark locked the door behind them. "He never even gave us a drink, or wished us Happy Christmas."

"Have a great Christmas day," Jules said hugging Amber as they parted.

"You too," Jules smelt of garlic and wine, "I hope that my boyfriend is still awake when I get back, I can't wait to open my presents."

"It's the middle of the night," Amber grinned.

"I don't care. I can't wait," Jules made a small dance of excitement, her trainers flashing wildly against the frost glittered pavement. "There is one really interesting looking box under our tree. I'm sure it is an engagement ring."

And then Amber was alone, walking through the silent streets, towards the empty apartment.

Stella would be with Rory, enjoying being together, while Amber had to spend Christmas day with her parents, listening to Ruby crowing about her wonderful job, wonderful life and the wonderful wedding that she was going to have.

Amber let herself into the apartment. Teddy launched himself at her in delight to have some company again, his tail wagging so furiously that it was almost a blur.

Outside a group of revellers were singing Christmas carols in drunken tuneless voices.

Amber went to the window and looked out, two couples; arms linked were weaving their way down the deserted pavement.

Amber picked up Teddy and held him to her chest; she had never felt so miserable and lonely. It was horrible to be alone at Christmas; it seemed as if everyone else had a partner, someone to be with, except for her.

Amber slid gratefully into bed. She was exhausted. It would be a miracle if she were not really ill on the night that she was supposed to be going to meet Ruby's boyfriend and his brother.

Ruby had organised Christmas Day, starting with the whole family heading off to mass at ten in the morning.

Amber hugged Teddy to her, she had better try to get at least a few hours' sleep before she had to get up and head over to her parents' house. Of course Ruby would be perfectly dressed and organised, with a pile of beautifully wrapped presents.

"Oh fuck," Amber crawled wearily back out of bed. She had forgotten to wrap her presents.

After what seemed like only a few moments Amber was grabbing her alarm clock to silence the dreadful shrieking sound. She would just have to close her eyes for a few moments before she had to get up and organised in order to be ready for when she was collected by the family on their way to mass.

"Ahhhhwww!" Teddy's sharp claws scraped across Amber's bare forearm as he leapt off the bed. "Oh shit!" Amber could hear the door bell ringing, its insistent note filling the silence of the apartment.

She had overslept. "Hi Daddy. Merry Christmas," Amber muttered blithely as she pulled open the door while hauling at Teddy's collar to stop him launching himself at her father in excitement.

"Not quite ready?" Jack Casey bent down to stroke the dog in order to not have to look at Amber disconcerted at her flimsy nightdress and tangled hair.

"I won't be a minute," Amber stumbled over the remains of last night's parcel wrapping frenzy in her panic to get dressed.

Amber hastily dragged a brush through her hair and pulled on an almost clean pair of jeans – the washing did not seem to be done with quite the same miraculous regularity while Stella was away – and unearthed a shirt from the pile at the bottom of the washing basket. "Ready," Amber clipped the dog lead onto a writhing Teddy's collar, heaped the pile of untidily wrapped parcels into her arms and followed her father out to his car.

"We are going to be late for mass!" snapped Pearl Casey as Amber scrambled into the back seat after abandoning the parcels into the car boot.

"I suppose you overslept," Ruby said smugly, leaning around from the front seat. Amber fought the urge to pull a childish face at her sister.

Ruby, as usual was immaculate, her dark hair shining, the glorious scent of an expensive perfume wafting in a fragrant cloud around her. "I was working late," Amber muttered petulantly, wrapping her fingers around Teddy's collar to stop him bouncing all over the car.

"I thought that the dog belonged to your friend!" Pearl Casey shot Teddy a look of pure dislike.

"Stella's away for Christmas and I couldn't leave him all alone for the day," Amber could hear the sullen tone in her own voice.

She slumped back against the car seat and stared resolutely out of the window. It was amazing how her mother and Ruby had the way of making her feel about twelve years of age again. "He will have to stay in the garden, I can't have him in the house," Pearl complained. "Doesn't everywhere look festive?" Jack Casey commented, trying to lift the frosty atmosphere that prevailed inside the car. "Hurry up Daddy!" Pearl snapped. "We are running very late!" she added pointedly.

Pearl was even more annoyed when they reached the church and found that the car park was filled to bursting point, "I'll drop you all off at the door and go and park,"

Jack was delighted to have an excuse to get away from the women who were all bristling with temper. The church was packed; whole families had come to celebrate Christmas together.

Amber was relieved when her mother spotted a pew halfway down the church, she would never have heard the end of it if they had been forced to stand up the whole length of the Mass.

Amber sank gratefully onto the hard wooden surface of the pew and let the glorious atmosphere of the festive mass wash over her. The Priest came out, resplendent in his purple robes and the Mass began. Amber felt a glorious sense of peace wash over her, tinged with a more than slight feeling of guilt that she did not attend Mass more regularly. It was just that life seemed to get in the way sometimes. She really should make more of an effort.

"Peace be with you. The Mass is over," announced the Priest making the sign of the cross and adding a cheery wave to the congregation.

It was time to go back to reality. Reality was that Teddy had discovered Pearl Casey's store of mints, left in the car to combat her bouts of travel sickness. Shredded pieces of wrapping paper littered the car. Pearl pointedly began to pick up the scattered bits of paper.

"Did you have to bring that dog?" Ruby said tightly, bending into the back of the car to help her mother.

Amber caught her father's eye and suppressed a giggle as they both watched the two large bottoms sticking out of the side doors, jiggling in unison as the paper was snatched up. "Wasn't that a lovely Mass?" Jack Casey sighed happily, as they finally drove away from the church, bringing back the feelings of peace and love that had washed over everyone during the service.

The rest of the day passed peacefully. Teddy, left to his own devices spent the day gazing enviously in through the glass patio door. He looked so sorrowful that eventually even Pearl relented and took him a plate of turkey scraps and gravy. "Time to open the presents!" Ruby said, appearing with a stack of beautifully wrapped parcels.

"I'll fetch mine," Amber hurried out to the car, wishing that she had spent more time wrapping her gifts.

"I've gone for an ecological look this year," Ruby handed everyone a parcel wrapped in brown paper with hand painted stars printed all over it, wrapped in brown string that had been teased into fancy bows.

"I've gone for a done-at-the-last-minute-look," muttered Amber under her breath as Pearl exclaimed, "Darling how lovely!" as she grasped the parcel that Ruby handed to her.

The Christmas spirit was definitely beginning to wear thin. Ruby always had to be top dog.

At least, a few minutes later Amber had the satisfaction of seeing the look of guilt in Ruby's face as she unwrapped the gorgeous cashmere sweater Amber had virtually sold her soul for. Ruby's gift to Amber had been an awful plastic makeup bag that had obviously been recycled from last year.

"Well," said Ruby, getting to her feet, as the James Bond film ended, "I really have to go. Roderick and I are going to his parent's this evening,"

Amber got to her feet, relaxed by an excess of Christmas spirit and wine at lunchtime. "It's been great today," she hugged Ruby carefully in order not to mess up her sister's immaculate hair.

"I'll see you in a few days' time; Ernest is looking forward to meeting you." Ruby disentangled herself from Amber's arms. Amber followed her sister outside and watched from the front door as Ruby got into her gleaming black Audi. As Ruby backed out of the driveway and drove away to the sound of classical music wafting from the half open driver's window Amber felt her smile fade. How on earth was she going to wrangle a night off work without losing her job?

CHAPTER TEN

Amber picked up the telephone, took a deep breath and began to dial her work number seven, three, nine, one, three........... four.......................two. Her fingers faltered on the key pad. Finally with a groan of frustration Amber slammed the receiver down. If only Stella were here. She would have no problem with making the call for Amber. She would just snatch up the receiver, dial the number and tell Mark Hardcastle, she was sick and would not be coming into work tonight. Thank you very much. Goodbye. Easy. Amber picked up the receiver again.

That was all she had to do, just dial the number and speak to Mark. What could he possibly do? He would know that she was lying. He would be furious. Maybe he would even sack her. Amber quailed at the thought. She could not get the sack. Not again.

Her last job had only lasted three weeks. The nursing home Matron had been a horrendous old dragon who bullied both staff and patients alike. Amber had hated the home with its all-pervading odour of urine. Amber had hated the job from the minute that she started, but beggars can't be choosers. There had been an enormous row when the Matron had discovered that Amber was sneaking extra sandwiches and biscuits to the residents at tea time. She had made a very unpleasant scene during which Amber had accused the Matron of neglecting her residents and being cruel to them. The result of which had been that Amber had been told to leave, in no uncertain terms.

There had followed a horrible few weeks of searching for work, which depressing as it was, only served to remind Amber of the fact that she had wasted her time at school, and what dead end jobs were available to those with few qualifications and even fewer skills, which was why Amber was so determined to cling to her job at the restaurant. It was a horrible job, but decidedly better than the nursing home and a million times better than being penniless and out of work.

If only Amber were not so delighted to be included in Ruby's exclusive inner circle of friends then she would never have dreamed of taking the night off. But the invitation was so rare. Ruby had always been the one with the glamorous circle of friends and the exciting invitations to exclusive venues.

By comparison Amber's friends had never seemed so interesting. Whatever invitation Amber was given, Ruby always seemed to be able to outdo her, with something far more alluring. And somewhere along the path of sibling rivalry Amber had inwardly thrown up her hands and surrendered. She had stopped trying to compete with Ruby.

Her sister's path of social and academic achievement had shot skywards while Amber's had spluttered into a freefall of drop out friends and hopeless exam results. It was easier not to try.

As the gap between them widened, Ruby heading off to university and a series of friends from well to do backgrounds and Amber into a series of dead end jobs and drop out boyfriends, they had less and less in common.

Finally Amber could only watch from the side-lines as Ruby excelled in everything.

The invitation to join Ruby and her fiancée and his brother for the evening hung over Amber, tormenting her like a precious unattainable prize. She just had to go. Ruby might never invite Amber again.

There was no escaping the fact – the telephone call had to be made. Amber took a deep breath, lifted the receiver and dialled the number with fingers that trembled. The telephone began to ring, the tones loud in Amber's ear above the drumming beat of her heart as it pounded against her ribs.

For long moments the telephone rang as Amber grasped the receiver in her sweat dampened hand. Then just as her courage failed and Amber was about to slam the receiver down – the telephone was answered. "Hello,

Grafton's," said the sing-song voice of Jules, Amber's friend.

"Jules, its Amber," her voice sounded high and tremulous, "I'm not coming in tonight, I feel terrible." It was not a lie. Amber really did feel dreadful. Somewhere during the course of willing herself to make the call Amber had forgotten how to breathe. Now each breath was short and ragged, rasping through a throat that had constricted with nerves. Her stomach had twisted itself into knots so that there was a burning ache down her right side.

"Oh Amber," Jules growled in exasperation. "Don't be such an idiot, Mark will never believe you."

Amber managed to stifle the whimper of fear that rushed from her lips. There was a rattle as Jules threw down the receiver onto the bar. Amber could hear the background hum of the restaurant, voices and the clatter of crockery and then rapid footsteps as Mark walked across the wooden floor. "Amber!" his voice was short and heavy with sarcasm.

"I'm not coming in tonight. I'm not feeling in tonight, I'm not feeling too good."

"Really?" Amber could imagine Mark's face; one eyebrow raised quizzically, his flabby lips twisted into a sneer of disbelief.

"I'm sorry," Amber gulped.

Mark gave a snort of derision. "Funny that you are sick just on the night that you wanted to take off."

"I'm sorry," Amber repeated weakly but Mark had slammed the receiver down. Amber puffed out her cheeks, sighing with relief at having made the call; the relief was soured by the dreadful guilt of having let Mark down and the nagging fear that she had not heard the last of their conversation. Mark had known that she was lying.

It was too late to change anything now, though. Amber was suddenly aware that she was still listening to the buzz of the dial tone; she threw the receiver down, wishing that she had never made the call. She would not be able to relax all evening now; in case she saw someone who would recognise her from Grafton's and tell Mark. But there was no going back now.

Amber forced the feeling of guilt to the back of her mind. Worrying would not change anything; she may as well enjoy her night out. Ernest could be wonderful; it might even be love at first sight, followed by a wedding that would outdo anything that Ruby could plan, followed by a life of luxury.

Maybe Amber would never have to go back to Grafton's and face the wrath of Mark.

Amber headed off to her bedroom with Teddy trotting behind, his eyes filled with mischief as he jumped up onto the bed with Stella's new makeup brush between his teeth. "Give me that back," Amber giggled, diving onto the bed and trying to wrestle the brush from Teddy's teeth as the puppy growled in playful annoyance. "Come on let it go, I haven't got time for messing around tonight."

Teddy released his hold on the varnished wooden handle of the new brush. "Oh bloody hell, it's ruined" Amber wiped the puppy spit off the handle which was now covered in marks where Teddy's teeth had clamped onto it, "Stella will be cross at you," Amber regarded Teddy sternly. Teddy gazed back solemnly before offering his paw to Amber. "Don't try to get around me that way," she chastised him. "You have got to help me find something to wear for tonight."

Amber slid off the bed and opened her wardrobe door, wincing at the jumbled pile of clothes that lay in a heap on the floor beneath the crammed hanging rail that was bent with the weight of garments that were festooned over it. "So?" Amber stood back, wryly surveying the scene. "What do you think Teddy?"

Half an hour later there were more clothes on the floor than in the wardrobe – and the pile was growing.

"This one?" Amber pulled a red flowered dress from the rail and held it against herself.

Teddy, exhausted by the proceedings had curled up on the bed. He opened one eye as Amber spoke, and then closed it firmly. "Obviously not."

Amber threw the dress onto the pile and sat down heavily on the bed, regarding the brightly coloured pile of clothes ruefully. Nothing was right. Everything was either the wrong colour, too gaudy, too tarty or just plain awful, all bought on the spur of the moment because Amber had liked the look of them at the time. What would Stella wear mused Amber, poking her foot at the heap of clothes, lifting the mishmash of fabrics wearily. Something understated, elegant......The ubiquitous black dress. God, how boring............but how right for the occasion.

Amber pulled a plain black dress from the back of her wardrobe. "This then?" Amber waved the dress in Teddy's direction. The puppy sat up opened his mouth and yawned loudly, before scrambling off the bed and heading out of the room. "I'll take that as a yes, shall I?" Amber pulled off her sweatshirt and jeans and stepped into the dress. It was one that she had bought years previously, probably for a job interview. "Good choice Teddy," Amber stepped back to survey herself in the mirror. The dress really did suit her, the square neckline showed off the shape of her neck and the plain style made her look.........What? Amber mused, gazing at her reflection in the mirror. Elegant, Amber grinned at herself, for once she really looked elegant.

The black dress, combined with her hair piled loosely on top of her head and a pair of Stella's black shoes really did make her look elegant. Satisfied Amber pulled on her grey coat and headed out of the door.

This was going to be a good night, Amber thought happily as the first taxi that she had waved at screeched to a halt beside her. Everything was going to be perfect, she thought, giving the driver Ruby's address and happily settling back into her seat.

Ruby lived in a glamorous apartment in the centre of the city. Amber fought down the feelings of envy as she walked across the foyer of Ruby's apartment block, her footsteps tapping on the Italian marble floor and echoing around the Grecian pillars and vast carved stone flower pots that overflowed with ivies and colourful plants.

She had only been invited here once before. Ruby had held a party to celebrate moving into her new apartment. The party had consisted of Ruby's work colleagues, and Amber, arriving in a short skirt and plunging top with a bottle of red wine in anticipation of a let-your-hair-down kind of night, had felt desperately out of place. She had spent the evening feeling very uncomfortable beneath the supercilious looks that Ruby's toffee nosed friends were throwing in her direction.

At the far end of the foyer Amber stepped into the lift and was swished elegantly skywards. Coming out of the lift on the top floor was like being in a five star hotel.

Amber set off along the long thickly carpeted corridor and rang Ruby's doorbell.

"Oh, come in," Ruby sounded as if she had completely forgotten that Amber was coming. Ruby led the way down a short corridor, her bare feet making no sound on the polished wooden floor and into an enormous lounge. Amber blinked at the vast expanse of neutral colours; the lounge was all white walls, pale beige carpet and furniture, with vivid silk cushions adding an occasional splash of colour.

At the far end of the room, sitting regally on the sofa, was another burst of colour. Pearl. "Hello Mummy," Amber stood uncertainly in the doorway, wondering if she dare tread on the gorgeous pale carpet. "Hello dear," Pearl frowned in Amber's direction. "What have you done to your hair!"

"Oh, I….." Amber put her hand uncertainly up to the mass of hair that she had so happily admired just a short time ago.

"It looks better down," Ruby agreed with her mother, smiling smugly in Amber's direction.

"I'll change it," Amber could feel the familiar feeling of uncertainty sinking into the pit of her stomach. Whatever she did it was never right, or good enough for Pearl.

Amber crossed the floor and stood in front of a mirror in an intricately carved gold frame and miserably pulled out the clips that were holding her hair in place.

"Well Ruby, I had better go, your father will be wondering where I am," Pearl said.

I bet he is hoping that you won't come back, thought Amber nastily, viciously tugging at her hair.

"I had a wonderful day shopping with you," Pearl continued, smugly. "And a wonderful lunch."

"I had a lovely time," Ruby said, walking across the room and handing Amber a hairbrush.

"It really is lovely that I have at least one daughter who enjoys taking her mother out for the day," Pearl whined.

Amber concentrated hard on brushing her hair, dragging the bristles so hard through her wiry hair that took her mind off her mother's sarcastic comments.

"Mind you, Ruby," Pearl crossed the room and adjusted a stray strand of Amber's hair, "I am thrilled that you are bringing Amber out with you! At least now she will meet a nicer class of people! It is time that she started to conform and get a proper job and a nice home like you have."

"I'm happy as I am," Amber hissed under her breath. It never did any good to answer back when Pearl was in full flow. She did not listen anyway.

The doorbell rang, saving Amber from more of her mother's comments. "That must be Roderick," Pearl sighed with anticipation, "such a lovely man!"

As Ruby hurried away to answer the door Pearl sighed with a martyred air. "You young things will be off out now. I suppose that your Daddy won't keep me waiting too much longer." Pearl glanced at her watch. "He was supposed to be here five minutes ago!"

She glanced up as Ruby came back into the room followed by a tall string bean thin man. "Roderick!" breathed Pearl, changing miraculously from put upon shrew to coquettish charm.

"Mrs Casey, how lovely to see you," Roderick enthused, rushing over to shake Pearl's hand.

Amber felt her jaw drop; she fought the urge to make pretend vomiting noises.

Roderick was a complete jerk. "And you must be Amber," Roderick crossed the room towards Amber, holding out his hand for her to shake. Amber put her hand into his, it felt clammy and limp within her palms. "Well, I am delighted to meet you,"

Roderick had the air of a dignitary on a meet-the-public occasion, enthusing over everyone while in reality not giving a damn about them. Amber pulled her hand away and fought the urge to wipe her palm across the fabric of her dress to rid it of the clammy feel of Roderick's palm. "And you managed to get the time off work. That's wonderful," his tone was patronising. "It's time we left." Roderick added, turning away from Amber now that he had given her a few moments of his time.

Ruby and Pearl leapt to their feet, grabbing their coats, Amber stood up. No wonder Ruby had wanted her to make up a foursome with Roderick's brother. Roderick was such a plonker that surely even Ruby must see it. She probably wanted Amber to come along to add a bit of life to the evening.

Amber followed them out of the apartment. There was no way that she was going to spend an evening with Roderick. As soon as she had been introduced to the delectable Ernest, Amber was going to drag him off to the nearest night club.

"Ernest will be here in a minute," Roderick snapped off his mobile phone and slid it into his jacket pocket. "Now then ladies," he said in the patronising tone that was already setting Amber's teeth on edge. "What can I get you to drink?"

"Here's Ernest now," Ruby nudged Amber as a tall, man walked across the crowded restaurant towards them, Amber was facing a bright light and Ernest was in shadow as he approached the table.

Amber watched him walking across the room; suddenly her chest was tight, her heart pounding fiercely against her ribs. "Hello Ruby," Ernest slid onto a vacant seat. "And you must be Amber," said Ernest holding out his hand for Amber to shake. "Hello Ernest," Amber said quietly, wishing that the ground would open up and swallow her.

The whole evening was a farce; Ruby had invited her out merely to make up appearances. It had nothing to do with rebuilding their fragile relationship. Amber had merely been a convenient person to be part of this awful façade.

Ernest had to be quite the ugliest person Amber had ever seen in her life.

CHAPTER ELEVEN

Stella watched Rory walk across the crowded restaurant towards their table. She noticed with a sense of satisfaction how the women cast surreptitious glances in his direction.

He looked extremely handsome in his dark grey suit and ice white shirt, his yellow tie, which would have looked too feminine on a lesser man, only seemed to highlight his dark colouring and blue eyes.

Stella gave a sigh of satisfaction; it was wonderful to think that a prize such as Rory was actually with her. Good looking, wealthy men were hard to come by.

And Stella should know, she had spent long enough trying to find one. Heaven knows, she could have written a book on the subject. Wealthy men came in all shapes and sizes, not many of them were suitable boyfriend material. There was Mike, with his flashy Lotus and a laugh like a hyena. And the very good looking Ralph, who when he stood up barely reached Stella's shoulder and she had to draw the line at going out with someone who had daintier feet than she did. And Sean, Mr Lying Bastard. A trail of wealthy mental and physical rejects wound back through the dark recesses of Stella's memory, some were clearer than others. Some had been so awful she had mentally erased them.

"When are you going to hand in your notice?" Rory sat back down opposite Stella and leant on the table, locking his eyes on hers.

"I........." Stella stammered. She loved Rory, he was gorgeous, but giving up her independence, a job that she loved, that she had fought long and hard to get, was too much to contemplate.

"For heaven's sake," he snapped, folding his arms aggressively across his chest and glaring at her. "What is there to think about? Women shouldn't work; they should stay at home and care for their men folk. You don't need to work. I'll look after you." Stella put down her knife and fork. "But I like my job, I love to be with you, but I enjoy working," she said patiently.

Rory grabbed his wine glass and gulped back the dark red liquid and then refilled it so hastily that some of the wine spilled out over the table cloth. A diminutive waiter shot forward with a damp duster, dabbing primly at the liquid as it spread slowly across the virginal white of the table cloth.

"Leave it," growled Rory and the waiter, looking as if he had been lashed with a whip, withdrew rapidly, a hurt look plastered dramatically all over his girlish face. "Stop denying it, Stella," he hissed, narrowing his eyes to glare at her. "There is someone that you are having an affair with at work isn't there?"

"Oh, Rory!" Stella drew her fingers across her forehead in an effort to straighten out the lines of tension that she knew must be crinkling her skin. "I've already told you, there's no one at work. No one anywhere except you. I love you. You know that. How could I want anyone else, It's just that I don't want to be dependent on you."

"If you say there's no one else then I believe you," he said, in a voice that made her think that he really did not believe her. "But I can't understand why you won't give up your job and be with me. You would have a great life. More money than you have ever had, all the time in the world to shop."

Stella smiled, his offer really did sound tempting. She wished that she could just agree with him. Just leave her job and go and live with him.

It was everything that she wanted. A gorgeous apartment, a handsome, wealthy man.

But giving up her independence.............? What if the relationship went wrong?

"I'll give you until the New Year to decide." Rory said gently, but Stella was aware of the veiled threat in his voice. Rory took her hand across the table and brought it to his lips and gently kissed each finger. "And if you still want to work, then I think that we will have to end our relationship."

Stella made her way wearily up the stairs to the apartment she shared with Amber, Rory's words ringing in her ears. There was no doubt that he meant every word, she had to leave work, or he would end the relationship. She hated the thought of leaving her job.

It had taken her years to work her way up to the position of authority that she now held. But it was not that that she minded as much as the buzz that she got from being in the magazine business, the pressure of having to produce the copy ready for a deadline. She loved the stress and the frayed tempers and then the glorious feeling of relief and satisfaction when everything went off to press, and then the delight when she saw someone reading the new issue. It was all addictive stuff.

But she hated the thought of losing Rory as well.

She was twenty six. Time was running out for her, soon marriage and children would have passed her by. Not immediately, granted, but soon enough.

Time slid by very quickly to those who were not aware of it. The last thing that she wanted was to still be sharing an apartment with Amber in another few years. It was time that she had a proper home of her own. A husband, children, maybe even a home in the country.

A dark cloud of gloom wafted over her shoulders as Stella shoved open the door to the apartment.

Amber huddled waiflike on the sofa, with Teddy, a picture of misery, her gloom a tangible thing that seemed to permeate the very air.

Teddy wriggled out of Amber's grip and hurtled across the floor, short hairy legs a blur of speed, his curly tail wagging furiously, yapping with delight to see her again.

"Had a good Christmas?" Stella asked, gently shoving Teddy away from her leg, his sharp needle like teeth were digging into her skin.

"You don't want to know," Amber said, wryly, getting up to help Stella with her bags.

Stella felt her jaw clamp tight with tension. She wished that Amber would lighten up; usually she was so bright and full of fun. Things could not be that bad.

The last thing that Stella wanted after all the hassle she was having with Rory and the quandary about whether she should leave her job, was to come home and have to put up with a flatmate constantly sunk in virtually suicidal despair.

Maybe she should leave her job and move in with Rory, at least she would not have to put up with Amber's constant stream of misery. "What is the matter?" Stella asked patiently.

Amber tried to speak but the words came out as a strangled sob.

Stella perched on the edge of the sofa. "What is it?" she asked as Amber leant forward, burying her head in Stella's shoulder. "My bitch of a sister," Amber said eventually in a voice thick with tears. "She asked me to go out with her boyfriend and his brother. I thought that she wanted to be friends with me again, but she just wanted me there for show. My date was gay!" Amber gave a stifled sob which turned into a snort of laughter. "Fucking bitch. The fucking bitch."

"Do you fancy coming shopping with me?" Stella asked the following morning Amber was still fuming about her cow of a sister," Rory has invited me to a party."

"Great. I'm not buying anything though," Amber said firmly, hoping that she would have the will power to stick to her words.

"Rory wants me to go and live with him!" Stella could not contain her excitement any longer. She had been keeping the news to herself, wanting time to think about the consequences and to slowly mull over all of the benefits before she made her decision. But the words had just bubbled out of her mouth, spilling into the air.

Amber shook her head violently. "He just wants you to look after him," she spat scornfully. "He's saving himself money, he can sack his cleaner, get all his laundry done for free, save on taxis because you will be driving him about when he's drunk – and what will you have in return? You will have no security, nothing, and then when he is sick of you he will just throw you out."

Stella glared at her friend, everything that Amber had said was rubbish, Rory was not looking at their relationship like that. He did not see her as just someone to make his life easier. Maybe he just wanted to see how well they lived together, maybe he wanted to marry her, but just was not sure. Maybe Stella would make him so happy that he would want to marry her at the first opportunity. Amber was just jealous because she could not get anyone nice. Stella smiled tightly, "I'm sorry that you see things like that," she said tightly. "But I don't think that is how our relationship is at all."

The two headed off into the packed streets, Stella was determined not to let Amber's words annoy her. She was entitled to her opinion, even if it was the wrong one.

Already the shops were emblazoned with 'Sale' signs and filled with determined looking shoppers, fighting for bargains.

Amber trailed after Stella through the streets, trying desperately to ignore the clothes and shoes that cried out to her to be taken home. She had made an early New Year's resolution. No more spending until her credit cards and new store card balances were at manageable levels. Probably in about three years' time!

Ignoring all of the cheaper shops Stella headed for her favourite exclusive boutique. She shoved her way through the bargain hunters and battled to a rail of slinky dresses. It would be lovely to spend the day mooching around the shops and picking out bargains, but today there was not the time. She needed to buy something and then head home, to get ready for the party that Rory was taking her to later.

"What do you think of this?" Stella pulled a dress off the rail and had the satisfaction of seeing the naked envy in Amber's face as she looked at the sleek caramel coloured dress. Amber would be better if she stopped buying tonnes of cheap junk and brought herself a few gorgeous pieces instead, thought Stella, holding the dress up to her front and examining her reflection in the mirror.

There was no point in looking any further, this was the dress. Rory would adore her in this. Even just held up against her, Stella could see that the dress flattered her pale colouring and that its slinky shape would mould itself to her body.

"Go and put it on," Amber said, enviously, tentatively pulling out a black dress covered with tiny sequins, before shoving it forcefully back.

Stella headed off into the changing room and put on the dress. Everyone turned to look at her when she headed out into the shop again to show Amber.

"You have to buy that!" shrieked Maddie, one of the assistants, abandoning the customer that she was serving and bustling across the shop. "It looks fantastic on you – and you could wear those brown strappy sandals with it," she said, recalling the last purchase that Stella made in the shop.

Stella looked at herself in the mirror, she had been right, the dress was

80

perfect. It clung to the contours of her body, skimming over her flat belly and the curve of her hips.

"You look lovely," Rory said approvingly, as Stella lowered herself into the passenger seat of his car, he leant over and kissed her gently on the lips, he tasted of minty toothpaste. "Don't forget you promised me an answer tomorrow," he glanced at his chunky gold Rolex. "Only five hours to go."

He slid the automatic gear stick into drive and entwined his long fingers in Stella's, driving one handed. "I hope that you are going to say yes, I thought that we could go to Zanzibar to celebrate."

Stella, wondered for the zillionth time what she was going to say to him. She watched the frost dusted city slide by, cushioned in the comfortable, squishy leather seats. Rory had switched on the seat heaters, making her back pleasantly warm, the feeling was one of infinite luxury and comfort, like being cosseted in a warm feather bed.

Leaving work was such a big step, but Stella was sure that Kevin would let her work from home, or she could go freelance, or maybe just cut down on her work load, let the pushy Sorcha take over. At first that would be hard, but maybe the benefits would outweigh the downside. She was sure of her decision by the time they reached the party.

Either side of the street outside the house where the party was held, expensive cars jostled for space.

Rory pressed the button on the ignition key and the car locks slid into place with an expensive clunk.

He led the way towards the house, a tall, imposing building, set back from the road, hidden behind a high wall. Tall elaborate wrought iron gates stood open to let the stream of people in to the garden.

Stella looked enviously about herself at the billiard table smooth stretch of lawn, surrounded by shrubs all dusted with a glittering of frost that shimmered in the lights from the house. Wide bay windows arched out towards the gardens and inside the house Stella could see that the rooms were full of people, clutching drinks and chatting in small groups.

She longed to have a home like this, somewhere gorgeous and elegant, filled with beautiful furniture and ornaments and constantly full of a stream of interesting, wealthy people.

And with Rory it was all possible.

"This is Stella," Rory introduced her to the tall, powerfully built man who opened the door to them, "Danny Lyons, he's building the new office blocks near your flat." Danny took Stella's hand, "Rory you have all the luck, what did you do to deserve such a beautiful woman?"

"Darling if you ever get fed up of him, I'll be waiting." Danny said longingly to Stella.

"Don't mind him!" a tall, willowy blonde emerged from one of the rooms and glided along the black and white tiled floor towards them. "I'm Norah, his wife!" she added, coming to stand beside Danny and poking him playfully in the ribs.

Stella smiled uneasily, unsure of how to react to Danny, or if she had offended his wife, or more importantly, if Rory would now be simmering with unspoken jealousy.

"Don't worry, he says that to all the pretty women, I hope he didn't offend you." Norah took Stella's arm and led her along the corridor to a study which was doubling as a cloakroom for the party.

"Leave your coat here," Norah told Stella, then gasped with delight as Stella removed her coat. "What a gorgeous dress, you look wonderful."

"Too wonderful, I'll be spending all night keeping the other men off her," Rory said, sulkily taking off his black wool overcoat and throwing it onto the pile, with very bad grace.

Stella bit her lip, she hated it when Rory got all jealous and possessive, there was no need. It was him that she loved and wanted to be with, there was no need at all for him to feel insecure and threatened. Surely he realised that now that they had been together for the best part of four months.

Stella wished that she had worn a plainer dress, then maybe he would not have to feel as if all the other men were chasing her. She hated the fact that he thought that she would be interested in anyone else. She had him. He was all that she wanted.

Norah led the way into one of the crowded rooms. "What can I get you to drink?" she asked, peering around the room for one of the black coated waiters who were circulating with glasses of wine and champagne.

"Champagne would be lovely," Rory told her as Norah waved frantically in the direction of one of the waiters.

Norah, having found drinks for them wandered off to circulate amongst her guests. Stella sipped the icy cold champagne and stole a furtive look at

Rory over the rim of her glass. He was smiling, happily, looking around the room to see if there was anyone there he recognised.

Stella felt herself relax, maybe she had just been imagining Rory would be angry about Danny flirting with her. It was only a bit of fun after all. And he had shamelessly flirted with those dreadful blondes at the restaurant the other evening. What harm was there in it? Surely he knew how much she cared about him.

Later on during the evening Stella began to relax, Rory seemed to be enjoying himself, he had wandered around the room, with her trailing at his elbow as he mingled with the dozens of people that he knew.

"Come and have a dance with me!" Danny emerged from the heaving throng of people who were cavorting in the centre of the room.

"Come on!!" yelled a dark haired woman, grabbing Rory. Laughing Stella allowed herself to be dragged into the centre of the room and began to sway in time with the music as Danny capered beside her. Stella, laughing with delight, looked at Rory and felt a jolt of dismay; he was glaring her in absolute fury.

CHAPTER TWELVE

Stella's heart skipped a beat, the music faded into insignificance, she was aware of Danny, arms and legs swaying like the tentacles of an octopus against the hazy background of the other dancers and of Rory, his face set in anger.

Shooting a tight smile in Danny's direction Stella walked off the dance floor towards Rory, who leant rigid with tension against the wall.

Anger seemed to almost ooze from his pores. He took a sip of his champagne, looking past Stella as if she were invisible. His mouth clamped into a tight white line when he took the glass from his mouth.

"Lovely party isn't it?" Stella spluttered incoherently. She had to say something anything to get him to talk to her, so that she could see what kind of a mood he was in.

"You look like you are enjoying it anyway," Rory snapped coldly, glaring in Danny's direction. "Why don't you go back and carry on dancing with Danny, you were obviously enjoying it."

"I only danced with Danny because he asked me," Stella could feel tears of frustration prickling at the back of her eyes. What was she supposed to do? One dance with Danny and Rory made her feel as if he thought that she was a total slapper, wanting to be with the first man who caught her eye. Refuse to dance and she was being miserable. It was impossible to win.

"I'm not doing anything with Danny, just dancing!" she could hear her own voice rising with hysteria.

Why was he being like this? She loved Rory. She did not want anyone else, but why did he get so jealous the minute she even had anything to do with anyone else. Rory made her feel so cheap.

"So, if you aren't up to anything why did you rush off the dance floor when I looked at you. You looked guilty to me. I saw you look at Danny, giving him that look, like I've got to go back to Rory now."

Stella felt a knot of tension twist in her stomach; she shifted uncomfortably, trying to ease the muscles that had cramped uneasily together.

"Rory, please stop being like this," pleaded Stella, one large tear rolled down her face, she dashed it angrily away; he was not going to make her cry again.

"Don't you start crying," Rory spat, nastily. "You won't get around me like that."

He spun around on his heel and marched away, his back taut with tension.

Stella hurried after him weaving frantically through the crowded party, barging people out of the way in her haste to follow him. She had to make him see sense, make him realise that Danny meant nothing, try to make Rory realise how much she loved him. Not anyone else.

The weight of his anger weighed heavily on her shoulders, he was impenetrable when he was like this, it was impossible to make him see that she was not interested in anyone else.

She followed Rory into the cloakroom, "I'm going home. You stay with Danny." Rory said coldly, grabbing his coat from the pile on the desk and pushing past her to get out through the door.

"I'm coming with you," Stella cried, she had to make everything alright between them again. She was not going to lose him this way, with him thinking that she was some terrible tart who would go off with anyone.

"I don't want you to come," he retorted, flinging his coat on and marching away.

Stella gave a cry of sheer frustration, pulling at the coats desperately trying to find her own. Finally she found it and dashed from the room, she dashed down the corridor and out of the front door, vaguely aware of the curious stares of the people as she barged past them and of Norah's startled cry.

Rory was in the car. Stella ran as fast as she could down the path and flung open the car door.

"You are not leaving me like this!" she snapped, furiously, flinging herself into the car.

For a moment there was silence, then from the direction of the house came the sound of bells ringing and cheering and inside the house Stella could see everyone hugging each other and kissing as the New Year was celebrated.

"Happy New Year," she whispered, grimly.

"Wouldn't you rather be in there celebrating with your new boyfriend?" Rory hissed, maliciously.

"You're my boyfriend. I want to be here, with you," Stella said, firmly, reaching across and talking his cold hand. It lay in hers like a dead thing, unmoving.

"Rory, please stop this," she said, quietly, forcing her fingers into his, "I don't want anyone else. I want to be with you. Surely you can see that."

"I thought that too," Rory said, reaching forwards, wearily and pressing the start button. "But when I saw you smiling at Danny………"

"Oh Rory," tears of pure frustration rolled down Stella's cheeks. What was she supposed to do? How could she get Rory to understand that she did not want Danny. Rory could chat to other girls without her putting him through all of this……….this shit. She just wanted everything to get back to normal again.

Next time she would make sure that she did not dance with anyone, talk to anyone that might make Rory angry, she would wear a plainer dress, cling to him. Anything to avoid making him jealous and causing a scene again.

It was her fault. It had to be, she had worn a sexy dress. She had enjoyed Danny's flattery, but it was all harmless fun, surely. She had never had a boyfriend who had reacted as possessively as Rory, but then she had never had anyone that she wanted as much as Rory. And she was determined that she was not going to lose him. Life would never be the same again, without him.

Rory snatched his hand back and shoved the gear stick into drive.

"Please believe me, there was nothing going on with Danny. Honestly," Stella could hear the desperation in her voice as she rummaged fruitlessly in her handbag for a tissue. "Please believe me. I am truly sorry if I made you think that I was interested in Danny."

Rory was silent, gazing intently at the road, as if he were scarcely aware of her presence.

Stella could feel panic rising deep within the pit of her stomach. Rory had been angry and jealous before, they had rowed before if he thought that someone was paying her too much attention, but he had never been as angry as this, or as immovable. Usually after he had made her feel guilty and cheap he relented and things went back to normal. It was because he loved her so much, he would tell her, that he hated the thought of her going off with someone else, being made a fool of.

But this time, he was so cold, so solid in his rejection of her. Stella found a screwed up tissue in her handbag and wiped her eyes, but the tears would not stop falling.

"Crying won't make any difference. You won't get around me like that," Rory hurtled around a corner, narrowly avoiding two drunks who were weaving across the road. "Get out of the fucking way," he growled, through clenched teeth.

Stella was relieved when he finally pulled into the secure garaging beneath his apartment, she had been sure that he was going to crash the car, he had driven so fast and aggressively.

"You can get a taxi home," he said, in a voice that was faint and full of menace. "I'm not going anywhere until we sort this out." Stella got out of the car and waited until Rory finally got out and slammed his door aggressively and then stalked towards the lifts that led up to his apartments. She followed silently, close to his heels, feeling his complete and utter rejection of her.

Rory opened the door and they walked silently into the apartment. Rory snapped on the light and pulled off his coat, ignoring Stella completely.

Stella took off her coat and walked slowly through the rooms. How happy they had been here, such a short time ago.

Now she had ruined everything. Why had she ever danced with Danny? How could she have been such a fool? She should have known that it was going to make Rory angry.

"I was going to tell you that I would leave work," Stella sank wearily down on the sofa and looked up at Rory. His face was closed, his eyes blank, mouth clamped into a tight line, white at the edges with tension. He hardly seemed to be aware that she was there.

"I'm going to bed," he announced suddenly, barely glancing in her direction.

"Rory we have to sort this out," she pleaded, leaping off the sofa, darting across the room and putting her hands on his shoulders.

He stood immobile, his face impassive, and unresponsive until finally she dropped her hands. It was useless. She might as well have been trying to get a response from a tree trunk.

"I'm going to bed," he repeated sullenly, turning away. "I don't care what you do."

From outside the apartment door came the joyous sound of revellers returning from celebrating the New Year, their laughter penetrating into the stony silence of Rory's apartment.

They should have been like that, Stella thought, bleakly, laughing together, delighted at the new life that was opening up for them, by now she would have told him that she was going to leave work, they should have been making plans for the future. Instead, their life was frozen, trapped in a misery of misunderstanding and pain.

"No, we have to sort this out. I'm not letting our relationship end like this!" Stella grabbed at his arm, holding tight onto the cool cotton fabric of his shirt, "I love you for heaven's sake!"

"Get off me," he growled, shaking his arm violently to dislodge her grip. Stella clung to his arm, she had to make him stay with her, make him realise how much she cared about him, make everything alright again.

Stella did not see the blow coming. She felt the whisper of air close to her face as Rory shot out his fist. His muscles moved beneath her hand as he wrenched himself out of her grip and grabbed her shoulder as he punched at her face. She heard a scream, but was not aware of making any sound, and then a feeling of lightness as she seemed to fall through the air. She heard a terrible crunching noise and was aware of an ornamental table splintering into pieces around her. Then there was silence. She was on the floor, her cheek throbbing terribly, Rory crouching over her, his face full of love and concern.

"Stella," he whispered hoarsely, putting his arm around her waist and pulling her gently to her feet. Stella was dimly aware of the room spinning lazily, dark spots dancing around the corners of her eyes and Rory, guiding her with the utmost tenderness, leading her to the sofa.

"Terrible accident, didn't mean to do that, jerked out my arm, hit you by mistake," the words drifted lazily into her consciousness, she wanted to close her eyes, sleep. Her cheek throbbed, it was an immense effort to bring her hand to the source of pain, when she forced her heavy lidded eyes to look at her fingers, they were sticky and red. Blood, she realised vaguely.

Rory knelt beside her, Stella was aware that he was white, and shaking, he was dabbing at her face with a pristine white towel, except that the towel was not white anymore, huge daubs of red covered the soft pile fabric as if it had been decorated by a modern artist.

"Hospital, this needs stitching," Rory was muttering to himself. Stella forced herself to sit up, fighting desperately to avoid falling into the enticing blackness that she longed to slip into.

"What happened?" Stella whispered, the earlier row was a vague memory that might never have happened. Gone was the frozen, angry Rory, in his place was a loving, tender man, worrying desperately about her. "I need to get you to hospital, you have cut your face," Stella could hear the panic in his voice.

Stella let Rory lift her from the sofa, supporting her gently with a tender arm around her waist as he reached with his free hand for her coat and arranged it around her shoulders.

"Can you walk?" he said, softly, leading her slowly towards the door. Stella nodded gingerly, wincing as the slightest movement of her head sent pain shooting through her face. She clutched the towel to her face, her whole body racking with shivers as shock began to grip her system.

The walk to the car seemed interminable, Stella was silent. Gradually the full impact of what had happened sinking into her realisation. Rory had hit her. Rory had hit her so hard that he had sent her flying across the room, she remembered the table crunching around her as the force at which she landed on it made it disintegrate into a thousand pieces around her. Had Rory had hit her so hard that he had cut her cheek. Or had she done that when she fell? She could not remember.

Neither could she remember, afterwards, the drive to the hospital.

She remembered Rory helping her from the car and leading her into the Emergency Department where the world swam dizzily back into focus, everywhere beneath the bright lights of the enormous waiting room, sat people. They crowded onto the benches around the edge of the room and squashed onto the plastic chairs in the centre of the waiting area all with a bleak, patient expression of desperation. Drunks, muttering uselessly to themselves sat amongst small children and old people.

"Sit down," Rory led Stella to a vacant seat, "I'm going to give in your details."

Stella wondered if she was going to be sick, the violent shivering that had racked her body had stopped. Now she just felt numb. She could see every pair of eyes turning with bored disinterest to see who had joined the ranks of the waiting masses.

"We have to see the Triage Nurse," Rory returned and crouched down beside her, his eyes were afraid, burning deep within his pale cheeks. "Come on that's you," the nurse, concerned about a head injury called Stella straight into be checked.

Rory helped Stella to her feet. It looked a dreadfully long way across the crowded waiting room to the open door inside which Stella could see the plump shape of a nurse watching her progress.

"She fell and cut her face, I don't think it is too much," Rory said, guiding Stella through the open door into the Triage Department.

"I think I'll decide that," snapped the nurse. "You can wait outside." She told Rory firmly. Rory hovered for a moment, then quailed beneath the nurse's steely glare and backed sullenly out of the room.

Stella fought a wave of nausea as she sank thankfully down on a chair.

"Now, what happened?" The nurse pulled Stella's hand, still clutching the blood stained towel away from her face. Stella saw her wince as she looked at her cheek.

"I fell over," she lied, Rory had not meant to hit her, he had said it had been an accident. It had been her fault anyway for making him angry.

"I see," sighed the nurse. Stella glanced at her and could see the disbelief in the plump woman's eyes. Stella slid her eyes away, staring instead at the comfortable roll of flesh above the nurse's belt buckle. Deftly the nurse undid a packet and dabbed at Stella's cheek with a damp wad, Stella winced as the antiseptic soaked into the cut flesh, making it sting.

"Hmmm," the nurse muttered. "This is going to need a few stitches. You're going to need a head x-ray and we will have to keep you in for observation, standard for a head injury. And no arguing," she said firmly as Stella opened her mouth to protest. "And I will tell you something else," said the nurse, sitting down suddenly beside Stella. "However much you love this man, any man who can do this to you isn't worth staying with."

CHAPTER THIRTEEN

Stella eased her painful fingers as the handles of her heavy shopping bags bit into the flesh. She dumped the bags onto the lift floor as the doors swished shut, thank goodness she would soon be home. Well. Home at Rory's.

She had spent the afternoon food shopping, battling against the tide of loved-up couples out celebrating Valentine's weekend. Valentine's Day was in the middle of the week, but the world seemed to have overdosed on romance.

Everywhere, in town, there were flower sellers displaying wilted, vastly overpriced cellophane bunches of roses. You could not possibly be in love, it seemed unless you had been brought out for an overpriced meal, been given an overpriced bunch of roses and received an overpriced piece of jewellery, preferably a diamond.

Stella was all for romance, but just for now they were taking things slowly. Things were not back on an even keel with Rory – yet.

After she had left hospital Stella had ended the relationship with Rory. He had been devastated, begging her for forgiveness until finally six weeks later Stella had pushed the dreadful events of New Year to the back of her mind and told him that they would try again.

Today she was going to cook supper to celebrate the resurrection of their relationship. Of course she had to give Rory another chance.

All that Stella had to do was to make sure that she did not attract the attentions of any other men. Easy.

And then everything would be fine. No more rows. No more flying fist accidents.

This supper would be the perfect start to seal the proper start to their relationship – again.

They had gone out for a few drinks, had dinner together, but this was the first time that they would have spent the night together since their relationship had resumed.

The leaving work question had never been mentioned again, presumably they would discuss that when their relationship was on a more level footing again.

Stella's indestructible shopping bags had been tested to their limit with all of the provisions that she had packed inside. Two wonderful pieces of fillet steak, delicious crusty bread, so fresh that the aroma of the cooling French stick filled the lift, making Stella's mouth water. Wine, a delicious red, the best that she could afford. And there was delicious ice cream for dessert, eaten at the table, or maybe in bed…..

The lift came to a halt at Rory's floor, Stella hauled up her bags and drooping with tiredness began the walk down the corridor to Rory's apartment.

A nice reviving cup of tea was much needed before she would have the energy to make a start preparing the salad and organising the sauce for the steak.

"Did you miss me?" she called, unlocking the door with the key that Rory had given her, and shoving it open with her knee. Rory was standing with his back to her, gazing out of the enormous picture window at the city rooftops. She saw his shoulders shrug. "Sorry I was longer than I thought I would be, I met someone from work."

Rory turned slowly towards her, Stella smiled at him, unable to read his expression, blinking in the bright sunlight from the huge window.

"Really?" he took a stride towards her, moving out of the brightness into the softer light in the middle of the room.

"Yes. Lynda, this girl that I used to work for when I first started at the magazine."

Stella felt the air in the room change, prickling with tension. Rory was moving towards her, as if in slow motion, Stella felt as if she were watching herself taking the salad out of her shopping bag, heaving a bag of potatoes onto the counter, while she was aware of her own voice, loud in her ears. The rhythm of her breathing had changed, becoming jagged, each gasp for oxygen tearing at her throat, her heart thudded painfully against her ribs, every fibre of her body tightened in panic, sensing the intense barely controlled anger within Rory.

"I was just getting some tomatoes and she tapped me on the shoulder, amazing that she recognised me. I haven't seen her for ages. She hasn't changed a bit, she could win a gold medal for talking. We went for a cof….."

"Don't lie to me!" Rory's voice thundered, he plunged forwards, grabbing for her arms.

Stella scrambled backwards, every movement seeming to take forever, as if her whole being was weighted down, struggling through thick treacle, that dragged on her limbs.

The bag of potatoes spilt open, cascading to the floor, they seemed to be in their own time frame, moving at normal speed, hitting the floor, bouncing and rolling, while she and Rory slowly came together. His hands grabbed her arms, his fingers vice like on her flesh, her feet still scrambling to take her out of his reach. One potato rolled beneath her foot, and over balancing she toppled to the floor, Rory still with his inhuman grip on her arms, toppled on top of her.

As she hit the cold, smooth terracotta floor tiles, the slowed down movie of her life stopped. Rory released his hold on her arms, struggling to his feet, yelling abuse. Scrabbling to get a grip on the floor she, half fell, half crawled out of his reach.

"You bloody liar," he screamed, his face purple with rage, eyes bulging. "Who have you been with?" He plunged forwards again.

Stella knew in that instant, with a dreadful clearness of reason that he was going to kill her. And in that knowledge, she reached a quiet still place within herself. Death held out its hand to her and finding a strength deep in her soul, she stood her ground, lurched back at him, screaming with as much force as he had.

"Rory, Stop it! Stop it! Stop it!" She saw him falter, hesitate for a split second and in that moment, grabbed at her car keys, flung so carelessly on the kitchen counter only moments before and ran.

Stella thought that she would never get the door lock open, the knob slid between fingers that were slippery with sweat and fumbling with panic. Finally the catch slid back and she wrenched the door open.

"Stella! Don't go!" Rory said so quietly that she half turned in surprise. Rory was leaning on the kitchen counter, as if his legs would not support him. "Please, I'm sorry. I didn't mean to frighten you," he wiped the sheen of sweat off his forehead with a shaking hand, "I couldn't bear the thought of you being with someone else."

Stella felt her hand freeze on the wooden door, watching him in disbelief. Only a few seconds ago she had been sure that he was about to kill her or do her serious harm, now he was as placid as a small child, that has exhausted himself in a tantrum.

As if by its own vocation she felt her hand begin to close the door.

Rory had not meant to hurt her, he had just been upset because he thought that she was off with someone else. If only she had not been late he would never have got upset. It was her fault. Yet again.

Stella looked at the chaos of the kitchen, the spilled potatoes, one still rocking gently to and fro in the middle of the terracotta tiles, surrounded by the debris of lettuce and tomatoes. The dinner that should have been. The meal that would have announced the new beginning of their relationship after Rory had put her in hospital with her injuries. That time she had been lucky. Whatever wrong Rory thought that she had done, he did not have the right to take his temper out on her. She valued her life too much. She might want, might really need a wealthy man to be her husband, but not at this price. Stella shook her head, numbly.

"No, Rory," Stella whispered, her fingers closed around the door once again and, the strength flowed back into them. Wrenching the door open wide, she shot out of the apartment and bolted down the corridor as fast as she could run.

"No!" she heard Rory yell behind her, but then she plunged through the open doors of the lift, pushing the button, her heart pounding painfully in her chest.

The doors seemed to take an age to close. Stella felt as if she were living a scene from a horror movie, at any second the villain would pound down the corridor and wrench open the door and then she would be found dead when the lift opened in the car park two floors below. But the doors swished closed and she was alone.

When they swished open a moment later she expected Rory to be standing there, or at least hiding behind the doors waiting to grab her, but as she bolted from the lift, no hands reached out to seize her.

Stella ran across the car park, back to her car, her footsteps echoing loudly around the concrete pillars. Then as she reached her car, she knew that he was there, she could hear his footsteps pounding across the concrete as he ran towards her.

She shoved her key into the door lock, sobbing in panic, vaguely aware of the concerned, curious glances of some shoppers returning to their apartment. Stella flung herself into the car and pressed the door locks just as Rory reached the car.

"Open the door," he yelled, hauling on the door handle with all his might. His face was purple, unrecognisable in his anger and panic, his eyes mere dark circles above burning cheeks.

"It's over Rory." Stella yelled, not giving a damn who heard her, or what they thought of her. She had to get away, out of this car park, away from Rory. Far, far away from Rory. She was calm as she pushed her key into the ignition and started the car, it might have been just any ordinary Saturday spent shopping.

Her mind, traumatised and terrified seemed to shut down, cutting out the dreadful sight of Rory, spittle flying from his mouth, yelling in temper, trying to bash his way into the car.

He cannoned off the front wing as she drove forwards, barely aware that he was there, her eyes seeking the exit sign.

Then a few moments later, the car surged into the pale afternoon sunlight and the car juddered, thumping into the kerb and bouncing gently to a halt as Stella burst into tears. She was trembling all over, her knees jerking frenziedly against the curve of the steering wheel. Too upset to notice the curious looks of the passers-by and the angry hoots of car horns from drivers annoyed that she was in their way.

Stella sobbed helplessly. Relief to get away from Rory, mingled with the dreadful knowledge of what could have happened and entwined with the regret of losing the relationship. It had to end now, she could never trust him again.

Stella hunted for and found a tissue in tucked in the side pocket of her door and wiped her eyes. She stole a glance at herself in the rear view mirror, her eyes puffy already from crying, her face white with terror. Nothing could be worth putting yourself through this for. She had longed for so much from this relationship and it had all disintegrated. Rory had been nothing but a violent bully. She would never marry him, never even see him again. A fresh flood of tears spilled down her cheeks, she must go home, she could not sit here, at the side of the road, it was pointless, she had to go on rebuild her life.

Sighing bitterly she started the car and pulled out into the line of traffic, heading to her apartment.

Stella pounded up the stairs to the sanctuary of her apartment. She shoved the key in the door and burst in. Amber looked up, startled, hastily sweeping a pile of papers together, a guilty look in her eyes.

"You ok?" asked Stella, momentarily forgetting her own plight, Amber looked so miserable.

"Sure," breezed Amber. "Just paying my credit card bills." She hastily picked up the pile of papers and took them to her room. "What are you doing back?" Amber asked, returning to the living room.

Teddy, hearing Stella's voice leapt from the sofa, where he had been taking an afternoon and hurtled across the room, a small ball of brown energy, tail waving furiously, his small teeth nipping at her ankles in a bid for attention.

Stella bent down and picked up the dog, burying her face in his soft fur, breathing in the warm doggy smell of him, he squirmed in her arms, small pink tongue working, desperately trying to cover her face in wet licks. He was so delighted to see her. If only Rory could have loved her as much.

The memory of her failed relationship clutched at her heart, Stella sank miserably to the sofa, releasing Teddy and covered her face in her hands.

"Stella," Amber's voice seemed to come from very far away, then Stella was aware of her friend sitting beside her.

A warm arm slid gently around her shoulders. "What's happened? What is it?" Amber asked gently.

"Rory………." Stella whispered his name, miserably, feeling the whole weight of the loss of him dragging her down into a deep dark place.

"Oh fuck!" spat Amber, viciously, "I told you……." Amber's voice trailed away as she decided not to continue to admonish Stella for trying to restart the relationship. Amber sighed, bitterly.

Stella felt the sofa move as Amber got up. "Put your head down," Amber said, gently, shoving a soft cushion onto the arm of the sofa. Stella let her head slide down into the soft fabric and closed her eyes as Amber wrapped a warm duvet around her shaking body. "Stay there for a while, I'll get you some tea and toast and in a while it will all feel ok."

"Thank you," Stella smiled faintly, she was not so sure that she would feel ok in a while, but it was nice to be mothered, to let Amber nurse all the feelings of despair away.

Teddy clambered onto the sofa and snuggled into the duvet, delighted that someone was going to join him in a snooze on the sofa, his favourite pastime.

In her handbag, dumped onto the floor beside the sofa, Stella's mobile began to ring. Lulled into a dreamy half sleep, by the warmth of the duvet and half a sleeping pill that Amber had slipped into her tea, Stella fumbled for the phone and switched it on. "Lo," she said, her voice thick with exhaustion.

"Hi, it's Rory, are we still on for tonight?" Stella was instantly awake, listening with disbelief. How on earth after all that had happened could he possibly think that they could continue with their relationship? The nerve and downright stupidity of him. "No, Rory," she snapped coldly into the receiver. "It is not on tonight, or any other night. I never, ever want to see you again."

"Don't be stupid, Stella," Rory's voice was icy cold, menacing. "You can't leave me. I won't let you."

CHAPTER FOURTEEN

Stella rubbed her sore eyes with her fingertips.

She longed to be home, out of this endless line of rush hour traffic. She blinked, trying to relax her eyes that ached with the effort of staring through the rain battered car windscreen at the endless line of tail lights ahead of her.

How was it that when you really wanted to be home that the traffic was always worse? The cars ahead of her in the queue seemed to have been stationary for hours.

Stella began to fantasise about reaching home, slamming the car door and running inside as fast as she could. She wanted to run a deep hot bath and then relax in the water and let the tension of the dreadful day melt away while she read the new book she had bought on her lunch break.

As days went this really had to have been one of the worst. Every bone in her body seemed to ache from where she had fallen on the floor a few dreadful evenings ago. Her temples throbbed with tension. The deep purple bruises that marked her arms were stiff and sore.

As she had dressed that morning she had seen the bruises in the mirror, each one the imprint of Rory's furious finger prints as he had exploded into that uncontrollable temper. Misery hung over her, like a black rain cloud sitting over the Mayo mountains.

Life without Rory seemed dull and featureless, the hope of a wonderful future snuffed out finally. Now indecision tormented Stella. Maybe it had been her fault again, maybe she was not treating Rory with the consideration that he deserved. Maybe she had driven him to attack her.

Finishing with him had seemed so right when she had discussed it with Amber. Stella could not believe that she had actually thrown down the telephone after Rory had rung to see if she was going out.

Did she really want the relationship to end? Really and truly?

Amber had been delighted; she had not doubts what so ever that Stella had done the right thing.

She had grabbed Teddy and sat with him on her knee waving his front legs like arms in a caricature of a delighted football fan celebrating a big win for his side.

"Thank goodness you have seen sense!" she had exclaimed. "He will always do that again." Stella had listened to her numbly, wondering vaguely where Amber had got her information from. What the hell did Amber know about violent relationships? "You would have always been waiting for him hitting you again. You would have become terrified of putting a foot wrong. And in the end you would change so much to keep him happy that you would not even be yourself."

Stella had nodded blankly, hardly able to take her words in. she had just wanted to be with Rory, curled up on his leather sofa listening to music, a glass of wine in her hand, living with the hope that she had finally found the security that she craved for. All of this was wrong, she could not be ending the relationship, he could not really be violent. Could he? And yet, beneath all of her sorrow and regret some part of her knew that she had done the right thing.

Sometime soon that part would grow, would envelope the part of her that longed for the relationship to work, and then she would be able to go forwards, look for another relationship. But not just yet.

For now she had to endure the feelings of misery and uncertainty, struggle through each day at work until she could return to the sanctuary of her bed. And the blissful release of sleep.

Sorcha and Kevin seemed to take great delight in her confusion and misery. Stella felt as if she could do nothing right at work, even the most simple of tasks seemed virtually impossible.

She had even submitted a reworked press release for a mascara product with the photographs for a new perfume.

Sorcha had spotted her mistake straight away and had made sure that she pointed it out to Stella just when Kevin was walking past. Her boss did not even alter his stride and for a long while Stella dared to hope that he had not heard Sorcha's crowing words.

But just when she had almost forgotten the incident Kevin had slid into her office and gently closed the door. Outwardly he had not appeared to be angry, but the cold disappointment in his voice, as he told her that the standard of her work was appalling and that it was time that she pulled herself together, or….. was worse than any yelling of abuse.

The fear of losing her job was worse than any verbal dressing down from Kevin, Stella could not bear the thought of being insecure once more. Not knowing where the next penny was coming from. She had done enough of that when she had been younger.

The rain battered against the windscreen in a fresh frenzy, huge hailstones mingled with the rain drops, pounding on the glass and the car body work sounding as if the metal and glass would cave in under the onslaught.

Out of the rain streaked windscreen the car tail lights inched slowly forwards, the line of red lights stretching as far as the eye could see into the distance of the dual carriageway. Surely this rain could not last much longer, Stella sighed to herself, maybe the morning would bring brighter weather, and everything would feel better then. She would feel more positive; she would put all of the bad things of the last few weeks behind her and move on with her life. Concentrate on her work.

She had to forget Rory. Show Kevin just how good she was at her job. Put Sorcha, with her simpering little side snipes into her place, show her once and for all who was boss. Tomorrow. It would all seem better tomorrow. But first she needed to get home and soak in a hot bath.

The car gave a lurch, momentarily the radio and windscreen wipers stopped and then started again, so quickly that Stella thought that she had imagined it. The line of traffic ground to a halt again. Stella braked and then the car was suddenly silent, the windscreen wipers stopped midway up the glass, the rain pouring unchecked down the sloping screen, quickly obliterating the view of endless red tail lights. Stella turned the ignition key, the engine spluttered and then was silent.

"No, no, no not now!" pleaded Stella, turning the key again, pumping her foot on the accelerator, hoping for some sign of life from the car.

The little car had never let her down before, it was like a friend, faithful and honest. How could it fail now, on what had to be the filthiest night ever, and just when she really needed to get home.

Without the heater blasting out hot air the car was suddenly freezing cold, Stella turned the key once more; she had to get the car started.

"Come on, you bloody thing!" Stella raged, thumping her fist on the centre of the steering wheel in sheer frustration.

The line of cars ahead began to move, the tail lights of the car in front moving away, their red glow flickering through Stella's rain covered windscreen as if they were mocking her plight.

The car behind flashed his headlights, the brightness reflecting in her rear view mirror and making her wince. Then from behind her came the noise of car horns, from frustrated drivers annoyed at being delayed further.

Stella jumped as a man thumped on her driver's window. Gingerly she wound it down, blinking as the rain poured in.

"Move out of the fucking way," a middle aged man snapped, rain dripping off the end of the newspaper that he had spread over his head.

"I'd love to," snapped Stella, sarcastically. "But the bloody car won't start."

The man wrenched open the car door. The icy rain poured in on top of her.

"Get out of the way," he growled.

Stella scrambled out of the car, feeling the rain immediately soaking her head and through the shoulders of her coat and through her best leather kitten heeled shoes.

"Fucking women drivers," complained the man, sliding into the driver's seat, while Stella watched in disbelief at how easily she had relinquished her car to him. He could have wanted to steal it or mug her, or anything. A thousand thoughts flickered distractedly around her befuddled mind, barely taking in that the car was immobile and would have been impossible to steal.

The man turned the car key aggressively, his bulk seeming to fill the small area in between the steering wheel and the seat. "Bastard thing won't start!" he growled between clenched teeth, glaring at Stella as if she had deliberately broken down.

"Yes," Stella whispered, close to tears, there were a thousand smart answers that she could have given him, but just at the moment she could not think of anything to say, she just wanted to get home and into some dry clothes.

Two men ran towards the stricken car, heads bowed against the rain that was soaking through their business suits

"Quick," one of them yelled, his voice almost lost in the traffic noise. The two of them shoved their shoulders into the back of the car, the big man leapt nimbly from the driver's seat and steered the car with one hand while he helped to push the car to the side of the road. The three of them bounced the car off the road onto the grass verge and then as quickly as they had appeared vanished into the rain swept darkness.

The line of cars began to move forwards, tyres sloshing through the puddles, leaving Stella standing on the grass verge.

Miserably she got back into her car; the seat was damp where the water from man's wet clothes had soaked into the fabric. Hopefully there would be reception for her mobile telephone to call someone to help her. Who on earth did she know well enough to ask them to come out and help her?

Stella reached over to the passenger seat and rummaged for her phone in her handbag. She looked up as a pair of bright headlights bumped up onto the grass verge and stopped behind her car. She watched through the rear view mirror as the lights were switched off and a man came towards her car. Hastily she jammed the car door lock down and inched open her window.

"I thought that it was you," Henry grinned at her from beneath the brim of a very battered looking cowboy hat. Stella's heart sank, of all the predicaments to find herself in this had to take the biscuit. Stranded on dual carriageway in the rain and he was the best Sir Galahad that life could provide her with.

Stella unlocked the door and opened it slightly. Henry crouched down beside Stella, shielding her from the worst of the rain. Water dripped slowly off the brim of his hat onto his corduroy trousers, Stella could smell the distinctive odour of horses above the tang of traffic fumes.

"I was driving along the opposite carriageway and I thought that it was you. I saw you standing in the road while the men pushed your car off the road. It took me a while to turn around and get back to you."

Stella twisted her lips into a polite smile, wishing that he had not bothered. She did not like Henry. She did not like anyone so obviously penniless and scruffy like he was. And she really did not like the way her heart seemed to beat at double quick time whenever he was around.

"Please don't let me delay you," Stella chanced a look at Henry; his face was dreadfully close to hers. She could see the rain drops glittering on the untidy strands of his hair where it curled unchecked beneath his hat.

"You aren't delaying me," his mouth was wide, his lips full, she watched them move over a row of perfectly even teeth, she did not dare look at his eyes, in case she discovered what was making her heart flutter so uncontrollably. "Come on I'll take you home, we will have to get a garage to come and tow your car in, and we can't do anything about it now." He reached in and took her hand; his skin was icy cold against hers. His hand was very big, gently clutching hers as if she were a tiny delicate bird that he was afraid to hurt. Stella let him pull her to her feet, then as if her skin was burning hot, he abruptly let go of her.

"Jump in to my Jeep," Henry said, reaching inside Stella's car and grabbing her handbag and keys. "Quick, get out of the rain."

Stella dashed for the Jeep, the heavy door gave a crunch of protest as she wrenched it open, she glanced back watching as Henry shoved down the lock on her car and slammed the door shut.

"You must be frozen!" Henry exclaimed, bursting into the driver's seat, a second later. "Here, you can wear this jumper of mine," he stretched his arm into the back seat, rummaging around in the darkness. "Take off your wet coat."

Stella did as she was told, pulling the heavy jumper over her head and grimacing with distaste at the smell of horses and dogs that wafted from the fabric.

"Throw your coat into the back," Henry told her, firing the engine into life. "Now you had better give me directions," Henry said as the Jeep jolted off the grass verge and surged out into the line of traffic.

Stella threw her coat into the back, narrowly missing the collie dog that was curled up on a pile of horse rugs. The dog lifted his head and regarded her balefully for a moment before lowering his head onto his paws, with a sigh.

"It's not far, turn off the dual carriageway at the next junction," Stella told him, thankfully.

There were limits to her endurance and sitting in this dirty, rattling Jeep was almost too much.

Heaven knows what was under her feet, she thought, tentatively pushing away a cardboard box full of Thoroughbred sales catalogues.

"Are you going to Fairyhouse, one of Rory's horses is running there?" Henry virtually had to shout over the rattling noise that the Jeep was making.

"Not sure," Stella shouted back, she should tell Henry that her relationship with Rory was over, but part of her held back. She did not want Henry to know that she had broken up with Rory. Something that she could see dancing behind his eyes, when she dared look at him, made her feel that Henry would be rather pleased to hear that she was single.

"Just here," Stella said a few minutes later, pointing at a gap between the parked cars where Henry could pull over close to her flat. "That was very kind of you," she smiled at him gratefully.

She scrambled from the Jeep as Henry turned off the engine.

"I'll walk you in," he said, hastily, leaping out of the vehicle before she could protest.

He shot around to the pavement with a coat which he held over her head as they ran towards the apartment block. Stella could feel the warmth from his body against hers as he hunched over her, protecting her from the rain.

Suddenly Henry was jerked away, the coat fluttered to the ground as a fresh onslaught of rain thundered down on Stella's head. Stella felt her mouth drop open, in the harsh glow of the streetlights Rory had hold of Henry's sweater and was shaking him like a terrier with a rat. "You bitch. You must have been carrying on with him while I was there." shrieked Rory. "I fucking knew you were seeing someone else, but not him!"

CHAPTER FIFTEEN

Stella felt disbelief mingle with an uncontrollable anger. In the harsh glow of the street lights with the torrential rain pouring down on them all, the scene had a surreal quality, as if she were watching a scene from a movie.

It was not possible that her ex-boyfriend was trying to accuse her of having an affair with someone like Henry. She did not even particularly like Henry. And she would never, ever have an affair with someone while she was in a relationship that just was not her style. Rory stood in the middle of the pavement, his hair slicked to his head with the rain, fists clenched as he roared, "I knew you were seeing someone else. You two timing bitch."

"Leave her alone!" Henry snarled, Stella noticed that the battered cowboy hat was askew on his head and that the rain had drenched through his shirt, plastering the fabric to his body.

She was surprised that even in these bizarre circumstances that she could still notice the minute details. She tore her eyes away from the swell of his arm muscles and the flat plane of his belly. "There's nothing going on between us. Never has been," he shook his head vehemently. Stella wondered if she could hear a note of regret in his voice. "Her car had broken down and I stopped to give her a lift."

Rory lowered his head, shaking it slowly, like a raging bull, about to charge, his eyes blazed in his pale face.

"Stop lying," he growled between clenched teeth. "You may as well admit it now." He swung a clenched fist in Henry's direction, blind with temper the punch missed by a mile.

"I wasn't seeing Henry," Stella yelled, astonished to find herself standing in front of Henry as if to protect him. "We finished days ago because of you acting like this all of the time." She told Rory. "Who I get a lift with is none of your business."

"Get out of my way," Rory snarled, he seized Stella by the shoulders and shoved her out of the way.

"Get off her," screamed a voice and Amber launched herself at Rory, her diminutive frame full of anger, tiny fists flailing in his direction. Rory, shocked by the sudden onslaught, stumbled backwards. "I was just walking Teddy," Amber said, putting her arm around Stella, "I heard that idiot screaming and carrying on." She glared at Rory who stood sullenly in the rain. "Go on you, piss off and leave Stella alone."

Rory shuffled his feet, all of his anger suddenly depleted. Then at the same moment all of them seemed to notice Teddy, who, released by Amber as she launched her attack on Rory, was now wandering around the pavement, weaving in and out of their feet. As if she had a sudden premonition of what was to come, Amber suddenly dropped to her haunches.

"Teddy, come here," Stella could hear the sudden panic in her voice. She saw Rory turn, look at the puppy, who was snuffling around close to his feet, and then in one movement he scooped the dog into his arms and shooting them a look that was pure malice, turned and ran with the dog in his arms.

"Rory. No!" screamed Stella, shooting across the road after him.

"Fuck off! It's your turn to get hurt now, Stella," Rory heaved open his car door, threw Teddy inside, like a rugby player passing the ball and before she could reach him, he had jumped into the car and slammed the door shut.

Stella stood in the street watching the car disappear into the distance with Teddy's small brown face looking at her out of the back window.

Fighting a dreadful feeling of nausea that was threatening to envelope her Stella slowly made her way back across the street, narrowly avoiding being run over by a car that hooted angrily as she almost walked into its path.

Amber crouched beside the wall outside the apartment block sobbing noisily, while Henry stood uncomfortably beside her looking shell shocked.

"Why didn't you stop him?" snapped Stella at Henry.

None of them could have prevented Rory from taking Teddy, none of them were close enough, but somehow she wanted to lash out at Henry, hurt him for being the cause of her precious dog being taken by Rory.

"I………." Henry shrugged helplessly, as if he knew that to argue with Stella would be useless, she was too distraught.

"He will kill the dog, I know he will," wailed Amber, covering her face with her hands. "He just wants to hurt you. He's a maniac." Stella felt hot tears of shock and hurt begin to trickle down her cheeks. She crouched down beside Amber.

"Come on, let's go inside out of the rain, we can't do anything out here," she said gently, putting her arms around Amber and trying to haul her to her feet. Amber got up, she stood beside Stella as limp as a rag doll, all of the life gone out of her.

"Rory, please don't hurt him," Amber whispered, miserably, burying her face against Stella's shoulder. Stella felt a warm pair of arms encircle the two of them. The damp cotton of Henry's shirt brushed against her face, she could feel the warmth of his arm against the icy cold of her cheeks and feel the hard muscle beneath the fabric.

"Come on. Let me take you inside," he said gently.

Stella launched herself backwards out of his grip. "Why don't you bloody well clear off. Haven't you caused enough trouble?" she snapped, furiously.

If Henry had not been around none of this would have happened. Why could he not have just gone when he had brought her home, like she had wanted? Why did he have to walk her home? If only her car had not broken down none of this would have happened.

Henry stepped back as abruptly as if she had punched him. "Fine," he said coldly. Stella glared at him, his face pale and set beneath the unearthly glow of the streetlamp.

"I'll go then," he paused, standing in the middle of the pavement, uncertainly, as if he were struggling to find something to say, some words that would make everything all right.

"Go on then!" raged Stella.

"Right!" Henry turned on his heel and walked away, the sound of his drenched clothes and the water sloshing in his shoes loud in the stunned silence.

Stella stared after him as Henry stalked across the road and got into his Jeep and drove away. Beside her she heard Amber sigh miserably.

"We should have got him to drive after Rory," she said, bitterly, turning away and walking towards the apartments.

Stella stood in the rain for a long time, watching the tail lights of Henry's Jeep disappear down the street. She wished that she had never, ever, ever met Henry Murphy.

"Oh God, Amber," Stella groaned, shaking her head in disbelief, turning around, but the pavement was deserted.

Amber had gone inside. Fighting back tears Stella made her way inside. Amber was in the lounge, pacing up and down, frenziedly as if she did not know quite what to do with herself.

"What's he done with Teddy?" she looked at Stella, her eyes wide and frightened, her hair hanging in wild disarray around her face. "You don't think that he will hurt him do you?" Stella winced, that scenario was too awful to contemplate.

"No," she shook her head firmly. "He might be a maniac, but he's not cruel to animals."

Stella hoped that she was right. Rory was angry enough to do anything to get back at her. Amber sank down onto the sofa and buried her head in her hands. Stella watched as the water from her clothes slowly dripped onto the fabric, making dark stains.

"Make him bring Teddy back," Amber pleaded, her voice almost lost in the sound of her sobs.

Stella stood in the middle of the room, uncertain as to what she should do, then suddenly she picked up the telephone and punched in Rory's number. After a few rings he answered.

"Stella!" he sounded delighted to see her number come up on his telephone. "Dinner tomorrow night?"

Stella frowned, had he somehow managed to erase the memory of the last few nights? Had he forgotten that he had attacked her – twice – and had just threatened someone who had helped her when her car had broken down – or that he had just stolen her dog?

"No Rory, we are not," she tried to keep her voice as calm and neutral as she could, "Rory. Could you bring the dog back please?"

"That bloody thing," he snorted in amusement. "Peed on the floor in my car. I threw it out by the new Sycamore Park Estate. Some kids went away with it."

Stella's mouth dropped open, she stared at Amber, who was looking at her expectantly, her eyes full of hope that he would bring Teddy back.

"I see," she whispered, struggling to speak for the enormous lump that had suddenly welled in the back of her throat.

"Come out with me again," she could hear Rory saying, "I'll buy you another dog, a nice pedigree one, not a scruffy mutt like that one."

Stella clicked the receiver down, there was nothing more to say to Rory. How could he have just let the dog go? Her precious little dog, Teddy. He might have been just a scruffy mutt in Rory's eyes, but to Stella and Amber he was an adorable part of their lives.

How could Rory have been so stupid? Had he done it just to hurt her? Stella opened her mouth again, but no words came out. She looked at Amber and saw the hope die in her eyes.

She walked around to the sofa and sank down; suddenly she did not feel as if her legs would support her.

"He let Teddy out of the car at the Sycamore Park Estate," Stella sighed.

Amber leapt to her feet. "Come on! We'll go and find him."

Stella pulled her back down onto the sofa. "We can't. It's almost midnight and I've no car. We will have to wait until morning."

Amber glared back at her. "First thing then, we will ring in sick and go and look for him."

Kevin was speaking, Stella could see his mouth opening and closing, but could not take in what he was saying.

Teddy had been missing for three days now and the belief that he would be found safe and well were beginning to fade. The harsh reality was hard to face. They were never going to see him again. He was out there somewhere, alone and frightened. Maybe he had been chased away by the children and was lying injured somewhere. Maybe dying.

Stella and Amber had spent every spare moment walking around the drab streets of the housing estate, looking for Teddy. They had knocked on countless doors, asking if anyone had seen the dog, but every reply had been negative. They had walked around the wasteland that bordered the estate, sinking ankle deep into mud and clambering over abandoned mattresses and old fridges, calling the dog's name and listening to the mocking replies of the grubby estate children who trailed curiously after them.

"So how do you think we should present this article?" Kevin asked, looking quizzically at Stella over the top of his half-moon glasses.

"Oh, I………," Stella began.

"About the health spas," Sorcha snapped, sarcastically, tapping a long finger nail against the pile of papers that she had laid in front of Stella before the meeting began. "Yes," Stella fought to get her thoughts in order, trying to banish the picture of Teddy lying, whimpering pitifully beneath a bush. "Perhaps we could do a top ten of the best spas?" she said, lamely.

Kevin clapped his pudgy, sausage like fingers together. "Excellent," he preened, pursing his fat lips together. "Now," he said, flapping his hands in front of him, "I think that Sorcha would do a great job of sampling them all and coming up with the top ten." He beamed across the table at Sorcha, who fought to control her cry of delight and just managed to turn it into a strangled cough.

Stella shuffled her papers, trying to hide her disappointment.

Normally that job would have been given to her, but she seemed to have lost all of the drive that had made her so good at her job. Sorcha had been snapping at her heels for long enough, now she was clearly over taking Stella, soon Stella would be the assistant and Sorcha would be given the editorial job.

The day dragged on, Stella stole yet another glance at her watch, time seemed to be standing still. There were hours yet before she could head out of the office into her car and head back to the Sycamore Park Estate, for yet another heart breaking search for Teddy.

"You've made a mistake on this article," Sorcha crowed, unable to keep the glee out of her voice. Stella almost choked on Sorcha's over powering perfume as the girl leant over her desk to throw the article in front of her.

Out of the corner of her eye Stella saw Kevin mincing past. She sighed bitterly, full of hatred for Sorcha. She had timed returning the article to Stella until Kevin was around. Stella had lost count of the times that she had altered things that Sorcha had made mistakes on, without even mentioning it to her. This was pure spite, Sorcha just wanted to show Stella at her worst so that she could weedle her way into Kevin's good books.

Finally the time came to leave the office, Stella tried desperately to string out the time that it took her to pack away her things so that she would not appear to be too eager to leave.

Sorcha looked up from her desk as Stella walked past. "Oh is it time to go already?" she asked loudly. "I'll just stay here and finish these. You get off Stella."

Stella clenched her teeth, yet again Sorcha had managed to make her look like a bad employee in front of Kevin. But she had to leave, she was due to pick up Amber from outside the apartment and then the two of them were going to spend the remaining hour or so of light walking around the housing estate hunting for Teddy.

Yet again the search was fruitless and as the darkness began to fall they had to admit defeat. They went back to Stella's car and sat shivering, aching with tiredness and misery as they drove home silently.

The door-bell rang. Amber leapt to her feet, expectantly and ran to open it. Stella listened, hopefully to the sound of voices coming from the front door, maybe someone had found Teddy and brought him back. She looked up a few moments later, longing to see Teddy wriggling with delight in Amber's arms, but instead Henry stood in the doorway.

Amber slid past him and disappeared into her bedroom and closed the door quietly.

Stella stood up, wondering why he had come.

"Hello," she smiled tightly.

"I came to say thank you," Henry said, stiffly, not returning her greeting. "Rory just came to see me. He would not believe that we were not having an affair."

Stella made a spluttering sound, the very idea was totally ridiculous, she could not stand Henry, let alone have an affair with him.

"And so," Henry continued, glaring coldly at her. "He's taken his horses away from my yard."

Stella snorted in disbelief at Rory's stupidity. "He took my dog and let him out of his car and now he is lost," Stella told him.

Henry was not the only one who had lost something because of Rory's stupidity.

"I've just lost half of my business," Henry continued, glared at her coldly, the muscles at the side of his jaw clenched with tension, before he added sarcastically, "thank you very much."

111

CHAPTER SIXTEEN

The roar of loud voices stopped suddenly. The apartment door slammed shut so hard that Amber's bedroom windows rattled. And then there was silence. Henry must have gone. Tentatively Amber got up from the bed where she had been sitting, blindly leafing through the pages of a magazine, opened her bedroom door and peered out. "It's safe to come out now," Stella muttered tightly.

"What was wrong with him?" Amber asked, although she knew full well what had happened. Their voices had carried through to her bedroom, through the paper-thin walls.

"Rory has taken his horses away from Henry's stables, half of his business," Stella muttered angrily. "Like that's my fault," she continued, her voice rising with temper.

"And Henry blames you?" Amber sat down at the opposite end of the sofa and looked at Stella, whose cheeks blazed red with indignation.

"He blames me for losing the business, just like you blame me for losing the dog," Stella met Amber's gaze.

"Don't be silly, of course I don't," Amber said, frowning as if the suggestion were complete madness. But deep down Amber knew that she was lying, if only Stella had not wound Rory up then he would never have taken the dog to get back at her.

Stella seemed to have given up on ever finding the dog, something that Amber could never do. Amber was determined to find Teddy. Somehow.

Finding Teddy might just be the one good thing to happen so far this year. Everything else had been pretty awful.

Ruby had been the start of everything that had gone wrong.

If only Amber had not been so delighted to be included in an invitation to join her sister's glamorous circle of friends then she would have never have skived off work nor would she have ever gotten involved with that gormless creep, Ernest. Oh how she regretted that evening.

Ruby's future brother in law had to be the ugliest man that Amber had ever seen. He was tall and stick thin, with a permanent hunch as if he wanted to hide his height.

When eventually Amber forced herself to look at Ernest's face she was reminded of an anaemic carrot, his face was so long and pointed and pale. The only thing that was right about him was his name. Ernest by name, earnest by nature. His watery looking grey eyes, had the eager expression of a besotted spaniel that hangs onto its master's every word.

Amber's heart had sunk into the soles of Stella's black shoes.

Ernest was dreadful. Ruby must have known how awful he was when she had asked Amber to join them.

Amber had stolen a look at Ruby over Ernest's frail looking shoulder, Ruby was watching them together. Ruby had looked away guiltily as she saw Amber looking at her, but not before Amber had time to see the look of amusement in her eyes.

And if spending the evening with the dreadful Ernest was not enough Amber still had to face the wrath of her boss, Mark Hardcastle when she returned to work.

Just as she had imagined, Mark had been dreadful. "Feeling better?" he had bellowed across the restaurant as Amber had arrived to start her shift.

"Yes thank you," Amber had replied quietly ducking her head to avoid the curious stares of the early diners who had turned to look at her.

Mark was never one to forgive and forget and all evening he had watched Amber like a hawk, criticising her every move until she longed to fling down her white apron and dash out of the restaurant.

Even Jules, usually Amber's compatriot in the war zone of the restaurant, had been decidedly frosty with her.

It had taken weeks until the atmosphere began to resemble anything like normal. It had also taken weeks to shake off Ernest's amorous advances.

After their meeting in the restaurant with Ruby and Roderick, Ernest had latched onto Amber with the ferocity of a limpet clinging to a rock. It had taken all of Amber's tact to shake off Ernest, who had telephoned daily for weeks after Christmas.

Watching Amber trying to get rid of Ernest had been the one thing that had amused Stella in the long dark weeks that while she was not seeing Rory. And now that relationship was well and truly over, Rory had taken their beloved dog, Teddy, in order to get his own back.

Losing Teddy had been the worst thing that had ever happened to Amber, worse than losing a job, or a boyfriend. It was like losing a child. She had adored the little dog. And now he was gone and the thought of him being out in the dark, alone and afraid was like torture to Amber. She was determined that someday, somehow she was going to find him and bring him home.

Stella smiled tightly, "it's nice of you to say that, but I still feel so guilty about it all."

So guilty, thought Amber that Stella had given up all hope of ever finding Teddy alive again. "Don't worry, you can make it up to Teddy when he comes back." Amber told Stella.

Amber spent yet another night drifting in and out of a restless sleep. Every sound from the dark streets became magnified, she could hear Teddy whimpering outside the apartment; hear his claws scratching at the door, begging to be let in.

At seven in the morning Amber abandoned any hope of getting any more sleep. She slid out of bed and opened the curtains, outside a man was walking a large black Labrador. Trotting behind the man was a small terrier, its short legs moving jauntily as it tried to keep up with the larger dog. Amber's heart gave a lurch and then sank again as she looked closer at the dog, it was not Teddy.

Amber wandered blearily into the kitchen and began to make herself tea.

Stella was already in the bathroom, Amber could hear the rush of the water as she showered, getting herself ready for work.

"Couldn't you sleep?" Stella came out of the bathroom, wrapped in a silky robe, rubbing her long hair with a towel.

Amber shook her head, "I keep thinking….." her voice faded away, it seemed silly to say that worrying about the dog had been keeping her awake, but that was the truth.

Stella made a sound that was somewhere in between a murmur of sympathy and a groan of guilt. "Better get ready for work," Stella grabbed a bowl of cereal and headed back to her bedroom.

Amber took a slug of her tea and sighed, she missed the easy camaraderie that had existed between them such a short time ago. Nothing was the same between them since the dog had disappeared. Amber padded back to her bed and curled up beneath the duvet, hugging the mug of tea to her belly.

Usually she enjoyed the mornings; after Stella headed off to work Amber would curl up in bed with Teddy, the two of them luxuriating in the warmth and comfort, until they felt like getting up. Lying in bed alone was not half as much fun.

"See you!" Stella called as she slammed the front door.

The silence descended again, Amber put down her tea mug and curled up, there was nothing else to do except sleep until later, but still she could not sleep. Memories of Teddy and the love that he gave would not let her rest.

Finally Amber abandoned her lie in and got up; at least she had plenty of time to get ready before her father arrived.

For the last few days Jack had been helping Amber to scour the streets, looking for Teddy. Today they were going to have another go, searching one of the estates close to the Sycamore Park Estate where Rory had dumped the dog.

"I thought that you had overslept again!" Pearl said petulantly as Amber clambered into her parent's car. "Sorry to keep you waiting,"

Amber bit her tongue, she had been looking out of the window waiting for them to arrive and had only kept them waiting as long as it had taken to leave the apartment and walk down the stairs outside.

She longed to snap back at her mother, but what was the point, Pearl would only get huffy and then the journey would be awful. At least she did not have to endure her mother for long, Pearl was going into town while Amber and her father searched for Teddy.

Amber shifted uncomfortably as the familiar nagging ache of tension knotted in her side.

"Ohhhhhwwww," complained Pearl so loudly that Jack jammed on the brakes. "There was no need to knee me so viciously in the back," Pearl complained.

"I was just moving my legs" Amber protested and then, seeing her father in the mirror, closing his eyes in a gesture of resignation, she clamped her mouth shut.

There was no point in arguing with Pearl. "Slow down Daddy!" Pearl snapped, crossly as they drove towards the city. Jack was silent, but the car slowed to a sullen crawl. Amber noticed that her father's fingers had tightened on the steering wheel. "We must change this car, Jack," Pearl began her relentless nagging again. "We have had it two years now. All of my friends will think that we have no money!"

"Ok," Jack said in a resigned tone, but Amber could hear the tension in his voice.

After what seemed an interminable journey Pearl was dropped off close to the shops.

Amber got into the vacant front seat. "I hope that you don't keep me waiting this evening," was Pearl's parting shot.

"Ok," Jack repeated patiently. "The last time I kept her waiting was nineteen seventy, she still hasn't let me forget it," Jack said almost to himself and then smiled guiltily at Amber, as if he regretted his disloyalty.

A short time later they drew into the genteel surroundings of Beechwood Park and parked the car on a quiet cul de sac.

Amber's heart sank, she had hoped that she would see Teddy trotting gaily down the pavement towards her. But the road was deserted.

"Come on," Jack said gently, unclipping his seatbelt and easing himself out of the car.

Amber shivered in the damp morning air.

They walked slowly along the pavement, past silent bungalows, hidden behind a mosaic of green bushes and shrubs. Teddy could be lying hurt and afraid beneath any of those bushes, thought Amber, peering over a low red brick wall.

They walked the length of the pavement, their footsteps echoing eerily in the deserted road.

At the far end was an oval of neatly trimmed grass, lined with shrubs. "That's it," Jack said, gently touching Amber's arm as if to guide her back to the car.

"Hush, listen," hissed Amber.

"What?" frowned Jack, listening intently.

"Listen," Amber repeated, her voice rising with excitement and then she set off at a jog across the oval of grass towards a clump of bushes. "Teddy?" Amber crouched beside the bushes, "Daddy, listen," Amber's voice was full of hope as she knelt down beside the bushes.

"I heard that," Jack bent down stiffly and peered into the dim light beneath the bushes to where the unmistakable whimper came from.

Amber crouched down and inched her way beneath the bushes, narrowing her eyes in an effort to see in the dim light beneath the canopy of dark waxy leaves.

Gradually her eyes became accustomed to the pale light and she could make out a faint animal shape beneath the tangle of branches. She crawled forwards, the damp earth soaking through the knees of her jeans, the whip thin branches scraping against her face and hands.

The animal shape unfurled, moving slowly. Amber stretched out her hand and touched the animal and encountered soft fur, too soft to belong to Teddy. As her hand moved over the animal it unfurled, hissing indignantly as Amber's hand closed over its fur. "

It's a bloody cat," Amber said miserably as she emerged from the bushes with the cat wriggling furiously in her arms.

Amber got to her feet and met the furious gaze of a short plump old lady who stood indignantly beside her father. "Just what are you doing with my Freddie?" demanded the old lady, her sloe black eyes glinting angrily, as she hauled the cat out of Amber's arms. "I thought that it was my dog," Amber protested weakly, aware of her father twitching with suppressed laughter beside her.

"Any fool can see that this is a cat," spat the old lady, her mouth closing firmly into a tight line as she darted Amber a glance of pure fury before stalking off with Freddie gazing maliciously at Amber over her shoulder.

"We are doing no good here," Jack said, gently. "Come on, I'll buy you some lunch."

Amber shrugged bleakly, he was right. There was no point in walking up and down the street, Teddy was not here. He was gone. Amber knew, suddenly that she would never see him again.

She trudged back to the car beside Jack, who, had cheered up at the thought of a warm pub and a good lunch. "You will feel better with a good lunch inside you," Jack said kindly, opening the car door to let Amber in.

Amber settled herself into the seat and sighed bitterly. Her father meant well, but she doubted that a plate of steak and chips would make the situation look any better.

She had adored Teddy. He was the best male thing that she had been around in a long time, reliable and adoring, who could ask for more. And now he was gone. She would never see his little button eyes looking at her again.

Although being in the pub did not make losing Teddy any easier, at least it was warm, Amber thought, sitting down in a corner, while her father went to the bar to organise the food.

"I've got you a brandy," Jack said, sliding into the seat beside her. "Food's on the wa......" he stopped speaking and stared at a group of women who had come into the pub.

"Thanks," said Amber, aware suddenly that her father was miles away, she followed his gaze to the women.

They were all elderly, chattering animatedly as if this was an exciting excursion for them.

Then as if she could feel Jack's eyes on her one of the women turned, the words fading on her lips as Jack's done. Her face lit up as if a dozen light bulbs had been illuminated behind her eyes as she lifted her hand in greeting.

"Kate," breathed Jack, Amber's presence completely forgotten as he shot to his feet, knocking the table and sending the drinks spilling across the wooden surface in his haste. Kate crossed the room towards him.

"Hello Jack," she beamed, taking his hands and planting a kiss on his cheek. "Is this Amber?" she asked, looking past Jack to where Amber sat, open mouthed.

"Ah, yes," Jack seemed to come back to earth. "We're just having lunch together." He still clung to Kate's hand as if he did not ever want to let her go.

"How lovely," Kate smiled gently at Amber, who, aware that she was staring at them, tore her gaze reluctantly away aware that she had witnessed a scene that she should not have. Kate and Jack were obviously in love.

CHAPTER SEVENTEEN

Stella lowered herself slowly into achingly hot water, which slopped dangerously close to the edge of the bath as she moved.

This really had to be the very best way to spend an evening in. Forget curling up with a good book, or a video. A hot bath with beauty treatments an inch thick on her face and over her hair was the ultimate way to relax.

Slowly, so that she did not slop the water over the edge of the bath, Stella reached over to the low table and grabbed her headphones and pressed play. She closed her eyes, letting the beautiful voice of Lucie Silvas wash over her. At least now she was in her own world, away from the ever present threat of the telephone ringing with Rory on the other end begging her to forgive him. Stella began to sing along to her favourite track on the CD, extending her long, slender limbs as she exfoliated each one with the expensive Christian Dior that a wealthy boyfriend had once brought her on a shopping excursion. She stopped singing, suddenly, aware that she could hear banging on the bathroom door. Scowling she pulled off the headset and sat up, slopping water out over the edge of the bath.

"Stella!" yelled Amber, hammering on the bathroom door once more.

"Yes!" Stella yelled in reply, through gritted teeth, what did Amber want now?

"Stella," Amber yelled again, her voice filled with urgency.

Stella heaved herself out of the bath, grabbed a towel and held it around herself while she opened the door.

"Stella" Amber almost fell in through the door as it opened. "Come out quickly. Guess who is here!" she squeaked excitedly, hoping from one foot to the other as if she could barely contain her energy. She stopped as she looked at Stella's head, her eyes narrow with annoyance from behind the thick green face mask, yellow fruit smelling slime sliding slowly off her hair. "Maybe you had better finish your bath first," her voice high with barely suppressed laughter.

Stella stepped back into the bath.

"But be quick!" Amber darted her head around the door again as Stella let the towel slide from her shoulders and clambered back into the bath. She pulled out the plug, watching regretfully as the hot water gurgled away down the plug hole. Whatever was exciting Amber so much she was not going to give Stella any peace until she had seen whoever had come for a visit. Stella could not imagine that there was anyone that she would like to see just at this moment, unless it was George Clooney, but she could not imagine that he was very likely to come calling, she mused, turning on the shower and gasping as a blast of icy cold water hit her in the face.

Drying herself quickly after the shower, Stella put on her dressing gown and sighing with annoyance went out of the bathroom.

"Nice singing," said Henry, his eyes widening with amusement as she emerged into the living room, still tying the belt of her dressing gown around her waist.

Stella gave an involuntary gasp of dismay. How could Amber have let him into the apartment? She must have known that Stella would not have wanted him here.

"Hello," Stella said, coldly, shooting a furious glance at Amber who was pawing at her cheeks like someone demented.

Henry leant against the back of the sofa, looking gorgeous in a dishevelled way, torn, faded jeans clung to the long muscles of his thighs and the collar of his shirt was frayed where it touched the long sweep of his neck. His eyes danced with amusement,

Stella cringed inwardly. How long had he been here, before Amber had hammered on the bathroom door. He must have heard her dreadful tuneless singing.

Uncontrollable anger sent prickles of heat all over her body, this really was dreadful.

Of all the people that could have come while she was in the bath Henry had to be the worst of them. And now he was standing in her lounge looking at her as if she were some really amusing comic turn.

"Henry's got something for you," Amber said, scratching at her cheek furiously and rolling her eyes at Stella.

"Oh yes?" Stella said coldly glaring in first Amber's direction and then at Henry. She wished that she were safely dressed in her business suit, feeling in command of the situation instead of feeling foolish and vulnerable, standing bare foot and damp in her oldest dressing gown with her hair all awry and without even a scrape of lipstick or mascara to cover the nakedness of her face.

Henry grinned, levering himself upright. "Something that you might like," he said, fetching a large cardboard box from the side of the sofa.

Stella frowned at Amber, as Henry bent over the box and began to tug at the strings that fastened it shut.

"Is he mad?" she mouthed at Amber, who ignoring her question, began animatedly pointing to her face. Then as something brown and hairy exploded from the box, Stella realised with a jolt what Amber had been trying to tell her. She still had some of the face mask smeared on her cheeks.

"Teddy!" the girls yelled in unison, as the dog bounded across the room, ears flapping, mouth wide open in a grin as he leapt from one of them to the other, unable to conceal his delight at seeing them again.

"You are wonderful," grinned Stella at Henry scooping up the dog into her arms where he wriggled furiously, trying to lick her face with his small pink tongue while his whimpers of delight rang loudly around the room. Henry, she noticed, above the wriggling dog, had gone quite pink and was grinning from ear to ear.

"Where did you find him?" she did not want to ever let Teddy go again, she stroked his wiry coat, revelling in the feel of his fur beneath her fingers. He smelt of dog shampoo, woody and clean.

"Some lads who do a bit of shooting found him on the wasteland behind the Sycamore Estate, I heard who had found him through one of the lads who works at my stables and went around to see if it was the same dog."

Henry watched Stella bury her face in Teddy's fur, long strands of brown hair sticking to the green face mask that was smeared on one of her cheeks and knew that the bottle of whiskey and crisp one hundred euro note that it had cost him to get the dog back had been worth every penny. Even if it did mean that he would have to live on toast and marmalade for the rest of the week.

"Let me cuddle him," pleaded Amber, taking the dog from Stella and gesturing with her head towards the bathroom, indicating that Stella should go and clean her face. "Yes, ok," Stella unwillingly released her hold on the dog and quietly slipped away back to the bathroom.

She closed the door and let hot tears of relief fall slowly down her cheeks. She had thought that they would never see Teddy again, imagined that he had died somewhere, all alone and afraid. And now he was back, safe and sound. Thanks to Henry.

A sudden picture of his amused expression flashed into her mind and Stella launched herself across the bathroom to the sink and peered into the mirror, barely stifling a cry of anguish.

She had come out of the bathroom in such a temper that she had not rinsed her hair, or face properly. A clump of yellow goo still clung above her right ear and a large smear of green face mask still remained on her face, now with numerous curly dog hairs stuck in it. And as if that was not bad enough, the green mask still remained in the creases at the sides of her nose and into her hair line at the temples.

What an idiot Henry must think she was. And he had heard her singing as well.

Stella scrubbed at her face with a flannel, rinsing every trace of the hair and face masks away, and then slapping face cream on with a hand that trembled with anger at being seen looking such a mess, she applied some foundation, mascara and a sheen of lipstick. Finally she combed her hair and slipped back into the jeans and tee shirt that she had been wearing earlier and then went back into the lounge.

Henry was sitting at one end of the sofa while Teddy sat at his feet looking up at him adoringly Amber sat at the other end, her face mirroring Teddy's expression of admiration.

"Ah," Henry looked at Stella appraisingly as she came back into the room. "You looked just as nice before."

Stella felt herself prickle with annoyance, what an idiot he must have thought she looked, in her tattered dressing gown with her face all smeared.

Now he was laughing at her. Somehow whenever she was around this man she seemed to make a fool of herself.

Amber leapt from the sofa as if it was suddenly burning hot. "Excuse me," she simpered. "Early night, I've got an important interview in the morning." She sidled towards her bedroom door, ignoring Stella's glared expression pleading with her not to go.

Stella did not want to be left alone with Henry, he made her feel uncomfortable. Gawky, as if her arms and legs were too big for her body and as if she had little control of them. And she did not like the way that her eyes strayed, as if by their own vocation, to gaze at the contours of his body or the planes of his face.

"You sit here," Amber indicated the vacant end of the sofa, like a sycophantic waiter guiding a tetchy client to the best seat. Stella sat down unwillingly as if she were at the dentist for a filling without aesthetic.

"It was very kind of you to find Teddy for us and bring him back, "Stella smiled, tightly, wondering how she could get rid of Henry, she hoped that Rory was not sitting outside the flat again. It would just cause more trouble if he saw Henry.

"Glad to be able to help," grinned Henry. "We seemed to have gotten off on the wrong foot," he added, looking around the room as if he were afraid to meet Stella's eyes. "Maybe we could be friends now."

"Sure," Stella shrugged, she could not see what on earth she would ever have in common with Henry, but it had been nice of him to bring the dog back.

"Would you like to come for a drink then?"

"Errrm……….well…….ok." Stella replied, caught completely off guard.

"Now." Henry said. It was a statement, rather than a question. Stella opened her mouth to protest and then closed it. What if Rory was sat outside again in his car waiting for a chance to beg forgiveness again? Stella hated the thought of another scene out in the street. But Henry had been very kind bringing the dog back; she owed it to him to at least try to be his friend. Just because he was scruffy and smelt of horses it did not mean that he was not a nice person. And just because she was looking for a millionaire and would never, ever, not in a million years, ever entertain a relationship with someone like Henry that did not mean that she could not go out for a friendly drink with him.

"I'll fetch my coat," Stella got up and went into her bedroom and pulled her coat out of the wardrobe. One quick drink could not hurt.

"Are you going out with him," hissed Amber, slipping into the room a moment later. "Yes," Stella said slowly, annoyed with herself to find that she was standing in front of her mirror, reapplying her lipstick and for some reason adding a squirt of perfume behind her ears.

Amber did a war dance around the room.

"Wonderful, he's really lovely," she hissed, excitedly, jumping up and down with excitement.

"No he's not," Stella snapped.

Amber gave a snort of amusement. "Oh yes he is. And from the way he was looking at you I would say that he is crazy about you."

"Well he is wasting his time," Stella hissed, angrily, someone like Henry did not have a chance with someone like her. There was no way that she would ever get involved with someone who had no money and no prospects. It just was not possible.

She had to protect herself, make sure that she never ended up scratching a living, struggling to make ends meet like her mother had. She simply had to marry someone who had some money, to protect her own future.

At least when Stella emerged from the apartment a few minutes later with Henry there was no sign of Rory, for the moment at least he had probably got bored of sitting outside waiting to catch a glimpse of her and then run alongside her begging forgiveness and asking for another try with their relationship.

Henry opened the door of his rusting Jeep to let Stella in. At least she noticed this time the floor was clean of the mass of newspapers that had littered it the last time that she had been in the Jeep.

"There's a pub just down here, isn't there?" Henry asked, gesturing down the road as he turned on the engine.

"Yes!" Stella yelled above the rattling that was coming from the bodywork of the Jeep.

Stella grinned in spite of herself Henry was such gentle easy company. It was a pleasure to be with him after her tense relationship with Rory where she had to watch everything that she said for fear he would get jealous again.

Henry pushed his way to the bar while Stella found a seat and tried to regain some of her hearing that she was sure had been damaged by the noisy vehicle.

Henry returned with two drinks and sat down beside her, grinning as he clinked his glass against hers. "Here's to friendship."

Stella took a sip of her drink and started as her telephone shrilled in her pocket. Her stomach tightened itself into a knot of tension as she fumbled for the telephone, its ringing loud in the half empty bar.

"Stella?" Rory was crying, his voice coming out in pitiful gulps. Stella swallowed hard, feeling Henry's eyes on her. "Please just come out with me, just once more. I miss y…."

Stella snapped off the telephone. There was no point in even speaking to Rory, sooner or later he would understand that she would not have anything more to do with him.

A second later the telephone rang again, angrily Stella snatched it up. She would have to turn it off altogether if he did not stop ringing, but somehow she was afraid to. Just in case Amber needed to telephone her. With Rory sitting outside the apartment so often the two girls were afraid of what he might do if he lost his temper again and had taken to having their phones with them at all times in case one of them needed help.

"Yes," Stella snapped into the mouthpiece, and then almost dropped the telephone in shock as a voice came through that she really did not expect.

"Hello Stella," said her mother.

CHAPTER EIGHTEEN

Stella pulled a wry face at Henry by way of apology for taking the telephone call when they were chatting. She moved to the doorway, where it was quieter, so that she could hear her mother above the hum of noise from the pub.

"Stella, can you hear me?" her mother repeated.

"Yes. I'm here," she answered shortly, chatting to her mother came second only to speaking to Rory in terms of undesirable telephone calls.

"I really need you to come home," her mother's voice was so loud that Stella could have heard it if she had lifted the telephone right away from her ear at arm's length.

Her mother had never got used to using the telephone; she still regarded it as some new-fangled piece of equipment, even in these days when there were computers, and microwaves and satellite television even in the darkest recesses of the Mayo countryside.

Listening to her bellowed speech Stella was instantly transported back to the small, cramped kitchen, with the ancient range that belched out smoke and covered all of the surfaces in a white powdery dust and the sink, so old that the enamel was worn away in places.

She could imagine her mother, Irene, wearing one of the awful, old fashioned, shapeless dresses that she always wore, sitting beside the range, holding the telephone, as if she thought that it would bite her, while the rest of the family crammed along the sagging sofa on their mobile telephones.

"Yes, I will. Soon." Stella was irritated by the request. She would rather walk through fire than willingly go back to Mayo.

"Your Dad is sick," Irene continued.

Stella closed her eyes, trying to blot out the words. Her father was always sick.

"It is serious," Irene persisted; ignoring the resentment in Stella's voice. "When will you come home?" her mother's voice was so loud that a couple of men who had come out into the fresh air for a cigarette grinned in amusement.

Stella felt as if she were sixteen again, telling her parents that she was getting a job and leaving home.

"I'm not sure; I'll have to see how things are at work." Stella glared at the men. "Bye," she whispered terminating the telephone call. She had no intention of going home if she could help it. She had escaped from that life. Made a new life for herself in the city. The trip back home at Christmas was enough.

Shoving her telephone back into her pocket Stella walked back into the warmth of the pub.

"Problems?" Henry asked as she sat back down at the table.

Stella shrugged in reply. "Just my Mum asking me to go home, my Dad is sick,"

"Oh dear," Henry said, sympathetically, gulping his drink down in one, "I guess you will need to get straight back to the apartment and head off home."

Stella shook her head, "No," she told him firmly, "I'm not going."

"But if your Dad is sick…." Henry drew his eyebrows together.

Stella sighed, shaking her head. "He's always sick, this is nothing new, Mum probably just wanted some excuse to try to get me to go there because I didn't go at Christmas."

"Don't you think that you should go?" Henry reached across the table and took Stella's hand gently, his fingers were long and smooth, the skin soft where it caressed hers. Stella let her hand remain in his, looking at his long fingers and the smooth clean ovals of his nails.

"Where do they live?" he asked softly.

"Mayo," Stella spat out the word, the very name made her shudder.

Henry looked at her, his gentle eyes roving over her face. Stella looked away, gazing at the row of bottles above the bar. Henry could not understand how she felt, how she hated everything about her background. "You should go," he said gently. "Maybe there is something seriously wrong with your dad. You shouldn't cut yourself off from your family completely."

Stella bit her lip, anger bubbling deep within her. What made him think that he had the right to tell her what she should do?

"Just go for the weekend, two days and then you can come back. It won't hurt you and it will keep them happy."

Stella took a sip of her drink, maybe he had a point, at least if she did make the trip to Mayo it would satisfy her mother, keep her off Stella's back for another six months or so.

"You are probably right," Stella nodded her head, "I'll go this weekend, just for Saturday night."

"I could drive you over there. If you like….." he smiled disarmingly. "You shouldn't risk taking your car not since it broke down on you. I'd be quite happy to stay in a B&B somewhere. I'm not very busy with the horses at the moment since…….." Rory's removal of his horses from Henry's yard went unspoken, but the memory of his terrible tantrums hung heavily in the air.

"Fine," Stella felt as if she had been totally railroaded into going to Mayo with Henry. At least if he was going to drive then she could sleep for the journey, instead of having to look at the dreary mountains and miserable bogs.

As Stella closed the door to the apartment Amber poked her head out of her bedroom. "Just thought that I would come in here in case you brought Henry back in for a coffee," she grinned, emerging from her bedroom and heading for the sofa where she snapped on the television. "Glad that you didn't, I was just watching a really good film." Amber stretched herself along the length of the sofa, sighing with pleasure.

Teddy scrambled up beside her and lay on his back with his head cradled in the crook of her arm, watching Stella warily through half closed eyes, in case she should shout at him to lie on the floor. When he realised that she was too distracted by her own thoughts to notice what he was doing he closed his eyes, drifting immediately off to a twitching, whimpering sleep.

"Isn't Henry lovely? Fancy him going to all that trouble to bring Teddy back," Amber grinned wickedly at Stella. "He's gorgeous isn't he?"

"If you like that kind of thing," Stella said huffily, she was not going to admit to Amber how gorgeous she actually did find Henry.

Amber would get all excited thinking that there was a new relationship on the cards. And that was not possible. Henry did not come anywhere close to Stella's very definite specifications for the type of man she was looking for.

"So, how did it go?" Amber asked, scratching Teddy's soft, hairless belly.

"Great," muttered Stella, sarcastically, throwing herself into the armchair, "I'm going to Mayo this weekend with him."

"What!" Amber exclaimed, sitting up so quickly that Teddy fell onto the floor. "You are a fast worker!"

"No I'm not," snapped Stella, petulantly, "I don't even like Henry, he just offered to drive me that's all. I have to go home. My dad's sick."

"Don't like him!" Amber gave a cry of amusement. "Well he's obviously mad about you. And you do fancy him. You go all pink every time you see him."

"Haven't you got an early shift at the restaurant in the morning?" snapped Stella, tight lipped with annoyance, Henry was cute, but she seriously did not fancy him and would not be interested in him. Ever. And as for going pink. It must have been a trick of the light.

True to his word, Henry arrived at the apartment on Saturday morning.

Darting warning glances at Amber, not to make any smart comments about them going away together for the weekend while Henry was there, Stella followed Henry outside to the Jeep, glancing furtively up and down the road to see if Rory's car was parked on the street again.

He had stayed away for days now and if it had not been for the daily arrival of an enormous bouquet of flowers and the twice daily telephone calls pleading for forgiveness she might have thought that he had gotten over her.

Amber watched from the window, grinning broadly.

Stella studiously ignored her, she had heard enough of her silly comments about the lovely couple that they made and how they should watch out and not go strolling in the hay fields together.

Henry heaved her holdall into the back of his Jeep, beside his own ancient leather bag.

The Jeep seemed to have acquired another layer of dirt since the last time she had seen it – and she was sure that the rust had spread.

"Let's go," Henry said, above the groan of protest from the Jeep as he slammed the rear door.

Stella got gingerly into the passenger seat, relieved that she had worn her dark coloured jeans and sweater. The inside of the Jeep was almost as dirty as the exterior.

The engine fired reluctantly into life, accompanied by a worrying sounding rattle that seemed to reverberate through the Jeep.

Stella looked longingly at her own car, tucked neatly off the road in one of the parking spots reserved for the apartment residents. She must have been crazy to let Henry persuade her that his rusty heap of junk was more likely to make the journey to Mayo.

They began the journey, the Jeep heading resolutely west.

There was little traffic, everyone with any sense, mused Stella was heading into the city to go shopping, to spend quality time wandering around the shops looking for lovely things to buy, instead of heading off into the back of beyond.

As the dual carriageways ended and the narrow, winding potholed roads began Stella began to be filled with a dreadful sense of foreboding, she hated the countryside.

She had grown up with undiluted countryside, in the middle of nowhere, miles from anywhere, and she had not liked it – one bit.

Now she lived in the city - the centre of all things, close to everything – and that was how she liked it.

Green fields stretched for miles at either side of the road, broken only by hedges and walls and endless herds of cattle and sheep. Not a shop in sight.

The Jeep sped through tiny villages where grim clumps of houses seemed to huddle together for warmth against the incessant Atlantic gales.

Henry peered over the stone walls and hedges.

"Isn't this beautiful?" he mused, jerking the steering as they headed towards the ditch when he spent too long gazing at the scenery instead of concentrating on the road.

Eventually they stopped for lunch in a small village café, Stella had been delighted at his offer to buy her lunch, she was starving, but eating in a hick town café, with plastic tablecloths and sauce in little packets was not quite what she had in mind, thought Stella as she stalked haughtily into the café, behind him. Henry did not seem to mind, he happily tucked into a vast plate of chips with a greasy sausage plonked unceremoniously on top by the fat woman who seemed to act as both chef and waitress.

Of course, thought Stella, miserably scanning the menu for Caesar salad this was probably the type of place that he was used to. Someone like Henry had probably never dined in anywhere even remotely nice.

They set off again, the sun now beginning to drop into the west hung above them like a beacon to mark the direction.

"I have to stop," Henry said, swinging the Jeep off the road into a lay-by. "This is all so beautiful."

He turned off the engine, heaved open the Jeep door, got out and leant against the long square bonnet gazing at the mountains.

Stella got out, she was not going to even look at the scenery, she hated the mountains, but she may as well stretch her legs.

"Look at that," Henry breathed in an awestruck tone, Stella looked. Below them, in a green valley a long lake shimmered, mirroring the green and greys of the mountains that surrounded it and the cloudless blue sky above. And across the lake, the mountains soared, timeless and majestic, clothed in a mantle of a thousand shades of green broken by glittering outcrops of granite. Stella looked at the brooding, forbidding slopes that had held her captive as a child.

"Beautiful," she admitted grudgingly.

It was the middle of the afternoon before they finally reached the village where Stella had grown up.

Nothing much changed in Abbeymoy, the wide streets were still empty, the inhabitants of the village sheltering inside behind twitching net curtains, gossiping about one another.

The shops were still the same, the butcher, a pathetic selection of meat displayed unimaginatively on silver platters and the general stores with its age old window dressing of faded boxes of breakfast cereal thrown together with plastic buckets and boxes of nails.

Stella shivered in spite of the warmth of the Jeep, how she hated returning to Abbeymoy.

The Jeep sped past the institution cream walls of the small school that

Stella had first attended, and then out onto the coast road.

"Not far now," Stella told Henry, quietly as the familiar feeling of gloom began to seep into her psyche.

"Fancy growing up around here!" Henry exclaimed as they reached the coast and the road turned westwards again, following the line of golden sand broken into small coves by the rocky headland and the blue, blue of the sea the horizon mingling with the blue of the sky. "Lucky you."

Henry wound down the window, letting the salt tang of the air blow into the vehicle, masking the all-pervading odour of horse and dog.

"Here," Stella pointed to a small laneway that wound between tumbledown stone walls. She had never brought anyone that knew her here. It would have been too embarrassing. But Henry did not matter; she could not have cared less what he thought about her. He lived in a hovel himself and probably had come from a similar background to hers. He would not look down on her for her simple roots.

The Jeep bumped along the potholed lane and then turned into the driveway of a small house.

"This is it," Stella said, quietly, hardly able to bring herself to look at the stark lines of the whitewashed cottage.

"OK, I'll come back for you tomorrow afternoon," Henry told Stella as she got out of the Jeep. He followed her out and handed her the holdall, "I'll head off and find somewhere to stay and do some exploring." He seized her shoulders and planted a warm kiss on her cheek.

"Thanks," Stella took the bag from him. "See you then," she added, turning away. She did not want him to come inside, at least not until she had looked inside herself and seen how tattered everything looked. Maybe if things did not look too bad she would invite him in tomorrow. But not now.

Stella waited until the Jeep had driven away before she put her finger tips to her face, she could still feel touch of his lips on her cheek.

Slowly she made her way into the cottage.

The door as always was open.

"Hello," she called, wrinkling her nose as the smell of the turf fire hit her as she walked inside, her footsteps echoing on the lino floor.

"Stella!" her mother, Irene, dashed from the kitchen, where she had doubtless been hastily tidying the room.

"Hello," Stella kissed her mother on the cheek as Irene enfolded her in a joyous bear hug. She could smell the turf smoke in her mother's hair.

"You look lovely," Irene, said looking at Stella, holding up her hands in a gesture of admiration, before shyly smoothing the collar of Stella's suede jacket as if she were afraid that she had damaged it while she were hugging her daughter.

"Would you like some tea?" Irene asked. "I don't have any of that cap-o-cheeno stuff that they are all drinking now," Irene bustled around the kitchen as if this was a state visit, stealing glances at Stella as if she could not believe that she was really there.

"Tea is fine," Stella wished that her mother would stop fussing over her. She should never have let Henry persuade her to come.

"Come into your Dad, he's been looking forward to seeing you." Irene said, as Stella drained the last dregs of her too milky tea. Stella followed her unwillingly down the corridor into their bedroom.

Her father had always been ill, for as long as she could remember, with a bad back that always prevented him from working and doing anything other than sitting beside the fireside day after day.

This was a waste of time, just an excuse to get her home for the weekend. Her father lay in the bed, dozing.

"Paddy," Irene said softly. His eyes opened briefly, closed and then opened with a start as if he could not believe what he was seeing.

"Stella!" he exclaimed, his voice weak but still filled with delight, wincing with pain as he slowly eased himself upright.

"Hello Dad," Stella went slowly across the room and bent to kiss her father. He looked terrible, harsh lines cut across his grey face. This time maybe there really was something seriously wrong with him.

CHAPTER NINETEEN

Stella walked into the kitchen and sat down heavily on the hearth beside the kitchen range.

A fire burnt in the grate as it did every day, winter and summer. The fire was essential in the old cottage to warm the water, on the rare occasions that the weather was hot, every window and door had to be opened to let out the stifling heat.

Today, despite the warmth of the air, Stella shivered, huddling beside the fire.

Stella gasped for air, as if she had been suffocated in the bedroom where her father lay.

She could only vaguely ever remember a time when her father had been healthy. She could vaguely picture him in a huge pair of fisherman's bright yellow over-trousers that covered his legs and ended somewhere up close to his chest, returning home in the first light of morning, from fishing trips up and down the Mayo coast.

Those memories were hazy, the predominant ones were of him lying in bed, or sitting in a battered armchair beside the fire, yelling at them for making too much noise or to fetch him something.

"What's wrong with Dad?" she asked, shaking her head as her mother offered her a cup of tea. Her stomach had twisted itself into a knot and there was a huge lump in her throat.

"Cancer," her mother whispered the word as if it were the most dreadful blasphemy. "Prostate….." Stella watched Irene picking up the teapot and then putting it down again as if she was not sure what she should do with it.

Suddenly Irene slumped down onto one of the low stools that the family used to sit around the table on and buried her head in her hands, weeping silently. Cancer…….. the very word made Stella shiver. But surely nowadays it could be cured. Thousands of people got cancer, they had treatment and then they were cured.

Stella got up and moved away from the warmth of the hearth, she pulled out a stool and sat beside her mother and gently touched her arm. "How bad is it?" Stella whispered, she could not say the dreadful word - cancer. That would only make it more real.

Irene lifted her head, gave a determined sniff and wiped her eyes with a tissue that she fished out of her apron pocket. "It's a stage four cancer, its spread into the bones of his pelvis," she said quietly.

"Spread?" Stella whispered. "Why didn't it get noticed before?" She was filled with an indignant rage; surely he must have noticed that something was wrong.

"He is always in so much pain anyway," Irene shrugged wearily. "So I suppose that masked any other signs."

"Is he ….." Stella struggled to find the words that she wanted to say. "Is he going to live?" she blurted out finally, there was no easy way to deal with this. No polite language to ask the dreadful questions.

Her mother shrugged her narrow shoulders, playing distractedly with a fork that she had picked up off the table and turned over and over in her rough, work worn hands. "How can they know?"

Irene stopped trying to dab away the tears and let them fall down her cheeks. "He starts radiotherapy next week and they say they will get the pain under control, but who knows……………"

The words hung heavily in the air. Irene got up from the table, the fork clattering down as it fell from her fingers. Stella watched her walk from the room, her shoes were tattered, looking as if they were years old.

"I've put your bag into your old room," said her mother, returning a few moments later.

"Thanks," Stella felt a jolt of annoyance twist in her stomach.

Why did her mother feel that she had to do everything, could she have not just left the bag in the hallway for Stella to move herself? "I'll just go down to my room, I want to change my shoes,"

Stella got up and went down to the bedroom that she had once shared with her sister.

Mary still slept in the room; Stella's old bed lay in the corner, untouched, the familiar faded quilt still covering it.

Stella changed her shoes and sat down heavily on the bed and stared at her surroundings, the lino floor, so dreadfully cold on winter mornings, and the bare, soulless walls. Now though a modern DVD player and computer sat on a table beside the window.

Everything was so familiar, and yet so dreadfully alien. It was as if she had never been away, the familiar sense of being trapped in a world that she did not belong in was so strong.

The door slammed and the sound of voices filled the silence of the house. Her brothers had returned.

Dragging herself unwillingly off the bed Stella went towards the sound of their voices. Her two brothers were sprawled on the sagging sofa, Patrick, a year older than Stella, sat with a cigarette tucked between his lips, smoking it without removing it from his mouth. Seamus, the nineteen year old baby of the family, his unruly hair covered in dust from where he had been plastering a wall for someone, had his head buried in the newspaper.

"Hi," Stella stood in the doorway, looking at them both.

"How ya doing?" asked Seamus, bending down to unfasten his boots, kicking them off. Irene picked them up and put beside the hearth.

"Fine," Stella said, tightly, sitting down beside the fire, struggling for something else to say, she had nothing in common with any of them anymore, their lives were so far apart.

It was easier when she came home at Christmas. They would soon return to the easy rapport that they had enjoyed when they were children when it had seemed that it was just the four of them against the rest of the world.

The cottage was usually busy, filled with a constant stream of visitors piling into the house to eat chunks of brown bread and drink the poteen that one of the neighbours brought regularly for their father.

At those times the cottage would be filled with the sound of laughter and merriment.

Mary, her sister came back later, she was fatter than ever, her enormous thighs squeezed into a tight pair of bright red leggings. She was a year younger than Stella, but her plumpness made her seem ten years older.

"How's life in the big city?" she asked Stella, amiably.

Mary always reminded Stella of a cow; she had that peaceful bovine quality, as if she were happy to let life drift by, needing nothing more than regular food and company.

She pulled out a stool from beneath the table and sat down, her wide bottom spilling over the edge of the seat.

She seized a slice of brown bread and spread butter thickly on it and began to chomp happily, looking at Stella as if she were some alien creature that she had just discovered in the kitchen.

"Great," Stella replied. That had exhausted all of their conversation.

After dinner the lads melted away from the room to go to the pub.

Stella heard the sound of their car engine dying away in the silent night air.

Mary disappeared to her bedroom to mess around on the computer.

"Your Dad would love you to sit with him," Irene said, gently, handing Stella yet another mug of tea. Stella stood up hesitantly, and went unwillingly down to the bedroom.

Her father was asleep, his breathing faint and shallow, for a moment his pain erased. Stella sat down in the armchair beside him. She watched his still form in the pale glow of the bedside light. His face was relaxed, the harsh lines that normally scored his cheeks smoothed away, Stella could picture him as the handsome man she had so loved when she was a child, before he had become bent and angry with pain.

After a while, when he did not wake, she slid quietly from the room, guilt at leaving him alone mingling with the relief at not having to talk to him.

Henry came back the following afternoon.

Stella fought the urge to stand outside with her bag packed, waiting for him to come and rescue her and take her back to Dublin.

Every hour seemed to drag. Mary's soft bovine snoring had kept her awake half the night and then she had woken with a jolt when Patrick and

Seamus had roared back up the lane in their noisy car, returning from the pub.

Stella had gone to Mass the next morning, sitting in the pew with the rest of the family, trying to ignore the curious stares of the locals who would no doubt be speculating about the kind of life that she led in the wild city.

And then she had sat with her mother, making polite, stilted conversation about the weather and her job, anything other than mentioning cancer. If it had not been so sad she would have laughed at the improbability of the situation as they sat chatting about how little it rained in the city, compared with out on the coastline.

Stella never thought that she would ever be delighted to see Henry, but when the sound of his Jeep could be heard, rattling up the lane, she breathed an audible sigh of relief. Soon she would be out of here, heading back home, back to the city where she belonged.

She invited Henry inside, because it would have been rude to do otherwise. He fussed over her mother, telling her how nice the house was and what a lovely spot it was built in. He might have been royalty for all of the fuss Irene made of him.

She embarrassed Stella dreadfully by telling Henry how pleased she was that Stella had found such a nice man. Stella cringed yet again, especially when Henry put his arm around her shoulder and told her mother that he had every intention of looking after her. Even her brothers and Mary came out of their shells in his presence. Patrick and Seamus chatted happily about their souped up car and Mary telling him about the latest game that she could play on her computer.

"I'd love to see the beach," Henry said, later, after they had drunk numerous cups of tea and listened to her mother, who had also bloomed under the beam of sunlight from Henry, rambling about the flowers that she intended to grow in her bare patch of garden. Unwillingly Stella got up, she did not want to stay a moment longer than she had to, but it would be rude to refuse Henry.

Henry walked alongside Stella up the beach, their shoes crunching on the golden sand. It was nice to be out of the house, away from her mother, flapping around everyone like a nervous, flustered hen, and away from her rough, uncouth, siblings with their country ways.

The tide was out and the beach stretched for miles ahead of them, high above, on the grassy headland was a patchwork of small fields bordered by grey stone walls each presided over by an identical small whitewashed cottage and the newer, sprawling bungalows built as second homes by wealthy foreigners and city dwellers. They looked incongruous beside the ancient cottages, too new and tidy, with neat gardens of low shrubs especially selected by garden designers to withstand the Atlantic storms of harsh winds and salty air, contrasted sharply with the old cottages, where every inch of garden was used to feed cattle or the inhabitants, neat rows of earth heaped up into potato rows alongside enormous cabbage heads and the lacy leaves of carrot plants.

"Let's sit here," Henry said, guiding Stella towards a long, low flat stone that nestled in a sheltered curve in the rocks. Years ago the rock had been used as a picnic table when they had been young, Stella remembered summer holidays spent on the beach, spreading out their simple lunch of home-made brown bread and strong cheese made by one of the local farmers. Long days where she had played with her brothers and sisters on the sand, bored, longing to be able to visit the city, to head off to the zoo, or to a holiday camp like the others at school did.

They spent their days teasing the city children who came to holiday at the nearby town and who headed out to 'their' beach in expensive looking cars with proper picnic sets and beach chairs. And then when they had got older, the long rock had been a famous spot for bringing a boyfriend or girlfriend too, perfect for romantic liaisons, hidden from the prying eyes of the village.

Henry stared out to sea, today it was cooler, the sea instead of the tropical blue of the hot days was a myriad shades of green which mingled with the white heads of the waves. Far into the distance the sea blurred to become part of the horizon, blending in with the grey of the gathering clouds.

Rain was coming. Stella recognised the signs in the sea, a skill learnt through a childhood spent listening to the men who made their living trying to harvest lobsters from the ocean.

They sat in silence, Stella wished that Henry would hurry up and have enough of looking at the scenery, drinking in the beauty of the sea ringed by the tall mountains. She wanted to get back to the city, back to pavements and traffic, back to reality.

"You should try to make things up between you and your Dad," said Henry, picking up a small stone and lobbing it down the beach.

Stella shook her head, "I can't," she whispered, bowing her head so that

Henry would not see her tears as she mourned for her lost childhood, "I hate him too much."

CHAPTER TWENTY

The Alsatian was absolutely enormous, and looked very cross. It stood in the middle of the pathway that led through the park barking ferociously at Teddy.

"Come on Sabre!" shrieked the diminutive woman who was tugging ineffectively at the dog's lead.

Sabre took another leap forward, straining at the thick leather collar around his neck. Teddy stood his ground, hackles raised, yapping furiously at the bigger dog, seemingly immune to the fact that his small head could fit quite easily into the Alsatian's gaping mouth. "I…Can't…..Hold…..Him," gasped Sabre's mistress, leaning back and digging her heels into the soft earth in an effort to hold the dog. "I'll go this way."

Amber jerked her head in the opposite direction, scooping Teddy up into her arms and marching quickly back the way she had come.

As Sabre's furious barking gradually faded into the distance Amber put Teddy back onto the ground. "Pick on someone your own size," Amber told Teddy, as he looked back up the path, his lips bared over a row of white teeth, as if he wanted to fight the big Alsatian. "This way Teddy," Amber jerked Teddy's lead as she led the way to a park bench. She sank down on the bench, stuffing her hands between the wooden slats and her knees to stop them quivering.

The encounter with the Alsatian had really shaken her up. Teddy finally deciding that the battle for dog supremacy was over, lay down and laid his head on his front paws, sighing loudly. "You would have loved to have taken on that big guy, wouldn't you?" Amber lent down to rub his head and then looked up slowly.

Across the park, oblivious to everything except his companion, was her father. He was walking straight towards her, his attention focussed on the person who walked arm in arm with him. A woman. And she definitely was not Pearl.

Amber instinctively leapt to her feet and darted away from the bench dragging Teddy behind her.

Amber could not face meeting her father, the scene was too bizarre to comprehend, her father with another woman. A girlfriend! A mistress! He must never know that she had seen him. What on earth would she say to him?

Feeling like some actress in a ridiculous spy movie Amber took refuge behind the enormous girth of an old sycamore tree.

Teddy, however had no plans of staying quiet, his thoughts were still on the big Alsatian. He strained against the lead, urging Amber to bring him back to the place where he had seen the big dog, so that he could finally show the wolf like creature who was really top dog. "Teddy, come here," hissed Amber, crouching down beside the tree and dragging Teddy close to her so that she could hold him better.

Voices came closer to the tree, her father and his lady friend, they sounded very cosy together.

"Let's sit here for a while my dear," Amber heard her father say in a gentle tone that she did not recognise.

From her crouching position she was sheltered from view by the dark waxy leaves of a sprawling rhododendron bush. Unable to resist glancing at her father Amber stole a look at the bench where she had been sitting a few moments before.

There, seemingly oblivious to everything else, sat her father, who seemed to be almost glowing with life and happiness and beside him was an elderly, but very elegant looking blonde lady, who was talking animatedly to Jack.

Amber's hand flew to her mouth to stifle an involuntary gasp of horror.

Her mother was a dreadful bitch sometimes; she nagged Jack and everyone around her relentlessly. But Jack. An adulterer? Somehow it just did not seem right. Her parents had been married for almost forty years.

Had Jack had this woman for all of that time? Playing her along on the side. Had Amber a family of half brothers and sisters that she had never heard of? Or was Jack going funny in the head.

Amber stumbled to her feet and lurched away from the tree, dragging Teddy after her as a myriad of questions and emotions threatened to swamp her.

Half an hour later Amber sat on a bench outside the café in the middle of the park, sipping a mug of hot chocolate.

Finally she felt calmer, she had over reacted. Surely her father had just met the woman by chance. They had just taken a stroll together. Amber had not witnessed some affair that her father was having. She had imagined how romantic they looked together. They were just two people sitting on a bench talking. She had completely misread the situation.

Amber drained the last dregs of her chocolate and got up. "Let's go home," she said to Teddy, as he trotted after her along the path that led to the park entrance.

It was beautiful in the park, the spring flowers in full bloom, celebrating the warm day. Relaxed at last now that she had decided that her father was not some serial adulterer, Amber wandered along, lost in her thoughts, admiring the beautiful blooms.

As she rounded the final corner towards the park gates a couple were walking towards her from the opposite direction. This time there was no doubting what she had seen. No chance to dash into the bushes and hide.

"Hello, Amber," said her father, guiltily shaking off his companion's hand.

"Hello Daddy," Amber's voice came out as a strangled squeak, her throat was constricted, making it hard to breathe let alone speak.

"Erm….," Jack stared at his shoes and then at some point beyond Amber's shoulders, as he struggled to find something to say.

"Hello Amber, I'm Kate," the blonde woman thrust out her hand in Amber's direction.

Amber took the woman's hand; her skin was cool and soft Against Amber's palm which felt as if it were on fire.

"Will you walk me to my car, Jack please," Kate asked, in a soft, husky voice, as she took Jack's arm and steered him away from Amber.

"Bye," Jack said, twisting his face into the semblance of a smile before he let himself be steered away by Kate.

They had disappeared from view before Amber finally shut her mouth.

"What is the matter with you?" Stella asked later that evening.

"Nothing," Amber said tonelessly.

Stella gave a snort of derision. "There has to be. You never just sit and stare at the television as if you aren't even seeing it."

Amber hugged her knees into her chest, "I don't know what the matter is. I saw my dad today with a woman, and I don't know how I should feel about it."

Stella was silent, watching Amber with a frown creasing her forehead. "Well, I guess you can be appalled by it. Vow to never speak to him again. Or you can be pleased for him," she said finally. "But don't forget if he was happily married then he would never have needed to find anyone else."

Amber sighed, puffing out her cheeks and letting the air escape through her lips, "I know that, but somehow it is hard to imagine my father that kind of stuff. All the deception. Being with someone else......" her voice trailed away to nothing.

Stella giggled. "Must be a bit like being a parent and finding your child has a boyfriend or girlfriend. You always imagine them to be pure and unsullied and it must come as a shock when you realise that they are human too and have feelings of love and lust just like the rest of us."

"That's it," Amber smiled faintly, "I just see my dad as the guy who potters about in his garden or sits in his chair letting my mum bully him. It's hard to imagine him being in love with someone."

"Are you going to say anything to him?" asked Stella, curiously, curling up in her armchair and looking solemnly at Amber.

"I haven't a clue," Amber shrugged helplessly.

"Oh God, please don't let that be Rory," Stella grimaced as the telephone rang. "You answer it."

Amber slowly picked up the receiver and held it gingerly to her ear, "Hello," she said, uncertainly, dreading hearing Rory's whining voice in her ear. Instead the voice that replied was far worse.

"Hello darling!" said her mother. "There is something that I need to ask you."

"What?" Amber gulped. Dreadful scenarios flashed through her mind,

Pearl was telephoning to ask if Amber had seen her father with another woman. Pearl knew that Jack was having an affair and the marriage was breaking up.

It was a moment before Amber realised that her mother was talking, desperately she focused on her voice. "Actually it is Ruby who should be telephoning you! But she is so busy with her work!" Pearl was saying, "Ruby wondered if you would come out with us at the weekend to choose her wedding dress and the bridesmaids ones. And she has something very important to ask you."

Amber began to giggle helplessly as the tension slid from her body. She was not going to have to lie for her father. The reality was so completely different. Ruby was going to ask her to be a bridesmaid. That had to be the question that she wanted to ask. Amber replaced the receiver and hugged her knees to her chest, grinning with delight. Finally she was going to be A Bridesmaid. How utterly, utterly wonderful.

Stepping into the Quality Brides shop was like a dream come true. Rails of gorgeous wedding dresses spanned either side of the shop, acres of shiny silk and sequins.

Amber breathed a sigh of pure delight as she reverently closed the shop door behind her, the whole place even smelt of romance.

Two young dark haired sales assistants glanced in Amber's direction and then went back to their conversation.

Amber pulled out some of the dresses, enjoying the luxurious feel of the satin and silk beneath her fingers.

A moment later a blast of cool air stirred the fabric of the dresses as the door opened again. "Amber, we're here!" Pearl's shrill voice reverberated the length of the shop. As Amber turned to see her mother and Ruby walking into the shop the shop assistants immediately jumped to attention and greeted the two women with broad smiles. Amber shook her head ruefully, she could have stood in the centre of the shop holding a fist full of one hundred euro notes and still the assistants would have ignored her. Pearl and Ruby both had a presence about them that just demanded attention.

As Amber walked towards them the door opened again and Jack slipped quietly into the shop.

"Hi Amber," he said quietly, his eyes meeting Amber's briefly before they slid guiltily away.

"I'm not really sure what kind of dress I want," Ruby was saying, her voice fading into the background as Amber smiled uncertainly at her father. She was afraid to speak to him, afraid that her voice would betray her feelings of confusion.

Amber turned away from the group that were clustered around Ruby, holding out dresses for her to admire, or turn her nose up at. Slowly Amber made her way down the rails of dresses, picking one out occasionally to look at it closer.

A pale blue long silk dress caught Amber's eye and she pulled it off the rail, holding the fabric against her body as she moved slowly towards one of the full length mirrors that were dotted around the shop. The dress was spectacular, a simple sheath of pale blue silk with tiny pale blue seed pearls embroidered into a pattern around the scooped neckline.

"Oh, that is lovely," yelled Ruby from the other end of the shop. "Put it on Amber."

Not needing to be asked twice Amber made her way into the changing room and put the dress on. It felt as beautiful on as it had looked. Feeling very beautiful she made her way out into the shop, where the commotion around Ruby ceased immediately as everyone turned to look at Amber.

"That is gorgeous," Ruby affirmed, "I'm definitely having that for the bridesmaids. Good choice Amber."

Amber changed back out of the dress and returned to the shop where one of the assistants took it off her. "I'll put this on the counter," the assistant said, virtually hauling the dress out of Amber's hands.

"I'll need that dress for all four of my bridesmaids," Ruby said with satisfaction. "But I still need to choose my dress." Ruby flounced in front of one of the mirrors in a long, tiered meringue-like creation that made her look like one of those old fashioned dolls that used to be delicately shoved over the toilet rolls to disguise them. Jack touched Amber's arm gently, "They are going to be hours," he said quietly, forcing his lips into a smile. "Come on, they can meet us at Fox's pub. I'll buy them lunch there later when they have chosen the dress."

Amber followed her father out of the shop. "We'll get a cup of coffee," Jack jerked his head in the direction of the pub.

Amber walked silently beside him keeping as much distance on the pavement between them as was possible, not trusting herself to touch him, let alone speak.

"You find a seat and I'll bring the drinks over," Jack told her as they stood at the pub bar.

Amber nodded shortly at her father, glancing at his face and then looking down at the dusty floor as his eyes searched her face imploringly.

Jack brought two cups of coffee back to the table and sat down beside Amber who fought the urge to move away so that his arm was not touching hers.

She ripped the top off a packet of sugar and poured it into the cup, stirring it violently.

"You will end up going through the bottom of the cup," Jack said, putting his hand on Amber's to stop her endless stirring.

Amber laughed shortly. "Oh Daddy," she said, sadly, squeezing her eyes shut tightly to stop the tears that were threatening to spill down her face. Amber forced herself to look at her father; his eyes as they moved over her face were filled with sadness and uncertainty.

"I wish that you hadn't seen me and Kate," he said softly. "It is hard to for you to understand that I love someone."

"It just ……," Amber's words faded on her lips, she did not know what to say, or how she felt.

She had expected her father to deny that there was any relationship between himself and Kate. Or even to say that he loved her as well as Pearl, but that had not been what he meant. He loved Kate. Not Pearl.

She had always known how difficult Pearl was to live with, how she bullied and belittled Jack, but it was still hard to imagine Jack doing anything as decisive as finding himself a lover. Someone with whom he laughed and joked and talked and kissed and made love.

"I've known Kate for a long time, but we only started……," Jack paused as he searched for the right words, before continuing primly, "seeing each other a little while ago." Amber took a sip of her coffee, the scalding liquid burning the back of her throat, she glanced at her father over the rim of the cup, he looked alive with happiness, his eyes glowing with an inner peace that Amber could never remember seeing before.

"It's ok," Amber said hoarsely, not trusting herself to speak, for fear that she would burst into tears. There was so much that she wanted to say to her father, but it would have to wait. Hopefully soon she would get the opportunity to tell him that she was pleased that he had found the love that he so deserved and that she understood why he had needed to find someone else.

"Kate makes me so happy," Jack said, smiling dreamily, "I had forgotten what it was like to be in love. She is very special and so....." The words died on his lips as Ruby and Pearl walked across the crowded pub towards the table where Amber and Jack were sitting.

"I've found a perfect dress," Ruby boasted, plonking herself down opposite Amber.

"Cream silk," Pearl sighed happily, still dreaming of the outfit that she would need to compliment Ruby's dress.

"The bodice is all covered in embroidery and tiny pearls, all sewn on by hand," Ruby continued smugly.

"By some child slave labour in China," muttered Amber under her breath.

"Now ladies, what would you like for lunch?" Jack handed the menu across the table to Ruby and Pearl. As Pearl scanned the menu, licking her lips greedily Ruby leant forward conspiratorially towards Amber. "And now," she said, "I want to ask you something."

"Yes," Amber buzzed with excitement, imagining herself floating down the aisle behind Ruby, wearing the gorgeous pale blue silk dress. Ruby was going to ask her to be her bridesmaid.

"What?" Amber exclaimed, sure that she could not have heard Ruby correctly.

"I said," repeated Ruby, sighing patiently, "I wanted to ask you if you mind terribly if I did not ask you to be one of the bridesmaids?"

CHAPTER TWENTY ONE

Stella turned off the car engine and sat for a moment listening to the peace that descended now that the boom of music from the radio and the hum of the car engine had been silenced.

After a moment the sounds of the city penetrated her conscious, the distant noise of traffic, a dog barking, the voices of a young couple as they walked past her car.

Stella sighed, for the whole of the journey back from Mayo she had managed to shut out her thoughts, with the loud noise from the radio, now she was back to reality and back to the dreadful guilt that gripped her like a clinging briar.

Her father had seemed so frail and exhausted; he had stayed in bed the whole weekend while she had been there. His treatment was going well, Stella's mother had told her, but he still spent the majority of his time in bed, too desperately exhausted to do anything else.

Stella had found herself heading off to Mayo after work on Friday, she had not wanted to go, but still was relentlessly drawn to her father's bedside, where she sat for most of the weekend, wishing that she could say what she felt, rather than the ridiculous stunted small talk that passed for communication between them. But somehow she could never find the words.

It was hard to frame the words when she did not know what they were herself.

She hated her father; he had made her childhood a misery, with his short temper and seeming lack of interest in anything other than sitting beside the fire.

And yet somewhere at the back of her mind she remembered a different man, a gentler, good humoured man who had laughed and played with them all. She had loved that man.

Stella got out of the car and headed into the apartment. As she opened the front door the telephone began to ring.

"Hello," Stella said in the cold, impatient sounding voice that she reserved for calls that she assumed were Rory.

"Stella, it's Henry." Stella felt a warm glow spreading slowly upwards from her belly, radiating heat.

"Oh. Hello," Stella heard the pitch of her voice change. Her voice seemed to think that she was delighted to hear from him, while her brain certainly was not. Now what did he want?

"I've been thinking about you. I know that you must be worried about your Dad," he was burbling, the words spilling out as if his mouth could not get them out quickly enough, "I thought that maybe you would like to go out, maybe go for dinner. Take your mind off things."

Stella cringed at the very thought of spending another evening with him. What was the point? They could never have any kind of relationship. They would never have any kind of relationship. He really was not the kind of person that Stella wanted to be with. Her brain shrieked "No!!!!" but before she could frame the word her mouth had said, "yes, thanks."

"Great I'll see you about eight."

Stella put down the telephone with a sigh. What had she let herself in for? Why had she not said 'No'. It was stupid to give him any encouragement; she did not want to get involved with Henry. She was looking for some glamorous businessman, not a poverty stricken horse trainer.

"Was that Henry?" grinned Amber, emerging from the bathroom and letting clouds of steam waft all over the apartment.

"Yes," Stella mumbled, "I've just told him that I would go out for dinner."

"Great stuff,"

"It isn't great stuff at all," sighed Stella. "It's terrible. Why the hell did I say yes?"

At just before eight o'clock the buzzer sounded to announce that Henry was downstairs.

"Come up," Amber said, dashing to the intercom before Stella had the chance to get to it. Stella sat on the sofa, rubbing Teddy's soft ears, listening to the sound of Henry's footsteps coming towards the door.

"You look lovely," mouthed Amber standing ready to open the door. Stella sighed, the last thing that she had wanted to do was to look lovely, and she had wanted to look ordinary as if going out with Henry was of no importance whatsoever.

She had put on her oldest jeans and a top that she hated, with only a minimal slick of makeup and yet, when she had looked in the mirror she seemed to glow with life.

The footsteps stopped outside the front door, but before he could knock, Amber opened it. "Come in," she breathed, simpering shamelessly at him.

"Stella," Henry grinned with delight, barely acknowledging that Amber was there. Teddy abandoned Stella and hurtled across the room, bounding up and down to get attention from Henry.

"He loves you too," Amber smirked.

Henry bent to pet the little dog.

"Are you ready then?" he asked, as tongue-tied as a youth on a first date.

Stella gazed at the dog, who was winding himself around Henry's legs, giving small cries of delight. She stole a furtive look at Henry and was horrified to find that he still looked as gorgeous as usual.

If only she did not fancy him so much. She was only ever attracted to sharply dressed men in dark suits and crispy cotton shirts with elegant silk ties and brightly polished shoes. It just was not possible that her heart could be fluttering so much at a man dressed in a baggy pair of cords and a shapeless hacking jacket, from which she could smell the unmistakeable odour of horse. And his hair needed cutting.

"It's ok if we bring Amber with us isn't it?" it was a statement, not a question. "No…." Amber began to protest.

"Nonsense," Stella told her. "Fetch your coat, you need a night out, take your mind of things."

"She has had a terrible time recently," Stella told Henry, firmly. There was no way she could trust herself to go out alone with Henry. He was too attractive and too unsuitable and just at the moment she did not feel as if she would be able to keep her emotions under control.

"Fine," Henry said, looking bemused.

They left the apartment together and walked out to Henry's Jeep. Rory's car was parked behind it. He got out of his car as they approached.

"Stella," Rory said, softly.

"Go away, Rory," Stella snapped, her voice quavering slightly.

"Leave her alone," snapped Henry.

"It's ok," Stella said softly, putting her arm on Henry's.

"Come back to me, Stella," Rory's voice rose to a plaintive whine.

"No," Stella said, firmly.

Henry unlocked the Jeep and they all got in.

"Stella!" Rory cried the note of desperation loud in his voice.

"Oh God," breathed Amber as the Jeep pulled away leaving Rory standing in the road watching them. "Why don't you get the Guards to sort him out?"

Stella shook her head, sadly, "he's just very sad about what he did. I don't want to make things worse for him by getting them involved. He will get fed up sooner or later."

Henry shook his head, angrily. "He's a raving nutcase. I think that he is bloody dangerous. You should do something about him. I am worried that he will hurt you." He seized Stella's hand and grasped her fingers for a few moments until she shook his hand away, without replying.

"Are you ok back there?" Henry called over his shoulder to Amber, who was perched on a pile of horse rugs. Fortunately they were new, still wrapped in their plastic covers and so did not smell of horse, but the plastic was slippery and every time Henry went around a corner Amber found herself sliding further and further off her makeshift seat. She began to wish that she had not come. It was not fair to play gooseberry with the two of them. Stella for some reason had seemed to want her to be there, it was as if she were afraid of what might happen if she let her feelings go.

Amber watched the two of them together, making stilted conversation, as if they were afraid of each other.

Henry led the way into the restaurant. He had a table booked, a third place setting was quickly laid out for Amber, who sat down, feeling more like a gooseberry than ever in the intimate surroundings of the dimly lit restaurant.

"Menu madam," Amber glanced up to take the menu and felt her mouth drop open. The waiter was absolutely gorgeous.

"And for you sir," he almost knocked over Henry's wine glass as he could not take his eyes off Amber.

"Paul?" Henry exclaimed, looking quizzically, "Paul Kennedy?"

The waiter tore his eyes away from Amber, "Henry Murphy," he gave an exclamation of recognition and shook Henry's hand.

"Well, Paul this is amazing" Henry grinned. "How are things? I knew you weren't racing much anymore, but didn't know what you were doing………" his voice trailed off.

Paul sighed, bitterly, "I wasn't getting the rides anymore, so I've had to find something to do to earn a living," he gave a wry wave of his hand to indicate the restaurant. "Got too cocky, missed rides, didn't respect the trainers, usual stuff," he sighed, humbly. "Got too successful, too quickly and couldn't handle it."

"Ah," Henry said, sympathetically.

"That's how it goes," Paul said, chirpily, handing a menu to Stella. "I'll be back to take your order in a while, would you like a drink now?" he asked, assuming his waiter role.

Henry opened his mouth, but nothing came out, he was too shocked to speak.

"We'll decide in a while," Stella told Paul, she was the only one of them who was not dumbstruck by Paul's appearance.

"Well fancy that," Henry mused, watching Paul walk away. I do very much, thought Amber, also watching Paul walk away. He had the smallest, neatest butt that she had ever seen.

"He was one of the best young jockeys that I have ever seen," Henry said, dragging his eyes towards the menu, "I wondered what had happened to him."

Racing again thought Stella, glaring at her menu, wishing that she had not come out. She should have stayed at home and rung her mother to see how things were with her father.

They ordered their food and then sat, waiting, making stilted conversation, each lost in their own separate worlds. Amber could barely eat the food that she had ordered. Her stomach seemed to have been filled with butterflies; she toyed helplessly with a beautifully cooked steak.

"Could you pass the pepper please?" Stella asked. Henry handed her the tall wooden pepper pot his fingers brushing hers. Stella jerked her hand away as if his fingers were red hot and had burnt her skin.

Paul returned to the table. "Is everything all right for you?" he asked, his dark eyes meeting Amber's.

"Fine thanks," Stella told him, Amber seemed beyond speech.

Eventually when their plates were cleared away and they sat sipping hot, strong coffee Paul came and pulled up a chair. "Mind if I join you?"

"Not at all," grinned Henry, shifting his chair around slightly to make room.

"I can take a break, now that the restaurant is almost empty," Paul explained.

"You seem to be doing well with the horses," Paul said to Henry.

Stella raised her eyes to the ceiling. Horses, that was all they could talk about.

"I've a great chaser at the moment," Henry told Paul. "She's called Hollyberry, I think that she could be a Grand National horse, she's just getting better from a nasty virus that has laid her low for a good while. But when she is on form....."

Stella looked at Amber to shake her head in annoyance at the boring conversation, but Amber was lost, gazing misty eyed at Paul.

"I haven't really been able to find the right jockey for her, she takes some riding," the conversation droned on, "maybe you would come and have a look at her?"

The other waiter's began to put the chairs up onto the now empty tables, casting annoyed glances at Paul for taking so long talking to Henry.

"I'd better go," Paul grinned, standing up and draining his coffee cup in one gulp, his eyes locking onto Amber's.

"So had we," Henry glanced at his watch. "It's getting late." Henry paid the bill and the three of them walked out into the cold night air.

Amber dragging herself away from the restaurant on feet that seemed to be made of lead. If only she had been brave enough to ask Paul for his telephone number, or slipped hers into his hand. He had clearly fancied her, as much as she had fancied him. How could she have missed out on such an opportunity? It was not as if gorgeous men came along every moment.

As they reached the Jeep, Henry suddenly gave an exclamation of annoyance, "Bloody hell," he snapped, reaching in his pocket and pulling out a business card, "I forgot to give this to Paul. Amber would you really mind running back with it for me?"

Amber gave a cry of delight and flung herself at Henry, seized the business card out of his hand and ran hell for leather back towards the restaurant.

154

CHAPTER TWENTY TWO

Amber glared at her reflection in the mirror. "Bloody hell," she grumbled. The yellow dress that she had picked out was completely wrong. It was gorgeous. That was the problem. The pale yellow fabric clung to the contours of her body, flaring gently out from her hips, skimming gently over her flat belly, the tiny, spaghetti thin straps showed off the creamy skin of her shoulders. She looked gorgeous in it. But………….. There was no way that she could wear it for a first date with Paul. It was too nice. Damn.

Amber wriggled her arm around her back to tug down the zip and let the dress slide down over her hips.

If only Stella were here, she would know exactly what Amber should wear. She might even suggest some casually elegant outfit from her own wardrobe. But she had headed off to Mayo again for the weekend.

Amber gazed longingly at Stella's bedroom door, she would have loved to have gone in and found something to wear, but after the fiasco with the lovely red dress she did not dare. She had got away with it the last time, but she might not be so lucky again.

Throwing the yellow dress on her bed Amber opened her wardrobe door again and peered hopefully inside.

"What am I bothering for?" Amber asked Teddy, who sat on the bed, watching her. Teddy cocked his head to one side, as if he were thinking. "He is probably just like all the other bloody men anyway. Use 'em and lose 'em. That's the motto men go by," she said, miserably, shifting the clothes from side to side as she looked. Teddy sighed and lay down on the bed, resting his head in his paws as he watched her.

"He probably won't even turn up," Amber pulled a pair of jeans from the bottom of the wardrobe. "These will do," she threw them onto the bed and pulled out a top to go with them. "I'm not going to go to any effort," Amber mused to herself. "Don't want to make a show of myself while I'm being stood up," she grumbled, pulling the jeans on.

Amber stood in front of the mirror and gave a groan of frustration. Even if he did stand her up and even if he did turn up and he was a complete bastard there was no way that she could go out dressed like a tramp. "You chose," she said, pulling off the jeans and slumping down onto the bed beside Teddy. The little dog gave a whimper of pleasure and wriggled onto his back, waving his legs in the air, hoping to get his belly scratched. Amber tickled the soft, hairless skin of his belly. "Ok," she sighed, a moment later. "Third time lucky." She pulled a pair of dark trousers out of the wardrobe and a simple shirt. "This really will have to do." She changed into the new outfit, applied a touch of mascara and lipstick and then smiled at her reflection. "Perfect," she grinned.

Of course there was no sign of Paul. Amber walked slowly up to the pub; a crowd hovered around the doorway, smoking furiously in the cool evening air.

Amber looked around at the faces to see if he was there. What had she expected? Had she really hoped that he would be there waiting for her? Still though her heart sank with bitter disappointment.

She wandered miserably into the pub, she may as well continue with her fruitless search. Inside the pub was crowded, the hum of noise unbearably loud after the relative silence of the pavement.

Amber moved through the drinkers, not even bothering to look to see if Paul was sitting down at a table. He had not come. He had stood her up, just like all of the others that she had got involved with. Men were such cruel bastards. They built you up, made you think that they liked you and then they dumped you, often before they even had a chance to get to know you.

Amber turned around and began to walk back out of the pub, she may as well go home, and there was no point in hanging around here.

A man was coming in through the door as she was going out, Amber could see his outline in the frosted glass. Amber stood back as the door swung open to let him pass. She stood back to let him in, staring at the floor, battered with misery. She watched a pair of smart shoes walk into the pub, topped by a trendy pair of jeans covering long legs.

"Amber?" a voice asked.

Amber looked up, "Paul?" She could not believe that he was actually here. He had come to meet her.

"Where are you going?" he asked, closing the door.

"I was going home," Amber replied, feeling as if she were living in a dream, she was so sure that he was not going to come. In her mind she had made him into the ultimate male bastard and now he was here. He had turned up. "I thought that you weren't coming," Amber muttered. Paul led her towards the bar.

"I said that I would come didn't I?" he said, huffily. "What sort of bastard did you think that I was?" his voice filled with indignation as he glared at her. "What do you want to drink?" he snapped, shortly.

"Coke," Amber snapped back, the whole evening was ruined now.

She had got into a temper because she thought that he was not coming. And now he had got into a temper because she had thought that he was not coming. It was impossible to win.

Paul brought them both drinks and carried them to an empty table, and then sat in a stony silence. "How could you think that I wasn't coming?" he asked, crossly, playing distractedly with a beer mat.

"You weren't here. I just thought that you would not bother coming."

Paul shook his head in disbelief. "But I told you I was coming. Did you really think that I would stand you up?" He took a long swig of his lager. "What kind of idiot did you think I was? Could you not see how I was looking at you the other evening?" Amber sipped her drink and looked miserably around the pub, she had ruined the evening. "I did think that you wouldn't come. Used to being stood up, I guess," she shrugged, bitterly.

Paul grinned suddenly, his face softening. "Anyone that stands you up must be stupid or something."

"I've met a lot of stupid men," Amber said softly and then smiled; the dreadful atmosphere that had existed between them had vanished like a morning mist as the sunshine breaks through.

When Amber looked up again the pub was almost empty. She had not noticed the time passing, or the ebb and flow of people around the pub.

The evening had passed by while she and Paul had been lost in a world of their own, talking about their lives, their hopes for the future, their likes and dislikes.

Paul, he had told her, had grown up in Kildare, surrounded by racing yards and horses. He was terrible at school, he had told her with a hollow laugh of regret, always sneaking off to go to the races with one or another of the trainers. And then when he had left school the racing yards were the only option, especially when he had no ambition to do anything else. He told her about starting to ride, learning to race, the success that came too early, before he could handle it. He told her with candour about how he had earned too much money, driven a fast car, thought that he was the best thought that he was indispensable. He had shaken his head, wryly at the memory. And then, when he became far too cocky, no one wanted him, there were other jockeys just as good who were reliable, nicer to the trainers and owners. And then no one would give him rides and he had fallen quickly from grace, the world that had put him on a pedestal had kicked it out from under his feet.

"We had better go," Paul said, suddenly, as the barman whipped their empty glasses from the table.

The pavement was deserted; everyone had long ago headed off home or to the chippy.

"I'll walk you home," Paul said, taking her hand. Happily Amber entwined her fingers around his.

They walked silently through the empty streets, there did not seem to be any need to fill the silence with mindless chatter, Amber resented every footstep that took them closer to home, closer to the moment when he would say goodbye and vanish into the night.

"This is where I live," Amber said, halting outside the apartment block.

"I don't want to leave you," Paul said huskily, gently he entwined his fingers in to her hair and drew Amber's face towards his.

For a long moment they stood, face to face, breathing in the same air, feeling the warmth from each other's skin and then, with infinite slowness and tenderness Paul gently lowered his lips onto Amber's. He slid his arm around her back, drawing her closer to him, so that every inch of their bodies touched.

"Now I really don't want to leave you," he whispered, when they finally came up for air.

"Don't then," Amber touched his face, softly as if she could not believe that he was real.

"Ok then, you've twisted my arm," he grinned, taking her hand and leading her in the direction of the apartment.

"Night," one of the residents said, as they passed on the stairs.

"Night," Amber said shortly, now everyone would know that she had brought a man back for the night.

The whole apartment block would be looking at her the next time that they saw her; the gossip would spread like wildfire.

Amber put her key into the apartment door, a bolt of regret shooting through her. She had vowed never to be used by a man again. Never sleep with someone just because she fancied them. And now here she was, putting herself straight back into that position.

Paul seemed to sense her hesitancy for he pushed open the door and led her inside, shoved the door shut and very tenderly began to kiss her once more.

Amber felt all of her hesitancy vanish. She knew that she would probably regret this in the morning. Paul would vanish. How could any man respect a woman who slept with them on the first date? But then maybe he would have vanished anyway and she would never have seen him again. She may as well enjoy herself.

Amber leant back against the living room wall, letting Paul kiss her, feeling his hands roving all over her body, while she kissed him back with equal passion.

Then suddenly Teddy exploded towards them barking furiously at the strange shapes that were moving around in the dark.

"Bloody hell, what's that?" Paul laughed as Amber switched on the light to pacify the small dog.

"It's ok Teddy," she picked up the terrier, cradling him in her arms, while his tail wagged furiously, his face filled with embarrassment at having barked at one of his own family.

"I'm getting jealous of all the attention that you are giving that dog," Paul said, huskily, taking Teddy out of Amber's arms and laying him gently onto the floor. "Show me where the bedroom is."

Taking his hand, Amber led him into her room.

Much later, when all was silent, Teddy pushed open the bedroom door with his nose and padded quietly towards the bed.

Amber and Paul lay entwined in each other's arms, their bodies covered only by the sheet that Paul had pulled over them before they had finally collapsed with exhaustion.

Teddy jumped up onto the bed, looking disdainfully at Paul, and then with a sigh of pleasure, he curled up in the small of Amber's back and went to sleep.

"Paul," Amber moaned, as she woke to feel him covering the back of her neck in warm, wet kisses. She turned and then gave a cry of disgust. Teddy, lay beside her on his back, licking her neck.

Paul lay beside her, sleeping.

Her cry woke him and he stirred, reaching for her and pulled her into his arms.

Teddy slunk guiltily away, landing with a thud as he jumped off the bed.

Amber saw him glance back regretfully as he slid out of the doorway.

Amber stared at the ceiling as Paul's began to doze once more. She had done it again. She had vowed that she would never sleep with a man on a first date again and she had done. How easy he must think her. He would wake in a while and make some excuse to leave and then she would never see him again.

As if he could sense her thoughts Paul stirred, sighing with pleasure as he slowly began the ascent into wakefulness.

"Hey," he said softly, propping himself up on one elbow. "You look gorgeous in the morning."

Amber wriggled out of his grip. What was the point of prolonging this? She may as well let him get up and head off, that was probably what he wanted to do anyway, he would just be looking for an excuse to leave.

"I'll make some tea," she said.

"Come back here," he pulled Amber back towards him and pinned her to the bed, covering her face in kisses until she giggled helplessly. Then he began to kiss her more slowly, his lips covering hers hungrily.

"I had better go," he moaned, a long time later, "I'm supposed to be working at lunch time."

"Right," she said coldly. Amber was prepared for the usual brush off, 'see you around then,' in a moment he would swing himself out of bed, pull on his clothes and then say those immortal words. She lay on the bed and watched as he dressed, trying to memorise the strong lines of his back, the muscles on his thighs and the way that the hairs on his forearms were standing up in the cool air. Finally dressed he sat down on the bed and pulled her towards him and whispered, "I really want to see you again. Would you come out with me tonight?"

CHAPTER TWENTY THREE

Amber did a war dance of victory around the apartment. This time things were going to turn out all right.

Paul had turned out to be a really genuine nice guy. He wanted to see her again – tonight. He had kissed her goodbye that morning as if he did not want to ever let her go.

Amber stopped jumping around and checked her reflection in the mirror. Tonight she wore the yellow dress that she had discarded the previous evening as being too dressy. It was perfect for the evening. The pale yellow colour of the dress looked gorgeous against her skin, she seemed to glow with happiness. Her eyes danced with delight, and for once, her curly dark hair seemed to hang in a sexy cloud around her face, rather than its usual wiry frizz.

Stella had rung from Mayo, her father's condition had not changed, she was going to stay a bit longer. She had sounded tired and miserable, her voice distant as if she were a million miles away, not just over a hundred.

And so, taking advantage of her absence Amber had decided to cook dinner for Paul. Not that it was going to be much of a dinner, she had found some pasta in the cupboard and some mince in the freezer and had plundered a bottle of red wine from the store that Stella thought that she had hidden. Hopefully Amber would be able to replace it before she came back. But, the apartment was empty and what was the point of sitting talking in a pub, when they could be alone together?

The whole day had gone brilliantly. Filled with happiness Amber had set off into town once Paul had left for work.

Life suddenly seemed very good, full of hope for the future.

Even the mountain of debt that she was buried under did not seem quite so big. Amber glanced at the clock, Paul had said that he would be here at eight, it was almost that now. Filled with nervous energy, she flittered around the room, brushing an imaginary crease out of the table cloth, straightening a fork that had gone out of line.

Teddy padded around the room, getting under Amber's feet, wondering why she was not paying him any attention. "Teddy, get in your basket," she ordered, finally, so filled with nervous energy that she felt as if she were about to burst.

The spaghetti was almost cooked and the mince, into which she had tipped a bottle of pasta sauce, simmered fragrantly on the stove. Everything was perfect - until the telephone rang. "Hello," Amber trilled happily into the receiver. Everything was going so well today, the call could not possibly be anything awful.

"Amber, this is Mark Hardcastle," Amber felt her heart sink, her boss always had that effect on her.

"Oh hi," Amber could hear the suspicion in her own voice. What on earth did Mark want?

"I need you to come into work tonight, one of the other waitresses has taken the night off sick," his voice was thick with sarcasm.

"I've made plans for tonight," Amber protested.

"Well you will just have to cancel them," Mark snapped, "Amber you owe me after you were off at Christmas."

Amber's teeth clenched as she remembered the awful date at Christmas when Ruby had tried to fix her up with Roderick's dreadful brother, Ernest. She had skived off work just for that......and now she was going to have to pay the price.

Mark, taking her silence for agreement snapped a curt, "come to the restaurant as quickly as you can," and then terminated the call.

Amber closed her eyes. "Fuck," she spat bitterly.

Cursing her stupidity Amber turned off the cooker. What was she doing? How could she be such a walk over? Then, filled with regret she went to the telephone, found the number of the restaurant where Paul worked and dialled it. "I'm trying get in touch with one of your waiters, Paul........."

She did not even know his surname.

In the heat of the passion the previous morning they had not even exchanged telephone numbers, Amber had been so sure that she would see him again.

"He is not here. Off for the night," came back the curt reply and then the telephone went dead as the speaker replaced the receiver.

"I know that," Amber growled, "I wanted a mobile phone number for him." Amber picked up her handbag. Maybe Paul would be outside when she went downstairs. She could tell him then that she had to go to work. He would understand. Amber stamped back into her bedroom, slamming the kitchen door hard behind her. It made her feel better, but it did not change the situation.

Her whole evening was ruined – by bloody Mark Hardcastle. Amber changed into the black skirt and white top that she usually wore for work and then left the apartment, slamming the door behind her and ran down the stairs out into the evening air.

There was no sign of Paul on the pavement outside the apartment.

Amber paced up and down looking longingly in both directions, hoping to see a sign of him approaching.

Maybe he was not going to come after all. Maybe he was just stringing her along, like all of the rest of the men she seemed to attract. But he really had seemed different. Amber fished in her handbag, she would leave a note on the door to tell him what had happened, ask him to telephone her later.

A car drew up alongside Amber. She abandoned her search for a scrap of paper and looked up expectantly, hoping that it would be Paul.

"Fuck," she hissed between her teeth as the side window glided down and Mark Hardcastle stuck his head out. "I thought that you might have a problem getting a taxi so I came to fetch you."

Amber glanced desperately back up the pavement again, still there was no sign of Paul, she shot a look of misery into her handbag. Why did she never have a scrap of paper when she needed one.

"Come on," Mark growled impatiently, drumming his fingers on the steering wheel.

Amber lingered a moment longer, torn between regret at her lost date and the certain knowledge that Paul had probably stood her up anyway and then with a low moan of despair she got into the car beside Mark.

Amber fastened her seatbelt and shoved her handbag down beside her feet, fighting the urge to scream with temper as the buckle on the front of it snagged against her tights.

She reached down and unhooked the metal from her nylon tights and as she looked up, there was Paul walking towards the apartment clutching a bottle of wine and a bunch of yellow flowers. Exactly the same colour as the dress that she had been wearing. As the car passed him Paul glimpsed Amber and their eyes locked together. "Stop," yelled Amber.

"No time," Mark grinned maliciously.

Amber slumped miserably into her seat. Paul had just seen her driving away from the apartment in Mark's car. He would think that she was going out with another man.

He had wanted to continue with the relationship. He had been coming to see her – with wine and flowers. For a moment Amber's heart soared with happiness before it plummeted straight back into the depths of despair. He would think that she was a real bitch, just heading off with another man. He would never want anything to do with her ever again. Her perfect relationship was over, before it had ever had the chance to begin.

Amber trailed miserably into the restaurant behind Mark.

Jules shot her a look of sympathy, raising her eyes towards the ceiling as Amber walked in. "He is an out and out bastard," hissed Amber as she squeezed past Jules on her way to the room where the waitresses left their handbags and coats. "He's never forgiven you for letting him down at Christmas time," Jules said quietly as Amber came back out into the restaurant, fastening her white apron.

"So I see," Amber said, miserably, "I've just wrecked the best relationship ever."

Oh Amber," Jules sighed with sympathy, before she darted away as Mark snapped his fingers at them from across the far side of the restaurant to indicate that there was someone that wanted serving.

As Jules weaved her way through the tables towards the customers who had just come in Amber leant against the bar and surveyed the restaurant.

It was very quiet. There were fifteen tables dotted around the wooden floor; only four of them were being used.

Mark surely could have managed without her tonight. "You are here to work, not just look decorative," Mark's voice said from behind the bar, making Amber jump, she had thought that he had gone into the kitchen to bully the chefs in there. "Here polish some glasses," he said, thrusting a cut glass wine glass in her direction and throwing a towel down on the bar.

Amber walked around to the other side of the bar and began to do as he had ordered, watching the light reflecting through the shimmering patterns.

How she loathed this place and its owner. He really was the most obnoxious man that she had ever met. The worst boss that she had ever had. He had just fetched her in tonight to prove a point, to let her know that she could not get one over on him.

She should never have skived the night off at Christmas time, Amber thought polishing one of the glasses so frenziedly that the delicate stem broke in her hand. Hastily she shoved it into the bin, hoping that Mark would not see it.

She should have been at home now, serving dinner to Paul, they would be sitting at the table, chatting, drinking the wine that he had brought with him, or maybe they would have been in bed. That was an even nicer scenario to imagine. And then bitterly she realised there would be no more scenarios like that. Paul had seen her with Mark, he must surely have thought that she had another boyfriend. Paul would never want her now. This was her life, standing in this crappy restaurant, night after night and being bullied by her boss.

"There's a big party booked tonight," said Jules, coming back to the bar and peering into the diary. "Dillon, sixteen of them," Jules tapped her finger on the diary. "They should be here any moment."

Right on cue the restaurant door opened and the large party of diners walked in. All men. All looking as if they were drunk.

"Oh shit," groaned Jules. "A stag party."

"I'll sort them out," Amber abandoned her polishing and flung her towel onto the bar. She grabbed a fist full of menus and headed off across the restaurant to where the men were hovering expectantly in the centre of the floor.

"You should have a table booked for sixteen. The name's Dillon," announced one of the men, taking off his coat and tossing it in Amber's direction.

Amber sighed. Great that was all that she needed, a big group of drunken men to contend with. "Would you like to sit here," Amber said, indicating the table that had been reserved for the big group.

"Would you like to sit here," grinned the man lecherously, patting his crotch.

"I'll hang up your coat," Amber said, blushing as the rest of the men laughed uproariously.

Amber handed out the menus and then staggered away to hang up the coats that the men had thrown in her direction.

"What a bunch of assholes," Amber complained, leaning on the bar beside Jules as the group of men studied their menus and made lewd comments in loud drunken voices.

"What did you say," snapped Mark, coming back behind the bar. "I'm going to take the dessert order from table nine."

Jules slid out from behind the bar.

"Nothing," Amber said tightly, grabbing her order pad and heading resolutely back across the restaurant to the rowdy men.

"Are you ready to order?" she asked, struggling to make herself heard over the roar of noise that was coming from the men. "I want a nice tender bird," roared one of the men.

Amber could feel her cheeks burning with temper and embarrassment by the time she had managed to get the order from the men. Puffing out her cheeks with relief she headed back to the kitchen to hand in the order.

It was a relief to be away from the awful men. But all too soon she was heading back across the floor with two plates in her hands and another one balanced on her arm.

"Steak, rare?" Amber asked, standing beside the table.

"Here!" yelled a fat bald man.

"Another steak rare?" Amber scanned the hungry looking faces.

"Mine!" yelled the man beside her.

As Amber reached to put the plate down in front of the man, a hand suddenly cupped her bottom, squeezing the flesh hard. Amber jumped upright with a shriek of temper and surprise, the plate that she was holding crashed to the floor as its contents upended all over the man beside her.

There was a long moment of shocked silence that seemed to reverberate around the restaurant.

The sound of Amber's hand slapping the man's face broke the silence along with her shriek of temper. "You filthy bastard," Amber yelled, going puce with temper. Then as if watching herself in a slow motion movie, Amber grabbed the water jug from beside the man and tipped it all over his head. "That will cool you down." The silence descended on the restaurant again, the calm before the storm.

"Oh Sir, I do apologise," Mark shot across the restaurant clutching a tea towel with which he began to dab ineffectively at the water that was dripping from the man's chin.

Amber backed away, feeling the icy cold water soaking through her blouse and skirt. Amber caught sight of Jules, standing by the bar, her mouth open in awe. "Get out!" spat Mark, glancing up at Amber, spittle flying from between his thin lips. "Get out and never come back!"

Outside the restaurant Amber sucked in a huge lungful of fresh air and then hitching her handbag onto her shoulder she began to run. Her feet pounded along the pavement as she hurtled away, wanting to put as much distance as she could between herself and Mark Hardcastle and his bloody restaurant.

Finally she stopped, exhausted. She bent over to ease the stitch that was now clutching at the muscles of her stomach. "Well done Amber," she told herself wryly, straightening up gingerly. She had messed everything up – yet again. And now she was probably going to be out half of the night trying to get a taxi home.

Amber stuck her hand up half-heartedly as a taxi sped past and then gave a snort of disbelief as the car screeched to a halt to let her in.

At least something had gone right.

Amber stood on the pavement after the taxi had dropped her off at home, listening to the sound of the taxi growing fainter and fainter. Slowly Amber turned and began to walk towards the apartment, her legs felt as if they were too heavy to move, each stride was an enormous effort. She felt as if all of her energy had been sucked out of her and replaced by a strength sapping numbness.

After a few strides she could go no further, Amber sank miserably down on a low wall in front of a house and began to weep, bitterly.

Tonight should have been so different.

It was meant to have been the start of her new life, a boyfriend who actually did seem to care about her. Except that the new relationship had never been given a chance to blossom. Now she was alone again. And jobless.

Amber stood up; she may as well go home. She could cry in bed, at least there she would be warm! She rounded the corner of the road and turned towards the apartment and then her stride faltered. A vagrant was sitting in the doorway of the apartment. That was all she needed. It was too dark to make out the man clearly. It certainly was not Rory; he always sat in the

168

comfort of his car while he did his stalking. Lying on the front doorstep was not his style. Fear crept slowly over Amber, making her heart pound, how was she going to get into the apartment past the man? The road was deserted. What if he attacked her? She stopped walking, waiting hesitantly, unsure of what she should do. The dark shape unfolded itself and stood up, "Amber?" said a familiar voice.

"Paul!" Amber yelled, and ran headlong into his outstretched arms.

CHAPTER TWENTY FOUR

Stella wondered if it would be rude to shove cotton wool in her ears to block out the sound of Amber's awful singing.

Ever since Stella had arrived home from Mayo, it had been like living with a banshee.

Amber could not sit still, she leapt around the apartment, singing tunelessly, bursting with excitement at having finally found what she told Stella, was the love of her life.

The fact that she was now out of work and had no money coming in did not seem to have had any effect on Amber's happiness.

Amber launched into a fresh burst of 'You are the love of my life.'

Teddy looked balefully at Stella.

The telephone rang and Amber stopped in mid shriek and bounded across the room.

No doubt it would be Paul on the other end and then the two of them would spend hours talking gooey rubbish to each other.

Stella held her breath as Amber reached the telephone, saying a silent prayer that Rory would not be on the other end of the telephone. He was still bombarding her with telephone calls, begging for another chance at their relationship.

"Hello," Amber snatched up the telephone, her voice full of excitement in case it was Paul. "Oh," the note of excitement faded, abruptly, "Henry, do you want to talk to Stella?"

Stella shook her head, waving her arms at the door and pointing to indicate that Amber should tell Henry that she was out.

There was no way that she wanted to talk to Henry. Stella could not risk getting involved with Henry. She knew that she was falling in love with him and she could not risk that. She had to find someone who was wealthy, someone who would protect her from the kind of life that she had lived as a child. Someone who would make sure that she would never be poor again.

"Here she is," grinned Amber holding the receiver in Stella's direction.

"No," mouthed Stella, glaring furiously at Amber.

"She is just coming," Amber spoke into the receiver.

With a face like thunder Stella snatched the telephone receiver out of Amber's hand.

"Hello," she tried to sound icily polite and failed miserably. Stella glimpsed Amber grinning at her and dropped her hand quickly; she had automatically been smoothing her hair as she spoke to Henry.

"Stella," she could hear the naked delight in his voice. "How are things out in Mayo?"

Henry was always kind and thoughtful. Rory never even gave her past life a thought and he certainly would not have cared about her parents.

Stella could just picture what Rory would have thought of the humble little house and her simple parents if he had ever met them.

"I just wondered," he continued, "if you would like to come for dinner with me?" Stella groaned inwardly, she really did not think that was a good idea.

Amber, eavesdropping unashamedly nodded her head furiously, mouthing, "Go on. Go on."

Stella shook her head, glaring at Amber, she did not want to go for dinner with Henry. She did not dare. What would happen if they were alone together and she let herself look into his eyes? Amber poked her viciously in the ribs.

"Say yes," she hissed in Stella's ear.

"Ok, lovely," Stella heard the words spilling out of her mouth as if they had a life of her own.

"Great," Henry sounded delighted. "Come over to my place, I'll cook for you."

She replaced the receiver, and turned angrily to Amber. "What did you make me do that for?" Stella snapped, irritably.

"You said "Yes" I didn't make you say anything except talk to him" Amber laughed, merrily.

"Oh God," moaned Stella, "I've just agreed to have dinner at his place. What have I done?"

"The right thing," Amber said, and danced around the room launching into an awful, tuneless rendition of 'Love is in the air.'

"For someone who did not want to go out you are making a big effort," Amber said, wryly, raising her eyebrows and looking quizzically at Stella, who was beautifully dressed in a dark pair of trousers and a creamy coloured top.

"Well," snapped Stella, tetchily. "You never know who you are going to meet when you are out."

"I thought that it was just dinner at his place," giggled Amber, her eyes dancing with amusement.

"Well I like to look nice." Stella glared at Amber. "For me."

Amber nodded her head solemnly.

"Of course," Amber said, seriously, trying desperately to suppress a smile.

Stella marched out of the apartment, filled with self-righteous anger. How dare Amber suggest that she had got dressed up to impress Henry? That certainly was not the reason; somehow she had just wanted to look nice for the evening. It was nothing to do with Henry.

There was no sign of Rory sitting in the street, in his car, breathing a sigh of relief Stella got in her car and headed out of the city.

She had soon left the bright lights of the city behind and sped along the narrow country lanes of Kildare. It was funny how different everything looked when you were driving yourself, rather than being a passenger. With Rory she had looked at the scenery, rather than the road signs. However, soon she found herself driving along the narrow potholed road where she had found Teddy that day when she had visited Henry's yard with Rory.

Stella missed the turn off to Henry's stables and before long was in unfamiliar territory.

"Damn," Stella cursed. Meeting a huge tractor on a tight bend in the road, she hastily steered the car into the hedge, hearing the thorn bushes scraping along the bodywork.

The road seemed to get narrower and narrower. "Shit, shit!" exclaimed Stella, now she was going to be late.

A short way further on she found a wide gateway and reversed into it to turn the car around. For one awful moment the wheels spun around, not able to grip on the slick turf and then suddenly with a lurch the car shot free and bounced out onto the road.

Stella shoved her foot hard on the accelerator, her eyes scanning the road for familiar landmarks. Over to her right, just visible through the green canopy of leaves she could see the huge mansion that she had admired before, Henry's cottage and stables were close to here.

She spotted the entrance to Thornhill stables, almost hidden in the bushy growth of the hawthorn hedge and slammed on the brakes.

The van behind her screeched to a halt, skidding and almost sliding into the bumper of Stella's car.

Stella felt a red hot blush flush over her face as the driver of the van honked loudly on his horn. In her rear view mirror she could see him waving two fingers in her direction in a rude gesture.

Slowly Stella drove down Henry's bumpy driveway towards his cottage, wishing that she had not accepted his invitation. What on earth had possessed her to say yes?

She enjoyed being taken out for dinner in slick city restaurants, not having it cooked for her by some country horse trainer.

This was only prolonging the agony of having to give him up. She could not have a relationship with Henry. How would she ever manage to find a suitable partner if she was involved with someone?

She would turn around, go home, and make sure that she did not talk to Henry again.

The drive way was too narrow to turn around on and she did not want to risk turning in any of the gateways that led off the lane, they all looked far too muddy to venture into and she could just imagine how amused Henry would have been if she had got stuck on his driveway, especially if she had to tell him that she was trying to bolt for home.

However, when she finally reached the stable yard in front of the cottage Henry's home stood in darkness, the stable yard was deserted. A black pall of disappointment rained down on her shoulders, surprising her with its intensity.

Not paying attention to what she was doing Stella drove into the middle of the yard, braked hard to avoid hitting a scrawny black and white cat and stalled the car.

She turned off the engine, looking around at the deserted looking cottage and yard.

Henry had obviously forgotten that she was coming.

He had gone out without her.

Stella scowled, miserably, suddenly wanting to see him very much.

The cottage was in darkness, the windows staring blankly out into the yard. From the stables a few horses stared out at her car, their ears sharply pricked eyes bright and intelligent, curious at who had driven into the yard. The black and white cat stalked back across the yard, jumped up onto her car bonnet, eyed her disdainfully through the windscreen and then settled down to wash itself, enjoying the warmth from her car engine.

Surely Henry would not have gone out and forgotten her. Stella thought, her pride not letting her believe that this was possible. He must be somewhere around, maybe there had been a power cut and he was in the kitchen, waiting for her to arrive. Stella got out of the car and walked across to the cottage, shivering in the brisk wind that cut across the pastureland and swirled around the yard, sending stray strands of straw skittering across the uneven cobbles.

Stella hammered on the back door, hearing the noise echoing around the silent cottage. Henry was not there, and then turning away she saw a light in one of the barns away from the stable yard. Maybe Henry was there.

Picking her way across the yard Stella made her way towards the light, grumbling under her breath about her own stupidity. Henry had not had the courtesy to wait in for her, why was she chasing after him? She should just get back into the car and drive away. Sod Henry. But still her feet brought her relentlessly towards the light, picking her way over the muddy patches and the patches of more awful substances that seemed to virtually fill the near derelict yard.

Lights from the mansion blazed through the woodland at the edge of Henry's gallops, shining across the sandy track and closely cropped turf. Stella paused to look at it, mesmerised as always by its beauty, before the chill evening wind made her shiver and carry on towards the light in the barn. Stella paused in the entrance to the barn, "Henry," she called, uncertainly.

"Fuck! Stella!" Came the horrified reply. Henry's head appeared from one of the stables at the far end of the barn.

"Shit! Is it that time already?"

Stella smiled tightly. "Yes," she said, irritably walking slowly down the length of the barn towards him.

The barn contrasted sharply with the unkempt cottage and stable yard outside. Inside it was immaculate. Large stables stood at either side of a wide corridor, each divided by smartly painted wood and tall iron railings. The stables were mostly empty, save a few at the far end, in which two pretty brown horses watched her approach.

"Sorry," confessed Henry, grimacing at his own stupidity, "I completely forgot about the time." He kissed her softly on the cheek; Stella could feel the coolness of his lips on her skin after he had released her from his gentle grip.

"This foal won't suckle," Henry told her stepping back into the stable. Inside the stable, knee deep in straw, stood an enormous chestnut horse, beside which was a foal.

"What's wrong with it?" Stella grimaced at the odd looking animal. The foal looked as if its legs were too large for its tiny body, and as if the head were too big for its short neck to support.

Henry gave a laugh of delight. "They always look like this, you will see, he will soon look like his head and legs belong to him." The foal took a step forward, wobbled on his long legs and fell, sprawling heavily into the straw.

Stella gave a gasp of sympathy and darted forward to help him. The big chestnut horse laid back its long ears and rolled a wild looking eye in Stella's direction.

"Don't come in," Henry warned, quickly.

Stella stopped; there was no way that she was going to go near that great orange brute.

"Woah girl," Henry ran a gentle hand over the chestnut mare's long neck, calming her with his voice and hands.

Stella watched, silently, enthralled at the graceful way in which he touched the mare and the way that she changed from a fearful mass of muscle, to a gentle creature by his presence.

"I need to get the foal to suckle," Henry, held the foal, supporting him while the gangly creature fought to control his enormous legs, his whiskery muzzle sweeping up and down the mare's hind legs and beneath her belly, while she stood patiently. "He has to learn to put his head beneath her belly and then upwards for her teats," Henry explained, gently trying to guide the foal while holding him up with his own legs.

Stella jumped back from the doorway as the orange horse let out an almighty squeal. "There," Henry said, grinning delightedly. "He's found the milk bar."

Once the foal had suckled, Henry moved away, the foal walked catching his long legs in the straw and tumbling down.

"Come and stroke him," Henry said, opening the stable door. Stella walked in, uncertainly, keeping one eye on his cross looking orange mother. "She won't mind," Henry said, seeing Stella looking nervously at the mare.

Stella crouched by the foal, he lay in the straw, all legs and enormous head, gingerly she stoked the warm fluffy fur of his belly and then touched his velvet soft muzzle, enthralled at how such a gangly creature could possibly grow up into something as huge as his mother.

"Oh bloody hell," exclaimed Henry suddenly, leaping to his feet, "I was so busy with the mare that I forgot to put the dinner on for you." Stella gave a short laugh; suddenly it did not matter anymore.

They walked slowly along the wide corridor, Henry turned off the lights and they walked, together across the dark yard and into the house. Henry closed the door behind them and then stood in the semi darkness, looking at Stella. She could sense the incredible tension that buzzed between the two of them. Then with infinite slowness he gently touched her cheek.

"Stella," Henry whispered, softly. "You look absolutely beautiful tonight."

CHAPTER TWENTY FIVE

Stella steered her car slowly along the rutted lane away from Henry's cottage, trying to avoid the deep potholes highlighted in her car headlights.

At the end of the drive she turned out onto the tarmac road, drove a short distance and then pulled over into a lay-by on the opposite side of the road.

She turned off the engine and threw open the car door, breathing in huge gasps of the cold night air as if she had been come to the surface after being under water for a long time. With movements jerky with panic Stella spun her legs out of the car and sat, with her head in her hands letting the cold air seep into her consciousness, bringing her back to reality.

Slowly Stella raised her head, far below the lay-by, through the trees, highlighted in the pale glow of the full moon was the gorgeous mansion. It stood, a proud, dark solid shape surrounded by the pale silvery sheen of the surrounding fields and gardens.

The round face of the moon reflected in the lake close to the house. And beyond the house, off to the right, were the sagging roof tops of Henry's cottage and the bulk of the barn behind it.

Stella levered herself to her feet and leant against her car bonnet, gazing longingly at the mansion. That was the sort of place that she wanted to live in. Not some tumbledown cottage like the one Henry lived in.

Stella ran a trembling hand over her forehead, feeling the tension in her skin, her temples throbbed. She had to get a grip on herself; she could not let herself fall for Henry.

She pictured a nightmare scenario, living in the battered cottage, becoming a bitter drudge, shabby and careworn like her mother. Stella shook her head to clear the scene from her thoughts. That could not happen.

Stella shivered, the cold bringing her back to reality. She got back into her car and turned on the engine and pulled out onto the road again, with a final look back at the mansion as it slid away out of the line of her vision.

She could not let herself get fond of Henry. That would lead to certain disaster.

Stella brought her hand to her cheek, she could still feel the touch of his fingers against her skin from when he had gently pulled her towards him, and brought his lips tenderly down onto hers.

The world had spun dizzily on its axis, as if she would fall, but his arms had encircled her, holding her as if he had the strength to support the two of them. He had kissed her so gently, his lips moving against hers as if she were the most precious thing that he had ever touched, while one hand gently cupped the back of her head.

She had felt the warmth from his body; felt the strength that lay within him as his body gently brushed against hers. And when they had drawn apart they had stood for a long moment, as if surprised and afraid of what was happening between them. Henry had moved away first.

"I don't know what we will have to eat," he had said, huskily. Stella had followed him into the kitchen, hardly aware of the chipped cupboards and grotty furniture. She had smiled as he had opened the fridge. On the bottom shelf was a leg of lamb, resting in a baking tray, ready to be put into the oven.

"Too late to cook that," Henry shrugged, wryly, crouching beside the open door and peering hopefully inside. "Looks like this is the best I can offer you," he said, puffing out his cheeks and letting out a huge sigh as he pulled rashers of bacon and two eggs out of the fridge. He had fried the rashers and eggs and while Stella sat on one of the rickety chairs, watching him.

Something happened to her when she got near to Henry, something that she did not like. She could not let herself fall for Henry. She had to cut him out of her life. Why then had she accepted his invitation to go to the raccs with him the following weekend? He had asked her to go with him. He had a horse running, he had told her, it should do well. It would make up for not getting any dinner. And she had accepted, eagerly.

But now she was cursing her own stupidity. She should have made some excuse, made sure that she had avoided Henry in the future. And now she had just got further into the mess, by accepting his invitation.

"What are you doing?" Amber asked as Stella headed into an expensive looking boutique.

"Just having a look," Stella quipped, holding the door open for Amber to follow her.

They were in town having lunch together. Amber was desperately job hunting. Or rather, as Stella thought, 'desperate at job hunting'. She did not seem to have any idea about what she wanted to do, except that she did not want to have yet another dead end job.

Stella had not had the heart to point out that with Amber's qualifications – or rather lack of qualifications – and her appalling work record – a dead end job was about all that she was going to get.

"What about this?" Stella pulled a tweed suit off the rail; she held the jacket up against her, looking in the mirror to see. The creamy tweed fabric highlighted her pale colouring, and the darker suede trim looked lovely against the colour of her hair. Amber narrowed her eyes.

"I thought that you didn't want to encourage Henry," Amber raised her eyebrows and looked quizzically at Stella.

"I don't," Stella snapped. "But I still want to look nice. I'll get a lot of use out of this suit," she told Amber, sincerely, ignoring her friend's sarcastic jibe and heading towards the checkout to pay.

Stella arrived at Henry's cottage at the appointed time a few days later. She parked her car close to one of the stables and got out.

"You can't park there," snapped the short dark haired man that she recognised as Henry's groom, Jimmy. "Go near the cottage,"

Stella got back into her car, prickling with irritation. What a rude bunch these racing people were. The car bumped across the yard to the cottage.

"Happy now?" Stella growled under her breath, but there was no sign of the short man.

The yard was a hive of frantic activity. Jimmy and a scrawny middle aged woman, with a leathery looking face, were shooting backwards and forwards across the yard from the barn to the ancient looking lorry that stood in the middle of the yard with its ramp down. Henry appeared out of the cottage, clutching a pile of brightly coloured satin jackets.

"Hi," he stopped hurrying and came across the yard towards Stella, greeting her with a kiss on the cheek. "We will be off in a minute," he said, glancing in the direction of the stables and then finally tearing himself away from Stella.

"Everything ready Kathy?" Henry yelled across to the leather faced woman, she gave him a thumbs up signal as she jogged back towards the stable yard.

A few moments later Jimmy and Kathy emerged from the stables, both leading enormous looking horses. Kathy led a pretty looking bay who walked politely beside her into the lorry. Jimmy hung onto the lead rope of a prancing grey horse, who had his ears flat back against his elegant neck and who seemed to roll his eyes to glare at Stella who shrank back against the wall in fright.

"Come on then," Henry said, as they all heaved up the heavy looking ramp, nodding briefly Kathy skulked back in the direction of the stables and Jimmy clambered into the lorry and settled himself down on the small ledge behind the driver's seat.

"After you," Henry held open the passenger door of the lorry for Stella to climb in.

Stella swallowed hard, she was not sure that her skirt and new high heeled boots were made for clambering up into lorries. Something akin to amusement danced in Henry's eyes.

"You will have to hitch that skirt up," he grinned.

Pursing her lips angrily Stella wriggled the skirt upwards and began the climb up into the lorry cab. Then much to her enormous annoyance, Henry put his hand onto her bottom and shoved her into the cab.

Jimmy gave a snort of amusement. "Nice legs," he grinned.

Glaring at him angrily Stella settled herself into the seat. She had expected to be driven to the races in the Jeep, that would have been bad enough, but to go in a lorry!

Stella would have enjoyed the journey, it was amazing how far you could see while high up in a lorry cab, but the whole way she was worried about how she was going to get down onto level ground again. Henry, however, had the solution.

"Jump down into my arms," he grinned, pulling open the passenger door when they pulled into the carpark at the race meeting.

Taking a deep breath Stella slid, very ungracefully down out of the passenger seat into his arms.

Henry took Stella into the race course, past the security guard and then went back to organise the horses for their races, telling Stella that he would see her in the parade ring, pointing in the direction of a grassy oval bordered by a white fence.

Stella began to relax, wandering happily around the race course admiring the outfits of the smartly dressed men and women.

At one edge of the course there were stalls selling everything from beautiful handmade leather handbags to gorgeous silky scarves.

Stella wandered around the stalls, losing herself in the pleasure of shopping until it was time to go and meet Henry at the parade ring.

Without her noticing the race course had filled up, there were people everywhere, wandering aimlessly, chatting on mobile telephones, gazing intently at the names of the horses written on tall boards beside the course book makers.

Stella made her way to the parade ring.

A crowd of people clustered around the edge of the ring, Stella shoved her way through and then hesitantly ducked under the rail. The horses were being led around a tarmac track that circled around the grassy oval, all bounding with energy and power. Stella took a deep breath and dived across the tarmac onto the grass, her eyes raking the groups of people, looking for Henry. At last she saw him and walked across the grass, hampered by her high heels which kept sinking into the soft turf.

"Hey, Stella, " Henry grinned with delight when he spotted her. "This is Eileen and Tom Joyce, the owners of Moody Man," Stella shook hands with them the tall, elegantly dressed man and his tiny, fragile looking wife.

"Hasn't Henry done a good job on him?" Eileen asked Stella.

Stella nodded, hoping that she looked knowledgeable; she did not even know which their horse was.

A red-faced man in a tight fitting tweed suit rang a bell, bellowing something unintelligible and from the low wooden building beside the parade ring came a line of jockeys, all dressed in brightly coloured silks, slapping short whips against their stick thin legs. "Here's Jamie, our jockey," Tommy Joyce stuck out a finely boned hand in the direction of a pale faced young man, who looked as if a strong breeze would blow him away.

The red faced steward rang his bell and the horses were led into the centre of the ring.

Jimmy was dragged towards them, clutching onto the bridle of the prancing, angry looking grey horse.

Henry legged Jamie up onto his back, Stella leapt out of the way as the horse began to caper, throwing his head up and down. Stella backed away quickly; she did not want to get in the way of those flying hooves.

The horses went out onto the course; Stella craned her neck to watch as they circled at the start of the race and then set off, a long caterpillar of colour against the green background of the surrounding farmland.

After what seemed only a few moments the horses were thundering past the winning post, with Moody Man in third place. Henry glowed with pleasure as Eileen kissed him as Tommy shook his hand at the same time.

"Now time to see what my horse can do." Henry said, once all the excitement had died down. Jimmy reappeared with the elegant bay horse.

"This is Princess Pushy," Henry told Stella as the horse walked around the parade ring. She was very different from Moody Man, calmly taking in her surroundings, gazing at everything through kind brown eyes, her ears sharply pricked, noticing everything that was going on around her, yet accepting it all fearlessly.

"I bred her myself," Henry said, proudly.

The jockeys trooped out once more, as Henry legged Jamie up onto Princess Pushy's back Stella turned as someone tugged at the sleeve of her jacket.

"Stella," Rory said. "How good to see you again."

Stella felt her heart give an uncomfortable lurch of fear as Rory towered over her, looking maliciously in Henry's direction. "How are you getting on with the prodigal son?" he asked nastily, jerking his head towards Henry.

"Fine thanks," snapped Stella, wondering fleetingly what on earth he meant, but before she had time to ask Rory continued, "I don't know what you see in someone like him when you could have been with me." Out of the corner of her eye Stella could see Henry glance in their direction, his expression full of concern.

"He is just a loser," Rory spat, and then seeing Henry approaching dropped his grip on Stella's jacket sleeve and with a final, defiant glare in Henry's direction, turned abruptly on his heel and stalked across the parade ring.

Stella heaved a sigh of relief, as Rory walked away. What a nasty shock he had given her, she had not expected to see him today.

"You ok?" Henry put his arm gently around her shoulder, Stella nodded, fighting the urge to lean against his chest and weep with fright. "Come on," Henry said, "let's go and see what Princess Pushy can do," they went out to the trainers stand and found a place to watch the race.

Stella was horribly aware of Rory's presence, a few seats away from them. The horses made their way down to the start line.

"This is her first proper race," Henry told Stella gripping her hand in his.

"She's done a few point to point races, but this is her first real race."

Far away on the other side of the course the race began, the horses surging away towards the first fence.

"Cod and Chips is Rory's horse," Henry told her, as the commentator began to reel out the names of the horses as they ran.

Princess Pushy was right at the front of the pack, her elegant cream muzzle, shoved resolutely forwards. Cod and Chips, Stella heard the commentator say, was in fourth place.

The horses surged past the stands, a blur of colour and movement, against the cacophony of noise from the crowd.

The horses took off as one to jump the solid looking fence nearest the stands, Henry's grip tightened on Stella's hand.

Princess Pushy had fallen, the elegant bay mare skidding incongruously along the ground before she scrambled to her feet, looking bemused. "I'd better go and see if she is all right," Henry said, distractedly, letting go of Stella's hand and shoving his way out of the stands. There was a roar of delight from the crowd as Cod and Chips surged over the finishing line ahead of all the other horses. "See," Rory, growled, coming to stand beside Stella, smirking smugly at her, "I told you that Henry was a loser."

CHAPTER TWENTY SIX

Amber wrapped her fingers around Paul's hand, savouring the sensation of his skin beside hers.

She chanced another look at him, hoping that she did not look too much like a besotted puppy.

He was truly, truly gorgeous, she concluded, trying and failing to suppress a grin of sheer delight.

It was hard to believe that finally things were going right.

She might be out of work – and penniless – with a mountain of debt – and Stella might well be getting pissed off with paying all the rent and buying the food and lending Amber money – but she had Paul. Paul.

Amber whispered his name, savouring the way that the syllables rolled off her tongue.

"Yeeeees," he said slowly, dragging his eyes briefly from the race horses thundering across the television screen.

"I really thought that I would never see you again," Amber repeated for about the billionth time since she had returned home from losing her job and found Paul still waiting for her outside her apartment. "I thought that you would think that I was seeing someone else. And that you would go away thinking that I was a complete bitch."

"I know," Paul replied, patiently, tearing himself away from the ferocious battle to the finish line that was taking place on the screen, "I saw you in the car. I was so upset that you had gone when I was looking forward to seeing you again."

"And tell me again what you thought," Amber could not believe that things had finally gone well for her. That Paul had waited all night for her to return. Because he thought so much of her and she could not stop wanting him to tell her the story of how he waited. And waited.

"I knew that it was Mark Hardcastle that you were with. I knew that you worked for him," Paul said, gently, tracing Amber's profile with his fingertips, "I guessed that he must have fetched you to go to work and I guessed that you had not been able to get in touch with me to tell me. I know how it is when you work in a restaurant – always on call."

"And you waited for me to come back," Amber sighed blissfully.

"Of course," Paul gently touched his lips to Amber's, before continuing mock dramatically, "I waited for hours, sitting out in the cold, all alone and miserable, not knowing when you would be back."

"I couldn't believe it when I saw you there," Amber smiled at him, "I thought that you would just go away and that I would never see you again."

Paul gave a snort of laughter, "I happen to think that you are worth waiting for."

Amber quivered with pleasure as Paul gently ran his hands over her body, drawing her closer.

"I'm glad that you waited," she whispered, huskily.

Much later Paul heaved himself out of bed. "I have to go to work," he said regretfully, tracing a flower shape across the flat plane of Amber's belly with one long finger.

"I had better go home," Amber said, drawing his hand to her lips and gently kissing each fingertip, "I need to start looking for another job."

"Here's the newspaper," Paul rummaged beside the bed and handed the crumpled newspaper to Amber. "Stay here for a while, come and meet me out of work if you like?"

"Thanks," Amber smoothed out the newspaper.

"Is Stella still seeing that race horse trainer, Henry Murphy?" Paul asked, opening the wardrobe door and pulling a white shirt off a hanger and sliding his arm into the sleeve.

"Yes," Amber smiled at the thought of the way that Stella tried to avoid any mention of her relationship with Henry and yet how she blushed furiously whenever he was around. "She is trying not to see him, but she can't keep away from him."

"Oh, right," Paul frowned quizzically at this piece of female logic. "It's just that I thought that I might call him up. Go and have a look at the horse he wanted me to ride."

"You should," Amber agreed, it would be lovely if she and Stella could go out in a foursome if the two men got together.

"I miss the horses," Amber watched as Paul slid his long, muscled thighs into a pair of black trousers, she had to wrap her hands beneath her body to stop herself from touching him.

"I was such an idiot," Paul sighed bitterly, sinking down onto the bed beside Amber.

He shook his head as if he could not believe his own stupidity.

Amber gently touched his back with her hand, wishing that she could soothe his pain away.

"I lost it all through being too cocky, too sure that I was the best, no one could manage without me, the trainers would all put up with the shit I gave them because there was no one better." He was so lost in his own thoughts that he barely seemed aware of Amber's hand, gently moving over the tense muscles of his back.

"Oh fuck," he sighed, bitterly and then visibly forcing himself to push away the regrets, he turned and enfolded Amber into his arms. "I had better go," he murmured softly into the tangled waves of her hair.

As the front door slammed shut Amber swung her legs out of bed and pulled on her clothes.

She wandered into the lounge with the newspaper tucked beneath her arm and settled down on the leather sofa with a contented sigh.

Paul's apartment was beautiful, brought, he had told her with his earnings when he was still a successful jockey.

The walls were covered with photographs of him riding horses, flying fearlessly over fences, or standing, mud splattered and grinning beside a sweating racehorse. In a corner of the room, behind the biggest television screen that Amber had ever seen, was a pile of boxes, filled, Paul had told her, with cups and trophies from his wins that he had never got around to displaying.

Amber gazed dreamily at the photographs; it was hard to imagine that this racing superstar was the waiter that she had so quickly fallen in love with.

Amber tore her gaze away from the photographs and opened the newspaper, forcing herself to concentrate on finding a new job. Amber scanned the half dozen pages of jobs, circling some with a pen, there was no way that she was going to have another dead end job, this time she was going to have a career, something that would challenge her – and pay well – for once.

Most of the job adverts wanted a current c.v sending in. That would need help from Stella, and some creative licence with Amber's employment record and qualifications. But there was one agency; close by that she could visit in the morning. There was an impressive list of job vacancies listed beneath the agency's name. They would surely find something suitable for Amber. Satisfied, Amber folded the newspaper and switched on the television, only another hour to wait before she could go and meet Paul out of work.

Amber set her alarm clock so that she would be awake early. Perhaps if she played her cards right Stella would help to produce a perfect c.v. before she went off to work.

Yawning she padded into the lounge and switched on the computer.

It was ancient and took forever to warm up, so while it clicked and whirred she clipped Teddy's lead on and took him to do a wee in the small garden area behind the apartment block.

Amber unclipped Teddy's lead and leant against the door frame as the little dog wandered around the dew soaked patch of grass. It would have been nice to have another few hours in bed. Amber was exhausted. She had met Paul out of work and then gone back to his apartment with him. It had been the early hours of the morning before she had finally managed to drag herself away from him.

By the time Amber returned to the apartment the computer had woken up sufficiently for her to be able to get into the word programme and slowly begin to type her c.v.

"I didn't know that you had a business studies degree," Stella said, peering over Amber's shoulder.

"Well, not actually," Amber said, glancing around at Stella. Even in her dressing gown, just after getting out of bed, Stella made looking gorgeous seem so effortless, "but I did apply to do it."

"Uh uh ," Stella gently pushed Amber's hand off the mouse and scrolled up and down the c.v. that she had written.

"I really want to do something good this time. I've had so many dead end jobs. It's time that I got my act together and started to think about the future," Amber leant back in the chair, with a heartfelt sigh.

"Interests, wine tasting!" Stella giggled, reading off the screen

"Well, that one is true," Amber giggled back.

Two hours later, with a much revised c.v. that Stella had made herself late for work helping with, Amber was in the offices of Billings and Rigg Employment Agency. "Good morning," said the snooty looking receptionist, slowly looking Amber up and down.

"Good morning," Amber squared her shoulders and met the older woman's steely gaze.

It was amazing the difference that wearing a smart suit made to your confidence, Amber thought, perching on the edge of the sofa that dominated the reception area.

"Miss Billings will see you in a moment," said Miss Snooty, with a tight smile, as she glanced briefly at Amber before resuming her machine gun speed typing, without, Amber was impressed to note, once glancing at her keyboard to see where the letters where.

There was a pile of magazines on the glass table in front of the sofa. Amber flicked through them as she waited, after a moments indecision she picked up a battered looking copy of Irish Business today, it would make a good impression if Miss Billings saw her reading a business magazine. It would make her look like a serious minded career woman.

Assuming what she hoped was a serious expression Amber slowly turned the pages of the magazine and a moment later was fighting a serious urge to yawn. The magazine was so boring. Full of lengthy articles on subjects that Amber had never even heard of.

Amber's eyes strayed longingly to the glossy pink cover of Cosmo, that looked far more interesting, especially the article on 'Sixty Nine ways to keep him begging for more.' Amber turned determinedly back to the business magazine; none of the technical words in the article that she was reading made any sense whatsoever. "Dammit," hissed Amber under her breath, throwing down the magazine and snatching up the copy of Cosmo, just managing to resist holding it to her chest like a long lost lover, with the sheer delight of finally having something interesting to read.

She was halfway through the 'Sixty Nine' article when the door behind the receptionist swung open and a short, dumpy woman with a short blonde helmet of hair barked Amber's name.

Amber tore herself reluctantly away from the visions of what could be done with an ice cube and followed Miss Binns into her office.

Miss Binns strutted across the expanse of revolting green and pink flowered carpet and positioned herself behind the enormous wooden desk. She held her hand out briefly for Amber to shake. "Sit down," Miss Binns had a booming voice and a handshake that made all the bones in Amber's hand feel as if they had been realigned.

Miss Binns must surely have been a man in another life. Amber had a sudden vision of her with a beard and fought an almost uncontrollable urge to giggle.

"So. What sort of position are you looking for?" Miss Binns waited with her pen poised over a sheet of paper.

Amber swallowed hard, forcing herself to concentrate, but the Cosmo article replayed itself relentlessly in her imagination. Paul would just love some of those positions.

"Position, ahem," Amber cleared her throat, desperately recalling the crash course in business-speak that Stella had given her that morning, "I'm looking for a change of direction."

"Have you an up to date c.v.?" Miss Binns jotted something down on her pad.

Amber handed her the very professional looking c.v. that Stella had created in a few minutes flat on the computer, and which the office supplies shop had bound into a beautiful presentation folder. Miss Binns turned over the first page of the c.v and began to read. Amber held her breath and hoped that she would remember everything that she was supposed to have done.

"I see your last position was in restaurant management," Miss Binns looked at Amber with her eyebrows raised expectantly.

"Yes," Amber smiled in what she hoped was a confident fashion. Well – Mark had left her in charge of the restaurant a time or two when he had to go out.

"And before that client management assistant at a nursing home."

"Yes," Stella had even managed to make up an impressive sounding title for what Amber had done in the nursing home.

"And a spell in retail, a factory, and in a Solicitor's office," Miss Binns looked at Amber's c.v. with a sigh and then slowly raised her eyes above the sheets of paper to survey Amber. "Quite a lot of jobs," she said after a moment's consideration.

"I've always felt that I should have a broad base of business experience to expand my experience of the cut and thrust of modern industry," Amber told her, relieved that she had remembered the line that Stella had told her to say in order to account for her constant switching of jobs.

Miss Binns smoothed her blonde helmet of hair. "I take it that you are computer literate?"

"Of course," Amber agreed with a short laugh. Wasn't everyone computer literate nowadays. She could surf the internet as well as anyone else. There were lots of buttons and stuff on the keyboard and screen that she did not dare go near in case the machine went berserk, but using a computer could not be that hard. Surely?

"And have you good typing speeds?"

"I'm fully acquainted with touch typing," Amber said. It was easy. You touched the keys and they typed. She was actually quite fast with two fingers.

"We need to do a speed test for your typing," Miss Binns said, reaching in her desk for a printed sheet of paper, "I'll let you type this up for me so that I can get an up to date typing speed. We need to be sure about all of our interviewees before we can recommend them to clients."

Stella looked up expectantly as Amber walked into the apartment. "How did you get on?" she asked looking at Amber over the rim of her coffee mug.

"They did not have anything to suit me," Amber replied, steadily.

Actually nothing at all to suit anyone who's typing skills were quite as bad as Amber's.

The speed test had gone very badly. Miss Binns had let Amber fumble out a few lines in her fastest two fingered technique and then had very courteously stopped the test and told Amber that they would be in touch

190

when anything suitable came up. They both knew that nothing would ever come up for Amber.

"That's a shame," Stella sighed, no doubt thinking about the rent that she was going to have to pay, as well as all the other bills while Amber was out of work.

"But I did find something else," Amber grinned.

"Oh yes," Stella put down her coffee mug and turned to face Amber.

"When I came out of the agency I was walking into town when I saw a job advertised in a window. I went in and I got the job."

"That is brilliant," Stella punched the air in delight at Amber's success. "What are you going to be doing?"

Amber reached slowly into her handbag, like a magician doing a complicated trick. "Customer mobile supply systems manager," she announced, importantly, unfurling a blue nylon overall from her handbag with a flourish. "Check out girl in the supermarket actually!"

CHAPTER TWENTY SEVEN

Amber glared at Stella. "Why won't you come?" she asked, gently. Stella shook her head, firmly, "Henry's just not my cup of tea. He's very nice, but I don't want to be with him."

"I'm not asking you to have anything to do with Henry," Amber said, a petulant note appearing in her voice, "I just wanted you to come and see Paul ride the horse for him. This could be the start of Paul race riding again."

Stella shook her head, firmly, shaking Teddy off her lap as she got off the sofa.

"I don't want to give Henry the wrong idea," Stella muttered, switching on the kettle, "I don't want him to think that we could have a relationship."

Amber watched Stella, as she lifted the tea caddy, and then put it down again, before lifting the coffee jar, beginning to open it and then changing her mind once more. She had been really affected by going out with Henry. More than she was admitting, maybe even to herself.

"He thinks the world of you," Amber told her. "You should just get on with things. Just go out with him and enjoy yourself."

"No," snapped Stella, firmly, slamming down the coffee jar and hauling the top off the tea caddy and shoving a tea bag into a mug. "I can't."

Teddy weaved himself around Amber's legs and plonked down, his small head resting on her feet, looking up at her in the hope that she would throw the ball for him.

"What else are you going to do?" Amber tried again. "Coming out for the day with Paul and I has got to be better than staying here."

Amber knew that she had won then.

She saw a fleeting look of fear flash over Stella's face. Since she had seen Rory at the races he had doubled his efforts to get her back, sitting outside the flat most nights, telephoning her constantly at all hours of the day and night and sending gifts of flowers and jewellery. A small heap of gold necklaces and pretty silver bracelets lay on the kitchen worktop, tangled incongruously into the cards, declaring undying love that had come with the flowers.

Amber knew that Stella was afraid; whenever she was home she wandered aimlessly around the apartment, unable to settle, listening for the telephone to ring that would either herald another bout of pleading from Rory, or another grim update on her father's health from Mayo.

Stella had thrown herself into her work to escape from the horrors that she found beyond the stark walls of her office.

Sorcha had been very firmly put into her place. Stella had turned the tables on her by working twice as hard and being twice as good at her job.

Kevin's boss had even offered Stella a promotion, which would make her Kevin's equal rather than working beneath him.

Amber, had no such ambition. She loved her new job, sitting merrily on the supermarket checkout with a constant stream of interesting people to talk to as she scanned their groceries and speculated on what kind of lives they had.

Paul would often come in to the supermarket and stand patiently in the queue for Amber's checkout, somehow he would have slipped a note into one of the things that he was buying, asking her to meet him for coffee, or making naughty suggestions that made her blush and giggle.

Stella brought a cup of tea back to the sofa and sat down wearily.

"Ok," she said, wearily. "You win, I'll come."

Paul picked the two of them up the following morning. Amber had dressed casually in a pair of jeans and a baggy sweatshirt. Her hair was being particularly un-cooperative and had stuck out at all sorts of angles, in spite of her dampening it down with water, and applying tonnes of stuff supposed to control frizz. Even so, her hair was as unruly as ever, and so Amber had stuck a baseball cap on the top of the whole mass, at least she could see without it blowing all over the place.

"You look nice," Amber grinned at Paul, nudging him to look at Stella.

She too was dressed in jeans, but still managed to look elegant and stylish. For someone who supposedly was not interested in Henry, she still seemed to make an awful lot of effort when she was going to be around him.

Paul still drove the flashy sports car that he had brought himself when he was earning a fortune as a jockey. He loved the car, but now, with his wages from working as a waiter, could barely afford to run the car, with the result that the petrol gauge constantly read empty, or dangerously near to it.

Today, however, after a good night at the restaurant he had earned a small fortune in tips and the petrol tank was full. Paul levered the front seat up so that Stella could climb into the small back seat, with her legs sideways along the seat. Amber put Teddy into the back with her.

"He's a good back seat driver," she joked.

Stella gave directions while Paul drove.

"This is lovely," breathed Amber, as they headed out into the countryside.

Soon they were bumping down the potholed drive to Henry's cottage. Paul grimaced as the bottom of the car scraped along the ground when it hit a particularly deep pothole.

"Oh my," breathed Amber, as the car came to a halt in the yard. "Isn't it absolutely gorgeous."

She got out of the car, breathing deeply through her nose to savour the warm country smell of horse manure and of the freshly churned earth that blew down from the gallops.

"Just imagine living somewhere like this," Amber turned slowly around, oblivious to Paul and Stella who were leaning on the car, watching her with bemused expressions.

Paul had grown up on a farm in the country, he took all of the fresh air and open space for granted, enjoying the convenience of the city and yet feeling totally at home when he came back to the countryside.

To Stella the countryside reminded her of her childhood, hand-me-down clothes and watching everyone all of her school friends doing all of the things that she longed to do and of vowing to escape and never return.

Amber moved into the centre of the yard and then slowly spun around.

"Look at that beautiful old building," Amber stopped revolving and stood still, awestruck gazing at the faded old stone of the barn. "Look at the colours of the stone…….and the roof." Amber gazed up at the stone barn, loving every inch of the battered old building, seeing incredible beauty in the stone, weathered to a thousand different shades of cream and grey, standing proudly beneath a slate roof, whose tiles were chipped and cracked with age.

"Just imagine the work that went into creating something like that," Amber mused, looking at the way the vast stone lintels had been placed in the windows high above the stable yard, in what would once have been grooms accommodation. "I would love to have somewhere like this, to make it live again," she breathed, enthusiastically, ignoring Stella's scathing looks.

"Old places are hard work, always needing repairing," Stella grumbled, remembering the draughty cottage where she grew up.

"So do new ones," scoffed Paul. "My flat is in a new block, only built last year, and there are things going wrong with that already."

"Imagine living in that gorgeous cottage," Amber said, enviously, looking across the yard to Henry's home. "It just needs some roses around the door and a few hanging baskets to make it look like a chocolate box picture," Amber said, dreamily. "Oh, look, Henry's here." Amber darted a look at Stella, a dark red flush had spread over her cheeks and she was staring determinedly at a blackbird who was trying to pull a worm out of the soil close to where Paul had parked his car.

"Hi, you are all very welcome," Henry came across the yard to join them.

Amber stifled a giggle as Henry, looking so hard at Stella, almost fell over Teddy who was trying to pull up a tuft of grass from between the cobblestones.

"Hi Stella," he said, kissing her softly on the cheek.

"Hi Henry," Stella replied. Amber could hear how her voice softened when Henry was around.

"It's lovely out here," Amber told him, indicating the yard and cottage with an expansive wave of her arms.

"Where is the horse that you wanted me to look at?" Paul asked, looking around the yard at the horse's heads that were gazing out at them.

"Henry?" Paul asked again, when Henry did not answer.

"Errr," Henry said, tearing his eyes away from Stella, "Sorry.......errr.... what did you say?"

Amber nudged Paul and hissed between her teeth. "Talk about lovelorn, look at the two of them."

"Horse? Which horse did you want me to look at?" Paul asked, nudging Amber viciously in the ribs to make her behave.

"Yes," Henry said, distantly as he dragged his attention back to Paul. "Horse....... Yes.........This way."

Henry led the way across the yard to one of the stables, yelling for Jimmy to fetch a saddle and bridle.

"This is Princess Pushy," Henry pulled open one of the stable doors. Paul and the girls followed him inside.

The elegant bay mare pushed at Henry with her elegant brown muzzle, hoping he would give her a treat.

"Is this the horse that fell when we went racing?" Stella asked, stretching out her hand gingerly to touch the mare's silky, soft neck.

"Just bad luck," Henry said, firmly, deftly undoing the fastenings on Princess Pushy's dark blue rug and sliding it off over her muscular quarters. "She ran in a few point to point races, I think that she has got a great future ahead of her, I think your style of riding would suit her," Henry told Paul, smiling as Paul ran an admiring hand down the mare's neck and rubbed her face, gently.

Jimmy shoved his way into the stable, using the saddle that he carried like a battering ram to shove them all out of the way. The mare was quickly saddled and bridled and then Jimmy led her outside into the yard.

"You can try her, see what you think," Henry told Paul, legging him easily up into the saddle.

Amber grinned at Paul, he looked so at home on the mare's back as he rode off across the yard, his legs dangling by her sides as he fumbled to put his feet into tiny stirrups.

Stella walked beside Henry as they toiled up the hill from the yard to the gallops.

Princess Pushy jogged in front of them. Amber had her heart in her mouth watching the two of them. The horse pranced, tossing its elegant head up and down, champing at the bit as if it wanted to rid itself of the burden it carried.

A blur of brown streaked from the undergrowth as Teddy hurtled from beneath a bramble bush, straight between the horse's legs and ran at full speed towards them.

Amber did not have time to be afraid before the mare gave a huge leap into the air with fright at the sudden appearance of the little dog. Somehow though, when they came down to earth the two of them were still together.

"I think maybe he had better go on a lead," laughed Henry, totally unconcerned as he fished a long piece of baler twine out of his pocket and tossed it to Amber.

Teddy wriggled furiously as Amber tied the twine to his collar; at least he was enjoying himself.

She hated every minute. She was sure that Paul was going to be thrown off and killed or at the very least injured at any second.

It was even worse when they started to go faster, Princess Pushy pounded around the gallops, her long legs a virtual blur with the speed that she was travelling at.

When Henry suggested that Paul try her over one of the jumps it was all that Amber could do to stop herself from falling onto her knees and clutching at his hand begging him to take Paul off the horse immediately.

Paul turned the mare towards the solid looking jumps, speeding along the gallops standing in his stirrups, crouching low over her neck. Amber felt her breath catch in her throat as they took off, soaring through the air, so high and so fast, in perfect harmony. And then as they landed Amber felt the most almighty jolt of adrenaline course through her body, this had to be the most incredible thing that she had ever seen. The most terrifying, but the most thrilling.

"That was amazing," Amber said as she jogged back down to the yard beside Princess Pushy.

Paul had been absolutely delighted with the mare, he had leant down to kiss Amber as he had ridden up beside them after he had jumped the mare. Amber could taste the sweat on his upper lip; his face was icy cold, his cheeks red from the wind. He was back where he belonged.

"She is a wonderful mare," Paul called back over his shoulder and then rolled his eyes at Amber, Stella and Henry were walking behind them their heads close together, seemingly oblivious to anything but each other.

As they neared the yard Amber heard Henry swear. "Fuck, I had forgotten about him." An elegant looking Range Rover was parked in the yard, its owner lolling casually against the bonnet.

"Hope I'm not interrupting you," the owner of the Range Rover strolled over to the gate to let them back into the yard.

"Not at all," Henry said, with a cool edge to his voice, he held out his hand for the man to shake. Amber could hear a note of tension in his voice. "These are friends of mine, just come to have a look at my mare." Henry said, introducing them.

"This is Derry Blake, one of Ireland's top trainers," Henry explained to Amber and Stella. Derry turned towards the girls; his lips were twisted in a smile that Amber saw did not reach his eyes. His eyes flickered briefly over Paul, registering that he recognised him and then back to the girls as if he had already decided that Paul was of no consequence.

Derry was one of the most handsome men that Amber had ever seen, elegantly dressed in smart tweeds and casual cord trousers, he smelt deliciously of expensive aftershave. Amber instinctively recoiled from him; he looked far too much of a charmer for her liking. Paul slid off Princess Pushy and nodded curtly in Derry's direction before leading the mare towards her stable.

"I can come back some other time," Derry said. "Although I thought that you were in a hurry to sell The Entertainer," he added, maliciously.

"Don't go," Henry snapped. "Stay. Let's get this over with." Amber turned to Stella, they should move out of the way, let Henry and Derry sort out whatever business they had to do. To her horror she looked at Stella and saw that she was absolutely mesmerised by Derry Blake.

CHAPTER TWENTY EIGHT

Stella's alarm clock was going off, its noise loud and insistent. She fumbled for the bedside table, made a grab for the clock and then realised that it was her telephone that was ringing. She was instantly awake. It was the middle of the night that had to mean bad news.

"Stella!!" Rory's hysterical sounding voice screeched in her ear.

Stella felt her mouth drop open with surprise. She had been expecting to hear her mother's hushed voice telling her some awful news about her father, that would mean she would have to scramble straight out of bed and begin the long, dark drive back to Mayo.

Stella caught sight of the clock, its red numbers glowing in the semi darkness of her bedroom. Two fifteen a.m.

"Stella!" Rory shrieked again, when she did not reply, immediately, his shrill voice was thick with alcohol. He was very drunk.

"You have to come back to me," he ranted. "Have too..........." Stella could hear the sound of him sobbing, "I can't live without you."

Stella propped herself up on one elbow, furious at having had her night's sleep so brutally disturbed.

"Rory," Stella said, trying to imply patience in her voice. "Listen to me. I can't go back out with you. The relationship is over. You have to understand that."

"I'm going to kill myself," he roared, sounding as petulant as a small child denied sweets.

"Ok Rory." Stella severed the connection on the telephone.

She could not bear to listen to him any longer. He had been telephoning her and waiting outside the apartment, harassing her at work as well ever since she had seen him at the races.

He had threatened to kill himself dozens of times as if he thought that this would make Stella change her mind.

Stella huddled beneath the bedclothes once more, shivering with nerves. Why could he not leave her alone, she really could not cope with this any longer. Maybe she should go to the Garda and complain about him, like Amber and Paul had been telling her too. She had really hoped that before long he would get fed up, when he realised that his threats were not going to make any difference.

Stella felt hot tears of frustration roll down her cheeks and onto the pillow. She hated the thought of what Rory was going through, hated the thought that she was causing him pain, but she could not resume their relationship.

He was never going to make her happy. And besides which, he would never actually carry out his threats of killing himself, that was all for attention, like a girl telling an ex-boyfriend that she is pregnant in the hope that he will go back to her.

There was no hope. The relationship was over. Forever.

Stella lay in the blissful place between wakefulness and sleep, cocooned in the warmth of the quilt. The telephone rang, dragging her once more into wakefulness.

"Hello," she said, impatiently.

"I'm going to crash my car off the motorway." Rory's voice was cold, filled with anger.

Stella dashed away the tears that flowed, how could he be so cruel to keep torturing her like this? Why could he not just leave her alone and get on with his life?

"Rory," Stella could hear the hysteria rising in her own voice. "Stop it, stop being like this. Just go home and go to bed. We can talk in the morning." Stella could not bear his unrelenting cruelty, twisting his life around so that she was responsible for his happiness.

"No Stella." Rory said his voice suddenly calm, almost jovial. "I'm going to crash my car now. And it will be your fault."

In the background Stella could hear the sound of Rory revving up the car engine.

This was ridiculous, tomorrow she was going to have to go to the Garda about him, make them stop him from keep harassing her, maybe they would be able to make him get some help.

"I'm going to drive off the motorway now," she could hear Rory saying, the car engine was loud in the background, screaming in protest as he drove it faster and faster.

"Rory. Stop it. Stop it!" Stella was panicking now. What if he really carried out his threat?

"It's your fault," his voice had a sing song lilt to it, rising at the end. "Your fault," he was silent then, Stella could hear the roar of the car engine, even the sound of the road beneath the wheels, then suddenly he spoke again.

"Bye Stella." His voice was icy cold and cruel.

Stella felt her heart pound in her chest as through the earpiece she heard a dull thud. Then a thousand different noises all joined together into one dreadful cacophony of sound of scraping, banging, metal tearing.

Suddenly the connection was severed and she lay in bed, shivering violently listening to the mundane noise of the telephone bleeping.

Stella slowly replaced the telephone on the bedside table. She was trembling all over. Surely Rory had not really carried out his threat to crash his car. Surely he would not be that stupid? Or cruel? Was he really prepared to kill himself in the hope that she would feel guilty about his death for the rest of her life? Stella turned on the bedside light and caught sight of herself in the mirror, wide eyed with shock, her face grey and pinched with fear.

"Amber!" she shrieked, "Amber!"

"Whaaaa?" Stella heard Amber stirring in the adjoining room.

In response to her cries Teddy shoved his nose around the bedroom door, hurtled across the floor and bounded up onto the bed to see what the matter was with his mistress. He shoved his small, cold nose into her neck, wriggling furiously, trying to cheer her up.

Stella was so shocked by the telephone conversation that all she could do was to feebly try to push Teddy away, but there seemed to be no strength in her arms at all.

"Teddy, get down," Amber came into the room, sweeping Teddy off the bed with a cuff of her hand and sitting quickly down beside Stella, her face full of concern and panic seeing Stella looking so upset. "What is it? What's happened? Is it your Dad?"

Stella shook her head numbly, her mouth opening and closing as she fought to frame the words.

"Rory......It's Rory. I think that he's just killed himself," Stella mumbled incoherently.

"Good!" snapped Amber, but then seeing the stunned, fearful look in Stella's face, she said quietly. "You don't mean that."

"He just phoned me, said he was driving off the motorway."

"Yes, but that doesn't mean that he was going to actually do it. He's just trying to get your attention."

"He did though." Stella gasped, "I heard him do it. His phone went dead."

Amber shook her head, trying to deny the facts. "Let me ring him," she picked up the phone beside Stella's bed. "What's his number."

Stella desperately fumbled with the phone. She could barely remember how to use it she was in such a state.

Amber shoved the phone up to her ear, watching Stella as it tried to connect. The unobtainable sound of the telephone bleeping was loud in the silent room.

"Now what do we do?" Stella asked, a few moments later.

They had been sitting silently on the bed, Teddy had snuck back onto the bed and lay sprawled between them, enjoying the unexpected attention, as they both stroked his fur distractedly.

Amber puffed out her cheeks and shrugged, "I dunno."

Stella was always the one who knew what to do about problems. It was impossible to sleep now with all the trauma.

Amber made tea and they curled at opposite ends of the sofa to sip the scalding liquid. "We will be worn out in the morning now," grumbled Amber, watching the hands of the clock slide slowly around.

"Maybe we should ring the Garda?" Stella whispered, bleakly. "Or the hospital?" Before they had time to ponder further Stella's telephone rang.

"I bet that is him," Amber growled, filled with uncontrollable anger. How could Rory be such a prick to put them through this trauma?

"Hello," Stella said, fearfully, afraid of what she was going to hear over the telephone. Amber concentrated hard on rubbing Teddy's ears, watching

Stella's reaction to the telephone conversation. She could hear the sound of a voice, muted, talking rapidly and Stella's stunted replies.

"Yes. Yes……………Yes…………Ok. Thank you." Stella put the phone down, shaking her head numbly while she brushed away the tears from her eyes. "He did crash the car," Stella said, wearily. "I can't believe that he would be so stupid. He's on his way hospital, in a serious condition. He managed to tell the ambulance men to telephone me before he passed out."

Even in the middle of the night the hospital was busy, like a small city living separately from the rest of the world, its inhabitants wandering aimlessly around dim corridors and sitting in small, bleak huddles.

Stella and Amber made their way to the Accident and Emergency unit.

There was a long queue of people waiting to talk to the bleary eyed receptionist, who sat behind a glass panel, speaking only through a small chink in the glass.

Stella and Amber joined the end of the queue, shuffling forwards at a snail's pace towards the receptionist.

Finally it was their turn.

"You have a friend of mine here, Rory McFadden, he was in an accident," Stella told the receptionist, lip-reading her reply above the angry buzz of noise from the seating area.

"We have to go through into the waiting room," Stella told Amber, walking through the waiting area, wide eyed in bewilderment.

The casualty department waiting room was crowded, row upon row of chairs were filled with slumped, bewildered looking youths, dripping blood from various parts of their anatomies.

Feeling as if she were living some bizarre nightmare Stella found them seats at the edge of the waiting room. It was ironic that the hope and dreams of her relationship with Rory were to end, in this drab, nightmare of a place.

At one end of the waiting room were double swing doors, through which a constant stream of people went in and out, nurses rushing in looking stressed and exhausted, patients walking in and then emerging bandaged and cleaned up.

Beyond those doors somewhere was Rory. He could be dead for all she knew.

The receptionist had not been able to give them any information.

Stella found a crumpled tissue in the corner of her coat pocket and dabbed at her eyes, uselessly. Nothing seemed to check the tears that persisted in falling at an alarming rate down her cheeks.

If only she had been nicer to Rory, maybe he would not have been driven to try to kill himself. If only she had been the kind of person that did not make him jealous and upset all of the time they could have had a great relationship. If only...... the words churned around and around in her mind, while she wondered desperately what was happening to Rory.

Pictures, memories and visions from a lifetime of television films and documentaries flashed through Stella's mind, she saw Rory bloodied and battered, being resuscitated, the Doctors giving him up for dead. If only........... she began to weep again, silently, sobbing, her shoulders shaking. As if she could read her thoughts Amber took Stella's hand.

"This is not your fault," Amber said firmly. "You did not make him crash his car. Whatever blame he tried to put on you. Remember that." Stella nodded her head, silently. It was true, of course, but somehow it was hard to believe.

An old lady, dressed in a huge baggy coat that reached almost to the floor, clutching a battered carrier bag to her chest, her enormous, bulbous red nose almost touching the grubby plastic.

Her eyes darted constantly from side to side, her mouth worked, talking to herself as she shuffled around the casualty department, ever watchful for the Security men who would haul her outside into the darkness when things quietened down and they had nothing else to occupy themselves.

One of the lads got up and began to shout, bellowing loudly that he had been waiting for hours.

Two burley Security men, hurried from their office beside the triage ward, outfaced by their bulk, the bellowing youth sat down glaring at them sullenly. Hearing their names announced over the tannoy, Amber seized Stella's hand. "Come on, we have to go in."

"Here," said Amber steering Stella through a set of double doors into the emergency department.

"You have to wait your turn," a skinny, exhausted looking nurse snapped at them, waving her arm at them as if to shoo them back into the waiting room. "We're here to see someone who was in an accident. Rory McFadden"

"In there," the nurse waved her arm in the direction of a row of curtained cubicles. "The third one."

"I'll wait outside," Amber said, her courage deserting her as they walked towards the cubicle.

Stella walked on as if she had not heard her, shoving back the brightly patterned curtain and disappearing inside. Rory lay on a high bed, with the metal sides pulled up as if he were an ancient old man in danger of rolling out of bed. A long cut ran diagonally across his forehead, a pretty young nurse was putting the final stitch into the cut to pull it all together.

"Stella," Rory grinned weakly, his face looked grey, in the patches that were not covered in purple bruises and bright red scratches.

"Is this your wife?" asked the nurse, gently clipping the end of the thread.

"Just a friend," Stella emphasised the word friend.

"He is very lucky, just a few nasty cuts and concussion. We will have to keep him in for the night. What a lovely man he is. Imagine driving off the road just to avoid running a cat over," the young nurse looked delighted that she was going to be looking after Rory for longer.

Stella smiled shortly. Rory obviously had not confessed to the fact that he had just tried to kill himself. Stella had lived through absolute hell the last few hours expecting that Rory would be dead, or at least would die of his injuries and now she had found out that he had merely got a few cuts and a bang on the head.

Stella stood by the foot of Rory's bed, numbly looking at him. She despised him for what he had put her through.

"I'll leave you to it for a little while," the pretty nurse said, smiling sweetly at Rory, before she swished back the curtain and disappeared. Stella sat down heavily on the bed, watching Rory silently, so filled with anger that she could not trust herself to speak. How often was he going to pull this stunt? Was he going to torture her every time that he felt miserable with threats of killing himself?

"I thought that you were dead," she muttered, bleakly, not able to bring herself to look at him. Instead she concentrated on the bleeping of machinery and moans that came from the other cubicles.

"I wanted to be," Rory said, gently. "I wanted to hurt you for leaving me. Punish you........." his voice faded away as he struggled to find the words to explain how he felt. Stella shook her head miserably, numb with tiredness and frustration.

"I drove the car off the embankment," Rory gave a short laugh at his own stupidity, which ended in a yelp of pain as bruised muscles protested. "Someone saw me and pulled me out of the car. There was a concrete bollard a few feet away, if I had hit that I would have been killed. Trust me to mess it up."

Stella burst into tears, searching frantically for a tissue and failing. She pulled a handful of paper towels from the dispenser and wiped her face on the coarse scratchy fabric.

"How could you put me through that," she whispered, desperately. Rory slipped his hand into hers; Stella jerked her hand away violently.

"Don't you touch me," she snapped, viciously.

"Stella," Rory said, his voice thick with tears, "I'm so sorry. I was so stupid." Stella nodded her head, unable to speak.

"I realised as soon as I had driven off the motorway that I had made a mistake," Rory gave a hollow laugh. "The car was rolling over and over, smashing to bits around me, and all I could think was that I wanted to live."

Stella made a faint snort of amusement. "Bit late then," she whispered, quietly, stealing a glance at Rory.

"I'm sorry for everything that I've put you through, I've been an idiot about everything," Rory's hand found Stella's and this time she did not snatch hers away.

"I miss you," he began and then feeling her hand withdrawing hastily added, "but I am going to get over you. I promise I won't bother you again." Stella nodded. She felt so sad, so utterly exhausted, too numb to speak.

"Get off home now," Rory said, gently, "I'll be ok," Stella stood up to leave as the pretty young nurse came back into the cubicle and began to fuss around Rory, plumping up his pillow and straightening the blanket that covered his legs. Stella grinned suddenly, turning to face Rory. "Yes, it looks as if you will be ok now."

CHAPTER TWENTY NINE

Amber knew that it was a hopeless idea. But maybe, just maybe she might be lucky. Paul had said that he thought that Princess Pushy had a good chance of winning or being placed in the race.

Paul had been riding the elegant mare for a few months and was really getting on well with her. She seemed to really try her hardest when he was riding her.

Amber walked slowly up the line of bookmakers, looking at the blackboards on their stands that listed the names of the horses that were running in the race. Beside each horse, the bookmakers had chalked in the odds that they were giving the horse in the race. Because she had fallen in her first race the bookmakers had not given her much chance of success and so the odds on her were very long. Paul had told Amber, when they arrived at the races that she ought to put a bet on the mare.

Now he had gone off with Henry to change into the brightly coloured purple and white silks that he was to wear in the race.

Stella had drifted off in the direction of a stall that was selling handcrafted handbags – as if she did not already have enough, Amber had thought.

Amber had been drawn relentlessly towards the double row of brightly coloured umbrellas that sheltered the bookmakers as they took fistfuls of money off eager gamblers.

At first she had only meant to put on a small bet, one of the bookmakers had a notice above the board giving out the odds saying that the minimum bet that he would accept was two Euros. That was plenty of money to gamble, Amber had decided, fishing in her jeans pocket for her purse, if the mare won she would get........she worked out the amount quickly in her head. A nice little amount. She could probably afford to buy a new top or two.

She opened her purse, inside it was crammed with the money that she had earlier taken out of her wage packet from the supermarket. The bulk of it was to go to Stella for the rent on the apartment and for her to buy food and pay the bills. While the rest, a pitifully small amount, was to pay for her bus fares and to try to make some impact on the frighteningly large balances on her credit card statements.

It hardly seemed worth paying anything into any of them as the pitiful amount that she did pay off every month barely covered the interest that was being accrued. The credit card people must have had a great laugh at her expense when her payments went into them. 'Take off ten Euros and then add twenty,' seemed to be their mantra.

Amber pulled out the money, a slender roll of crisp notes. She closed her fist around the notes as if they were alive; her skin seemed to tingle with the touch of the money.

Paul had said that the mare stood a good chance of winning. It would be a shame to lose out on the chance to gain so much money if she did win.

Amber quickly worked out that if the mare won, she would have enough money to pay off all of her debts and still have some left over. In her mind she already had the left over spent on the pretty cream dress, dotted with the tiny pink flowers that adorned the mannequin that Amber could see from her place on the checkout at the supermarket.

Amber walked in a daze along the line of bookmakers, being jostled from side to side by the frenzied throng of gamblers, desperately looking for the best odds on the horses they wanted to bet on.

It would be sheer stupidity to gamble all of her wages. The mare could lose the race. There were so many other good horses in the race. Nothing was certain. She should just bet a few Euros and then if she lost it would not matter.

"Jockeys up," came the announcement over the tannoy, blaring loudly close to Amber.

The race was about to start. In the parade ring the jockeys were being thrown up onto their horses ready to go down to the start of the race.

Amber cringed, guiltily, she should have been back in the parade ring to wish Paul good luck, instead she was still with the bookmakers deciding what to do.

The announcement spurred the gamblers into a fresh panic, they swarmed everywhere, shoving money in the direction of the bookmakers, who snatched it eagerly from outstretched hands, shoving it into cavernous black leather bags and muttering the details to their assistants who jotted down the amounts on a huge ledger.

Amber joined one of the queues, being shoved forwards by the swell of people, thrusting towards the red faced bookmaker, sweating with the effort of having to take the money so quickly.

Suddenly Amber was at the front of the queue, her purse in her hand. The bookmaker looked at her, if a cartoonist had drawn him he would have given him the face of a pig, he had a huge round, red face, with large ears and a wide long nose like a snout.

"Yes, Darlin'" he bellowed, twitching with the urgency of getting her money before the race began.

"I want to put……." Amber's fingers closed on the roll of notes. She would just bet ten Euros, that was enough, "this on Princess Pushy," she thrust all of her money into his hand.

"Count that," the bookmaker, casually tossed all of her money to his assistant, who counted the notes, casually and then threw them into the depths of the leather bag. The bookmaker handed her a ticket.

"Two hundred on Holbrook," yelled the man behind her, shoving forwards to push Amber out of the way.

Amber looked yearningly at the bag, wishing that she was still clutching her money. It had seemed to jump out of her hand into the bookmakers as if it had a life of her own.

It was too late now though, she could not get it back, Amber tore back to the parade ring, dodging past people in her haste to get to Paul before the start of the race. The horses were just beginning to go out of the parade ring onto the course.

Amber ducked under the guard rail and hurtled across the turf.

Jimmy was leading Princess Pushy around the parade ring.

Paul, astride her on the impossibly small looking saddle looked decidedly ill. His face was a curious shade of grey-green and his lips were clamped tightly shut as if he thought that he would vomit if he opened them.

Amber skidded to a halt.

"Paul," Amber shrieked, waving to attract his attention. Paul looked, and managed a small, nervous smile. "Good luck."

He had been so full of himself in the lorry on the way to the races, sitting in the passenger seat, beside Henry, his feet propped up on the dashboard, reading the newspaper, laughing and joking with Amber and Stella who were squashed onto the narrow ledge behind the seats. Now he looked terrified.

"Don't worry," Henry said, coming to stand beside Amber. "He will be ok once he starts racing."

Amber nodded, slowly, she hoped so.

"I'm going to find Stella and head up to the stands to watch the race," Henry told Amber, his eyes already scanning the spectators looking for Stella.

The parade ring began to empty.

Amber bleakly followed the line of people out onto the stands. There circling below them, close to the stands, were the horses and riders, getting ready for the start of the race.

Amber craned her neck to see Paul, standing on tiptoe to look above the heads of the other spectators who all seemed to be either very tall, or wore ridiculously large hats, making it impossible for her to see anything.

Finally she managed to get a glimpse of the horses and their riders. They were all walking in a large circle, chatting to one another, their demeanour relaxed as they lolled casually in their saddles.

Then she spotted Paul, riding apart from the other jockeys, every line of his body oozing tension. And then the horses began to walk forwards for the start of the race, the starter dropped his flag and the race began.

Amber could hardly bear to watch. Her hand ached with the loss of her money. How she wished that it were still in her hand, ready to give to Stella, rather than being gambled on the strength of the outcome of a race. How could she have been so bloody stupid? Before the race began she knew that the money was lost, but still, at the back of her mind was the hope, the dim possibility that maybe, just maybe he could win and then she would go home with her pockets crammed with money.

It was sheer anguish watching the race, her emotions veered wildly from wild hope, when her heart thumped so hard that it was hard to breathe, as Princess Pushy shoved her way to the front of the runners, her long legs raking over the ground, shooting over the fences like an equine missile.

Then sinking into the agony of despair as the other runners swept past her at the final fence and surged on towards the finish line, leaving her to toil up the hill alone, trailing in last.

"Brilliant, she did great" gasped Henry. "She needed that run to give her the experience. She will probably get placed the next time."

Amber had not even been aware that he was nearby.

"They didn't fall," Stella grinned, shaking Amber's jacket sleeve with excitement. "He's safe, thank goodness."

"Come on, we had better go and find Paul," Henry dragged at Amber's sleeve and then darted off across the stand, hand in hand with Stella.

Amber watched them go, feeling sick. What had she done?

A whole week's wages gone, in a few moments. And she did not even have anything to show for it. What on earth was she going to say to Stella? Maybe she should say that she had been mugged and the money stolen? How could she have been so stupid?

If only things had been different, she would now have been celebrating and congratulating herself on how clever she was, instead of cursing her own stupidity.

Amber trailed after Henry and Stella, letting herself jostled by the spectators who were dashing back to the bookmakers to collect their winnings, clutching betting tickets aloft, their faces split with broad grins of delight.

Princess Pushy was being led around by Jimmy. Paul had gone to weigh in after the race and get changed. Henry patted the mare.

"She has it in her to be a champion," he beamed, hugging Stella to him. Amber glared resentfully at the mare, who stood with her head down, sides heaving, her enormous body was a network of veins that stood out beneath her sweat darkened coat.

Amber had lost all of her money because of Princess Pushy losing the race.

Paul jogged across the grass towards them, his hair, still wet from the shower was slicked to his head.

"She was brilliant," he grinned, slowing to a walk, his face, red from exertion glowed with delight. He grabbed Amber and swung her around. "Next time you will be able to win a fortune on her you'll see," Paul grinned, Amber swallowed hard to stop herself from crying. How could she explain to him that she had just lost what to her was a fortune?

"You have a good mare there, Henry," Derry Blake sauntered up to them. He shook hands with Henry and nodded curtly at Paul.

"You rode her well," Derry sounded surprised as if he had not thought that Paul would have been capable of riding her at all. "I'll pick up the horse that I bought off you in a day or two."

Amber could see the regret in Henry's eyes; he obviously had not wanted to sell The Entertainer.

As if he picked up on this Derry added maliciously, "I'm sure that he will improve no end when he comes to my yard."

Amber could see Henry struggling to find a reply; he was no match for Derry's razor sharp disdain.

His eyes roved casually over Amber, dismissing her of no consequence and then lighted on Stella.

"Stella," he said, silkily, brushing past Amber to seize Stella's hand and bring it to his lips. "How lovely to see you again," he reminded Amber of a snake, slithering gracefully, hypnotising its victim, ready to pounce.

"We had better load Princess Pushy on the lorry, we should be getting home," Henry said, there was a note of desperation in his voice as if he had been outfaced by a stronger rival and knew that he stood no chance.

"Perhaps I will see you at the Murtagh's party." Derry slowly released Stella's hand as if he were unwilling to let her go. Stella was speechless, as bemused by Derry's megawatt charm as a gauche child.

It was almost midnight when they finally got home after driving back to Henry's to put the mare in her stable and then driving home. Stella went out when they got back to the apartment to take Teddy out for a walk.

"See you in a little while," Stella said, pulling an unwilling Teddy out of the door, he had been cosy and warm curled up in his basket and did not want to go out into the cold night air.

The door closed and Amber collapsed onto the sofa in panic. How was she ever going to get out of this scrape? Why was she so stupid with money?

Stella had laid a line of newspaper around the kitchen in case Teddy had an accident. One section was stained dark where the dog had wet it. Bleakly Amber went to clean it up, she could not sit still, thinking of what a fool she had been. Scooping up the newspaper she shoved it into the bin and then paused. There, on the floor in front of her was her salvation.

Amber slowly crouched down as if she had found gold inlaid into the floor. On her hands and knees Amber began to read the advert that she had seen on the newspaper. Amber read the newspaper advert slowly, an enormous feeling of relief seeping slowly through her body, like sinking into a hot bath after being out in the cold. 'Consolidate all of your loans into one simple repayment. Borrow enough to pay off all those annoying loans and have cash back to treat yourself.'

Tomorrow she would go to the offices of the loan company and fill in the simple paperwork, just like the advert said.

After tomorrow she would have no more awful credit card bills, just a small repayment. She would have money again. It was the answer to all of her prayers.

CHAPTER THIRTY

Amber picked one of the chocolates out of the crisp tissue paper and put it gently between Paul's lips. "This is the life," she sighed contentedly, lying back so that her head rested on Paul's shoulder.

"Mmmmm," Paul agreed, his mouth full of chocolate, he swallowed quickly. "Wine, chocolate and the whole place to ourselves," he grinned, wickedly.

Amber put another chocolate into her mouth smacking her lips with pleasure as she chewed, savouring the gorgeous flavour of the expensive treats.

Life was very good at the moment. Paul was wonderful. And the job at the supermarket was far nicer than anything that Amber had ever done before. No one complained when she chatted to the customers and there were always the new lines of clothes being brought into the ladies section of the shop, just across the store from her seat at the checkout.

It was lovely to be able to afford to buy the chocolates so that she could spend an evening in with Paul, eating and drinking the lovely bottle of wine that she had found in the off-licence. It had been expensive, but now that she had got rid of all of her credit card debts things were a lot easier.

The girl in the loan agency had told Amber what her monthly repayments would be – for the next five years, they did seem rather expensive, but the end of the month was a long way away. And it had seemed worth spending the money on chocolates and wine.

After all it was not every night that she got to spend time alone with Paul.

He had the night off from work, now that he was racing again; he had cut his hours down at the restaurant. He was only working a few nights a week rather than every night. And it was not every night that Stella went out, leaving them with the place to themselves.

Stella emerged from her bedroom looking like a film star in a slinky gold dress that fell to her ankles, the soft fabric draping itself around her body like a second skin, clinging to her curves.

"Wow," breathed Paul, gasping as Amber elbowed him mock jealously in the ribs. "Behave!" Amber hissed.

"The Murtagh's party is supposed to be a really good do," Paul said, his voice tinged with jealousy, "I've never been asked, never good enough for that kind of crowd," he mused. "But of course now that you are mixing with the Henry Murphy." Stella gave a snort of derision.

"Yes turning up for parties in a bettered old jeep really gives a good impression," she mocked, grabbing her bag from the table. "I bet Derry Blake won't come in a battered old car," she added wistfully.

"Henry's worth two of him" snapped Paul irritably, heaving himself upright to glare at Stella.

"I'll walk you out," Amber said, getting to her feet and popping another enormous chocolate between Paul's teeth to shut him up before he could annoy Stella further. She followed Stella out of the door and down the stairs into the cold night air.

"You look lovely," Amber said, pausing in the doorway as Stella buttoned her coat over her dress.

Stella smiled wryly. "Henry probably won't even notice."

Amber shook her head, with a smile. "Of course he will notice, he never takes his eyes off you."

"Really?"

"You know he doesn't," Amber grinned. "Surely you can see that he is crazy about you."

Stella winced, "I don't want him to be crazy about me though," she sighed, "I think he is lovely, but I don't want to get involved with someone like him."

Stella was silent, leaning against the doorframe, looking out at the semi darkness.

"But you are involved," Amber said, gently. "Can't you see that?"

Stella kissed Amber softly on the cheek. "'Night,"

Amber leant against the doorframe and watched Stella get into her car.

"Don't hurt him," Amber whispered as the car pulled slowly out of its parking spot.

Paul stretched luxuriously as Amber sat gently down on the sofa and leant over him, kissing his mouth gently. He had been drifting off to sleep, lulled by the heady wine and the warm flat. He ran a leisurely hand around the back of her neck, drawing Amber closer to him.

"I hope that Stella is very, very late back," he muttered huskily, sliding his tongue in between Amber's lips.

"Very, very, late," agreed Amber, wriggling so that she was lying on the sofa, stretched out beside Paul, every inch of their bodies touching. She gasped as he slowly undid the buttons on her shirt and slid his hand inside, caressing her skin.

"Do you think that we might be more comfortable in my room?" Amber whispered, nibbling gently on the soft skin beneath Paul's ear.

"Definitely," he agreed, whimpering as Amber's fingers travelled slowly down his chest and came to rest tantalizingly at the waistband of his jeans.

"Come on then!" Paul shouted suddenly, tipping Amber onto the floor with one deft movement and darting towards the bedroom.

Teddy, thinking that this was a great game that he would love to join in, leapt from his basket and ran yapping across the floor. Paul shot into the bedroom with Amber hot on his heels dragging Teddy, clinging to her jeans with his tiny, needle sharp teeth after her.

"Sorry mate," Paul said, a moment later, depositing Teddy outside the bedroom door and closing it firmly in his crestfallen face. "You are not welcome in here."

"We should send Stella out more often," Paul said, throwing himself onto the bed and watching Amber with his hands propped behind his head. "You are some floozzie," he grinned, as she began to take off her shirt and jeans.

"I wonder if she is enjoying herself," mused Amber, taking off her socks and getting into bed.

"I bet she is," Paul replied as he pulled off his jeans. "The Murtagh's parties are pretty legendary, all the posh, rich crowd go. Stella will feel right at home."

"Hmmmm," Amber mused, gently stroking Paul's face, "I prefer a bit of rough."

A few moments later the silence of the apartment was broken by the door buzzer sounding. Teddy exploded into a frenzy of barking.

"Who the fuck is that?" groaned Paul, rolling irritably away from Amber.

"I'll get rid of them, whoever it is. Wait there," Amber wrenched back the bedclothes and hastily dressed again. "Hang on," she snapped, as the buzzer sounded again.

"Yes," Amber pressed the intercom.

"Amber, its Ruby," came back her sister's tinny sounding voice.

Paul appeared naked in the bedroom doorway. "Whoever it is – get rid of them," he growled.

"I can't," whimpered Amber miserably, screwing up her face in anguish. "It's my sister,.."

Paul ran one hand through his hair in a gesture of frustration.

"This had better be important," he growled, snatching his jeans off the bed and beginning to pull them on, whimpering softly all of the time, so that Amber giggled. Teddy sat watching him, his head on one side, wondering why he was making such a strange noise.

"You are too young to understand," Paul said, bending over to scratch Teddy's whiskery face.

Amber pulled open the door and stood watching for her sister appearing. "You had better come in," Amber said, hoping that she did not sound too resentful at being disturbed by her sister.

She hoped that this was not just a social call, it would have been awful to have missed out on a luxurious night of pleasure with Paul. But somehow she knew that it could not be. They had never been close, even when Amber lived at home.

"Sit down," Amber said, graciously, catching Paul's eye as he came back into the room, dressed once again. He pulled a sad clown's face at Amber, behind her sister's back, turning his lips down and hunching his shoulders and then rubbing his eyes as if her were crying. Amber shot him a warning look.

"This is Paul, my boyfriend," she told Ruby as Paul sat down with a barely audible sigh.

Ruby shot a tight smile in Paul's direction.

"How are things?" Amber asked, thinking how bizarre it was that she was now making polite conversation with her pain in the ass sister, when she wanted to be back where she had been a few minutes previously – back in bed with Paul.

"I shouldn't have come," Ruby's voice cracked as she spoke, clearly struggling to hold back the tears that were threatening to spill down her ashen white face.

Amber sank down onto the sofa; this was obviously going to take some time.

She forced the muscles at either side of her face to unclench, already she was filled with tension.

Ruby had never done anything for her other than be horrible, and now all of a sudden she wanted Amber. The flood bank of tears finally broke and Ruby began to sob pitifully into a white handkerchief.

Amber looked up helplessly at Paul. He shrugged, and mouthed, "what's the matter with her?"

Amber shrugged, pulling a face at him to indicate that she needed help.

"I think that I'll leave you two alone for a while," Paul grinned apologetically, grabbing his coat from the back of the chair where he had flung it so gaily just a short time ago, before Ruby had interrupted them.

"Paul!" Amber pleaded, furious at him for deserting her, but with an apologetic wave of his hand and a kiss blown in her direction he was gone. The door slammed and above Ruby's sobbing noises Amber could hear his footsteps pounding down the stairs.

After what seemed like ages Ruby blew her nose and looked at Amber. "I'm sorry, I've ruined your evening," she sniffed.

"Yes you bloody have," Amber longed to say, resentful of the intrusion and seething that of all the times in her life that Ruby had to need her, that she had picked this one. Amber longed to tell her sister about all of the times that Ruby had hurt her, all of the times that she had needed someone to talk to and Ruby had never been there for her.

But instead she said, "it's ok."

"I couldn't go to anyone else," Ruby rummaged in her handbag and pulled out a mirror and gazed at her ravaged reflection with a small gasp of misery. She dabbed furiously at the smudged mascara that stained the skin beneath her eyes. "I don't want anyone else to know," Ruby continued sullenly.

Amber swallowed hard, moistening lips that were suddenly dry, with her tongue. Ruby must have found out about their father seeing Kate. Amber would have to confess to knowing all about the affair. Ruby would be furious that her perfect world had been shown for the sham that it was.

"It's just too embarrassing," Ruby continued.

"Well," Amber began, trying to frame the words to explain to her sister that Amber was happy for their father. Happy that he had found love with someone, even if it was not their mother, "I suppose it is, but….."

"What's too embarrassing," spat Ruby. "You don't even know what I'm talking about."

"Erm…..No," Amber grabbed Teddy who was trying to climb up onto the sofa beside her, glad of the distraction. Ruby knew nothing about the affair. Amber had nearly blown it. "So what is the problem?"

Ruby laid her chin on her chest, studying her entwined hands as if she had never seen them before. "I didn't want anyone else to know that I have a problem," Ruby said quietly. "What would everyone think?"

Amber looked at her, wide eyed. Ruby was from a completely different planet.

When Amber had a problem the whole world knew about it, she told everyone from the person she was serving at the supermarket, to the person that she sat next to on the bus. Ruby was so busy striving to create her perfect world that she hated the thought of anyone realising that beneath the façade of success that anything could be wrong.

"But I had to tell someone. So it was either you or the Samaritans,"

Amber shook her head slowly, longing to tell Ruby to pick the Samaritans the next time she had a problem and leave Amber alone. "So what is the problem?" she asked, feeling her reserves of patience rapidly running out.

"It's Roderick," sniffed Ruby, "I think that he is seeing someone else."

"What?" Amber spat, incredulously.

"I think that Roderick is seeing someone else," Ruby repeated.

"But what on earth makes you think that?" Amber frowned.

Ruby sighed, bitterly, her mouth worked as she tried to find the words that she was looking for. Finally she spoke, "I found a text message on his telephone."

Amber nodded slowly; somehow she could not picture Ruby snooping around her fiancées possessions.

"He was in the shower and the phone bleeped to say that there was a message," Ruby began, "I don't know why I looked at it. But I read the message and it was from this woman, Olympia."

"But surely," Amber crossed the room and sat beside her sister. "Couldn't it have been from someone that he worked with?"

"Saying 'see you at Murray's. Can't wait' that could not have been anything work related, could it?"

Amber shrugged bleakly, "maybe it was a mistake, someone sending a text to someone else. Just a wrong number."

Ruby looked imploringly at Amber, "I hoped it was that," she sniffed, tears spilling down her cheeks again. "But there was an entry in his diary yesterday. 'Lunch at Murrays'."

Amber could hear her own breath, loud as it rushed past her lips. She knew what she was going to hear and yet could not bear to hear Ruby speak.

"So I went to Murrays, peeped into the restaurant. He didn't see me. Roderick was there with this woman."

"His sister? Work mate?" Amber desperately sought an answer that would take away the awfulness of what Ruby was saying. There had to be a reasonable explanation. Roderick could not be seeing someone else. Ruby was marrying him in a few weeks' time.

"With his tongue down her throat?" Ruby spat vehemently.

Ruby jumped up from the sofa as if it had suddenly become burning hot. She began to pace around the room, filled with the boundless energy that comes with naked fury.

"The bastard," Ruby spat, pacing from wall to wall, covering the space in a few paces.

"What are you going to do?" Amber asked, watching her sister pace.

However much she disliked Ruby Amber would never have wished anything like this on her. Not the pain of rejection, especially just before her wedding.

All of the wedding plans would have to be cancelled.

Amber thought of all of the money that had been spent on the perfect dress, the gorgeous bridesmaid dresses, that Amber had picked and would not be allowed to wear, the glamorous reception booked. The list was endless.

Beneath the mantle of sympathy a tiny sliver of nastiness fought itself to the surface. Ruby had finally got her comeuppance, for once it was Ruby's world that was about to come crashing down around her smug shoulders. Ruby's world was not so perfect now.

"What are you going to do?" Amber asked, imagining a new horrific landscape that they would have to pass through. Cancelling the wedding, the embarrassment of returning the dress, all of Ruby's smug friends knowing that she had fallen in love with a love rat.

"Do?" Ruby stopped pacing and looked at Amber.

"Well surely if he is seeing someone else you can't go through with the wedding." Amber spoke as if Ruby were a small child in the throes of a tantrum.

Ruby leant over the back of the sofa and glared at Amber, "I only told you because I needed to get this off my chest," Ruby said, coldly. "If Roderick wants other women that's his business. I'll get over it. I have to marry Roderick. I want everything that he can give me. I'm not going to do anything."

CHAPTER THIRTY ONE

Stella stole a look at Henry. He looked gorgeous in his tuxedo, tall, elegant and impossibly handsome.

As if he sensed her eyes upon him Henry glanced at Stella, who looked away shyly.

"I'm really glad that you agreed to come with me," Henry said.

He almost had to shout above the rattling and squeaking that the Jeep was making. "This should be a great party," he said, turning the Jeep in between a tall set of gates. Stella caught a glimpse of the outline of rearing lions and tall proud stags set into the ornate ironwork.

"I hope that there will be plenty of people here that I can talk to about bringing their horses to me to train," Henry mused, joining the tail end of a long queue of cars and Jeeps that were jammed along the wide, straight, tree lined avenue that led up to a magnificent four square house set on a rise above them. "I could do with a bit of extra business since.........."

Henry's voice trailed off, the unspoken truth that it was because of Stella and Rory that he had lost the best part of his business, hung momentarily in the air between them.

Stella suppressed a sigh, losing Rory's horses had made things very difficult for Henry, a huge part of his income had vanished. Losing a few horses would not have mattered to a big trainer. Someone like Derry Blake.

Stella found her thoughts straying to Derry. He fascinated her. If only Henry could be like him. Wealthy and powerful, just the kind of man that she wanted. Henry was lovely, kind, very handsome, but so, so terribly poor. That was obvious in every part of his life, his tatty Jeep, his tumbledown cottage, his shabby clothes.

But Stella knew that she was falling in love with him. Had fallen in love with him, hopelessly, but every fibre of her intellect rebelled against that love. She had to have someone wealthy. Had too. There was no way that she was ever going to end up like her mother, scratching a living, always having to worry about where the next penny was coming from, making do with second best. But she was not going to end up with Henry. No way. Not under any circumstances. But she could go out with him – without things having to get serious. That was alright. But she must never let Henry know how she felt about him. The relationship had to be light, friendly, just loving friends.

The long line of vehicles finally crawled closer to the mansion.

A man, wearing a florescent jacket and waving a powerful torch frenziedly in the air was directing the cars into a field, through a muddy gateway in the post and rail fencing.

"We'll go a bit closer, I think," Henry mused, winding down his window as they neared the florescent jacketed man.

"Everyone has to go into the field," he snapped, jerking his torch in the direction of the gateway. "Oh, sorry, didn't realise that it was you, Henry, you go on up to the house, park in the courtyard."

Henry grinned. "Cheers, Fintan." He gave the man a thumbs up signal. "How's Geraldine?" he asked, ignoring the angry hoot of a car horn behind the Jeep.

"She's a lot better now, thank you for remembering," the man grinned, moving quickly away to direct the car behind them into the field.

Winding up his window Henry drove on towards the house.

"We will go around the back of the house, into the old courtyard," Henry said, as they reached a fork in the driveway. "That way goes up to the house," Henry told Stella, pointing to a gracefully curving drive, lit by flickering flares, that wound around a velvety smooth expanse of grass, broken only by tall, ornate yew trees, each trimmed into a precise rectangular shape. "This drive would have once been used for carriages," he explained, steering the Jeep along a driveway that curved away from the house, through parkland dotted with ancient trees before it led beneath a huge archway into a vast cobbled courtyard.

"These would have been staff houses at one time," Henry jerked his head in the direction of the cottages that lined the edge of the courtyard. "Times have changed now," he added with a wry laugh. "Now the rich folk have to take every penny that they can out of these big old money pits they call houses. The Murtagh's rent these out as holiday cottages."

He parked the Jeep beside an ornate fountain that tricked water over a woodland nymph carved in stone and into a huge circular pond. "Very upmarket holiday cottages, though," Henry mocked lightly, glancing at the large chandelier that they could see hanging in a room of one of the cottages.

"Come on, we'll go in the back way," Henry shot around and opened the door of the Jeep for Stella to get out. The door gave its now familiar screech of metal against metal, as he wrenched it open and then banged it shut, forcefully.

Henry led the way to a door, half hidden in the dark shadow cast by the towering, square house. He shoved his shoulder against the door, barging it open. It gave way, unwillingly, obviously it had not been used very recently.

"Hang on," Henry mumbled.

Stella stepped into the darkness of a cold, damp room. She could hear Henry fumbling around the walls. "Light has to be here somewhere," he muttered. Stella blinked as Henry found the switch, flooding the room with light. "This was once the servant's quarters," Henry told Stella, seeing her look of wonderment at the shabby, damp rooms. "I don't think that the Murtagh's ever come down here," he shook his head, sighing at the abandoned rooms, with their peeling paint and piles of unidentifiable cardboard boxes and rubbish. "I used to spend hours down here when I was a child," he sighed at the memory.

"Nice," Stella said, politely.

Henry grinned, taking Stella's arm.

"It was all in use then, there were servants still here when I was a kid. These were old kitchens and laundries," he said, dreamily, remembering his past. "I used to come and play with the cook's children when I was little."

They walked along echoing corridors towards the sound of the party that filtered down from above them. Stella musing over everything that Henry had told her. His parents had probably worked here, that was why he knew the place so well. Maybe his mother had been one of the maids.

Henry led the way up a narrow wooden flight of steps, shoved open a door and helped Stella out into the midst of a crowded party in the most luxurious house that she had ever seen.

Stella fought to close her mouth that had gaped open in amazement.

"Hello Henry!" someone yelled, as Henry shoved the door closed behind them. Stella felt as if she were like Alice in Wonderland as a uniformed man carrying a silver tray laden with tall, slender cut glass champagne flutes, bore down on them.

"Thanks," Henry seized two of the glasses and handed one to Stella. "Cheers," he grinned, clinking her glass against his.

Stella took a long swig of the champagne, gasping as the ice cold bubbles hit the back of her throat, tingling as they hit the roof of her mouth.

"This is gorgeous," Stella breathed, overawed by the sheer opulence of the house. They were standing in a huge domed hall; acres of creamy marble floor seemed to stretch forever at either side of them. A dozen double doors led off the hall, all standing open to reveal luxurious rooms, filled with heavy wooden furniture and glittering crystal chandeliers.

The whole downstairs of the mansion was filled with what seemed to be the most elegant, beautiful people that Stella had ever seen. They moved with a self-assurance and confidence born of wealth and power, as if they had been gilded at birth with an aura that set them apart from everyone else.

"Here's the Murtagh's," Henry seized Stella's hand and began to lead her across the marble floor towards a middle aged couple. "Cecilia and Gerald," Henry introduced them to Stella.

"Oh, Henry," giggled Cecilia, "Cess and Gerry, please." She had a rich gravelly voice that sounded as if she had a dozen plums in her mouth.

Stella tore her eyes away from Cess, aware suddenly that she was staring. Cess was magnificent, she was tall and plump, but the gorgeous red silk dress that she wore only seemed to highlight her voluptuous figure, skimming over her waist and plunging to reveal the creamy skin of her glorious breasts. Dressed in a baggy pair of jogging bottoms wandering around a supermarket she would have looked common and vulgar, but dressed in a way that brought out the best points of her body. She was an imposing sight.

Beside her Gerry cut a dashing figure. He was so tall that he seemed to hunch over as if to bring himself back to the level of his companions. He was as thin as Cess was fat. Dressed in ordinary clothes, sitting on a bus he would have cut a nondescript figure.

It was amazing, thought Stella, taking a long swig of her champagne as Cess and Gerry glided away to meet more of their guests. How wealth transformed someone's image, from the commonplace to the extraordinary.

Together Henry and Stella wandered around the beautiful rooms, filled with beautiful people. In one room an enormous mahogany dining table creaked with the weight of food that it carried, huge turkeys, dressed salmon, the biggest side of beef that Stella had ever seen, with vast bowls of lush salads and a steaming dish of tiny potatoes, swimming in butter. Music boomed from a darkened room, from which sweating couples emerged to clasp glasses of champagne off the waiters, which they gulped down like lemonade.

"Maybe you will have a dance with me later?" Henry suggested, shyly, looking warily towards the flashing lights that could be seen inside the dark room.

Stella's favourite room was an enormous lounge, three huge squashy sofas were arranged in a rectangle around a cavernous fireplace, all around the edge of the room were dark wooden book shelves, crammed with books of every description.

"Shall we go and get something to eat?" suggested Henry, "I don't think I ate since this morning," he frowned, trying to remember when he had last eaten.

"No, you go," Stella said, she felt too excited to eat, "I'll just wander around on my own until you come back," she smiled at Henry, who lingered, uncertainly for a moment, torn between his hunger and his desire to stay with Stella.

"Ok, then," he said, the hunger winning. "Are you sure that you will be ok?"

"Yes, fine. You go on." She virtually had to push Henry in the direction of the food.

It felt strange, suddenly, not to have Henry beside her. Stella felt curiously naked, as if she had forgotten her handbag, or to put on her shoes.

She wandered off down a long hall, exploring the house, squeezing past groups of people who all seemed to be chatting animatedly about horses or racing. The hall was lined with enormous portraits, originals in oil, in gorgeous ornate frames. One, a picture of a blonde man, astride a huge grey hunter looked oddly familiar. Stella paused to look at the picture, fascinated by how familiar the man looked; maybe he was the ancestor of someone famous, or something.

"You're with Henry Murphy, aren't you?" a willowy blonde came to stand beside Stella, gazing up at the picture.

"That's right," Stella nodded, warily, not sure of who the blonde woman was.

"Lucky you," she breathed, looking Stella unashamedly up and down. "He has never even given me a second glance," she sighed, turning to gaze up at the picture.

"Do you think that could be one of Henry's relatives?" the blonde asked, wiping an imaginary bit of dust from the frame and examining the tip of her finger.

"Maybe," Stella said, lightly, was the woman implying that Henry's relatives had come from here? Maybe she meant that they were servants who had worked here, maybe she meant that Henry's ancestors had been the illegitimate results of liaisons between the servant girls and their aristocratic masters. Maybe that was why the woman mentioned a likeness.

"Stella," a familiar smooth voice said, beside Stella, she turned and smiled up into the handsome face of Derry Blake. "How careless of Henry to leave you alone," he said, silkily, resting one arm on the wall above her, trapping Stella.

"He's just gone to get something to eat," Stella replied, seeing, out of the corner of her eye, the blonde woman slipping away.

"Come on I'll get you a drink, someone as gorgeous as you should not be left alone," Derry cupped his hand around the small of her back and guided Stella across the room. "Bottoms up," Derry handed her a glass of champagne.

Stella sipped the champagne and watched Derry over the top of her glass. There was something dangerous about him, dangerous and intriguing. Derry leant forward and whispered, huskily, "I would love to fuck you," Stella felt her mouth drop open with the sheer effrontery of the man. Then as she opened her mouth to frame a reply Henry slipped his arm gently around her waist and drew her possessively to him.

"Thanks for looking after Stella," he smiled, tightly at Derry.

"My pleasure," Derry smiled back, his eyes narrow with dislike at Henry having interrupted him. "Any time," his final words were directed straight at Stella.

The night wore on; Henry finally claimed his dance with Stella as the music slowed from a booming disco beat to gentle romantic songs. They swayed slowly around the dance floor.

Henry was lovely to dance with, he held her tenderly, his cheek resting gently against Stella's hair. Stella leant against his body, letting the music take them around the floor. She felt so safe, so protected by him. So comfortable.

And then all too soon they were outside, clattering down stone steps onto a gravel forecourt.

Dawn was just breaking bright purple and pink streaks spanned across the horizon, mingling with the remnants of the darkness and the pale grey sky of morning.

"Henry, your tie," laughed Cess, hurrying out of the front door with Henry's bow tie draped in her hand. Henry gave a sigh of disgust at himself for being forgetful. "Excuse me," he released his grip on Stella's hand and ran lightly back up the steps. Stella stood and watched him, smiling faintly, luxuriating in the warm feeling of being with him.

"May I give you this," Derry was at her elbow, he slipped a business card, embossed in black and gold lettering on heavy, expensive feeling card, into her hand, "I meant what I said. Call me."

CHAPTER THIRTY TWO

Stella watched Henry running lightly down the stone steps towards her, his reclaimed bow tie clutched in his hand. He looked gentle and kind, and very happy, shaking his head in mock anger at himself.

Behind him, standing at the top of the steps, stood Derry, staring intensely at Stella, his face impassive, amusement glittering in his eyes. "Good job Cess found my tie," Henry laughed, seizing Stella by the hand, "I'd have been looking for it all over the house. This way," Henry led the way along a path that ran around the edge of the house, towards the courtyard where they had left the Jeep. "I need a good woman to look after me," Henry blurted suddenly, not looking in Stella's direction.

Stella glanced quickly at him. Had she heard him right?

"And I know just the one for the job," he put his arm around her shoulder and drew her towards him. Stella leant against him, briefly, soaking up the strength from his body, before she pulled gently away. If he meant her – he was in for a big shock. She enjoyed his company, he was wonderful, gorgeous, but she had no intention of making him her life partner. It was not possible, she had to find someone who could protect her from the poverty that she was so afraid of.

The field where everyone had parked their cars was empty now, save for a lone Range Rover, which was left beside the gateway.

"I really enjoyed last night," Henry said, pulling out of the driveway onto the main road.

"So did I," Stella agreed, truthfully. She had indeed had a wonderful time.

Stella laid her head against Henry's shoulder and let herself be lulled into a doze by the jolting and rattling of the Jeep.

This whole situation was crazy, she was falling in love with someone that she could never be secure with.

Tomorrow she would have to pull herself together. Be firm with herself and never see Henry again. It was not fair, on him, or her.

She woke as the Jeep jolted down the drive to Henry's cottage. "Hungry?" Henry asked, as Stella sat up, rubbing her eyes, sleepily.

"Very," she grinned, all of that dancing had made her starving.

The driveway down to Thornhill Cottage was gorgeous, the early morning light shone on the branches of the trees and the grass as if it were all freshly painted especially for them. At either side of the drive, cowslips and honeysuckle danced in the faint breeze, their delicate heads almost hidden by the lush growth of grass.

From a distance even the cottage and yard looked pretty, the dawn light shimmering on the silvery grey of the rooftops and setting the ancient stonework alight into a thousand different colours.

The yard was silent, as Henry drove in and turned off the engine.

Henry's old black Labrador, George padded stiffly out of one of the hay sheds awoken by the noise of the Jeep. He stood in the centre of the yard, and gave a single bark of welcome, his whole body moving as he wagged his tail in delight at having his master home.

"Morning George," Henry crouched down to rub the old dog's head and pat his portly body.

For a long moment Henry looked longingly towards the stables, where the horses looked eagerly over their stable doors, expecting their breakfasts.

One banged hopefully on the door with a tiny, elegant hoof, demanding food.

Stella could see Henry itching to go and check the horses, to make sure everything was ok with them all after he had been away for so long.

But then, he turned abruptly away, "I'll get you some coffee," he said, giving a final, lingering look around the stable yard before walking decisively towards the house. "The grooms will be here in a little while." Henry said, talking as if to reassure himself that his precious charges would not be deserted for much longer.

Stella's car was still parked beside the cottage, where she had left it the night before. "I'll get my bag and get changed," Stella told Henry, reaching inside her tiny evening bag for her car keys.

"Oww, I like you in that dress," Henry said, stroking her waist, regretfully. "Mind you," he smiled, suddenly, "I like you in anything."

"Thanks," Stella smiled faintly, embarrassed by his words.

This was all moving too fast for her, in a direction that she did not want it to. Stella grabbed her bag off the back seat of her car. She should leave as soon as she could, being with Henry was not doing either of them any good.

He was obviously falling in love with her, and she was letting him – and she was enjoying the feeling.

She could not let herself love Henry. It would never work. Stella shook her head to clear the sudden vision of the cottage with hanging baskets swinging from beside the battered wooden door, except that now it was brightly painted and herself, humming to herself as she hung out a line of gleaming white washing. Then, as in the movies, when the happy music screeches to a halt, she stopped the vision. Good heaven's what was she thinking of? She was going to have a smart, new town house, with a brand new car sitting on the drive, a good looking husband in a suit, and tonnes of money in the bank, swanky holidays every year. That was what she wanted.

"I'll put on some coffee," Henry said as Stella headed upstairs to put on her jeans. "Need any help?" Henry called up the stairs.

"No thanks," Stella yelled back, hastily, wrinkling her nose at the delicious smell of frying bacon rashers that was drifting up the stairs towards her.

A moment later she hurried back downstairs, before Henry decided to come up to give her a hand to change.

"Yes," Henry nodded, as Stella walked into the kitchen. "You look just as gorgeous in jeans." He darted quickly back to the toaster, where the toast he had been making had got stuck. Thick black smoke poured from the toaster making Stella cough. She darted forwards, pulling the toast out, giggling at his hopelessness.

"Come here," she said, mock bossily, taking the frying pan out of his hand and pushing him gently in the direction of the table. "You set the table; I'll do the girly stuff."

"How on earth do you manage, really?" she smiled, happily, poking at the bacon rashers with the metal spatula.

"I like burnt food," Henry mocked, pretending to be hurt.

He was very close to her suddenly. "Well actually George does," he said, softly.

Stella was intensely aware of his closeness, it was as if the heat from his body were radiating towards her.

Her eyes were level with his mouth; she concentrated hard on watching his lips moving over his even, very white teeth. His breath smelt of mint, as if he had cleaned his teeth – in anticipation of kissing her.

As if he read her thoughts Henry gently lowered his head, for a long moment their lips were inches apart, the anticipation tingling in the very air between them.

And then, infinitely slowly and tenderly, Henry lowered his lips onto Stella's.

"I should......erm.......the bacon," Stella said a moment later, turning slowly away. Her body felt as if it were limp, all the tension gone from it.

"Yes," Henry answered dreamily, his arm still lingering on her waist. "Right," he seemed to be forcing himself to concentrate, surfacing back to reality as if he had been under water.

"Here," Stella forked bacon and eggs and the freshly made toast onto two plates.

After they had eaten Stella cleared away the plates, Henry shot out into the yard, unable to keep himself away from checking out the horses any longer. "I'm sure that Jimmy and Katy will be able to manage without you for a while longer," Stella smiled, watching him go.

Henry shrugged, self-effacingly, "I know," he shook his head, wryly at his own inability to trust anyone but himself. "It's just that they are all I have."

Stella watched him go, shaking her head at her own insanity, falling in love with someone whose life was as precarious as Henry's. This had to stop. She could not keep falling deeper and deeper in love with Henry.

A short while later Henry returned, Stella had washed up and tidied the kitchen. "Right then," Henry said, sternly, "I have delegated. Jimmy and Kathy are in charge for the morning." Stella smiled, raising her eyebrows and looking at Henry quizzically. "Let's go wild, head off for a walk, and just enjoy the sunshine." He seemed amazed that he had managed to tear himself away from his responsibilities, even for a few hours.

"Come on then," Stella helped herself to a coat from the pile that hung in the hall. "Right." Henry grabbed another coat and followed her outside.

Even George looked surprised to see Henry heading out of the yard without the horses. After a moment, he bounded after them, delighted to be going for a walk. It was gorgeous to be outside in the fresh air, the coolness of the early morning still lingered, but with the promise of a warm day later, when the sun rose fully.

Dew still dampened the grass, clinging to their shoes and leaving a trail of footprints across the fields.

They walked silently, savouring the silence, while George padded stiffly behind them, his thick black tail waving in delight.

Behind them some of the horses were coming out onto the gallops, Henry paused, turning to look, unable to not watch his prized horses working, and then after a moment he tore himself away.

"Madly Deeply looks like he is going well, should be ready for Clonmel," he muttered, ducking under the post and rail fence that bordered his land and holding out his hand to steady Stella as she followed him.

They followed a path that wound through the woodland, winding steadily uphill, through the ancient oak and sycamore trees. It was warm inside the woodland, no breeze stirred the leaves.

Henry stripped off his coat and flung it over his shoulder.

"This is wonderful," Stella took in a deep breath of the earthy woodland scent as they padded along, their footfalls muted by the peaty earth.

"There's a fairy fort up here," Henry said, leading the way as the path forked, turning sharply up the hill.

He grabbed Stella's hand, pulling her up the steep incline, winding through the ancient, thick trunks of the trees, into the shadowy dim light of the canopy made by the leaves.

At the top of the hill the trees thinned out into a grassy field and there on a small incline was a circle of trees around a circular mound of rocky earth.

They reached the fairy fort and leant against one of the silvery trunks of the sycamore trees, taking deep breaths of air into lungs that protested with the effort of the climb.

"Oh, there's my house," Stella said, looking at the scenery once she had got her breath.

"Your house?" smiled Henry, gazing in the direction of the mansion that Stella so often admired when she was travelling to Henry's cottage.

"I would love to live somewhere like that," Stella mused. Henry shook his head, snorting faintly with amusement, "I think that maybe you will. One day."

Stella turned to face him.

"If I win the lottery maybe," she smiled, wryly.

"You should have a house like that," Henry said, cupping his hand gently around the back of her neck and drawing her gently towards him. Stella let herself step into his arms.

"I want you so much," Henry breathed softly, cupping her chin in his hand and tilting her face up to meet his.

The soft green canopy of the leaves of the tree made an almost mystical shelter from the outside world.

Gently Henry unbuttoned Stella's shirt, sliding his cool hands around her waist, stroking her smooth skin, as if he could not quite believe that she was real.

"Take off your jeans," he murmured, his long fingers already fumbling with the button.

Stella felt intoxicated by the heat and pure unadulterated lust for him.

She slid quickly out of her jeans, wanting to be entwined against his skin, revelling in the feel of his lips against hers, in the pure pleasure of longing for another body. Henry cupped her buttocks, naked in her tiny lace thong and drew her to him once again. She could feel his cock, pressing urgently against her belly. Then reluctantly pulling away from her, Henry slipped out of his jeans, grinning unabashed by his nakedness.

"Sit down," he whispered hoarsely, pulling apart from Stella and helping her to sit beside him, handling her as gently as if she were made of fine cut glass. Slowly they unfolded their limbs until they lay side by side, cushioned by the warm grass that made a deep comfortable bed for them.

"Stella, Stella," Henry whispered, gently, pulling her towards him so that they lay, every inch of their bodies touching. "Jesus. You are so lovely," he murmured.

Stella ran her hands over his skin, feeling the firm swell of his muscles beneath his skin, letting her hands play across the smooth plane of his back and then onto the firm athletic muscles of his belly, sliding relentlessly downwards.

The sunlight played on her face as Henry slowly rolled Stella backwards, the grass prickled momentarily and then all external sensation was lost as their bodies became one, entwined, hungry for each other. Their hands grasped each other, fingers entwined, lips locked onto one another until they were breathing the same air, the sweat from their bodies mingling, dripping onto the crushed grass.

And then the telephone rang.

For a long moment the shrill noise of the telephone did not penetrate their consciousness as they lay, lost in each other.

It was Stella who heard the telephone first, recognising its shrill note.

She lifted her head, listening.

"Oh, sorry," Stella scowled, "I have to answer that, it might be my Mum."

Henry rolled away, lying with his hands behind his head, gazing up at the sunlight filtering through the leafy canopy.

"Yes," Stella snapped, irritably switching on the telephone, lying on her belly to speak into the phone.

"Stella, it's your Mum. Please can you come home. They have just taken your Dad into hospital……"

"Ok, I'm on my way," Stella snapped off the telephone, and shoved it back into her jeans pocket, the earth felt suddenly very hard beneath her body, the grass prickly. "Henry," Stella said, quickly, rolling to face Henry, who lay facing her, his head propped on one elbow.

"I know," he said, before she spoke. "You have to go home." Stella nodded, already reaching for her knickers. She felt suddenly embarrassed about her nakedness, wanting to get back into her jeans and shirt as quickly as she could.

Henry watched as she dressed, as if he wanted to savour every moment of seeing her body.

"Come on, please," Stella, snapped.

He did not seem to appreciate the urgency she felt.

She had to get away, get to her car, drive to Mayo. Now.

Half an hour later she was hurtling away from Henry's cottage, belting her little car up his drive as fast as it could go. The dread of the hours yet to come mingled uncomfortably with the sense of relief that she now felt. Her mother's telephone call had just saved her from making the biggest mistake of her life.

CHAPTER THIRTY THREE

Stella found that she was trembling all over; she drove like the wind, wanting to put as much distance as she could between herself and Henry.

How could she have been so stupid as to let herself get carried away like that? She had wanted him so desperately.

Stella shook her head, wiping a sweat dampened hand across her forehead, reliving every gorgeous, terrible moment of her encounter with Henry. What would they have been doing now, if it were not for that fateful telephone call from her mother?

They would probably have been lying in each other's arms, like a pair of lovebirds, billing and cooing at each other. What path would her life have travelled along then? She would have doubtless become Henry's official girlfriend. And then what………?

The love making with him had the promise of being delicious, something that would have been hard to walk away from once she had been with him. Thank goodness that had not happened. She had been given a second chance to get a grip on her emotions. She could not let herself get carried away. Must not.

Falling in love with Henry was just not an option.

She pictured her mother, a shapeless, careworn figure, dressed in shapeless awful clothes, a skirt, so old that the hem drooped, and an ancient jumper, threadbare at the elbows. heaving bags of turf in from the shed, carting water up from the well, her face haggard with the exhaustion of caring for her husband and running the house with no money, no prospect of a better future.

That was where being in love with a poor man got you.

And that was not for Stella. Ever.

Stella pulled to the side of the road. There was no point in going back to the apartment, she had everything that she needed, her toilet bag, makeup, she could borrow spare clothes from her sister. Heavens above, what was she thinking of? It was doubtful that anything of her sister's would even fit her, even if she could bring herself to wear the dreadful junk that her sister clothed herself in. The best option was to buy something in Westport, that at least would save her the time of having to go into the city. Then she telephoned the apartment to make sure that Amber would look after Teddy for a few days.

Amber was obviously making the most of having the apartment to herself, she sounded drowsy as she answered the telephone. "Heylo," Stella could hear Paul in the background, saying something about the ice cream melting and bedclothes.

"It's Stella," there was a scuffling noise as if Amber was thumping Paul to make him behave.

Stella could imagine the two of them lying in bed doing just what she had been about to do.

Except that she had been about to do it under a tree, out in the open.

She prickled with an unexplainable anger, Amber just drifted through her life without a care in the world. Messing around with a no hope job in a supermarket, with a waiter for a boyfriend. Amber was going to end up nowhere in life if she did not buck up her ideas, have a bit of ambition, ditch the waiter and get herself a man with a future ahead of him.

"Listen," Stella said, huffily, "my Mum rang. I need to go home. Will you look after Teddy for a few days?"

"No problem!" Stella could hear the barely disguised delight in Amber's voice at having the apartment to herself for a few more days.

The telephone call made Stella started the car and headed west. A few more miles further down the road the telephone rang. She pulled over to the side to answer it.

"Stella?" it was Henry, she could hear the sound of horse's hooves clattering along tarmac in the background. "I just telephoned to see how you are?"

Stella felt a jolt of pleasure at hearing his voice, he was so kind and thoughtful, concerned for her well-being.

"I'm ok," she replied, knowing that she was anything but. If only he knew what just the very sound of his voice did to her and how hard it was going to be to tell him that she could not see him again.

"I enjoyed last night," Henry continued, "and this morning!"

"Henry, I have to go," she ignored his quip about their morning stroll and what had happened between them.

Stella wanted to be alone with her thoughts, just talking to him distracted her. "Listen, best of luck with things at home."

"Ok, look I need to go," Stella severed the connection.

It was the middle of the afternoon before she headed into the village.

It was only a few weeks since she had been here, but already everything looked different; the village looked brighter in its summer mantle.

The village shop was festooned with the buckets and spades and rubber balls that would be brought by the holiday makers that descended on the village in the summer months.

Even the dull looking houses looked more cheerful, the bright sunlight glittering on their paintwork.

The village café, which only opened during the summer months, its owner headed off to a villa in Spain, that an aunt had left her, during the winter, returning during the summer to lay out gleaming plastic tables and chairs onto the pavement for the holiday makers to enjoy burgers and cokes out in the sunshine.

Even the whitewashed cottage looked bright and cheerful in spite of the tragedy that had taken over the lives of everyone who lived there.

Stella parked her car out on the grass outside the cottage and dragged her small overnight bag out of the back seat.

Patrick came out to greet Stella. "Mum is at the hospital with Dad," he said, quietly, his face was pinched with tiredness.

Stella was silent, unsure of what to how to frame the questions that swirled around in her mind. Was their father dying? The Doctors had all sounded so positive about him getting better. They had seemed so optimistic that they would be able to control the cancer.

"He got really sick," Patrick told her, sensing her feelings. "Something to do with the bone cancer, calcium from the bones was getting into his blood stream and it made him sick. He couldn't keep down his painkillers." Patrick's voice trailed away as he remembered the dreadful night that the family had just gone through, watching their father. "Hypercalcaemia," he said finally, his lips twisting around the unfamiliar word that the Doctors had said was wrong with his father.

"What does that mean?" Stella asked, afraid of Patrick's reply.

"They will put Dad on a drip, get his pain back under control and use some drugs, bisphosphonates to sort out the calcium problems." Patrick took Stella's bag off her and led the way inside. "We will go down to the hospital now that you are here."

Seamus and Mary were slumped on the sofa, hands cupped around mugs of tea, looking for all the world as if they had been up at an all-night party. Except that they had been up all night and it had been no party.

An hour later they were all walking through the dim echoing corridors of the hospital. "Primrose Ward," Mary read aloud, scanning the long list of wards on a map of the hospital.

"This way," Seamus headed off down a long corridor. Then as they saw the sign, 'Primrose Ward' above the door Patrick's steps came to a faltering halt. "I think that I'll go and get some coffee first," he said, gazing through the glass doors into the ward, where patients lay surrounded by the winking lights and bleeps of machinery. "Me too," Patrick and Mary spoke together. "You go in, Dad will love to see you,"

Mary opened the door into the ward, leaving Stella no choice but to go in.

Stella walked slowly down the ward, gazing at the beds that lined either side of the room, afraid of intruding on the patients that lay there.

Her father lay in a bed halfway down the ward, his eyes closed. He looked relaxed in sleep, all of the pain smoothed away from his face.

Her mother sat in an armchair facing him, her hand entwined in her husband's. "Hello Mum," Stella said softly. "Oh love, you are here," Irene smiled, getting stiffly to her feet. Stella hugged her mother; she could smell peat smoke in the fibres of her blouse.

"How is he?" Stella perched on the edge of her father's bed.

He had lost more weight and his skin had a grey tinge to it.

Irene opened her mouth to speak, but all that emerged was a half strangled sob. "The others are down in the café," Stella gently touched her mother's arm. "Why don't you go and get a cup of tea with them. I'll sit with Dad."

Irene nodded, her lips twisted together as if she were afraid to speak in case she began to sob. Unwillingly she released her grip on Paddy's fingers and walked away down the ward.

Stella eased herself into the chair that her mother had just vacated and watched her open the doors and walk away from the ward.

There were a lot of people in the ward, visitors coming and going, crowding around the beds, chatting to the patients, nurses hurried up and down the ward, their rubber soled shoes creaking on the lino floor.

Stella looked everywhere except at her father. She felt a fraud being beside him, as if she were playing the role of a caring relative, when in reality she had no feelings. She was frozen inside where he was concerned.

"Stella," his familiar voice startled her.

"I felt rough last night," Paddy said, his hand moved across the bedclothes in Stella's direction.

Stella smiled tightly, unable to bring herself to meet his eyes. He always felt rough, even before the cancer there had always been something wrong with him.

"Have you come all the way from the big city just to see me?" Paddy smiled, teasing gently, as he struggled to sit up.

Stella nodded, watching him for a moment and then jumped to her feet to rearrange his pillows so that he would be more comfortable.

"I love you Stella," Stella heard her father whisper as she leant over him.

"I love you too," the words had escaped from her mouth before she had the time to stop them.

It was evening when a Doctor came to Paddy's bedside. "We have the calcium under control," he said, looking intently at Paddy, as if he were some unusual specimen, "and the pain. We will monitor things for a day or so, but he should be able to go home soon."

240

Stella went into the kitchen and lifted the blind up from the window.

The blind clattered up nosily, behind it the window was misted with condensation, a long crack stretched from one side to the other.

Outside it was already bright; the early morning sunshine glittered on the sea. Stella stood at the window, gazing out at the small, windswept garden behind the cottage, the stunted plants, that her mother tried so hard to cultivate, withered by the constant battering from the Atlantic.

Beyond the garden, small fields, bordered by stone walls formed an untidy patchwork down to the golden gleam of the sea shore, white breakers charging up onto the sand marking the passing of time.

The cottage was silent, everyone else still slumbering.

Stella made tea, in two mugs and padded softly down the corridor back to her mother's bedroom. The dawn light had begun to slowly filter through a gap in the curtains, casting a dim light over the bedroom.

Irene opened her eyes, smiling faintly, she still looked exhausted, huge purple smudges marked her cheeks beneath her sunken eyes. Stella handed her mother one of the mugs of tea and sat down beside her.

"Paddy was....is a wonderful man," her mother said, taking a sip of her tea.

Stella sipped her tea, wondering if they were speaking about the same man.

He had never seemed very wonderful to her. He had always been bad tempered, shouting at them to be quiet, always ill, spending days in bed, or propped on the sofa while her mother ran errands, bringing tea to him, coaxing him to eat with little titbits.

They had always been poor, wearing hand me down clothes.

Stella had always blamed him for not working, not being able to give them the things that they so obviously needed.

Her mother was always too busy, running around after her husband to look after the children, give them the attention that they all so desperately craved.

"You probably don't remember him before he became ill," Irene reached for Stella's hand, mindlessly moving her fingers over her daughter's fingers while she spoke. "He was such a good father, always playing with you, helping with the nappies and feeds." Stella felt a tinge of regret for the man who she wished that she could remember. "But then the accident changed him."

"I never knew he had an accident," Stella said, taking a sip of her tea and looking at her mother over the rim of her mug.

"He never made much of a fuss about it, it was not something that he brought up again," Irene said, smiling gently at Stella. "The ironic thing was that he saved the lad's life and ruined his own life in the process,"

"What are you talking about?" Stella asked, quizzically, she did not remember anything about her father being injured in an accident. She did not remember him ever being anything other than a frail sickly man.

"Some lads had come down from Dublin for the weekend," her mother said, quietly, her voice tinged with pride. "They went out on a boat into the sea, got into difficulties. Your father was out in his boat, checking the lobster pots. He went to help, rescued one of the lads that had fallen in the sea. He was drowning, panicking. Your father saved his life."

She smiled at the memory, shaking her head, bleakly remembering the proud man that her husband had once been. "Your father got pulled into the sea by the lad who was panicking, he saved him but got trapped between the two boats. Damaged his back, harmed his insides. He was never the same again."

Stella wished that she had remembered the accident, but she had been so young.

"Of course after that he was never really able to work much," her mother continued. "There was never enough money. He was so proud. He hated not being able to provide for you all." Irene shook her head at the memory, "I never minded," she said, "I loved him so much. We were happy with our simple life. We had each other. Even if he was sick he was a wonderful man. We were very happy together."

"I never knew any of that," Stella whispered, humbly.

"He is a very proud man," her mother answered. "He was never going to say, I was injured and now I need pity. He must have seemed angry to you, but it was because he was so often in pain and angry at himself for not being able to give you the things that he wanted to."

A strand of sunlight shone through the curtains, Stella watched the dust dance in the chink of light, coming to rest on the simple furniture.

"He loves you so much," her mother said.

CHAPTER THIRTY FOUR

Amber looked into her purse. Under the circumstances it was the most ridiculous thing that she could possibly have ever done. She knew that there was no money in it, other than a twenty Euro note and a handful of dingy looking coins. But still she looked.

"Well?" the huge man seemed to tower over Amber, his huge bulk seeming to fill the doorway.

Even Teddy had been terrified of him, when he had come up the door of the apartment Teddy had yapped furiously, guarding Amber from the stranger.

Then as the man had glared at him, the small dog had thought better of it and slunk away, bushy tail between his legs, to hide, embarrassed at his failure, in his basket, leaving Amber to deal with him alone.

"I don't seem to have enough money," Amber said, hearing her own voice, high and afraid.

"Not good enough, darling," the man rested one arm on the door frame; he was very large and very intimidating.

Amber wished that she had pretended that she was not in, when he had rang the doorbell.

He had sounded pleasant enough when he had spoken into the speaker, "Nigel," he had introduced himself, from the loan agency. "Your repayment seems to be overdue, I wondered if there is a problem? Can we have a quick chat about it?"

Nigel had a high, squeaky voice, he sounded as if he were about twelve years old. "Sure, come on up," Amber had grinned cockily into the speaker.

There was a bit of a problem with the repayment. Basically the repayment had gone on a rather nice handbag and a matching pair of shoes.

They were the just the thing that she had needed for going to the next race meeting.

Paul was due to ride one of Henry's horses in a big race next week. Actually buying the shoes and handbag was saving money. The dark brown leather bag and the shoes with the fancy stitching and inlaid snakeskin would go perfectly with a cream coat that she had bought years ago. So she would not need to buy a new outfit, just update an old one, thereby saving a fortune, even if it had meant spending the repayment money.

Nigel had sounded like the kind of lad who would understand all about people having problems with repayments.

She would soon smile and flirt her way out of this little problem. Tell him that she would give him the money next week.

Nigel, when he appeared at the door to the apartment did not somehow quite look like a Nigel. More like a Fang, or a Basher. He was enormous. At least six feet tall and almost as wide, with a huge head that seemed to rise straight out of his shoulders.

"So," he leered, as Amber gulped at the sight of him. "What's the problem with this repayment then?" He had a wide mouth with a dazzlingly white row of teeth, one of which glittered with a tiny gold star that had been embedded in its centre. His eyes were hidden behind huge dark glasses, making it impossible to read his expression.

Except that Amber did not need to read Nigel's expression. He oozed anger and menace.

"Well, I, er…" Amber felt her face alter from a petrified white, to a terrified red. "You should have deposited the repayment in our office at the end of last month," Nigel growled, he lowered his chin, so that he could look at Amber over the top of his dark glasses. His eyes had the cold, merciless look of a shark.

"I forgot," Amber said lamely.

"Uh uh," Nigel grunted, thick dark eyebrows raised over the top of his dark glasses. "Well, I'll take it with me now."

"Right," Amber glanced desperately at the top of the stairs, would she be able to dodge past Nigel and escape?

Nigel looked as if he were well used to stopping people from escaping, so she ditched that as an option.

Maybe Teddy could seize him by the throat and maul him into submission so that he would let her off the payment. Teddy was watching the proceedings from his basket, one eye open, wearing a guilty expression.

That did not seem like a viable option either. "I'll fetch my purse."

As she opened her purse Nigel seemed to grow, expanding until he filled the doorway, rather like a volcano about to explode.

Amber swallowed hard.

"I'll take that," he reached forwards with a huge paw-like hand and incredible delicacy, seized the single crisp note from her purse. "Thank you." Nigel stuffed the twenty Euro note into a brown envelope and wrote her name on the front of it. "So," he sniffed, menacingly. "What are you going to do about the rest of the money?" Amber opened and closed her mouth. What was she going to do about the money? The twenty was all that she had in the world, heaven knew how she was even going to get to work in the morning, without her bus fare.

Nigel answered for her. "I'll call in two days' time. You be here with the money. Or I will have to pay you a little visit at work," with that he turned and stomped off down the stairs.

Amber leant against the door frame, feeling as if Nigel had punched every inch of her.

Now, Amber wondered, what was she supposed to do? She had never dreamt that the loan company would be so heavy handed about wanting their money back.

Paul came later, clutching a carrier bag of Chinese food and a bottle of wine.

Amber swallowed her pride and asked him if she could borrow some money, "I've left my bank card at work by mistake," she shrugged, wryly, "I just need to borrow enough to get to work."

Paul grabbed a thick wad of money out of his pocket, "I just got paid for riding a horse that belonged to a friend of Henry's," he grinned, delightedly.

Amber could not take her eyes off the money.

There was enough there to pay off her monthly repayment, but she could not bring herself to ask Paul.

It would be too embarrassing to confess to him what an idiot she had been letting herself get into a mess with money again.

They ate the Chinese and then Paul headed off, he needed an early night, he grinned, he needed to be at the gallops early in the morning.

Amber lay awake all night, turning over and over in bed, fitfully, wondering hopelessly where on earth she was going to get the money from.

She wished that Paul had stayed the night that would have taken her mind off the impending sense of doom that she felt. But then, she decided, it was probably a good job that he had not, she would have probably ended up asking him for the money.

Amber could not settle at work. She made mistake after mistake, handing out the wrong change, scanning groceries twice and throwing tinned stuff on top of delicate boxes of eggs when she was helping to pack the shopping.

All day she kept casting furtive glances to the end of the line of people queuing to come to her check out, expecting at any second to look up and see Nigel standing beside her, his hand open ready to take the money out of her till. Even that seemed a terrible temptation, all that money, just sitting there in front of her. Surely no one would miss the little bit that she needed? But she could not bring herself to do that. Eventually the clock slid around to the end of her shift and Amber slid thankfully off her seat and headed out of the supermarket.

The streets were crowded as Amber began the journey home.

It was a short walk to the bus stop; usually Amber enjoyed watching the people who hurried along the pavement, couples arm in arm, families laughing together.

Tonight though she felt exhausted, as if every stride were an immense effort, the crowds jostled against her and Amber felt too weak and miserable to resist, letting herself be pushed from one side of the pavement to the other, like a piece of driftwood in a restless sea.

Amber reached the bus stop and sank down thankfully onto the hard plastic, graffiti covered bench. She longed to be in bed, longed to cover her head with the quilts and wait for the oblivion of sleep that would take her far away from the cares and worries that had weighed on her ever since the debt collector's visit.

A car drew to a halt beside the bus stop, "Amber," yelled an impatient voice. Amber felt her heart sink. Things really could not get any worse. "Amber!" Ruby yelled. Amber got to her feet, forcing a smile to twist her lips upwards. Ruby was absolutely the last person that she wanted to see.

"Hurry up and get in before I get clamped or get a ticket for being in the

246

bus stop," Ruby leant across the passenger seat and thrust open the door for Amber to get in. "Come on!"

Amber stifled a groan of pure despair as she slid into the aeroplane cockpit like interior of Ruby's swanky car. This was the last thing that she could bear, listening to Miss Successful bragging the whole journey home about how great things were for her. Fine talk coming from one who was about to marry a man who was already messing around with other women.

"Have you just finished work?" Ruby flicked on the indicator and pulled straight out into the line of traffic, ignoring the hooting and flashing headlights from the cars that had jammed on their brakes to avoid crashing into her.

Amber thought of a dozen witty replies, surely it was fairly obvious that she had just finished work. Did Ruby think that Amber usually wandered around in a blue nylon overall? It was not exactly high fashion. Instead she said tightly. "Yes, a few minutes ago." Amber just was not in the mood for quick witted conversation.

"Are you enjoying your new job?" Ruby pulled out onto the wrong side of the road to overtake the car in front.

"Yes thanks," Amber closed her eyes as Ruby's front wing almost grazed a car coming in the opposite direction. Her sister had to be the world's worst driver.

"Are you still seeing Paul?"

"Yes,"

"Still getting on with Stella?"

"Yes,"

"Did you buy anything nice recently?"

Amber gave a hollow laugh. "No."

It was unlikely that Amber would be buying anything – ever. She was going to be in debt forever, living in fear of what the ferocious debt collector was going to do to her if she did not pay up.

Amber gazed out of the car window, watching the world glide past from within the gilded cocoon of luxury that was Ruby's car.

Outside the car people walked by, or drove in their cars, they all had normal lives,

Amber felt so bleak and lonely, she had to be the only person in the world who was so stupid as to get herself into such a financial mess. If only she had not gambled all of her money at the races. If only she had not got involved with the company that had promised fast easy access to money that would consolidate all of your debts into one small monthly repayment. If only she had saved her wages for the repayment. If only. If only. Now she really was in a mess.

Amber felt hot tears slide down her cheeks yet again. She had told everyone at work that she was starting with a cold in order to explain why she was constantly wiping her nose with a tissue. The supervisor had even asked if Amber had wanted to go home. Home that was a joke. How could she go home – and lose a day's wages. She needed every cent that she could earn.

"Surely you must have been looking in the shops to see what you could wear for my wedding," Ruby started again.

"No," Amber replied quietly.

"No?" Ruby exclaimed. "But you really need to start looking now. I hope that you aren't going to show me up on my wedding day by wearing something awful."

Something old was the unspoken meaning behind Ruby's words, something that might have been worn once before.

"No of course not," Amber felt weak with misery. She would never be able to afford to buy anything new for Ruby's wedding. Besides which if she did not pay the debt collector then it was likely that she would be wearing a black eye for the wedding. Or maybe even two.

"What is the matter?" Ruby asked sharply, swerving over to the pavement, the car jerked to a halt and Ruby switched on the interior light.

"I'm fine," lied Amber, Ruby was the last person that she would ever dream of telling that she had problems.

Ruby never got herself in a mess. Her life ran like clockwork, always perfection, even if her fiancée was seeing someone else. Not even that could mar the perfection that was Ruby's life.

"No you are not," Ruby said sternly.

"I am. Of course I am," Amber protested, hastily wiping the eye furthest away from Ruby, with the back of her hand. Her tears were falling fast now, splashing off her cheeks and trickling down her neck.

"No you are not," Ruby repeated in a school teacher voice. "What is it?" she continued more gently.

"I'm in such a mess," Amber said quietly, surprised that the words had come unbidden from her lips.

"What kind of a mess?" Ruby asked, her voice so gentle that Amber turned to face her, not recognising this side of her usually brash, loud sister.

"Money," Amber gulped, and then the words tumbled from her mouth as if they would never stop.

And then she was telling Ruby all about the mess that she was in, everything from the credit cards that she could not pay, to Nigel, the enormous debt collector who was threatening all kinds of violence if Amber did not repay the money immediately.

Finally the words dried up and Amber was silent. Ruby was silent, her hands gripping the leather covered steering wheel as she gazed out at the orange glow that bathed the streets around the car.

"You bloody idiot," sighed Ruby, finally breaking the silence. "How could you be so stupid?"

Amber opened her mouth to reply, but no words came. There was nothing to say, she had been stupid. Amber stifled a sob, burying her face into a sodden tissue. She had been a bloody idiot, but Ruby's words hurt terribly, especially when Ruby was about to marry someone in what she knew was merely a marriage of convenience. She was marrying Roderick to gain social standing, business contacts and for financial reasons, nothing to do with love. How stupid was that?

"Oh Amber," sighed Ruby, in that superior way that reminded Amber so much of her mother.

Ruby swivelled around and grabbed her handbag off the tiny back seat, rummaged in its leather depths for a moment before pulling out her chequebook. Amber dabbed at her eyes as Ruby opened the chequebook and briskly wrote Amber's name on a cheque. "How much do you owe?"

"Bloody idiot," she shook her head as Amber whispered the amount.

Then in large extravagant handwriting Ruby wrote out the amount that Amber owed and signed her name with a flourish.

"Here," she ripped out the cheque and shoved it towards Amber.

Amber looked at the cheque. She could pay off the debt agency, be free of money worries. Start afresh. And make sure that this time she did not mess her finances up. It was nothing to Ruby. On her vast salary it was peanuts. And no doubt it made her feel very smug and virtuous to bail out her hopeless sister.

Amber clenched her hands into fists; there was no way that she could touch the cheque. No way that she was going to let Ruby, Miss Perfect, know that Amber could not manage to sort out her own problems.

Nigel was coming back in a few days expecting her to have the money to repay the debt.

Amber had never hated her sister more in her life as slowly she lifted her hand and grasped the cheque.

CHAPTER THIRTY FIVE

Amber shrugged helplessly, "I don't know where he is."
Henry glanced at his watch yet again. He had been growing more and more agitated as the morning wore on. "Try ringing Paul again," he said, trying to make his voice sound bright as if he were not concerned. But Amber could tell by the anxious glances that he kept darting to the end of the driveway that he was hoping to see Paul's car appear at any moment.

"I knew that he would let Henry down," Stella said, huffily, coming across the yard with yet more mugs of tea. They seemed to have been drinking tea constantly for the last few hours. "He said he would be here first thing," Stella handed a mug to Henry, who slopped a good part of his onto the cobbles a sure indication of the agitated state he was in.

Amber turned away, gazing up at the woodland behind Henry's stable yard. How peaceful it looked up there, the woolly green heads of the towering oak trees standing proudly as they had for generations.

Stella's hand was shaking too, Amber noticed, she was as brittle as thin ice, snapping at everyone tetchily. Stella had not wanted to come. It had taken all of Amber's powers of persuasion to get Stella to accompany her.

"I'm going to end it with Henry," Stella had said, that morning as the two of them ate breakfast. "There's no point in carrying on with this."

"Why?" Amber had asked, shaking her head in bewilderment, the two of them had seemed so involved with each other. They were meant to be, anyone could see that. "I'm getting too fond of him," Stella said, there was more than a touch of bleakness in her voice.

"What?" Amber spat, incredulously, surely you were meant to get fond of someone when you were in a relationship with them.

"He's not for me." Stella said, flatly.

"Of course he is."

Stella shook her head. "No." For a long while she was silent, sipping her tea, resting her elbows on the table. Her expression looked desperately sad.

"My mother loved my Dad," Stella said, quietly. "After he was injured they had nothing. Mum says that she never regrets that. She loved him and was happy with him. And that it didn't matter to her that they had nothing."

Amber smiled, faintly. "Well, surely if you love someone nothing really does matter, whether you are rich or poor, sick or healthy. The love is there whatever."

Stella glanced up at Amber, her eyes narrowed with annoyance. "No. I don't believe her. How can she have been happy living like that? Struggling all the time?"

Amber was silent, afraid to answer. Afraid that if she did, she would say something that Stella did not want to hear.

"So," Stella put drained the last of her tea and put down her mug decisively. "I'm going to end it with Henry." There was an air of finality in her words that made Amber realise that she was not going to change her mind. Stella had decided what she was going to do and that was that.

"Please don't do anything until after this weekend though," Amber pleaded. "Henry is so wound up about this big race. Paul was with him a few days ago, getting ready to ride the horse in the race. He said Henry is like a cat on a hot tin roof, he can't settle. If they win this race he is hoping that more clients will come to him. It will make life a lot easier for him."

Amber saw a frown flicker across Stella's forehead. "You owe it to him." Amber told her. "It's because of Rory he lost so much business in the first place."

Stella's jaw clenched. "If you are going to end it with him, please wait."

Stella sighed. "Right," she snapped, crossly. "But once this race is over."

Amber began to wish that she had not persuaded Stella to stay with Henry until after the race. She was as taut and tetchy as could be, her face pale and drawn.

"What has happened to Paul?" Stella repeated, she rested her hand on Henry's arm, touching the fabric of his jacket as if she wanted to imprint the feel of him into her memory. Amber shook her head, shrugging miserably. "He was just going out with some mates last night," Amber saw a wry look flash over Stella's face.

"He's not the kind to get blind drunk and end up sleeping in a gutter somewhere." Amber said, loyally, but still, at the back of her own mind, prickled a seed of doubt.

Where was Paul? He had told Amber that it was a lad's night out.

He had not been out on his own since they had started to see each other. He had seemed to prefer spending time sitting quietly in a corner of the pub with Amber, sipping a coke, or curled up at the apartment watching television with her, or if Stella were out, curled up beneath the duvet, their arms and legs entwined. She had almost had to force him to go out with his friends.

In fact when one of them had telephoned to ask him to come he had initially refused.

Amber had made him ring back and say that he would go. Now she regretted her rashness. What if he had gone off with another girl? Maybe at this moment he lay beneath someone else's duvet, licking ice cream off her belly.

"We will have to go," Henry said, getting jerkily to his feet. "We can't wait any longer."

Amber pressed the redial number on her telephone, listening bleakly as it rang momentarily and then switched straight to a recorded message of Paul's voice brightly saying he was sorry that he could not come to the telephone. "Where are you?" Amber hissed, before saying into the mouthpiece, "Henry is going to have to leave. He can't wait any longer for you. Please telephone me, or him."

Maybe Paul was with someone else and did not want to talk to her.

If that was the case maybe he would just telephone Henry, he would not have to have anything to do with Amber, if he did not want to.

Kathy led Princess Pushy across the yard and into the battered horse lorry, her face like thunder. "Will you be able to get someone else to ride her?" she snapped at Henry, shooting a glance of dislike in Amber's direction as if it were her fault Paul was not here. Henry nodded, following the woman and the horse into the lorry and shutting the partition as Kathy ducked underneath it.

"There is usually someone around without a ride," he said, running lightly down the ramp and heaving it closed. "It's just that she goes so well for Paul. She really likes him." The undertone was that it was as well that Princess Pushy liked Paul, because just at this moment in time, no one else did.

Stella walked across the yard, carrying the empty tea mugs.

Amber climbed into the passenger seat of the lorry, looking back to see Stella gazing around the yard as if this were the last time that she would ever see it.

Amber began to feel sick, a sharp pain dug into her side, like a stitch, as if she had been running a long distance, she shifted uncomfortably, digging her fist into her side to try to ease the pain.

What a nightmare of a day this was turning out to be.

Paul had gone missing and Amber did not know if she was ever going to see him again. And it looked as if Stella had no intention of ever seeing Henry again after today either. She had been true to her word, standing by him for the race that meant so much for him. Helping to ease the stress that he was under, but tomorrow she was going to end it all, so she had told Amber.

Stella climbed into the lorry, flashing a sympathetic smile at Henry.

"It will be ok, you'll see," she smiled, talking gently to him.

Amber could see Henry visibly relax when she was around. She soothed him, just like Paul had seemed to sooth Princess Pushy.

It was as if she lifted all of the clouds that surrounded Henry when she was around.

Amber wanted to shout at her, to shake her, anything to make her not leave Henry. They were so right together. Any fool could see that.

Henry started the lorry. "Maybe he will meet us at the races," he seemed to speak more to reassure himself than anything else.

"Don't worry," Stella reached across and put a gentle hand on his knee. "You will find someone else, if Paul doesn't turn up."

Henry smiled, bleakly at her, "I know, it's just that I had such hopes for the two of them."

Amber stared fixedly out of the window, cursing Paul, and Stella. She was going to break Henry's heart when she dumped him. And why? Because of some silly idea that she had of finding a rich man. She thought that she would not be happy if she were with someone who had nothing.

Love did not work like that. Love came whether you were ready or not. It was so obvious how much they cared about each other.

Stella was going to be lost without Henry, she was being ridiculous.

Why break your own heart, because your head is leading you in a different direction.

The races were already crowded when they arrived. Kathy went to get the horse ready, grumbling sourly that they had left things very late and that Princess Pushy would not be relaxed and warmed up enough.

"She will be ok," Stella snapped at her.

Amber grinned, in spite of her own misery, Stella protected Henry like a mother hen, shielding him from any more anguish that Kathy was trying to stir up.

"Go and declare Princess Pushy, we will meet you in the parade ring. There will someone around who will ride her. Go and look in the Weigh Room."

Stella gave Henry a gentle shove in the direction of the Steward's offices.

People were pouring into the races as Amber and Stella walked into the concourse.

This was one of the biggest races of the year. And Henry had been convinced that Princess Pushy had stood a good chance in the race. She had been working so well with Paul riding her. But now…….

Amber trailed miserably after Stella across the race course. She wore her new boots and carried her matching handbag, the whole outfit did look beautiful, it should do after all of the trouble it had got her into, thought Amber, catching sight of herself in the reflection from the glass in the Owners and Trainers bar.

Paul would have loved her in this.

They had all been so angry at him, but now Amber was beginning to get frightened. What if he had been in an accident?

Stella had been so convinced that he had gone out and got drunk and was just sleeping it off somewhere. But that was so unlike him. But they had never seemed to consider that.

Amber glanced at her watch, they would be home in a few hours' time and then she would have to telephone the hospitals to see if he was lying there, injured. Injured. The very thought made the pain in her side grip again.

Stella and Amber leant on the guard rail around the parade ring, watching the horses walk around, delicate hooves barely seeming to touch the tarmac as they danced with excitement. Amber could feel the anger that seemed to emanate from Stella, as she stood silently watching the horses go around.

"I've found someone," Henry dashed up to them, alight with excitement. "Toby McEvoy's horse has been pulled out; he was lame this morning, so Toby has agreed to take the ride on Princess Pushy."

Stella grabbed his hand, kissing him with delight. "Brilliant!" she exclaimed, the relief loud in her voice.

"Great," agreed Amber, feeling very much as if she should not be with them. After all it was her boyfriend that had caused all the trouble.

Henry put a kind arm around Amber's shoulder and squeezed her gently. "Don't worry, I'm sure that there is a really good reason why Paul isn't here. He wouldn't just let us down. He's not that kind of man."

Amber smiled gratefully, ignoring the look of scorn on Stella's face. She obviously thought that Paul was exactly the sort of man who would let anyone down.

Kathy brought Princess Pushy into the parade ring. The elegant mare looked fabulous. She walked calmly around the ring, her delicate ears sharply pricked, taking in all that was going on around her.

"I hope that she goes well for Toby," Henry fretted, twisting a lead rope between his fingers, Stella took his hand, squeezing his fingers gently.

The jockeys trooped out of the Weigh Room, their brightly coloured silks billowing in the fretful wind that had blown up.

"Good afternoon," Toby shook hands with Henry and nodded politely at the two girls.

"She's a good mare," Henry began, taking Toby to one side to tell him how to ride the race.

Amber glared at the jockeys bowed legs, she did not like him at all, and neither did Princess Pushy from the way that she laid back her ears and kicked out with a hind leg when Henry legged Toby up onto her back.

"Steady my lady," Kathy tried to soothe the mare as she jogged, tense beneath Toby's weight.

The horses began to go out onto the course, Kathy struggling to keep control of Princess Pushy, who was prancing sideways, tossing her head up and down, thoroughly upset by the stranger that was on her back.

"She doesn't like Toby," wailed Henry, miserably.

"Paul!" screamed Amber, not sure whether to be delighted or furious. Paul ran across the grass towards them, grim faced. A huge black eye swelled on one side of his face.

"Where the fuck have you been?" snapped Henry as Paul slithered to a halt, panting for breath.

"In the Garda cells," he gasped.

CHAPTER THIRTY SIX

Stella wanted to hit Paul, to give him a black eye to match the one that he already had. How dare he let Henry down? And being in the Garda cells. That was just what she would have expected.

Amber looked as if she were about to burst with pleasure she was so delighted to see Paul back and even Henry looked relieved to see him, even if it was too late for him to ride the horse.

"Garda Cells!" exclaimed Henry and Amber, in unison.

"What the hell were you doing in the cells?" Henry frowned.

Paul brought his hand up to his face as if his black eye were really hurting him.

"I went out with some lads last night," Paul began. "We were in a bar and I heard some lad, a jockey he was, bragging about ....stuff. And so I hit him. And he hit me back."

"What?" Henry said, incredulously. "Bragging about what stuff?"

"Come on," Paul said. "They are going down to the start," he looked regretfully at Princess Pushy who was cantering away from the parade ring, looking very unhappy, swishing her tail and bucking as if she wanted to rid herself of Toby.

"Bragging about what stuff?" Henry persevered as they walked towards the Owners and Trainers stand.

Paul stopped, ignoring the angry glares of those who had to squeeze past them on the way to the stands. "You remember when the trainer Morgan

Flynn had some horses poisoned?" Henry nodded.

Amber and Stella looked at each other; this was all stuff that they had never heard of.

"His horse fell and killed a jockey. And then afterwards some of his horses got poisoned and died."

Henry nodded. "Go on."

"Well this lad who was bragging was someone who had once worked for Morgan, he had got the sack for stealing and decided to get his own back. The accident was the perfect cover; everyone thought that the poisoning was something to do with that."

"And so you hit him and ended up in a cell for the night?" Stella could hardly keep her temper.

"But I tried to phone you, it wasn't answering."

"My phone got broken," Paul pulled his telephone out of his pocket to show them. "And this morning I just wanted to get here as quickly as I could. I hoped that I would make it before you had to give the ride to someone else."

"Well you didn't." Stella snapped, how could he be so stupid as to let Henry down. Why could he not have just walked away, not got involved in the fight?

"I would have made it," Paul grinned, disarmingly. "But the Garda stopped me for speeding!"

"Oh God!" Henry started to laugh.

"I thought that you were dead," Amber threw her arms around Paul, who locked his lips against hers as if it were months since they had seen each other rather than just an evening.

They hurried up onto the stands, Henry running lightly up the steps to a place where they would all be able to see the race. Stella pushed her way in so that she was standing beside him.

At the far side of the course they could see the horses circling as they waited to start the race.

It was easy to spot Princess Pushy, Toby was riding her apart from the others, trying to get her to settle, but the mare jogged, tossing her head up and down. Even from across the race course they could see the white patches

259

of foaming sweat beneath her saddle patch and on her graceful neck.

Stella glared at Paul, he should have been riding the mare. She knew him and went well for him. He owed it to Henry not to let him down. Henry had stuck his neck out to give Paul a second chance when no one else would, when all of the other trainers would not let him ride for them. And this was how he had repaid Henry.

Paul was looking across the race course miserably, his face full of guilt, his eyes never leaving the frenzied shape of Princess Pushy.

The Steward who started the race climbed up the starter's stand.

The horses began to form a ragged line across the track. Princess Pushy lashed out at another horse, her powerful back legs raking into the air, sending Toby sprawling up her neck.

The starting flag fluttered downwards and the horses plunged forwards towards the first jump.

"Oh shit," gasped Paul, as Princess Pushy refused to start, turning sideways as the horses shot away from her. One of the stewards cracked a long hunting whip at her bottom and she jumped forwards in surprise, scooting after the other horses.

"She's racing," breathed Henry, relief sounding in his voice as he gazed, with narrowed eyes at the brown caterpillar of horse's legs that was surging around the track towards them.

Princess Pushy caught up with the horses; they could see the familiar colours of the silks that Toby wore, merging with the other jockeys as they soared over the first jump. Around the track they went.

"She's there," Amber pointed un-necessarily, at the heaving mass of horseflesh and grim faced jockeys. The horses thundered past the stands and then surged on around the course, soaring over fence after fence as they raced.

"Two fences to jump," the commentator's voice bellowed out of the loudspeaker. "They are rounding the home turn."

"She's in second place," Henry said, incredulously, gripping Stella's hand so hard that she winced.

"Princess Pushy coming up on the outside," screamed the voice of the commentator. "Only the final fence to jump. It's Late Again closely followed by Princess Pushy." The commentator was hoarse with excitement, his voice rising higher and higher. Stella stood on tiptoe to watch the horses rushing towards the final fence, Late Again's chestnut face appeared over the jump, with Toby flying through the air alongside him.

"Princess Pushy has refused, Toby's gone over her head," shrieked the commentator, "Late Again wins the race," he bellowed as the chestnut horse surged past the winning post alone.

"Oh fuck," Paul gasped, sinking down into his seat. "She'd have won if I had been riding her."

Stella glared at him. "If you hadn't been so stupid," she snapped.

Henry sank down beside him, speechless with misery.

The stands began to empty as people dashed down to get drinks and place their bets before the next race.

"Hadn't we better go down to Princess Pushy?" Stella could not bear the utter misery that emanated from Henry. Henry shook his head, bleakly, "Kathy will deal with her," he sounded totally defeated.

"Come on, I'll get you a drink," Paul gave Henry his hand and hauled him to his feet.

After a moment, Henry sighed, bitterly and then, shrugged. "Ah well, maybe next time we will have better luck," he said, quietly and headed off down towards the Owners and Trainers bar, his shoulders hunched with misery.

The bar was crowded; everyone was congratulating the owners of Late Again, a syndicate from a pub in Galway who were already very drunk. The bar heaved with the happy throng.

They found a quiet corner away from all of the merriment in which they could drown their own sorrows.

Paul pushed his way to the bar, while Henry sat on a bar stool at one of the high tables and watched the merriment enviously.

Stella prickled with anger at Paul and Henry.

It was all Paul's fault, but yet Henry seemed to just accept the terrible thing that had happened and was putting it behind him and moving on.

Stella could barely bear to be near Paul, or Amber who was so delighted to be with him. In Stella's eyes he had lost Henry the race.

A few moments later Paul came back, with the glasses clutched in his hands.

"Henry," Paul grinned. "There's a guy at the bar who wants to talk to you about putting a horse with you - and in having you train it – and me ride it – if I can turn up on time," he joked, delighted to be imparting such good news.

"Excuse us," Henry said, smiling at Stella, "I'll just see what this man wants; I'll be back in a few minutes."

Stella glared at Paul's back as he wove his way through the crowds beside Henry.

"There should be scorch marks in his coat from the way you are looking at him," Amber said quietly, sipping her drink.

"He deserves it," Stella said coldly. "He lost that race for Henry. He ruined the day." Stella seethed with anger. Amber gave a short laugh.

"For someone who doesn't care about Henry, you seem to be caring an awful lot about how he feels." Amber raised her glass mockingly at Stella.

"Paul obviously doesn't care very much about anyone," Stella retorted, turning to glare at Amber, her eyes narrowed with sudden hatred. Paul was no good. Amber would be able to see that if she had any sense what so ever.

"I don't know why you bother with him," spat Stella. "You should get yourself a better boyfriend."

"Better than being a waiter and part time jockey I suppose," Amber retorted, spitting out the word 'waiter' vehemently.

Stella was silent, staring across the bar at Henry and Paul, who were talking animatedly to a short, balding man with very large teeth. "He's going nowhere Amber," Stella said, the words forced out through her clenched teeth. "He will let you down and break your heart."

"Just like you are going to break Henry's when you finish with him," Amber hissed venomously, watching the sudden look of guilt that flashed across Stella's face. "That's my business," she growled sullenly.

"Well, Paul is my business," Amber snapped back, full of hostility.

"You didn't mind me looking out for you when you had no money," Stella said acidly.

"You didn't mind me looking after you when Rory was stalking you. Or mind me looking after your dog when you went away," retorted Amber, fighting the childish urge to bawl and pull Stella's hair.

"Well thanks for that," Stella shrugged, tartly.

Both stunned by the ferocity of the hostility that darted between them Stella and Amber sat in sullen silence waiting Henry and Paul to return. "You aren't really going to finish with Henry are you?" Amber asked suddenly, breaking the silence.

"I have too," Stella answered, looking at Amber, her eyes filling with sudden tears. "I can't carry on with this."

"Because you've fallen in love with him?"

Stella nodded, bleakly, "I can't stay with him. I just can't. Being poor…………" her voice trailed off. It was too hard to describe how she felt. Why she felt that she had to finish with Henry before it was too late.

Amber shook her head, silenced by the intensity of her sadness. Stella was being such a fool. How could she give up a man who clearly worshiped her and who she so obviously felt so much for? The whole thing was crazy.

"Well, it looks as if I've got myself a new client," Henry grinned, returning a few moments later. He pushed himself up onto the bar stool and took a long swig of his drink.

"I hope some good has come out of today then," Stella said bitterly, glaring at Amber, who glared back, through narrowed eyes.

"Maybe we should head off," Amber said, putting her hand on Paul's arm, urgently. "Oh, right," Paul sensed the tension in Amber. "See you soon, Henry," he nodded in Stella's direction, "Stella,"

Amber slid off her chair. "Bye Henry," she pecked Henry gently on the cheek. "You are a real nice guy." Then without saying a word to Stella she grabbed Paul's arm and strode out of the Owners and Trainers bar without a backwards glance.

"What was all that about?" Henry frowned, gazing at Amber as she shoved her way angrily through the bar, barging past the group from the Galway syndicate, sending one man's glass flying.

"I told her that Paul was no good," Stella said tartly.

Henry frowned, quizzically. "What on earth for?" Henry stared at Stella as if he could not believe what he was hearing.

"Because he let you down, because he will let her down," Stella replied sullenly. Henry smiled, touching Stella's face with his fingers, tracing a line from her high elegant cheekbones to her chin. "Leave them to sort their own relationship out. It's none of your business. No matter what you think. And as for me…." He gave a snort of laughter. "Well, today turned out ok anyway." Henry drained his drink. "Come on, we had better head off, Kathy will be ready to leave now."

Stella slid off her stool and followed Henry out of the bar, the sound of merriment followed them out of the door. They drove home in silence;

Kathy lay in the space behind the passenger seats, snoring softly.

"I'll finish off," Kathy woke up as the lorry air brakes hissed on as Henry stopped in the yard at his cottage.

"Come on, we'll go inside." Henry helped Stella down from the lorry.

It seemed a life time since they had been in the yard during the morning, waiting for Paul.

Stella felt as if she had aged a thousand years, the journey from the lorry to the house seemed as if were a hundred miles long, every stride seemed to be an immense effort. She could not go inside with him. Stella could not trust herself to be alone with him again. If he were to kiss her once then she would be lost and then this time there might be no going back. She had to end the relationship. Now. While she still could.

Henry shoved open the cottage door and stood back to let Stella pass.

"Henry," Stella said, suddenly, her voice sounded very tired, almost mechanical. Henry leant down and kissed the soft skin on her neck.

"I think we should go up to bed," he muttered, moving forwards to gently enfold her in his arms. Stella felt herself waiver, her whole being cried to be with him, to go to bed with him, to become part of him, to stay beside him forever, where she belonged. But she could not.

"Henry," she spluttered, "I have to end this," she wriggled out of his grasp, glimpsing his shocked, white face, highlighted in the soft light from the hall and then she was charging across the yard, hurtling towards her car as if she thought that he were going to grab her and make her stay. Make her listen to sense. Make her love him. But he did not. She reached her car, fighting to shove the key in the lock, slamming the key into the ignition while Henry stood in the doorway, his face closed with shock.

She drove away from Henry's yard, wondering if this time she really had made the biggest mistake of her life.

CHAPTER THIRTY SEVEN

Stella threw the remains of her sandwich into the bin at the side of her desk.

Actually there was rather a lot of sandwich uneaten, but she just did not seem to have any appetite at all.

Stella sat up quickly as Sorcha came into her office, she must not let Sorcha see how upset she was, otherwise she would start to undermine her position again, by criticising her work.

Stella did not want to go down that particular road again, it been hard enough the last time when she was upset about Rory. Now she was upset again, about Henry and Amber, but this time she had to keep things under control, not to betray how terribly upset she felt.

Sorcha picked up a typewritten feature from Stella's desk.

"Do you want me to check this?" she asked, her lips twisting into a snide smile.

"No thank you," Stella smiled back brightly feeling her teeth grate together with the effort. "It's fine. I've checked it myself."

And she had, very carefully, anything to keep her mind off the horrible thoughts that churned around.

The memory of Henry's gorgeous, too handsome face when she had told him that she did not want to see him again.

And Amber, her very, very best friend – who now hated her, with a vengeance.

If only she could unsay the things that she had said, Stella thought, miserably forcing her unwilling mind to focus on checking the article that she had just written. But it was too late, for going back. She had found a new apartment and was moving out.

Amber had been shocked into silence when Stella had told her that she was moving out. Amber had been keeping a frosty silence ever since they had rowed at the races, but she had been speechless when Stella had broken the news to her.

There had been days when they had scarcely said a word to each other, apart from. "here is your mail," and "I'm out tonight." They had shared the apartment, acting like polite strangers, other than when Stella had come in that night from the races and Amber had said, "you didn't really finish with Henry did you?"

"Yes," Stella had replied, unable to believe herself that she had actually done the terrible deed. How her mouth had said those words while her heart had screamed out for her to stay with Henry.

"You bloody stupid idiot," Amber had said, her hand full of toast, halfway between her plate and her mouth.

Amber had frozen, glaring in disbelief at Stella then she had laid the toast down and silently got up and left the room.

After that they had hardly spoken, after a week Stella knew that things would never be the same between them again.

They had been friends for two years, since Amber had come to share Stella's apartment.

They had liked each other immediately and living together had been easy, but now there could be no going back. Stella could not change her mind and Amber could not forgive her. Too much had been said and too much ill feeling had passed between them to ever be forgotten. After a week, Stella telephoned an agent and asked if there were any other apartments or house shares available. As if it had been fated, there was a house, in Ballsbridge, where the girls who rented it were looking for another to share it with. They were, the agent had told her, all lovely girls, all around the same age. They would get on brilliantly, so the agent said. And none of them had any objection to Teddy being there, as long as he would not chase the cat that belonged to one of the other girls.

Stella had gone straight around to the address that the agent had given her.

The house was lovely, an old Edwardian house, set in a tiny garden.

One of the girls, had answered the door when Stella arrived. "Hello, you must be Stella, I'm October" she had a clipped, posh sounding accent, very polite and correct, that matched perfectly with her neat oval face and precisely trimmed bob. October was very pretty in an elfin kind of way, with enormous brown eyes that scrutinised her from beneath her fringe. "The others are all out," October told Stella. "They are all very nice girls, I'm sure you will get on with them."

She showed Stella around the house. It was gorgeous, spacious and airy, with a shared kitchen and lounge downstairs. Each of the girls had their own bedroom,

Stella's one was at the back of the house, looking out onto a lovely garden with a paved patio and an inviting looking swing seat beneath a cherry tree. Her room was far larger than the one at the apartment and had a small en-suite.

Stella could not think why she had stayed in the apartment with Amber for so long. Here at least she would be mixing with a nice set of girls. They would be able to introduce her to a new set of men, maybe now she was on the right track to finding a thoroughly nice millionaire.

Stella had told Amber that evening. Amber had been in the shower when Stella had come in from work. Stella stood in the living room waiting, unable to settle, slowly pacing the room, listening to the sound of the water running, as she had tried to frame the words to tell Amber that she was moving out.

Stella had arranged for the lease on the apartment to be put into Amber's name if she wanted to stay. Now that her sister had sorted out her money problems she should have no problem paying the rent. That was just like Amber, someone else always picked up the pieces when she got into a mess. Maybe Paul would move in with her to help pay the rent, or if not she would just have to find someone else to share with.

The water stopped running and Stella knew that the time had come to tell Amber. A moment later the bathroom door had opened and Amber had come out wearing a dressing gown, a towel swathed around her head.

"Hi," Amber always forgot that they had fallen out when she saw Stella, launching into a bright conversation until halfway through getting her words out she would remember and the sentence would falter and die on her lips.

"Amber," Stella heard the words escaping from her mouth as if she were watching a video of herself. She could have stopped if she had wanted to, but still she went on, wishing that she was saying different words, asking for forgiveness, telling Amber that it was all a terrible mistake, that they should repair their friendship, put everything behind them, but still she did not. Her voice went on, "I've found another place to live. I'm moving out at the weekend."

A tendril of Amber's hair had escaped from the towel, Stella watched a drop of water slide down it until it spilled onto the shoulder of her dressing gown.

"I see," Amber said coldly, her eyes narrowing with dislike. "Thanks for telling me," she turned away, her mouth clamped into a tight straight line, her jaw thrust resolutely forwards.

There was no sign of Amber in the morning when Stella got up. She was in the kitchen when Amber returned from walking Teddy.

"Hang on, let me take your lead off," Amber's voice came from the front door, a moment later Teddy bounded into the kitchen.

"Teddy!" Stella bent down as the little dog hurled himself at her, leaping at her legs, his sharp front paws clawing at her calf muscles.

"Hi," Amber said, shortly coming into the kitchen, she leant against the door frame, with a half-smile playing on her lips, unable to not be amused by Teddy's antics.

"So when are you going?" she asked, staring fixedly at Teddy, not able to look at Stella in case she started to cry – again.

"I'll pack up this week and be out on Friday," Stella stood up, if only she could bring herself to put her arms around Amber and tell her how sorry she was. Everything would be back to normal.

"What about Teddy?" Amber said, sullenly.

"He's my dog," Stella said, quietly. Amber gave a snort of derision.

"You might have found him, but I've spent more time with him than you," Amber said coldly.

"Yes, well…." Stella could not think of a reply. They had shared the dog; he was a family pet, when she and Amber had been each other's family.

"He's still my dog," she finished lamely.

"Suit yourself," snapped Amber, adding "bitch," quietly under her breath.

By Friday Stella could not wait to move out of the apartment and make a fresh start.

The atmosphere in the apartment had deteriorated into one of open hostility.

Stella woke on Friday morning with a sense of relief. At last she was going to be away from Amber and make a fresh start. She would at last put the nastiness of the last few weeks behind her.

There was very little to move, just her clothes and personal possessions. They were already packed away in the new luggage bags that she had bought especially. She may as well make a good impression when she arrived at the house.

There was no sign of Amber when Stella left her bedroom. She must have been out walking Teddy. Amber has spent the last week cradling the dog as if she could not bear to let him out of her sight. Looking at Stella coldly as if she thought that she was about to take her child away from her.

Stella could not wait to get out of the apartment; the atmosphere was poisoned with the bad feeling that oozed between the two of them.

As soon as Amber returned with Teddy she would leave. Stella carried her bags downstairs and packed them into her car. Then there was nothing more to do but wait for Amber to come back. Stella sat on the sofa and looked around the room. She had been very happy here, there were such good memories tied up in these walls.

Amber pushed open the door. "So you are going then?" she held Teddy in her arms, the small dog wriggled furiously, trying to get to Stella.

"Yes," had Amber thought that all of this was a joke? She sounded so surprised.

"I'm ready to go, I was just waiting for you coming back," Stella heaved herself to her feet, not daring to look at Amber, she was aware of her bleak expression and that there were tears pouring down Amber's face. "I'll bring Teddy out."

Stella groped her way to the door, blinded by the tears that were flowing furiously down her face.

Her car was parked outside against the pavement, filled with her boxes and bags.

Amber let out a strangled sob, burying her face in Teddy's fur.

"Here," she spluttered, pushing the dog towards Stella. Teddy squirmed delightedly in Stella's arms, enjoying the attention, trying to shove his wet nose into her neck to lick her.

Stella longed to put her arms around Amber, tell her that everything was alright. To bring her bags back inside the apartment and spend the rest of the day laughing about how stupid they had been. But it was too late.

Amber folded her arms. "See you then," she mumbled thickly and then before Stella had a chance to reply, turned on her heel and dashed back into the apartment.

Numbly Stella put Teddy into the car, he put his front paws on the dashboard, peering through the windscreen excitedly dying to know where they were going to. His curly tail waved furiously as he glanced at Stella, his mouth open, panting eagerly.

"Right then," Stella said, feigning decisiveness that she did not feel as she slid into the driver's seat and shoved her key into the ignition.

A short time later she was pulling up outside the new house in Ballsbridge. The drive outside the house was jammed with expensive looking cars, a small Mercedes sports car, a flashy looking Mini Cooper and the one that she knew that belonged to October, an exotic looking Lotus sports car.

Stella left her own car outside on the road; it would have looked very nondescript beside the expensive cars that belonged to her new housemates.

Hauling one of the bags, with Teddy beneath her arm Stella made her way up the drive, skirting carefully around the sports cars. She rang the bell balancing Teddy on her hip as she did so.

A moment later the door swung open.

"Yes?" a tall, willowy blonde girl stood aggressively in the doorway. In her arms was an enormous fluffy grey cat, which took one look at Teddy and seemed to grow to twice its size, emitting loud hissing and yowling noises, before it exploded from the girl's arms and vanished into the house.

"I'm Stella," Stella gulped, quailing, beneath the girl's furious gaze, "I'm moving in today. And this is Teddy,"

"Julia," the girl eyed Stella coldly, she held out a cold, limp hand for Stella to shake, dropping the contact as soon as she could. Her hand reminded Stella of one of the dead fish that she had hauled from the boats on the beach in Mayo years ago, when she was a child. She pronounced Julia as if it were Juli-yah.

"You had better come in," she made it sound as if she were doing Stella the most enormous favour, letting her cross the threshold of the house. "That was Gucci your………" she looked Teddy up and down as if she had never seen anything like him before, "dog" she finally decided, "upset. I thought when October said you had a dog that you would have something like a Labrador, something nice. I didn't realise that it was a mongrel," she made it sound as if Teddy were the most revolting mutt ever created, rather than the most adorable sweet little dog.

"October and Xanthe are in the lounge," Julia waved her hand in the direction of the lounge, before wordlessly heading off in search of her cat.

Stella sighed, holding tight onto Teddy who was wriggling with impatience; hopefully Xanthe would be nicer than Julia.

She was not.

Xanthe took one look at Teddy and shrieked, "that dog has to live outside. There's a kennel in the garden."

Xanthe got to her feet, fluttering her long hands in agitation, her long dark waterfall of hair swinging from side to side as she gestured agitatedly.

October smiled languidly at Stella.

"Whatever," she sighed, passively, "I think that there is a chain out there," she gestured in the direction of the garden. "The last people in the house had a dog."

Stella nodded, this had to get better.

They had got off to a bad start.

She took Teddy outside into the garden and attached the chain to his collar and left him yelping furiously, annoyed at having been left and headed back into the house. "I'll give you a hand to bring your things in," October said as Stella came back into the lounge.

"Where do you come from?" Xanthe asked still fluttering around the room, looking agitatedly out at the garden and wincing dramatically every time Teddy yapped. "Mayo, but I've lived here for ……….."

"Mayo!" exclaimed Xanthe, turning her green eyes onto Stella, "Mayo? I didn't think that anyone actually came from Mayo!"

271

CHAPTER THIRTY EIGHT

Amber turned the pages of her diary, counting slowly. There had to be some mistake. She could not possibly be that late with her period. But, conscious of an ever sinking feeling deep in her belly, she knew that she was late..

"Bloody hell," she mouthed, miserably, that really was all she needed. She could not be pregnant. It just was not possible; fate would not be that cruel, surely. And yet the dates were there, in black and white. She was very late.

Amber sniffed hard; she was not going to cry again.

Amber missed Stella and Teddy terribly. Life just was not the same without them.

She missed Stella's easy company, telling her about the silly things that had happened at work. How they would have laughed. She could tell Paul and he would roar with laughter, but somehow it just was not the same. It was wonderful to have a kind, loving boyfriend, for once in her life, but Amber missed Stella, like hell. Missed curling up with her on the sofa, Teddy sprawled between them while they watched some girly programme on the television. And girly gossip, bitching about the people that they knew and the people that they worked with.

Somehow when she said the same things to Paul it sounded nasty and snide, another girl understood. Well, all other girls that was except Della her new flat mate.

Della was….well, Della was like a lady wrestler, with lots of makeup on.

She was enormous. Not in the pudgy fat kind of enormous, just solid, hefty, with thighs like tree trunks and strapping forearms that a navvy would have been proud of.

And she had no sense of humour whatsoever. She merely went to work, or she sat in front of the television, her solid face, impassive behind a thick layer of orange makeup.

At least Amber had thought when she first met Della, she would never have to worry about having her boyfriend pinched.

Della did not look as if she were interested in anything, except watching television and eating chocolate. She could consume bar after bar, her jaws moving with the rhythmic slowness of a bovine while her eyes never moved from the flickering images on the television screen.

Della was absolutely the complete opposite of Stella.

And just at this moment Amber missed Stella terribly.

Stella would have made Amber feel as if she could cope with this awful pregnancy scare.

Amber could imagine her snatching the diary and counting the dates, her long fingers tapping the pages as she turned them. And then she would have dismissed the scare as irrelevant, "you're only a few days late, don't worry," and sent Amber off to the shops to rent a girly video and buy a bottle of wine, or she would have helped to do something about it. "I'll be Godmother. I'll baby sit. I'll help you find a crèche. I'll help you tell the father." Telling the father…… . that was an awesome task.

Paul was gorgeous.

He was the best thing that had ever happened to Amber. Even if Stella had not thought so.

He was kind, considerate, infinitely good looking. Very sexy.

But telling him that she was pregnant. If she was. Assuming that she was, from the dates in her calendar and from how sick she suddenly felt, that was something else altogether.

To Amber the thought that she might be pregnant was scary, but not terrifying. She wanted children. Someday.

To have a baby as an unmarried mother and hold down a job and rear a child was not a dreadful prospect. She would cope, she knew that.

But Paul was another prospect altogether. He was carefree. Just getting his life back together. He was getting more work as a jockey. He was grateful now at having been given another chance, working hard and conscientiously to prove that everyone was right to have faith in him. How would her react to the tie of having a baby around. Amber did not expect that he would suddenly go down on one knee and propose to her. But she did not want to lose him because he did not want the tie of having a baby around in his relationship.

"What's up?" Della removed the wrapper from another chocolate bar.

"Nothing," replied Amber, it was silly to even think about pregnancy and babies. She was only a few days late, she had not even done a test yet to see if she was pregnant. Even if she did feel rather sick.

It could have been the thought of going out to see Henry that was making her feel sick, thought Amber, as the buzzer sounded, to announce that Paul had arrived.

They were going out to Henry's cottage today; Paul was going to ride Princess Pushy for the last time before their big race next week.

Amber had been dreading meeting him again, after Stella had dumped him so cruelly.

"I guess that is Paul," Amber shoved her diary into her handbag and went to the intercom.

"Right," Della said her mouthful of chocolate.

"Hello," Amber said into the intercom.

"Hi sexy," Paul's voice filled the apartment. Amber felt herself go pink with embarrassment, but Della never gave any indication that she had heard him.

"I'll be down in a minute," Amber grabbed her coat, "I'll see you later."

"Right," Della chomped in reply, heaving her feet luxuriously onto the sofa and changing the channels on the television.

Of course if could have been the smell of all of that chocolate that was making her feel sick, pondered Amber as she ran down the stairs to the front door.

Paul was sitting on the wall outside. He got up as Amber slammed the door, opening out his arms for her to leap into.

"God, I missed you," he mumbled, trying to kiss her at the same time.

"Can't we just go inside and go to bed?" Paul turned Amber back towards the apartment. "I'd rather ride you than Princess Pushy."

"No," laughed Amber. "Your horse needs you," she shoved him in the direction of his car. "Besides which we couldn't get to the bedroom for all of the chocolate wrappers that Della has littering the floor."

"Yack," said Paul, opening the car door, courteously for Amber. "Yes, she does rather look like one," laughed Amber as he slammed the door shut.

The sick feeling returned as they sped out of the city.

Amber wondered if it were possible to feel terrified and delighted all at the same time?

Paul chattered as he drove, but Amber felt miles away, living in a world where she was breaking the most earth shattering news to him. The yard was deserted when they arrived at Henry's yard.

"Where is everyone?" asked Amber, straining to look through the car windscreen. "They will all have gone home," explained Paul. "They work in the morning, doing the stables and stuff and then go away for the afternoon and come back to do the evening stables later on." Amber nodded; the whole place looked abandoned and uncared for.

The old Labrador barked a greeting as Paul parked his car next to Henry's Jeep. He turned off the engine and an unearthly silence descended on the yard.

"Where's Henry?" Amber whispered, it was so quiet that it seemed wrong to even talk.

Paul shrugged. "Let's try inside," he said as they walked up the path to the cottage. The curtains were half closed, giving the cottage an eerie, deserted feeling. Paul hammered on the door, "Henry knows that we are coming," he frowned. "He can't be far away, his Jeep's here." Paul fished his telephone out of his pocket and dialled Henry's number. They could hear the telephone ringing inside the cottage, the noise echoing around the rooms.

Amber felt a surge of panic grip her insides like an iron fist, she darted a look at Paul and saw that he was as afraid as she was.

Something must have happened to Henry. Something was very wrong.

Paul tried the door and it swung open, the cottage felt damp and lonely. "Maybe he's inside," Paul spoke as if things were normal, as if maybe Henry had overslept or had got engrossed in a pile of paperwork, his calm voice betraying the panic that they both felt.

Amber followed Paul inside the cottage. She was sure that they were going to find Henry dead. Losing Stella had unhinged him so much that he had taken his own life.

The television was on in the lounge, the sound faint over the noise of their breathing. Paul pushed open the door. Amber gave a sigh of relief. Henry was alive; he sat on the sofa watching the television.

"'Lo," he grinned foolishly in their direction, his eyes blinking slowly as he tried – and failed to focus on them. On the floor beside him was a half empty bottle of whiskey, a beautiful cut glass tumbler lay on its side, a small pool of liquid seeping slowly into the grubby looking carpet.

Henry looked terrible, his face was pinched and grey, the clothes that he wore seemed to hang off his body as if they had been made for someone several sizes larger. He was very, very drunk.

"Henry?" Paul said, his voice filled with relief.

"She's left me you know," Henry stumbled over the words. "Left me," he shook his head as if he could not believe what he had just said. Amber brought her mouth up to her hand to stifle a sob. Stella had done this to Henry. She had left him and broken his heart.

The smell of whiskey reached Amber's nostrils and suddenly she knew that she had to get out of the room. She dashed outside, retching miserably on her knees on the muddy patch of grass that served as a lawn.

After a while Amber felt better, she picked herself up, wiping the mud from her now damp knees and walked back inside, ignoring the curious glance that Paul shot in her direction.

"You ok?" he frowned.

"Mmmm," Amber said, trying hard not to breathe the whiskey fumes, she pulled out a chair from beneath the dining table and sat down.

"Where did you say the coffee was?" Paul asked as the kettle whistled on the gas cooker. Henry said something unintelligible.

Paul went into the kitchen; Amber could hear him opening cupboards as he looked for the coffee. After a moment he reappeared in the doorway, shrugging his shoulders at Amber, helplessly.

Amber grinned. "Leave the domestic stuff to me," she was glad of the excuse to get away from Henry, it was awful to see such a wonderful man so broken in spirit. "Make yourself one," Henry shouted merrily. Amber found the coffee jar, made three cups and took them back into the lounge.

"What the hell are you playing at?" Paul snapped at Henry, shoving the coffee cup into his shaking hand.

Henry shrugged. "Just thought that I would give it a try," he laughed, fumbling for the whiskey bottle and shaking it gently. "Seemed to work for my father," he gazed at the liquid in the bottle for a moment before laying it down gingerly.

"Drink that coffee," ordered Paul. "You'll feel better. Whiskey isn't the answer." Henry did as he was told and sipped at the coffee, miserably. "My father was an alcoholic," he said, suddenly, "I always vowed that I would never touch it. But after Stella......."

Paul seized the bottle and went into the kitchen. Amber could hear the sound of liquid glugging down the plughole.

"Don't touch it again, all right?" he handed Henry another cup of coffee.

"Come on, we need to work Princess Pushy." Paul hauled Henry to his feet. "I just want Stella back," Henry said as he followed Paul unsteadily out into the yard.

"Well drinking isn't going to get her back now is it?" Paul said, gently. "I don't understand why she left me. I was crazy about her. I thought she was crazy about me."

Amber wiped her hand across her eyes, furiously dashing away the tears. How could she tell Henry that Stella had been crazy about him?

"I just need to nip to the chemist on the way home," she told Paul as he drove along the driveway from Henry's cottage, a lot later. "Della used all my makeup remover. I'll have to buy some more."

Paul sat in the car, reading the racing newspaper, while Amber went into the shop. She brought a pregnancy testing kit, feeling as if everyone in the shop was staring at her, shoved it deep into her handbag and then with a new bottle of makeup remover in a paper bag, went back to the car.

Amber went into the toilet and opened the packet. According to the instructions the kit was easy to use. Amber followed the steps on the instructions and then sat on the edge of the bath to wait. The moisture soaked through one square, lighting up a blue line and then as it soaked through into the other square the next blue line lit up immediately.

Amber stared at the two boxes, each with a bright blue line. The test was supposed to take a few minutes. This was too soon. There must be something wrong with it. But she knew that there was nothing wrong with the kit. There was something wrong with her. She was pregnant.

CHAPTER THIRTY NINE

Amber decided that this was probably not a good time to tell Paul she was pregnant.

He was writhing around on the ground clutching his thigh muscle where seconds earlier Princess Pushy has lashed out with a hind leg and kicked him.

"Fuck!" he yelped, his face contorted in pain.

Kathy grinned. "She's a bit tetchy this morning, I'd stay away from her back end if I were you."

"Thanks," Paul said bitterly, scrambling painfully to his feet. A long dirty mark scored the front of his jeans where the mare's tiny iron shod hoof had made contact with his leg.

"Lucky it wasn't a few inches further over," Henry grinned, coming across the yard, his arms full of the brightly coloured silks that Paul would wear when he raced Princess Pushy later. "Amber would be really upset."

Amber met his eyes and grinned back.

Henry looked a different man from the one that they had found drunk almost to the point of being unconscious. The sparkle that had been in his eyes when he was around Stella had gone, but the dead, lifeless look that had been there the last time that

Amber had seen him had gone too. Now he looked rather lost and bewildered, but calm almost resigned to the fact that Stella had left him.

Kathy led Princess Pushy into the horse lorry. Paul hobbled over to the ramp to help Henry push it closed.

"Fuck, fuck that hurts," Paul complained, leaning against the side of the lorry, wiping away the beads of sweat from his forehead with the back of his hand.

"Come on, you can be get loads of sympathy later. You have got a race to win now," Kathy slapped Paul hard on the arm, making him yelp again.

Henry's Labrador, George, waddled across the yard and shoved his nose into Amber's hand, his dark eyes gazing at her imploringly, pleading for attention. Amber rubbed his wide, square head, gently, she missed Teddy terribly. Paul had told her that she should get another dog, but Amber did not want to, not yet.

She would be busy enough in a few months' time without having the extra work of a dog as well.

Amber gave George a final pat, she did not even want to think about the baby. If she did not think about it then it would not seem to be real. She would have to tell Paul, sometime, but finding the right moment was hard.

Amber was sure that he would not be very happy about finding out that he was going to be a father. Somehow the responsibility of looking after a tiny human being did not seem to be part of his lifestyle. He was so full of life, carefree, just restarting his career as a jockey. He had all of his life in front of him now.

While for Amber, she was starting to live her life with a new life, something that she was going to be responsible for forever.

Amber was sure that she would lose him. He would freak out completely. Their relationship was too young for such a big change. How could she have been so stupid to let herself get pregnant?

That was easy to answer, one time without a condom; she had told him that it was ok. No way that she could get pregnant, she counted the days diligently, except that somehow she had miscounted, or something.

One thing was certain. Something had gone wrong and she was pregnant now.

And she was going to lose Paul as soon as he found out that she was pregnant. Sure, he would be delighted at first. He had proved that he was fertile, that he was doing it right. But then, once the weight of the responsibility had sunk onto his shoulders – he would be off – quicker than a race commentator could say – 'They're Off."

Amber scrambled into the lorry and settled herself into the passenger seat, Kathy lit up a cigarette behind her, making Amber want to heave, she wound down the window, fighting waves of nausea.

"I'll get someone to give you a massage on that ……. ." As they reached the top of the drive a small, white car, like the one that Stella drove came along the main road towards them. For a moment Henry froze, the words dying on his lips. "Leg," he finished lamely as he realised that it was not Stella driving towards them.

Amber wished that there was something that she could do to ease the pain that he was feeling.

It was a dreadful thing to lose someone that you loved. She would probably be feeling the same way in a few weeks' time, once Paul found out about her being pregnant.

It was not going to be possible to keep the news from him too much longer. Her waist line was expanding at an alarming rate. This would probably be the last time that she was able to wear her size eight jeans.

Paul and Henry went off to find the course physiotherapist when they arrived at the races, while Kathy got Princess Pushy ready for her race.

Amber wandered onto the racecourse alone. They were early and the tarmac concourse was deserted, only the a few stewards and early spectators wandered around, shivering in the bitter wind that drifted around the buildings.

Amber went inside and got herself a cup of hot chocolate in one of the restaurants. She could not face coffee or tea any more, but somehow the sweetness of the chocolate was just what her body seemed to crave.

While she dreamily stirred her chocolate Amber looked up as another couple came into the restaurant. She recognised the man instantly, Derry Blake, how on earth could Stella have thought that he was attractive when she had someone like Henry in love with her?

Derry glanced in Amber's direction, his cold eyes flickering over her momentarily then sliding away as he dismissed her as of no consequence. His companion was a pretty red head, whose china blue eyes never left Derry's face, until another man joined them.

The other man was tall and very thin, elegantly dressed in a smart black over coat, with a smart Fedora hat tipped over his eyes. He put his arm possessively around the woman who now looked anywhere except at Derry.

Amber curled her lip in distaste. Derry and the woman were obviously having an affair, she disliked him intensely. He had no respect for anyone.

Amber made the hot chocolate last for ages, enjoying the warmth of the restaurant, until it was time to go out and watch the horses parade at the start of the race.

It was bitterly cold outside after the warmth of the restaurant. Amber pulled her over coat further around her, drawing the collar together at her neck.

There were more people now on the concourse, the atmosphere bright and cheery in spite of the cold wind that darted sly gusts around the corners of the buildings, sending abandoned race tickets and litter scooting across the tarmac.

Amber could see the brightly coloured umbrellas of the bookmakers, like brightly coloured beacons beckoning her towards them.

Amber turned hastily away. She did not dare even go near them.

Ruby had helped her out of the financial mess this time. She would not do it again.

Amber had to keep control of her own life.

Amber found Henry in the saddling enclosure. Kathy was holding Princess Pushy in one of the saddling stalls, while Henry buckled the saddle into place.

The mare excited by the tense atmosphere swished her tail and laid back her ears as Henry pulled the girth straps tight.

"How is Paul feeling?" Amber asked, gingerly rubbing the velvet soft hair on Princess Pushy's nose.

"A lot better now," Henry pushed the last strap into place. "The Physio gave him a good massage on that leg, hopefully that will have un-knotted the muscles."

Princess Pushy rushed out of the saddling stall as Kathy tugged gently on her lead rein. "Come on, we'll go to the parade ring," Henry said, watching Princess Pushy capering as a sheet of newspaper, caught by the wind, skittered across the grass, frightening the highly strung mare. "You ok," he shouted to Kathy as the tough wiry little woman hauled on the mare's bridle to bring her under control.

"No problem!" she yelled back between gritted teeth.

The parade ring was already full. Owners and the trainers of the horses huddled in groups, watching their horses and surreptitiously eyeing up the competition.

The twelve horses that were competing in the race walked around a tarmac path that circled the edge of the parade ring, while the spectators crowded against the white guard rail around the edge, trying to pick out the winner of the race.

Princess Pushy looked thoroughly upset by the noise and commotion that went with a big race. She jogged sideways, her tiny hooves beating a rapid tattoo on the tarmac, flecks of foam flying from her mouth as she champed restlessly on her bit.

Amber saw Derry Blake and the owners of the horse that he was training, standing close to herself and Henry. Derry was resting his hand gently on the red haired woman's bottom, as he stood beside her husband.

What a bastard he is, Amber thought, shooting him a glance full of hatred. Any woman who had anything to do with that creep needed to have her head examined. He was pure poison.

The jockeys trooped out of the Weigh Room.

Paul looked like a stranger in his racing clothes, his body unfamiliar in the white breeches and dazzling purple and white silks, his face unrecognisable beneath his skull cap. He dropped a gentle kiss onto Amber's lips.

"Ok?" he asked, full of concern. "You look frozen."

He hugged her to him for a moment; Amber let herself lean into him, soaking up the warmth from his body. Loving him was too painful, when she was bound to lose him when he found out about the baby.

The bell rang, loud above the hum of conversation in the parade ring, signalling that it was time for the jockeys to get onto their horses.

Kathy led Princess Pushy towards them, bracing her elbow against the mare's shoulder to steady her.

In one swift, graceful movement Henry threw Paul up into the saddle and the mare bounded forwards as he fumbled for his stirrups, then with a suddenness that surprised Amber, the mare shot sideways, surprised by an innocuous piece of litter that blew along the ground from the edge of the parade ring. Amber glimpsed the movement out of the corner of her eye, but before she had time to react the mare's enormously powerful muscular quarters had hit her in the back, knocking the wind out of her body and sending her sprawling to the ground. A second later Henry was helping Amber to her feet.

"She's ok. Aren't you Amber?" she heard him say, seeing Paul's concerned face looking down at her from the horse as she nodded in agreement.

"I'm ok. Go on. The horses are going onto the course," she said, struggling for breath.

Amber bent over as a spasm of pain shot through her tummy and then was gone as quickly as it had come.

"Are you ok?" Henry put his arm gently around Amber's waist, his kind eyes full of concern.

"Just winded," Amber managed to gasp, she let out her breath slowly, "I'm ok," she straightened up slowly, kneading her side.

"Sure?" Henry was oblivious to the fact that the parade ring had emptied and that all of the spectators had gone off to watch the race.

"Yes, honestly," Amber lied. Henry needed to go and watch the race. They had spent so long preparing for this race; she was not going to deny him the chance to see it. She followed Henry to the Owners and Trainers stand and climbed high up the steps so that they had a good position to watch the race from.

The pain had subsided to a dull throb, she longed to sit down somewhere quiet. But there was no chance of that now.

The horses were already racing; Amber could see a brown blur topped by a kaleidoscope of colour at the far side of the track. Amber swallowed hard, she was sure that she was going to be sick; beads of sweat had broken out on her forehead.

"She's in fourth place," Henry whispered beside her, his voice filled with wonderment.

Amber glanced up to see the horses thundering past the stands. She glimpsed Paul's face for a split second, filled with concentration and determination.

Once the race was over she would find somewhere to sit down and wait until the pain had passed, Amber thought as the horses shot around the track, away from the stands. It seemed to go on forever as Amber fought the waves of pain and nausea. As if it was coming from far away Amber could hear the voice of the announcer, echoed by Henry's voice, rising higher and higher with excitement. "Second place, she's in second place," then what seemed like an eternity later. "She's going to win. She's going to.........." She's won!" Henry bellowed beside her.

"Come on!" Henry yelled as Princess Pushy thundered past the winning post. "Let's go and lead her in." dragging Amber by the arm, they shoved and barged through the crowds.

Paul rode Princess Pushy off the track, his red, mud-splattered face split into a broad grin.

"We did it!" Paul yelled over the deafening thunder of noise, shaking his whip in the air.

Henry grabbed Princess Pushy's bridle, the mare's bay coat was wet with sweat, plumes of breath came from her enormous nostrils, she was exhausted, but proudly tossed her head as if to acknowledge the cheers and clapping of the spectators.

A man shot out of the crowd and grabbed Henry's hand, pumping it furiously as he shouldered his way through the crowd in his desperate attempt to stay beside Henry. "I've five horses, I want you to train them for me, telephone me. Here's my card," he shoved a crumpled business card into Henry's pocket. "I'll come and talk to you in the Owners and Trainers bar later," he let go of Henry's hand and was immediately swallowed up by the tide of spectators who all wanted to touch the mare, her jockey and trainer.

"This way. Look this way," the photographers yelled from all directions around them, as a barrage of cameras clicked and whirled around them.

Princess Pushy, her nervous energy expanded stood quietly in the place reserved for the race winners, between a grinning Paul and Henry, her ears sharply pricked, as if she were showing the cameramen how beautiful she was.

"Brilliant!" Henry grinned above the roar of noise. "You rode an amazing race!" "Brilliant!" Paul grinned back. "You did an amazing job of training her!"

Paul hugged Amber to him, kissing her on the cheek as the cameras clicked and whirled once again. And then, as quickly as they had arrived the cameramen darted away back to the track to photograph the next race.

"Come on, I think we should go and celebrate after Paul has weighed in," Henry told them, giving Princess Pushy a final pat before Kathy took her back to the lorry.

Paul released his grip on Amber's shoulder and suddenly her legs crumpled as Amber slid to her knees.

"Paul," her voice was a strangled whisper as another dart of pain shot through her stomach.

CHAPTER FORTY

"Where is Stella?" Amber croaked, she ran a tongue that felt as if it were three sizes too big over lips that felt cracked and dry. "I need Stella," Amber wailed, vaguely aware beyond the waves of pain that tore at her stomach of Paul's pinched white face gazing at her. She could not read the expression in his eyes. "Stella," she whispered again, longing desperately for her calm control. Stella would know what to do; she would be able to make the pain go away.

"It's alright," Paul's cool hand passed gently over Amber's sweat dampened forehead, smoothing away the tendrils of wet hair that clung to her pale skin. "A nurse is coming."

Amber opened her eyes again, forcing herself to focus, trying desperately to ride the pain, rather than tense against it, but it was too strong for her, too frightening to control.

The room was very bright; the powerful lights in the ceiling seemed to penetrate her eyes, making her head ache.

Amber turned her head; she was surrounded by machinery, tubes and pipes, red lights that winked. Hospital. But she had no memory of arriving, or the journey.

A door opened, Amber could hear noise from outside her room, voices, someone yelling, and someone else in pain. Amber closed her eyes.

"This will stop the pain Amber and then we can have a look at what is going on," said a female voice. Amber winced as a needle was inserted into the back of her hand and then felt her face split into a daft grin. The pain had miraculously gone, but then so had any sensation except a disconcerting feeling of floating.

Tentatively Amber looked at Paul. He looked terrified, Amber groped for his hand, his fingers closed gently around hers, stroking her fingers distractedly as he watched the nurse work.

"Excuse me Dad," the nurse said, leaning over Paul to lift Amber's top. Amber saw his eyes widen, his mouth dropped open as if he were about to speak, but then he closed it again, biting his bottom lip as if he were afraid of what he might say.

"I'm just going to do a scan," the nurse said. "See what is going on."

She smeared an icy gel over the slight bulge of Amber's belly and then deftly began to work the scanner. A moment later the unmistakeable sound of a super-fast heart beat filled the room.

"That's his heart," Paul's voice was filled with awe.

"His!" laughed the nurse, switching off the machine and handing Amber a wad of tissue paper. "Typical man!"

"Well the baby is ok at the moment," said the nurse, suddenly serious, "I imagine that the Doctor will want to keep you in hospital for a few days, just in case there are any problems."

And then she swept from the room leaving Paul and Amber alone.

"I'm sorry that I didn't tell you before," Amber whispered, when the silence between them grew to be an almost physical presence. "There never seemed to be the right moment to say 'I'm pregnant.'"

"Pregnant," Paul said, slowly as if he were speaking a new language and he was having trouble getting his tongue around an unfamiliar word. "How the hell did it happen?"

Duh. Amber wanted to laugh out loud. How did he think it happened, she thought fleetingly, but somehow the atmosphere did not seem right to make jokes.

"I suppose the night when we didn't use a condom," Amber said gently.

The whole scenario had an air of unreality about it.

Only a short time ago she had been worried about paying her debts, now the whole landscape of Amber's life had altered. Pregnant. A baby. The baby that was part of herself and Paul, created out of the love that they had felt for each other, but something that would alter Amber's life forever.

Getting rid of the baby was never going to be an option. And yet the thought of having it in her life was terrifying.

Yet again Amber wished that Stella were there, she would tell Amber how easy it was to rear a baby – as if she knew! It will be just like having another puppy; Amber could almost hear her saying. It just needs love and feeding and changing. And at least we won't be mopping its puddles up off the floor; at least a baby did its business in a nappy.

Stella was always looking on the positive side of everything. If Stella were here Amber would not be feeling so desolate and afraid.

Paul looked grey faced; he shook his head in disbelief, making Amber afraid. This was too much for him to take in. It had been a bad way for him to find out that she was pregnant. To have her dropping to the floor, clutching at her belly, just when he had won the big race of the day and was looking forward to an evening celebrating his success. From the look on his face when she had moaned, "get me to hospital I think I'm having a miscarriage," he must have thought that she was joking.

Through the waves of pain that were rocketing through her body Amber had read his expression, he was thinking stop messing around Amber, don't play jokes on me now.

But then as Henry had scooped her off the floor and yelled at someone to bring them to hospital his expression had changed. He had realised then that this was no joke.

"Oh," was all that Paul said, after what seemed an interminable silence. Amber clutched at his hand, trying to hold him physically, fighting the terrifying feeling that mentally he was a million miles away, lost in his own world. Maybe lost forever.

Exhausted by her ordeal Amber's eyelids became too heavy to hold up and she dozed, aware of Paul's presence beside her, aware that he was just sitting, looking at her, but looking at her as if he was not seeing her any longer.

Each time that she opened her eyes the fear that Amber had felt over the possibility of losing the baby was replaced by some nameless fear over Paul. He did not seem angry, or delighted, or scared, or anything. Merely silent.

Amber was glad when a nurse came and told her that a bed had been made ready for her on one of the wards, she would have to stay in hospital for a few days, until they were sure that she was not going to lose the baby.

Amber was not allowed to walk to the ward, instead Paul pushed her in a wheelchair, following the straight back of the nurse who guided them through the dim, deserted corridors.

Even in the middle of the night there was activity on the ward.

Nurses moved around the beds, their uniforms rustling, rubber soles squeaking against the lino floor, speaking in hushed tones to the patients as they administered medicines or a reassuring word.

A bed had been found for Amber, beside the window. "I'll let you get into bed," the nurse told Amber before turning to Paul, "Amber needs to rest now. You can come back tomorrow." Paul nodded.

Amber saw the relief at being told to go shining in his eyes, he was glad to be going away from the hospital, away from her. Amber could feel him sliding away from her, like sand on a beach, she could not hold him, she was losing him piece by piece.

A pregnant girlfriend was too much to cope with.

"Do you want me to tell anyone that you are here?" Paul asked, kissing her chastely on the forehead as he prepared to leave.

Amber wanted to grab his arm, cling to him, plead with him not to stop loving her. Instead she said, "no, I don't want anyone to know."

It was hard enough to cope with her own feelings, and Paul's without having to deal with the wrath of her mother and Ruby's smug pity.

Amber stayed in the hospital for two days, lying in the narrow bed, being poked and probed by a succession of doctors and nurses.

Paul came dutifully every evening, bringing grapes and flowers, to sit beside her bed shuffling his feet and making stilted conversation about the weather.

Had it not been so sad Amber would have found it funny that they were having such inane conversations when usually they had discussed everything under the sun. Eventually a nurse had come and told Amber that she could leave.

Paul came that evening; Amber was desperate to get out of the hospital and back home.

They walked out into the pale evening sunshine, two tense strangers talking about anything except reality.

Paul found a taxi, gently guiding Amber into the back seat, before getting in himself, sitting slightly apart, gazing out of the window, while a black cloud of fear settled heavily on Amber's shoulders.

"Paul, are you ok?" Amber had asked, fearing that he was anything but ok.

"Just give me time to get my head around this." Was all that he had said, in a tone that she could not read.

Amber could have understood anger, or coldness, but his voice sounded as if he were a stranger, discussing the weather.

Paul walked Amber to the apartment door, in silence, Amber terrified to speak, afraid of the demons that might be unleashed if she began to question Paul about his feelings, she just had to wait. Wait and let him come to terms with what had happened. He had been so delighted when he had seen the blob on the scanner screen and yet now he seemed so angry with her.

"Will you be ok now?" he asked gently as Amber pushed open the door.

"Yes," she answered tonelessly. She did not feel very ok. She was terrified, terrified of losing Paul, terrified of losing the baby, terrified of what the future might hold.

Paul wrung his hands together as if he were uncertain what to say, or do, he hovered for a moment, seeming to decide whether to come in with her or bolt.

"I'll talk to you soon," he said, choosing the latter.

Then he was gone, running lightly down the steps and disappearing through the front door.

Amber listened as the door slammed shut and then wearily made her way into the apartment.

"Oh you're back," Della sprawled in one of the armchairs surrounded by the debris of her life, chocolate bars, crisp packets and the television remote control.

Amber suddenly had no energy to move; she slumped down in the other armchair and tried to lose herself in the mindless programme that Della was watching.

Della, humming tunelessly to the theme tune of her favourite television soap unwrapped yet another chocolate bar.

Amber gritted her teeth, her nerves stretched almost to breaking point as the cellophane rattled and then Della long teeth crunched down onto the chocolate, chomping loudly, still humming while she ate. The urge to rush over to the sofa and force the chocolate bars into Della's mouth until she choked was very strong. Amber wondered fleetingly how long she would get in prison for murder by chocolate bar. Probably not very long, considering the strain she was under.

"Do you want one of these?" Della rattled a chocolate bar under Amber's nose.

"No," Amber almost heaved.

It was strange the odd things that happened to your body when you were pregnant. All of the things that she had once loved to eat, she now hated. Chocolate was suddenly the most revolting substance in the world. As were Chinese takeaways, once almost her staple diet.

"Suit yourself," Della said, shoving the remains of the bar that she was eating into her mouth.

Amber's stomach lurched uncomfortably; she closed her eyes to block out the sight of Della chewing.

"Are you ok now?" Della stopped chewing and turned to face Amber, as she spoke great waves of chocolate fumes made Amber want to cover her nose and mouth with her hand so that she could not smell her breath.

"I think so," Amber forced herself to smile. It was not Della's fault that Amber could not bear to be near her, she should try harder to like her new companion.

"Good," Della gave Amber the thumbs up signal, "I've no problem with living with a baby in the apartment. Don't mind even babysitting."

"Thanks." It was hard to imagine life with a baby.

There was so much to consider, so much responsibility. Amber had never imagined a scenario with her looking after the baby with Della. She had always pictured herself with Paul, the three of them as a family. Life as a single mother had never occurred to her.

The clock slid at breathtaking speed around to midnight.

Paul always telephoned at around ten o'clock if they were not together to say 'goodnight'. Tonight however there had been no telephone call.

Ten sped around to eleven o'clock. Amber dialled Paul's number and got his message service. A leaden chunk of fear slowly sank to the pit of Amber's stomach.

Where was Paul? Della heaved herself out of the armchair and said "Goodnight," as she headed in the direction of her bedroom.

Amber sat silently, watching the clock slide around, fingering her telephone, willing it to ring. Paul must not leave her. Not like this.

Amber could not bear the thought of life without him. She would do anything to keep him. Get rid of the baby, if that was what it took. She would do that. Anything.

Amber picked up her telephone again, checking to see if the battery and reception were working. They were fine. Everything was fine. The reason that Paul had not rung, the reason that Amber could not get him on the telephone was that he did not want to speak to her.

He was gone. She had lost him. He was never coming back.

CHAPTER FORTY ONE

Stella clipped the chain back onto Teddy's collar. "You can come in later on," she whispered, gently rubbing his soft ears. "I'll bring you in when they've all gone to bed."

Stella had taken to creeping downstairs once everyone had gone to bed and bringing Teddy inside to her room.

She found it comforting to drift off to sleep with him curled in the small of her back.

Most mornings she woke early to find her arm around his small, warm body, drawing much needed reassurance from his presence.

She stood up, biting her lip miserably as Teddy whimpered despondently.

"I don't think that he likes being chained up," Henry's voice said, suddenly, making Stella jump. Henry came out through the French windows and walked down the path towards her. "He had a better life when you lived with Amber."

Stella drew herself up to her full height. "He will get used to it," she said tensely, completely thrown by Henry's sudden appearance and at the way that her whole body quivered with delight at him being there.

"I doubt it," Henry said wryly, walking past Stella and crouching down beside Teddy who squirmed with delight, pawing at Henry and jumping up to lick his face. "How did you know where I was? Did you want something?" Stella asked, stunned into confusion, her panic making her defensive. Henry stood up slowly, one hand still dangling at his side for Teddy to lick.

"Amber told me where you had moved to. I just wanted to tell you that…….. ." He was silent for a moment, looking at Stella as if he wanted to absorb every particle of her.

Stella was silent too, gazing back at him, longing to take the two strides that separated them and fall into his arms.

Henry looked cold, impenetrable and Stella dropped her eyes. "Tell you that Amber has been in hospital."

Stella felt a jolt as if she had put her fingers into the electric socket.

"What?" she exclaimed,

"She's had a threatened miscarriage."

"Miscarriage?" repeated Stella slowly. "Miscarriage? I didn't even know that she was pregnant."

"Came as a bit of a surprise to Paul too," Henry smiled, tightly. "He just found out that he was going to be a father in the same moment that he found out that Amber might lose the baby."

"How did he take the news that he was going to be a father?" Stella swallowed down the lump in her throat that was making it suddenly hard to talk.

Henry shrugged and pulled down his mouth. "They broke up."

"God, that is awful," Stella could not bear the thought of Amber being miserable.

A tense silence fell between them, Stella longed to touch Henry, wished that he would come and take hold of her.

She could not move, afraid of what would happen if she took a step forwards.

She had to get over him, the pain was too great to go through all of that again.

"Just thought that you would like to know."

Stella nodded. "Thanks for letting me know, it's kind of you to come and tell me." Henry shrugged. "It gave me an excuse to come and see you," he said, so quietly that Stella wondered if she were hearing things. "I miss you," he said.

Stella met his eyes and looked into their loving depths. One step was all that it would take and she would be back in his arms.

"I……. ." she began.

"Stella!" Xanthe shrieked from the open French windows. "Your phone was ringing. It's Derry Blake for you!"

Stella watched a myriad of emotions flicker across Henry's face, his eyes grew hard, the love that she could see reflected there fading and being replaced by a coldness as he stared back at her. Stella could not move, it was as if she were rooted to the spot, hating to see the coldness in his eyes.

"Hadn't you better go and take that call," Henry said coldly, his eyes blazed with hatred.

Stella moved towards the house, her limbs felt heavy as if she were fighting her way through treacle. Her telephone had been left in the hall; Stella picked it up conscious of Henry walking past her, bitterness oozing from the straight line of his back and his tense, set jaw.

"Hello," her voice sounded flat and dead.

"Hello, I couldn't speak to you earlier, I was entertaining a client," Derry said. Stella watched Henry walk out of the front door.

Stella wanted to drop the telephone as if it were red hot.

She wished that she had never telephoned Derry Blake. She had not even really meant to telephone him. It was not the kind of thing that she did, asking a man out.

She had turned his business card over and over in her hands, just looking at it, wondering what it would have been like to go out with someone as sleek and desirable as Derry, but she could not pluck up the courage to speak to him on the telephone.

She had picked up her mobile a few times and then dropped it, losing courage at the last moment.

Sorcha had come into her office, and that had stopped her trying to telephone during work hours. Peter Shaunnessy, the Chairman of the company wanted to see Stella, Sorcha had told her. Stella had gone up to his office feeling sick. No one got to go to Peter's office unless it was really important. He must have been going to sack her, maybe he had found out that she was fiddling her expenses and the Guards were waiting for her.

Peter's office was on the top floor of the building. It was enormous, taking up the same amount of room as the office that all of the journalists that worked for the magazine were crammed into.

Peter had asked her to sit down on a vast leather armchair, and had told her that Kevin, her boss, had suffered a nervous breakdown and was going to be off work indefinitely. And he wanted Stella to take over Kevin's role.

She had gone back down to her own office feeling as if her luck had turned. She was a powerful, independent woman; she could ring Derry Blake if she wanted to. It had taken her long enough to pluck up the courage, until finally she had decided that she definitely needed to let her life move forwards.

It was no use regretting the past, she had to forget about Henry, he was not what she wanted.

And she had to forget about Amber, they had fallen out, there was no going back. So finally she had reached for her telephone and dialled his number. He had told her that he could not talk to her at the moment, but that he would ring her back, in the evening. Now he had and at a very bad moment.

"But now you have my full attention, as someone as gorgeous as you deserves," Derry was saying, his voice smooth as warm chocolate and as sickly sweet. "Would you like to come to the races with me?" Derry continued, oblivious to Stella's stunned silence on the end of the telephone.

Out of the window she could see Henry getting into his Jeep, his face cold and set.

"Err, yes lovely." Stella was barely aware of what she was saying, listening to the familiar sound of the Jeep rattling and screeching as Henry started it up and drove slowly away.

"Right then, maybe you will meet me at the races. You can park in the trainers car park, I'll tell the steward there to expect you."

Stella heard herself agreeing as Derry gave her directions and made the arrangements to meet her at the races, while her throat constricted miserably and her heart pounded, dully against her ribs.

"Right," Stella put down the telephone, she should have been feeling delighted, she had just got an invitation to the races with Derry Blake.

He was just the kind of man that she had always been searching for, wealthy, good looking, powerful and yet.....Stella sighed, remembering how she had felt standing in the garden when Henry looked at her.

Stella did not look forward to going to the races. There was no feeling of dread, as if she had been going for an exam, or a much feared dentist appointment, it was just that there was no buzz of excitement. It should have been thrilling to go out with Derry, but she felt nothing.

The spectre of Henry weighed heavily on her shoulder.

She thought of Amber often, wondering how many weeks pregnant she was or had been. Why had she never told Stella, maybe she had not found out until after Stella had left.

She wondered if her pregnancy continued, or if she had miscarried.

Stella longed to go and see her, but somehow she was too afraid of the reception that she would get.

If things had gone wrong, Amber would have accused her of gloating.

Stella buried herself in work and in creating a new life for herself, anything to block out the memories of her old life.

Stella arrived at the races. As Derry had instructed her she drove into the Owners and Trainer's car park, her small car looking incongruous amongst the large cars and four wheel drive vehicles.

She walked across the car park and into the race course and straight into Henry who was being interviewed by a television camera. A large crowd had gathered around him, jostling the camera man and his sound assistant.

"How do you think Princess Pushy will do in the big race on Saturday," the interviewer was asking Henry.

Stella stopped, jerked to a halt like a dog reaching the limit of its leash.

As if he knew she were there Henry turned to look at Stella, their eyes meeting over the crowd that had gathered around him.

"Henry?" the interviewer questioned him again.

Henry shot a cold glance at Stella and then dragged his eyes away; she could see him gathering his thoughts, forcing himself to concentrate on what the interviewer was saying.

"His Lordship is very important all of a sudden," Derry's voice dripped sarcasm.

He took Stella's arm, spinning her around to face him, and then kissing her full on the mouth.

Out of the corner of her eye Stella could see Henry falter again as the interviewer asked him another question.

"Come on," Derry took Stella's arm. "The owners of the horse I've got running have a hospitality box. We will go up there. Nicer than mixing with all the riff-raff." He smirked as Henry dashed by trying to escape the hoard of journalists that were pursing him.

The hospitality box was hot and airless.

"J.T. and Olivia Burke," Derry introduced Stella to the owners of the horse that was running in the big race of the day.

J.T. was short and was almost as wide as he was tall, with a shiny bald head and tiny eyes that reminded Stella of a pig that they once had in one of the sheds when she was a little girl.

J.T. slapped Stella's bottom as he was introduced to her, "Derry's a lucky man," he chuckled. He had a laugh that reminded Stella of the noise that the pig made just before they fed it.

His wife Olivia, was a feisty looking red-head, with so many freckles that she looked as if she were tanned. She was slender and pretty, with a hard, sharp little face and cold eyes that never left Derry.

"Are you Derry's girlfriend?" she asked, moodily, the moment she and Stella were alone.

"Just a friend," Stella replied. Olivia visibly relaxed, becoming instantly friendlier towards Stella.

J.T. and Olivia's horse, Bamboozle, came third in the race.

Afterwards J.T. and Olivia got steadily drunk. Olivia leaned provocatively forwards to reveal the tops of her freckly breasts as often as she could.

Stella sighed, wishing that she had not come. Derry had virtually ignored her all day.

"I think that we will head off," Derry took Stella by the hand.

"Derry," murmured Olivia, huskily, pressing herself up against Derry and running her hand around the back of his neck. "I'll see you very soon. I hope."

"Of course," Derry put his hand on the small of her back and slowly let it slide downwards, "J.T. is a lucky man." Then releasing Olivia abruptly he turned, opened the door and guided Stella outside. "Silly tart," he hissed, nastily, as he led Stella across the race course. "I just need to check the horse and then I'm going to bring you for a lovely dinner to make up for having to put up with J.T. and Olivia," Derry slid his arm around Stella's shoulder, suddenly attentive and tender.

They headed out of the course and into the lorry park.

"No point in standing around in the cold," Derry stopped at the most enormous lorry Stella had ever seen. "You can wait in the lorry while I go into the back to check the horse."

He guided her up the steps of the sleek blue and gold lorry into the most sumptuous living accommodation that Stella had ever seen. It was like being inside a really plush miniature house, with a tiny elaborate kitchen along one wall, with an eating area opposite. A pair of silky curtains hung open to reveal a bedroom area with what looked like a shower beside it.

"Handy for the grooms to sleep in if they have to travel long distances," Derry explained, airily. "Make yourself at home, I'll just go and check the horse."

He disappeared through a door into the back of the lorry where the horses travelled.

Stella wandered around the living accommodation, fingering the pale wood of the kitchen units and the plush velvets of the seats.

"Come and see the amazing entertainment system in the bedroom," Derry said, brightly, as he returned.

Stella followed him through the curtains into the bedroom.

"Sit down, watch this," he grabbed the remote control from a small recess above the bed and flicked a switch.

Immediately the living accommodation filled with soft music. "What is your favourite kind of entertainment?" Derry sank onto the bed beside Stella. Before she had the time to answer, Derry cupped her chin in his hand and covered her lips with his, kissing her gently. "I wanted to do that all day," he whispered, slowly unfastening the buttons on Stella's shirt.

"I'm sorry, but I......" Stella pulled his hand away from her shirt. "This is a bit soon for me," Derry was gorgeous, infinitely sexy, but every time Stella closed her eyes, she saw Henry's hurt face as he looked at her from the centre of the crowd of journalists. She could not sleep with Derry until that memory had been erased.

"Just relax," Derry's hand was persistent, travelling now up her leg, sliding up her skirt, his lips strong against hers, his weight forcing her backwards onto the soft plush bed cover.

"Stop it," hissed Stella, finding a strength she did not know she possessed. She shoved Derry away from herself and scrambled to her feet.

"You don't know what you are missing," Derry drawled, the sound of his cruel laughter followed her as Stella fled through the living accommodation, bumping into the kitchen units in her haste to escape.

Stella climbed hastily down the steps out of the lorry, her face on fire with fury and indignation. Her skirt was wrinkled around her thighs, her shirt hanging loose and her hair flew in wild disorder around her face. Hastily Stella tucked in her shirt, trying to pull down her skirt and tidy her hair all at the same time.

Then out of the corner of her eye she glimpsed a familiar pair of shoes. Stella stopped and slowly straightened up and looked at Henry, his eyes met hers impassively. "I hope that you had a good time with Derry," he said coldly.

CHAPTER FORTY TWO

Stella glanced up from her magazine as the doorbell rang, expecting one of the other girls to leap to their feet to go and answer it.

"Not for me," October shrugged.

"Nor me," Julia, raised her eyebrows expectantly at Stella.

Xanthe merely continued to apply another layer of glossy pink lipstick, pursing her lips and blowing a kiss at herself in the mirror that she held in her hand.

"I'll go then," Stella sighed, putting down her magazine and levering herself to her feet.

Stella walked to the front door her bare feet padding softly on the wooden floor; it was probably yet another politician canvassing for their votes.

The girls had taken to sending Stella out to answer the door as a joke, letting her stand for hours listening to their boring speeches.

Stella grabbed a sweatshirt from the bottom of the stairs, pulling it over her head as she turned the door lock. Her flimsy pyjamas were not suitable for standing in the cold listening to speeches. At least now she would not be half frozen by the time she had escaped from whatever politician was waiting outside to bore her.

"Hel…," she swung open the door. Henry stood on the doorstep, "lo," she finished lamely, feeling her cheeks flame with colour. The last time she had seen Henry she had just escaped from Derry Blake's clutches and had been in a terrible state of disarray. Henry eyed her coldly, his lips curling with distaste.

"Not out with Derry tonight," he spat coldly.

"Is Amber ok?" Stella said, a dart of fear shooting through her once she had got over the initial shock of seeing him.

There must be terrible news for him to come to the house. Maybe she had lost the baby or maybe died herself.

"She's fine, her and the baby. Don't know why you are asking me, you don't seem to have any interest in her; you've never even been to see her."

"I wanted to," Stella mumbled guiltily. She had wanted to go and visit Amber; it was just that she had not been able to pluck up the courage, afraid of the reception that she would get after the last time they had met.

"Too busy shagging Derry Blake," Henry spat coldly.

"Is that all you wanted?" Stella said miserably, he hated her with such intensity.

"No actually I didn't want you at all."

Stella glanced up at him, but he was looking beyond her, down the hall.

Stella spun around to see what he was looking at.

Xanthe sashayed down the hall, her blonde hair swinging in time to her strides, her impossibly high heels tapping a tattoo on the wooden floor. Stella felt her mouth drop open. Xanthe wore the shortest skirt that she had ever seen, revealing a gorgeous pair of tanned, toned legs and the best part of her knickers.

"Hi Henry," Xanthe breathed sexily, pouting her full glossy pink lips towards Henry, Stella saw him swallow hard before he puckered up to kiss her.

"Ok then gorgeous, let's go," Xanthe grabbed Henry's arm, swinging him around with careless grace and marched him off down the drive.

Stella leant on the door; she did not dare move for fear that her legs would not support her. Open mouthed she watched Xanthe grab Henry's bottom and squeeze it playfully. "My car, I think," Xanthe steered Henry towards her Mercedes.

Stella could watch no longer. She shut the door and leant against it breathing hard. What a bitch Xanthe was. She had no right to go out with Henry, even if Stella did not want him.

Stella went back to the living room.

"Did you know that Xanthe was going out with Henry?" she stood in the doorway, looking at the other two girls.

Julia looked up, her hand continued to stroke Gucci, the cat, rhythmically. "Yes of course. Why shouldn't she?"

Stella looked from one girl to the other. "I'm going to go out for a while," she said, suddenly she could hardly bear to be in the house.

She had ended her relationship with Henry, but it was not right for Xanthe to go straight out with him. That was not right, surely. She had really thought that Henry had cared about her, but he had replaced her so quickly and with someone as awful as Xanthe.

"Don't be long," October said. "Don't forget that we are having some friends around later."

"Should be lots of lovely men for you to meet," Julia added, her plumy voice grating on Stella's nerves.

Stella closed the door; they just treated men and relationships as if they were of no importance, moving from one to the other with no thought for anyone's feelings.

Stella went upstairs to her room and looked into her wardrobe for something to change into. Her new room had a wardrobe that stretched the whole length of one wall, with rails set at different heights for hanging coats and dresses and skirts all separately. Beside these were the shelves where she had put her shoes and sweaters and underwear, each neatly organised, instead of crammed together like they had been at the apartment.

Stella fingered the row of dresses, each seeming to symbolise a fond memory of her past life.

On impulse she pulled out a red dress, smiling as she pulled it towards her. It smelt vaguely of her old apartment, the heady scent that Amber sometimes wore and the joss sticks that she burned when she had been smoking and did not want Stella to know.

Stella slipped the dress off its hanger and held it up to herself and looked at herself in the mirror. The red dress was beautiful; the colour looked fabulous against her skin, making her hair look as if it were alive with a thousand different colours.

Stella stroked the front of the dress, moving slightly. The fabric was still slightly marked with the stain, if you looked really hard. Stella smiled at the memory, Amber had thought she hadn't known she had borrowed the dress and somehow got beer spilled down the front of it. Of course she had not minded. She gave a small laugh out loud at the memory of how Amber had tried to conceal the damage from her.

Stella slipped out of her jogging pants and pulled the sweatshirt over her head.

302

The red dress would be perfect for tonight, and somehow it comforted her, bringing back happy memories of a life now lost to her. Stella fetched her coat and headed outside to her little car. She would go and see Amber, make things up with her, before the girl's party.

Amber at least had a grip on reality; she would never have gone out with Henry after Stella had finished with him. That would have been an unwritten rule between them.

The girls at the house seemed to have their own rules for everything; they did not care about anyone except themselves.

The city streets were quiet and Stella was soon parking her car outside the apartment. How familiar everything looked, the square brick building slumbering beneath its mantle of ivy and Virginia creeper. Stella got out of her car and stood outside the building, suddenly afraid. She leant against her car, the cold metal chilling her skin. What would she say to Amber? She really did not know.

She stood looking up at the building, mulling over the things that she should say – and the replies that Amber might give her. How easy it would be to march up to the doorway and press the buzzer of the intercom and talk. How they would laugh when Amber saw Stella wearing the red dress. They would joke about how Amber had tried to conceal the damage from Stella. Maybe she would even tell Stella how the damage happened. It was bound to be a long and funny story. Amber was brilliant at telling a funny tale. But maybe Amber would not want to talk to her. The row would start up again. Maybe things would not be good with Amber being pregnant.

Maybe she should leave. Just put this stage of her life behind her and move on. Forget Amber and her pregnancy. She was better off without Paul, no matter how much Stella knew that it would be hurting Amber.

Stella got back into her car and put her head into her hands. They had been such good friends. She missed the easy companionship, missed the love and trust that they had felt between them. But that was all wrecked. Amber would not want her around. She had her own life to lead.

Stella started her car and headed back to her new home. The beautiful building lay elegantly before her, the drive and road outside crowded with expensive looking cars. This was what she had wanted, to move in elegant, wealthy circles, meet a lovely millionaire.

Stella took a deep breath, smoothed back her hair, applied a fresh coat of lipstick and then went into the house to join the party.

"Stella!" cried Julia as Stella walked back into the house. "Come and meet some lovely people." Stella followed Julia into the lounge. It buzzed with noise and music, people filled every space, crowding together and spilling out onto the lawn through the open French windows.

"I sent your dog over to one of the neighbours, couldn't bear that yapping while we were having our party," Julia said over her shoulder. "I've shut my cat in your room. Gucci can't bear parties. I hope you don't mind," she continued, handing Stella a tall blue coloured drink that a girl, dressed in a very short waitresses outfit was carrying on a tray. "Drink that and you won't mind about anything."

October threaded her way through the crowded room to Stella.

"We have loads of people who are just dying to meet you," October seized Stella's arm and led her to a group of people. "This is our new housemate, Stella," October thrust Stella into the centre of the crowd of people.

"Hello," Stella said, knowing what it must feel like to be a specimen in a zoo.

"Hell-ooo," a tall, red haired man grabbed Stella's hand and held it up to his fleshy mouth.

His face was the same colour as his hair and his eyes were almost transparent behind thick round glasses. "My name is Rupert."

Stella's hand felt wet where Rupert's thick lips had suctioned onto the skin. "I'm in property; let me introduce you to everyone."

Rupert slid his hand into the small of Stella's back, possessively as he introduced the circle of faces. "Liam," Stella smiled at a foxy faced man. "He's into hotels. And this is Miranda," a horsey faced woman glared at Stella.

"His wife," Miranda spat, in a warning tone.

"Lovely," Stella shook hands with her; she had a grip like a vice, probably from hauling her horses around on the hunting field.

"Devon," Rupert continued, spinning Stella around the circle of people. "He's an investment banker," Stella smiled at the short, dumpy man, his head topped by a mass of grey curls like a judge's wig, hardly daring to shake his hand for fear that another possessive wife was going to leap at her. "He's not married," Rupert said, as if he could read Stella's thoughts.

Devon let out a loud bray of laughter. "No point in taking your own sandwiches to a picnic, eh? Never got married, still testing the girls out. Amazing how quickly a fat wallet will open a girl's legs." Devon let out another bray of laughter, his piggy eyes looking Stella slowly up and down.

Stella felt as if he were undressing her with his eyes. And it was not a pleasant feeling.

She took another swig of her drink, the blue liquid tasted of cranberries and something sour that she could not identify.

"And what do you do?" asked Miranda, gripping her husband's arm as if to remind Stella that he belonged to her. Stella looked at the group did they all think that she wanted to be with them, just because they had money?

"I work for a magazine."

"Oh," exclaimed Rupert, his piggy eyes lighting up momentarily. "You're a publisher."

"No," Stella shook her head, "I just work there."

"Ohhh," the light of interest in Rupert's eyes flickered and died.

The hum of conversation started again, talking about people and places that Stella had never heard of. They all seemed to be trying to outdo each other with tales of the wealth and houses that they possessed and the amazing faraway places that they had visited. Stella felt completely left out of the conversation.

It was as if they had examined her, discovered her to be someone of no consequence whatsoever and now were not interested in her.

Stella finished her drink, excused herself and went in search of the waitress with the tray of glasses. She hated this party. These people were dreadful, completely self-obsessed, full of their own self-importance. Not caring about anyone for their own personality, it was all about possessions and wealth. Had she really wanted to be part of this? Belonging to people like this?

Stella groped her way outside. The whole house seemed to be moving as if its foundations were shaking.

There were people crowding in the hall, Stella was aware of blurry shapes, their faces merging into a mass of colour and eyes that all seemed to be watching her.

The front door had two locks. It took Stella quite a while to locate the right one, her fingers kept slipping off the round knob and then she was not quite sure which way to turn it to open it. Was it left to open? Which way was left? Then slowly she pulled open the door. It was very difficult, she needed the support of something solid to help her to stand up which made it almost impossible to manoeuvre the door open and actually step through it.

Eventually Stella managed to open the door and groped her way out into the front garden.

The fresh air felt icy on her skin, Stella gulped in huge breaths, feeling the coldness tingle on her tongue, sucking it into her lungs.

She took wavering steps out onto the lawn, feeling her shoes fall as she walked onto the grass. Each blade of grass seemed to prickle beneath her feet, the dampness soaking into her skin, each sense intensely alive. There were car headlights, swinging into the drive, their beam bouncing off her brain and hitting the bone at the back of her skull.

In that moment Stella knew without doubt that she was going to be sick. The feeling of nausea grew in her belly, growing more and more fierce with every passing moment.

The trees at the edge of the garden spun wildly, the sky and trees merging into a continuous blur of colour as if she were on a roundabout that was going too fast. Stella sank slowly to her knees, retching violently onto the grass.

The garden stopped spinning so wildly. Stella blinked, trying to focus her eyes. A pair of shoes appeared at the edge of her vision, brown shabby looking brogues, a pair that she was sure that she recognised, but somehow could not place. A second pair appeared, sandals with long, narrow feet inside them, the toes wriggled, the bright pink nail varnish on their tips dancing as Stella tried to focus.

Slowly Stella raised her head, bringing her hand to her mouth, which suddenly felt damp. It took and immense effort to raise her head, past the two pairs of shoes, on upwards as she scrambled clumsily to her feet, past trousers and a pair of brown legs, a shirt and a tanned tummy and then on upwards, conscious that Xanthe was gazing at her with an expression of distaste Stella looked straight into Henry's amused, yet horrified face.

CHAPTER FORTY THREE

Amber woke on the morning of Ruby's wedding feeling absolutely dreadful. She had woken feeling dreadful ever since the pregnancy was confirmed, spending the first moments when she first opened her eyes waiting for the terrible waves of nausea to subside enough for her to feel well enough to make the dash from her bedroom to the bathroom.

But this morning it was worse.

It was not just the nausea, but a dreadful feeling of loneliness and despair. The novelty of discovering that she was pregnant had given way to a dreadful realisation that she was going to go through this whole experience alone.

At first she had thought that maybe Paul had just wanted to think about what had happened, come to terms with it on his own.

Then after she had given him a few days alone Amber had tried to telephone him and found that his mobile was always switched off. She had left messages, humorous at first, gradually becoming more panicky and desperate, until she had realised he was not going to contact her again.

She was alone.

"Time that we got up baby," Amber said, gingerly inching herself off the mattress. She had discovered that if she moved slowly enough then the nausea was not as bad as it would have been if she had just got out of bed normally.

"Bloody Ruby's wedding, and we haven't got a thing to wear," Amber had taken to talking to herself as if the baby was actually with her. Somehow it made her loneliness seem less daunting.

307

"What can I wear?" Amber moved her hands slowly over her body, feeling the unmistakeable changes that were happening to her. Amber's breasts, once tiny, indistinguishable dots on her chest, were now a sizable asset.

It was a shame that Paul was not around anymore to enjoy them, thought Amber, wrenching open her wardrobe door with a vicious tug.

Even thinking about Paul made Amber miserable. Amber tried desperately not to think about Paul, but relentlessly he filled her thoughts, day after day, however hard she tried.

It was hard to be without him, all of the fun seemed to have been drained out of Amber's life. She had felt so sure that they would always be together. He had been her soul mate, there would never be anyone else that she would love as much.

If only she had not become pregnant they would still have been together. But somehow Amber could not resent the tiny new life that grew within her.

The baby was part of Paul, part of the special time that they had shared together.

If Amber did not have Paul, at least she would have his child.

At first, after she had almost lost the baby and when she had lost Paul, Amber had been afraid. The thought of being alone was terrifying. Her heart felt as if it would break with misery at losing Paul.

She had ached physically for him, spending days just sitting, hoping that he would come back, waiting to hear the sound of his footsteps, her heart lurching with hope each time the telephone rang, hoping, longing that he would come back.

The pain had gradually lessened to a dull ache, being without him was dreadful, but at least she had the energy to eat and go to work.

It was almost as hard to be without Stella. Amber missed her terribly. And Teddy.

Stella would have known how to help Amber get over the loss of Paul. She would have made everything seem ok again. Della was hopeless, Amber would never have even dreamed of trying to tell her how she felt.

Amber caught sight of herself in the mirror that hung behind the wardrobe door. It was incredible how her body had changed in just a few short weeks.

Amber's belly was a pretty sizable asset as well; unfortunately, her waist line had disappeared almost as soon as her pregnancy was confirmed, another reason why Amber was missing Stella. Her constantly expanding wardrobe of gorgeous clothes would have bound to have been the perfect place to find a suitable outfit for the wedding. Now all of her clothes were gone, along with her fabulous selection of shoes, handbags and scrumptious accessories.

Instead Della's clothes were piled into Stella's once tidy wardrobe. Amber doubted very much, judging by the outfits that she had seen Della in that there would be anything suitable for her to wear even if she could find something to fit her.

Della's clothes would have swamped Amber even now that her body had expanded with her pregnancy. Finding something to wear was an impossible task, nothing felt right any more. Or if it did it was too scruffy, too dressy, too tarty, too anything other than suitable for the Ruby's perfect wedding.

Eventually Amber settled for a rose pink dress in a floaty kind of fabric that swirled around her when she walked. It skimmed her body, rather than clung to it, disguising the slight swell of her belly.

Her old grey overcoat did not really look right with the dress, but Amber could not do anything about that. She added an enormous vibrant silk pink rose that she had once borrowed off Stella and forgotten to give back, pining it to the lapel of her coat to give it an air of festivity and then wrapping a double row of silvery necklaces around her neck Amber finally stood back to admire her handiwork in the mirror,

"Ok baby," Amber gently stoked the slight swell of her belly. "That is as good as it is going to get."

Della sprawled in her favourite armchair, the television, tuned into a Saturday morning children's programme blared with laughter and inane chatter.

"Switch on the kettle before you go will you," Della said, in between mouthfuls of toast from the pile on the plate that rested on her knee.

"Sure," Amber walked across and turned on the kettle. "Can I get you anything else?" Amber asked, hating the sarcastic note in her own voice. "More toast?" and then added under her breath, "arsenic, powdered glass?"

Amber hated the way that Della treated her like a servant.

She collected her handbag, thinking longingly of Stella. If she had been there Stella would have been examining Amber's outfit, adjusting the way that the rose was pinned onto her coat, adding another necklace, stepping back to admire her handiwork, while all the time she would have kept up a steady stream of conversation.

Instead, Della was just a dull lump who only thought of herself and where her next mouthful of junk food was going to come from.

"Yeah, throw some more bread in the toaster for me will you," Della's eyes did not move from the television screen, where a bunch of children were throwing water filled sponges at a giggling young blonde presenter.

Amber's sarcasm was totally lost on her.

Amber viciously shoved more bread into the toaster, "I hope that it chokes her, don't you baby?" Amber muttered, under her breath, then to Della she said, "I've got to go now, can you manage to butter the toast and make the tea yourself?"

"I'll be ok," Della said through a mouthful of toast.

"I'll be off then," Amber winced as she looked at the clock. She was supposed to be at her parent's home now!

"Bye Amber. Bye baby," Amber hissed through clenched teeth as her words fell on deaf ears, Della was totally absorbed in the childish antics that were happening on the television screen.

Outside, parked half on and half off the pavement was a taxi, the surly looking driver drumming his fingers against the steering wheel in an impatient gesture.

"Where too love?" he snapped, glancing at Amber in the rear view mirror.

Amber gave him the address and then lurched back into her seat as the taxi driver hurtled out into the traffic in his haste to get going.

He screeched to a halt outside Amber's parent's house, throwing Amber back into her seat, she struggled out of the taxi, paid the driver and then taking a deep breath walked slowly through the neat garden to the house.

As Amber got closer to the house she could hear the high pitched shrieks of Ruby and Pearl as they bickered over the wedding preparations.

Amber felt her heart sink. Why had she bothered coming to the house? She should have stayed away. It would have been far more peaceful to spend the morning at home and then meet everyone at the church, rather than be in the middle of what sounded like a war zone.

Inside the house was a scene of utter chaos. Clothes were draped all over the banisters and strewn across the hall table, where Pearl had tried on the numerous new outfits that she had bought for the wedding and then discarded. A bright red hat had been abandoned on top of Pearl's prized bowl of spider plants, the long thin leaves poking out from beneath the hat brim, like some bizarre hairstyle.

Most of Pearl's best shoes were abandoned on the rungs of the stairs. A makeup bag had been upended on the hall table, the lipsticks and mascara scattered around the carpet. An expensive looking suitcase stood at the foot of the stairs, for a fleeting moment Amber wondered if Ruby had changed her mind about marrying Roderick. Maybe finally she had the sense to see him for the cheating love rat that he was.

Then Amber realised that the suitcase was there in preparation for Ruby's honeymoon. She was determined to go ahead with the wedding, no matter what a scum bag Roderick was.

He would provide Ruby with the perfect life that she so craved.

Amber glanced up the stairs as Pearl yelled, "Jack, what have you done with my new suede handbag!" from the bathroom she heard Ruby shriek, "Mummy, for God's sake will you help me with this corset!"

Amber grimaced; maybe she should slip quietly away now before she got involved in the wedding preparations. A movement caught her eye, Amber grinned as she saw Jack sitting serenely in the lounge, slowly turning the pages of the newspaper. "Hi Daddy," Amber grinned, kissing her father on top of his head.

"Welcome to chaos," Jack smiled gently, patting the seat beside him, for Amber to sit down. "How are things?" Jack asked, gently, his dark eyes full of concern. Amber had told him about losing Paul and that Stella had gone, but she had not mentioned her pregnancy, afraid of her parent's reaction. To tell them would make everything real, at the moment the pregnancy still felt like a crazy dream, like a fantasy that she was living out. She would tell them, or at least tell Jack first, when the time was right.

Amber shrugged, not daring to speak, for fear that she would begin to cry. It was better not to mention how much she missed Paul – and Stella, that way she could keep all of the hurt inside.

"Great," Amber said, smiling brightly. "My new flat mate is very……. unusual. We are getting on really well. I don't miss Stella at all."

Jack nodded seriously. "That's good."

"And I'm not missing Paul either, things are already looking up on the love front again, plenty of offers," Amber lied, staring at her hands.

"Bad as that is it?" Jack said, softly, taking one of Amber's hands in his.

A huge lump fixed itself in Amber's throat, making it impossible to speak. She nodded, "Daddy," Amber's voice was little more than a whisper, "I've got something to tell you."

Jack squeezed Amber's finger's tightly, "I've got something to tell you too," he said softly.

"Jack! Jack!" Pearl shrieked from upstairs.

Jack started and then smiled a gentle smile of regret at Amber. "We'll talk later," he said, touching her cheek with his fingers and then plodding resignedly in the direction of his wife.

"What did you want to tell me?" Amber touched her father's arm as they stood outside the church waiting for Ruby to have yet more photographs taken as she got out of the white Rolls Royce.

Jack shot a glance in Pearl's direction. "You probably won't like me very much after this," he said, in the resigned voice of someone who has reached the end of their tether and has no option but to face up to all of the nastiness that is ahead of them, "I'm going to leave your mother after the wedding." Jack's eyes roved over Amber's face, to judge her reaction, "I love Kate, and I want to be with her. I deserve some happiness for the rest of my life," he plunged on recklessly, without waiting for Amber to speak.

"Daddy," Amber bit her lip, shaking her head gently in disbelief, "I love you, I wish you all the best of luck in the world."

Jack grinned delightedly. "What were you going to tell me?" he hissed in Amber's ear.

"I'm pregnant!" Amber whispered back, watching her father's stunned expression change into one of fury. She swallowed hard. It had been a terrible mistake to blurt it out like that to her father.

"That bastard Paul dumped you when he found out didn't he?" Jack spat, his eyes blazing with fury. Amber's fear turned to relief, her father was furious at Paul for deserting her, not at her for being so stupid as to get pregnant.

Amber saw Pearl shoot a curious glance in their direction. In a moment she would be hot footing over to them to find out what was going on.

"It's ok Daddy, I'm ok without him. I can cope."

Jack hugged Amber gently, whispering gently into her ear, "I love you too and I wish you all of the luck in the world."

Ruby walked slowly up the aisle on Jack's arm.

Pearl leant out from her pew at the front of the church to watch their progress from beneath the most enormous hat that Amber had ever seen.

Ruby winked delightedly at Amber as she glided past her figure voluptuously curvy in a tightly fitting cream silk dress.

Amber felt bitter tears of loneliness prickle at the back of her eyes. No one would want her now that she was going to be a single mother. She was destined for a life of loneliness. She would die a bitter old maid. She would never find anyone to love.

At the end of the aisle Roderick turned to look at his bride to be, his face softening as he smiled gently at her.

The Priest walked out in front of the alter, looking at them and clearing his throat in readiness for the service. At the back of the church the enormous wooden door creaked shut, there was a thud as the huge latch banged heavily into place. Amber saw the Priest look up as someone came in late.

"You are all very welcome," the Priest began his service.

"Move up, let me sit down" whispered a familiar voice beside Amber. She stifled a cry of surprise as Paul shoved her with his hip as he pushed into the pew.

"Sorry I'm late," he whispered, reaching for Amber's hand.

"Are you staying?" Amber said, unable to believe that he was truly here.

"Yes. Definitely. I promise," he whispered.

"Thank you," Amber whispered back, slipping her hand into his.

CHAPTER FORTY FOUR

Stella thought she was going to cry when Xanthe told them all her news. They were all in the lounge when Xanthe announced she had something very important to tell them.

"You've actually got engaged!" shrieked October, jumping to her feet and dashing across the lounge to throw herself dramatically at Xanthe, kissing her theatrically on both cheeks.

"It's only taken six months to wear him down!" Xanthe flicked back her long blonde hair and gave an enormous self-satisfied smirk.

"Well done," Julia said in her husky voice. "Can't believe that you have beaten me. I was sure that Clifden was going to propose to me before you got around to it." Xanthe plonked herself on the sofa. "Well I had to kind of guide him into it." Xanthe smirked.

"How did you manage it?" October clapped her hands together in delight, as if obtaining a marriage proposal was a huge game.

"Actually Daddy took him out to lunch and pointed out to him what a huge asset I was."

"And what huge assets Daddy has," chortled Julia, pushing her wide mouth into a pout.

"Quite!" Xanthe roared with laughter.

"Absolutely," agreed October, examining her long finger nails and flicking an imaginary piece of dirt from beneath one of her red talons,

"That is wonderful news," Stella forced herself to say. As long as she concentrated hard on the pile of press releases that she had been flicking through then she would not cry.

It was hard to imagine that Henry and Xanthe were going to be married.

Only a few months ago Stella had been with Henry. She could have carried on with the relationship, but she had let him go. Stella had decided that Henry was not the man for her. She worked hard to rid herself of his memory. Stella had thrown herself into a busy schedule of evening classes, riding lessons, anywhere that she thought there might be the possibility to meet someone suitable for a relationship. She had plenty of dates, with some lovely, wealthy men, but somehow she had lost the determination to find someone. Everyone got compared to Henry whether she liked it or not. No one yet had matched up to him. No one had made her heart sing like he had when they were together. Dumping Henry had been a huge mistake.

"Look at this," Xanthe got up and flounced over to where Stella was sitting, she waved her hand at Stella.

"Isn't this just the most gorgeous ring that you have ever seen?"

Stella put down the press releases, suppressing a sigh. "Very nice," Stella glanced at the ring.

"Here," Xanthe wrenched the ring from her finger. "Try it on," Xanthe thrust the ring in Stella's direction.

"Thanks," Stella took the ring from Xanthe and slipped it onto her finger, she twisted her hand, watching how the ring reflected the light into a thousand shimmering shafts of colour within the ring.

"So," Julia said, holding out her hand for the ring as Stella pulled it off her finger. "Where is the wedding going to be? Have you set a date yet?"

Xanthe leant forwards, delighted to be holding court as her ring was passed around. "Well, I thought that abbey in Mayo where Pierce Brosnan got married, and then the reception in Ashford Castle."

Stella somehow could not see Henry being very comfortable with all of the swanky arrangements that Xanthe was describing.

"I'm going to get Tamara Brennan to organise everything. Only the best for me." "Tamara Brennan," October and Julia gasped in unison. "She is The wedding planner," October said enviously.

"Well," smirked Xanthe. "Of course Daddy is going to pay for everything.

"Have you set a date yet?" Julia continued.

"I thought in a couple of months' time. No point in waiting." There was a ripple of laughter from the girls.

"You will give Tamara an ulcer getting everything organised in that short time." October said.

Xanthe shrugged diffidently. "She will be earning bloody good money from my father, and she will just have to work hard for it."

"Quite," agreed Julia, and the conversation drifted on to the silk dress that Xanthe was having designed for her and the absolute fortune that it was going to cost to fly in the special flowers, from Thailand that Xanthe had already picked out for her bouquet.

Stella only half listened to the conversation.

Two months. Two months, she wanted to shriek in bewilderment. Two months and then Henry would be lost to her forever.

She was horrified at how the finality of his wedding distressed her. The relationship had been over for months, she had a string of new boyfriends, a new life, and yet still, hearing that he was going to be married made her feel as if her heart would break all over again.

"I'm going to be late for the gym," Stella got slowly to her feet.

She wanted to rush from the room, and throw herself onto her bed and cry and cry and cry, but she could not. Henry was Xanthe's boyfriend now.

Stella had given him up. For a good reason. He was never going to be the man that she wanted to marry. She knew that. But why then did it hurt so much?

Stella collected her bag and headed off to the gym.

The gym had taken her mind off Henry; there she could exercise away the hurt that ending the relationship had caused. Henry was not right for her and the sooner she grasped that the sooner she would feel better.

After a couple of hours in the gym, Stella had walked, peddled, rowed, pushed and pulled on every machine available. She was starving, exhausted, purple in the face and drenched with sweat. She felt calmer, the desperate sadness that she had felt had settled into an aching numbness in the pit of her stomach.

Stella showered and then went out into the changing room, finally stopping the incessant movement that she had used to escape from the pain of thinking about Henry.

Sighing she leant her forehead against the mirror, feeling the cold glass against the aching heat of her skin. Then slowly Stella straightened up and looked at herself, she had to stop thinking about Henry all of the time. Just had to.

There was little that she could do to repair the ravages made on her looks by the gym. Her complexion would take a while to calm down from the fiery red to its normal pale pink and her hair, in spite of her ministrations with the hair drier and brush, still somehow managed to look as if she had been dragged through a hedge backwards.

After a final glance in the mirror Stella decided there was nothing she could do to improve her appearance, she was red and sweaty and that was that.

Quickly she dressed, shivering now in the cool air of the changing room and then hurried outside to her car.

"You look awful," said a voice as Stella left the gym and headed across the car park towards her car. Stella felt her heart start its familiar pounding.

Henry looked gorgeous; he had got his hair cut since she had last seen him, probably due to Xanthe's cajoling. The style suited him, showing off the neat shape of his skull. "Thanks," she smiled faintly, wondering if Henry was aware of the feelings seeing him wrought on her. Henry stood a few feet away from her, his eyes flickering incessantly over her face.

Stella longed to move into his arms, to feel the warmth of his body against hers.

"Have you been to the gym?" he asked, un-necessarily, since she was dressed in trainers and jogging bottoms.

"Yes," Stella took a stride backwards, not trusting herself to get too close to Henry. Stella found that she could not tear her eyes away from him. Even the shabby clothes that he wore could not detract from what a handsome man he was.

Stella wanted to burn the image of him on her memory, hold him there forever.

"You look too thin," he said, suddenly.

"As if that is any of your business," Stella snapped, suddenly hostile, she wanted to get away from him. Being so close to him was too painful; she loved him too much, even now.

"You made that very clear," Henry snapped back, coldly, shoving his hands into the pockets of his baggy cord trousers.

"I have to go," Stella could feel the panic rising in herself, she had to get away from him, before her emotions betrayed her.

"Me too," Henry glanced towards the hospital at the edge of the car park. "My father is sick. We haven't spoken for years. He wants me now he is dying."

"Maybe I'll see you at the wedding," Henry began to walk away, his lips clamped in a tight, hard line as he looked back over his shoulder at Stella. She opened her mouth to speak, but instead broke into a run, wanting to get to her car before the turmoil of her emotions exploded and she began to cry.

After all that had happened between them he still expected that she would go to his bloody wedding.

A week later Stella sat in an editorial meeting. She had thrown herself into her work with a frenzied enthusiasm in order to block out the dreadful feelings of pain and regret that she felt. From now on she was going to concentrate on her career, forget Henry, and eventually meet someone suitable to marry.

"So ideas for the special summer issue?" Peter Shaunnesy said, looking at the feature editors that were sitting around the vast boardroom table. Stella fingered the brochures that she held, waiting for an opportunity to speak.

"I'd like to do a piece on this," Fleur Lombard, the editor of the social diary, held up a large glossy mock-up of a magazine page. "The Thornhill estate."

Stella felt her eyes widen in disbelief. There, in Fleur's hand, was a picture of the gorgeous house next door to Henry's cottage. The house that she loved so much.

The photograph on the glossy mock-up was taken from a distance and showed the whole of the house, surrounded by its fantastic gardens and the parkland around it. "Lord Thornhill the owner died a few days ago. He was an alcoholic, damaged all of his liver and everything with his drinking. He was hugely wealthy, old money, you know," Fleur glanced at Peter to judge his reaction to her idea. Peter pulled an interested face and she continued. "The estate and the title has passed onto his son, they were estranged for years, seems the old man didn't like his son training racehorses."

Stella closed her eyes, gripping the edge of the table as the room swayed uncomfortably.

She could hear Fleur shuffling more mock up pages. "I thought that we could do a piece on the estate and the new owner."

Stella opened her eyes and looked desolately at the new mock up page that Fleur held. The page showed her gorgeous house, and super-imposed in front of the house was the new owner of the house. Henry.

CHAPTER FORTY FIVE

Stella walked unsteadily back to her office.

The corridor seemed to stretch for an eternity, the creamy coloured carpet and walls blurring with the swirling mass of brightly painted modern art that her boss collected.

Every step seemed an immense effort as if she had been struggling up hill, her breath sounded loud in her ears, each intake roaring as she gasped to suck it in.

Finally Stella reached the door to her office, fumbled desperately to turn the handle and then almost fell into the cool silence. Slowly she closed the door behind her and sank to her knees with her back against the cool wood.

Henry. The Henry that she had loved so desperately and given up because she was afraid of living in poverty for the rest of her life had just inherited a fortune. Henry, the man that she had given up because he was not the man that she had wanted -was the man that she wanted.

Stella threw back her head and let out a mournful wail of desperation.

Stella could remember very little of the meeting after the social editor had put up the mock up page with Henry on it, standing in front of Thornhill House. Just immense pain, she had wanted to run from the board room, hide somewhere dark to come to terms with what had happened.

She had survived the meeting though. As she crouched on the floor trying to compose herself Stella marvelled at her own powers of endurance. As if from afar she had watched herself sitting at the board room table, surrounded by the other editors and journalists, nodding her head at the required moment, making the appropriate noises to make everyone else in the room believe that she was totally engrossed in her job, instead of dying inside.

At some stage too she remembered suggesting a feature on the perfect wedding day makeup for all skin tones, for her own pages, which had been approved by the boss. Now it was over and she finally faced the devastation of her life.

"Fuck, fuck, fuck," groaned Stella, clambering to her feet an interminable time later.

Every muscle ached with the enormous tension that cramped her body.

She had loved Henry so, so, so much. She had given him up because she could not have borne seeing that love die as they struggled to make a living, as she began to resent him for not being able to provide for her and probably their children's needs.

Now he had Xanthe.

They were going to live together in the gorgeous house that Stella had loved so much.

Henry was lost to Stella forever, all because of her own fears.

Stella straightened herself, smoothing down her skirt that had wrinkled up around her thighs as she crouched on the ground and tilting her chin walked slowly to her desk, sat down and took a deep breath. Life had to go on. She had fucked up – big time – now she had to get on with life – forget Henry.

Stella's day seemed to go on forever; she was exhausted by an all pervading sadness that seemed to soak into her very bones, making every task an immense effort.

Finally though, the end of the day arrived.

She waited another half an hour, making sure her boss would realise that his faith in her was justified. That he had promoted the right person, that she was conscientious and dedicated to her job.

The extra half an hour Stella put in at her desk dragged slowly, the clock hands seeming to be determined to linger for as long as possible on the numbers.

Finally she closed down her computer, listening with relief as the final notes of the shut-down sequence sounded.

She had not expected to find any peace at the house, but the level of excitement was far greater than she had ever imagined, or could stand.

Xanthe had returned from spending a few days at her father's villa on Lanzerote, where she had been topping up her tan and relaxing before the onslaught of having to hassle the wedding planner over the trivia of her wedding.

"Hey, come and listen to what Xanthe has just found out," October greeted Stella at the front door.

Shrieks of excitement could be heard coming from the lounge, Gucci the fat cat slinked past along the hall, glanced disdainfully at Stella and then headed upstairs out of the way of the noise.

Stella followed October towards the source of the noise.

"Listen to this," October pinched Stella's arm in her excitement.

"Tell Stella, Xanthe," she begged, pulling Stella towards the sofa. They all seemed to have forgotten that Stella had ever been anything to do with Henry and the thought that she might have still felt anything for him had never occurred to them.

"This really has to be the most exciting thing ever," Julia crouched on the floor, at Xanthe's feet, clapping and exclaiming with delight, "Henry has just inherited his father's mansion."

"Oh?" Stella feigned delight; she sat down on the sofa, looking out through the French windows at Teddy, who seeing the girls in the lounge was straining at the end of his lead, yapping sporadically.

Xanthe leant forwards, "Henry fell out with his father years ago, seems like the old man did not his career plan. Threw him out without a penny, but he let him live in the old cottage, hoping that he would soon get fed up of earning his living. But he didn't and they never spoke until just before the old man died."

Stella stared fixedly at Teddy, straining against his chain, wanting to get into the house; she began to feel very sick.

It really was all true. Henry really had just inherited the gorgeous Thornhill House. "Henry's father was an alcoholic, seems like he had some very fixed ideas and Henry was as stubborn as he was."

"Anyway," Xanthe said, tiring of talking about Henry, "I'm going to get Tamara to organise the most fantastic girl's night out, my last fling before I get married."

October and Julia's eyes widened in anticipation, "I want all of my very best friends – about two hundred and fifty of them – and you can come too Stella if you like," Xanthe added quickly, remembering that Stella was there, "I want to take over Neo's for dinner and then a VIP night of partying."

Stella felt her own eyes widen enviously. Neo's was the most fabulous night club, and the most exclusive. Its membership list was said to read like an edition of the Irish Who's Who. The nightclub had only opened recently and was reputed to be an exact replica of a street in Pompeii, complete with slave girls serving the drinks. Peter, Stella's boss had been invited to the grand opening a few months ago and had returned to work wearing a real gold slave bangle that the owners were giving out as souvenirs.

"Fabulous," Julia and October's voices echoed each other. "Unfortunately," Xanthe began, "I promised Daddy that I would go and watch his horse running, so I'll have to suffer that first before I can enjoy myself." She raised her eyebrows skywards in annoyance, tutting in disgust. "You will all have to come with me for moral support," Stella felt herself nodding in agreement, wondering why on earth she had complied with Xanthe's order.

"I hate this," complained Xanthe, bitterly as they trooped into the race course. "It's so cold and boring," she moaned, dramatically pulling the fur collar of her full length mink coat together at her neck and shivering theatrically.

"I don't," Stella said, quietly, her words lost in the bitter wind that seemed to blow straight from Siberia. "It's the best fun ever."

Stella looked eagerly around her, letting Xanthe and the other girls hurry off to the hospitality box that Xanthe had persuaded her father to hire for them.

Stella had missed coming to the races. She strode purposefully off towards a programme seller, eager to see which horses were running today. She had become fascinated by racing while she had been with Henry and it would be interesting to see if any of the horses that she had seen before were running today.

Stella brought herself a programme and flicked through the pages, recognising many of the names of the horses and their trainers and jockeys. She really ought to come to the races, Stella decided, even if she was not involved with Henry any longer, it was still a brilliant day out.

The thought of being with Xanthe and all of her braying friends did not hold much excitement for Stella so she wandered off towards the parade ring to watch the horses.

As she crossed the tarmac towards the parade ring Stella caught sight of a familiar figure in the centre of the ring, watching the horses go around. She felt her stride falter, uncertain if she could bear to see Henry. But it was too late, as if he could sense her presence from a great distance Henry looked up and caught her eye. Stella felt her mouth spilt as if of its own accord in a wide grin, her hand raised in greeting.

"Hi," Henry mouthed. Stella smiled back. She leant against the parade ring, watching the horses go around.

"Come in," Henry beckoned Stella into the grassy centre of the ring. Uncertainly Stella ducked under the rail and went across the grass towards him.

Henry introduced her to the elderly couple who were standing with him, "Rosie and Connor Flanaghan they have a horse running later on," Stella smiled politely at the couple who were dressed in identical tweed jackets and felt hats. Rosie wore a tweed skirt that revealed calves knotted with varicose veins, while Connor wore tweed trousers in the same fabric.

"What should I bet on in the race?" Connor boomed.

"Let's go and watch them parade over here," Rosie suggested tactfully, seeing the way that Henry was looking at Stella.

"What?" Connor roared, scowling at his wife, his long moustache bristling as she led him away, "I want to talk to Henry. Where are you taking me too, woman?"

"Come along," Rosie boomed back, Stella caught Henry's eye and smiled. "You can talk to him anytime. Henry's busy now."

"Good to see you," Henry's voice was deep and sincere, his eyes roving over her face as if he were afraid that she would disappear if he looked away.

"And you," Stella said, sadly, she missed him terribly.

Whatever chance she could have ever had of restarting their relationship was lost now. He was going to be married to Xanthe, he was not interested in Stella any longer.

She had rejected him and he had found love elsewhere.

"I'm sorry about your father," she said, dragging her eyes away from his face and turning to look at the horses as they walked around the ring, heads bowed against the wind. Out of the corner of her eye Stella could see the jockeys beginning to come into the parade ring, the race would begin soon.

"Thanks," Henry said sadly, looking at the churned turf beneath his boots. "We kind of made up before he died, two stubborn fools that was the trouble."

"I heard that you inherited the house," Stella said, quietly, it seemed weird to call the magnificent mansion merely 'a house'. Henry nodded, looking sideways at Stella, "I'm a lot better proposition now aren't I?" he said, bitterly.

Stella opened her mouth to speak, but no words came out, she did not know what to say. It was impossible to explain to Henry how she felt.

"Is Amber…Paul.. ?" Stella blurted out.

"Amber's fine. Paul and Amber made up," Henry said his eyes meeting Stella's. "Not long now until she has the baby. Paul's not riding today. He won't leave her."

Stella bit her lip and looked away. Lucky Amber. How wonderful it must be to have someone with her like that.

"I was wrong about him wasn't I?" Stella whispered, quietly.

"You were wrong about a lot of things," Henry said bitterly.

The steward rang his bell for the jockeys to mount.

Kathy pulled Henry's horse towards them. "This is I Agree, isn't it?" Stella said, remembering the horse from one that she had seen at Henry's before. Henry nodded, looking at a tall elegant man who was walking towards them.

"Here comes Xanthe's father, he owns the horse," Henry said, stretching out his hand to greet the other man.

"Good luck," Stella said, she had no business being with Henry now; he needed to talk to his future father in law.

Stella made her way out of the parade ring, dodging easily between the horses as they were led around. Funny, she thought, how afraid of the horses she had been when she had first started to come to the races. Now she moved amongst them as easily as if she had grown up with horses.

She made her way up to the hospitality box. The girls were already partying in earnest, completely immune to the racing that was going on outside.

"Tamara!" Stella heard Xanthe yell, as she shoved her way through the heaving throng that was packed into the gaudily decorated room. "Tamara!

I ordered Lanson champagne, this is Moet!" Stella cringed inwardly for the poor Tamara, having to be at Xanthe's beck and call would not be pleasant, no matter how much she was charging.

"There you are," Xanthe screeched, catching sight of Stella. "What have you been doing?" Stella took a glass of champagne from one of the flustered looking waitresses.

"Outside. Watching the racing."

"Ohhh," Xanthe gave her a look as if she thought that actually watching the racing beside her fiancée was the most bizarre thing to do.

"I'm going out onto the balcony," Stella said, walking past Xanthe. "Your father's horse is running."

"Ohhhh. Yeah" Xanthe breathed, as if she had completely forgotten about the races. "I had better watch then," Xanthe said screwing up her face in distaste.

Stella opened the balcony door, letting in a blast of icy cold air.

"Eweuch," Xanthe grimaced.

"It's cold out there," Stella shrugged. "Stay inside then."

"No," Xanthe said with the affected air of a martyr "I had better come out and watch. Tamara!" she bellowed back over her shoulder. "Bring my coat will you!" Stella leant against the balcony wall, immune to the bitter cold, soaking up the atmosphere of the race course.

Below them the spectators yelled and roared encouragement at their respective horses, while far away on the course the horses sped over the jumps.

"Fuck," complained Xanthe. "It's like waiting for nail varnish to dry. How bloody boring."

She leant over the guard rail, tipping her champagne glass slightly so that a drop of the golden liquid spilled out, falling and splashing on the top of a flat cap. Xanthe stepped back, giggling gleefully.

Then tiring of this game she leant over the balcony again, scanning the crowd. "No sign of Henry," she mused. "Goodness, who is that?" she shrieked, in such a loud voice that the man below them turned and looked up. "Coooeeee," Xanthe yelled, waving wildly, "I wouldn't mind a bit of that!"

Xanthe pointed at the man. Stella looked at the people milling below them. The man that Xanthe had waved at had stopped and was looking up at them a broad grin splitting his far too handsome face. Stella looked straight into the highly amused eyes of Derry Blake.

CHAPTER FORTY SIX

Stella whooped in delight as Henry's horse, I Agree charged past the winning post seven lengths ahead of the other runners in the race.

"What a horse!" she exclaimed in delight, remembering watching the horse when she had first known Henry. Then it had barely wanted to canter round his gallops after his other horses. Henry had worked a miracle training I Agree to win a race in such a style.

"Oh super," Xanthe mumbled sarcastically, craning her neck to look through the crowds at the ramrod straight back of Derry Blake as he walked through the spectators. His horse, Stressed Up had come second.

"You had better go and be with your father and Henry," Stella said, trying to catch Xanthe's eye and get her attention. "He will be getting awarded his trophy," Stella told her, adding, "and getting his photograph taken. I saw that the Irish Tatler were taking pictures of all of the winners."

The words were hardly out of Stella's mouth before Xanthe wheeled away from the balcony rail and almost knocking Tamara out of the way, yelled, open the door. Now!" at Tamara. "Quickly!" she yelled, her voice rising in temper as Tamara fumbled with the catch of the sliding door. "I have to go to the winning post….enclosure … thing," Xanthe squawked, barging her way through the hospitality box in her rush to get to Henry and get her photograph taken. "Drink more champagne everyone!" she yelled, barging out the door with Tamara hurrying in her wake.

Stella shook her head, as Xanthe's strident shrieks faded into the hum of noise from her party friends, the fact that they were at the races seemed to have passed most of them by.

Not one person had gone out onto the balcony to watch the races, or had even glanced at the overhead television that was relaying each event live. All that they seemed to be interested in was chomping their way through the canapés and champagne like a hoard of hungry locusts and trying to outdo each other with the tales of expensive holidays and clothes.

Stella looked quickly around the room, there was no one here that she wanted to be with, she longed to be beside Henry, sharing his victory, proud of the brilliant job that he had done on the horse.

"I'm going to congratulate Henry," Stella touched October gently on the arm. "Really?" October smiled gently.

Not bothering to reply Stella walked through the hospitality box, down the stairs and into the fresh air. Outside on the tarmac all of the spectators were hurrying towards the winners' enclosure to see the winning horse.

It was difficult to get to the winners enclosure, the crowd around the outside was like an impenetrable wall, everyone wedged in together, shoving good naturedly to try to get a glimpse of the winning horse and his trainer.

Stella shoved her shoulder into the crowd. "Excuse me," she said, firmly and to her surprise the crowd parted, letting her through, suddenly she found herself at the edge of the winners' enclosure.

Inside, beneath a tented awning that flapped listlessly in the wind, were the winning horses and those connected with them. I Agree stood proudly in between Henry, the jockey, Xanthe, and her father. Xanthe posed for the cameras, grinning broadly and pouting as they clicked and whirled wildly.

Henry caught Stella's eye. "Well done," she mouthed, giving him a thumbs up signal, genuinely delighted that he had been so successful, for a moment all of their problems forgotten as she shared his delight in the success of the horse.

Then Stella's delight turned to repulsion as she glanced past Henry and saw Xanthe flickering her long eyelashes at Derry Blake, who shot her a seductive smile, full of invitation.

Kathy led the horse away as the winners' enclosure began to empty, Stella felt the full blast of the wind again as the crowd around her dispersed as everyone headed back to watch the next race.

"We'll head off to the Owners and Trainers bar," Henry said, he put an arm around Xanthe's father's shoulder as they walked away.

Stella felt her heart sink, she had loved being part of the racing scene. Now she was an outsider, that world was lost to her forever.

"Would you like to come with us to the Owners and Trainers bar?" Rosie Flanaghan waved at Stella, who nodded gladly and jogged after them.

"Who is that?" Xanthe hurried up to join Stella, she pointed discreetly at Derry who was walking ahead of them in the direction of the bar, chattering to the owners of the horse that he had trained.

"Derry Blake, a racehorse trainer," Stella told her.

"Daddy should put his horses with him," Xanthe said wistfully.

"Fetch us some drinks," Xanthe ordered Tamara, shoving a fist full of money in her direction. She seemed to have forgotten that Tamara was supposed to be organising her wedding and was using her as a maid instead.

"Tamara," Stella heard her say, "I must insist that the Priest wears black shoes, otherwise the colour co-ordination will be ruined."

Stella stood uncertainly on the edge of the group of people. She did not want to talk to Xanthe, and felt that she could not talk to Henry......... . .

"Who is your friend?" asked a silky voice at her side.

"Hello Derry," Stella did not turn to acknowledge him. "That's Xanthe I share a house with her. She has just got engaged."

"Ahhhh," Derry's voice was devilish, filled with the promise of mischief.

Stella saw Xanthe glance in her direction, watched her spin around, Tamara still talking to her as Xanthe stalked across the room towards Derry.

"Hello," Xanthe preened, holding her hand out seductively for Derry to kiss.

"Well," Derry took her hand in his and brought it slowly to his lips, never once taking his eyes off Xanthe. He kissed her hand, his lips lingering on her skin. It was a gesture filled with erotic promise. "Where have you been hiding all of my life,"

"I should think that she was at school most of your life," Stella itched to say.

"I'm here now," Xanthe said, making no effort to remove her hand from Derry's. "What are you doing getting engaged? What a terrible waste, especially when I have just found you."

Xanthe giggled, flirtatiously. Stella began to feel very uncomfortable, the sexual tension buzzed between Xanthe and Derry. What the hell was Xanthe playing at? Derry Blake was pure poison; he did not give a damn about anyone or anything.

"It's time that we left for Neo's" Tamara gently touched Xanthe's hand.

"I'm busy," she shot back, nastily, jerking her hand out of Tamara's reach.

"Neo's?" Derry mocked, putting on an impressed face.

"Xanthe's having a party there," Tamara smiled, politely professional.

"Ahh," Derry said silkily. "Maybe I will see you later," his eyes locked onto Xanthe's, filled with forbidden promise.

"It's a private party," Tamara said, "Xanthe's hen night." Derry gently brought Xanthe's hand to his lips and kissed it once more, his eyes roving seductively onto Tamara.

"Girls only night? Sounds perfect." his voice held a challenge that Tamara could not stop him going to Neo's. "I'll see you later ," he smiled at Xanthe, before spinning on his heel and walking away. Stella glared at Derry, he even had the audacity to stop and talk to Henry. She was filled with anger as she saw Derry congratulate Henry, shaking his hand and nodding in Xanthe's direction. No doubt telling Henry what a lovely girl she was.

The dinner at Neo's was an exclusive affair for fifty of Xanthe's closest friends before the party afterwards to which everyone else had been invited. Stella had been surprised to find that she had been invited to the dinner, but then realised afterwards that October and Julia had probably arranged it so that Stella could drive them home afterwards.

"Isn't this gorgeous?" October said, looking around the room. Stella nodded, Neo's was truly fantastic, acres of white marble seemed to stretch in every direction, tall columns stretched up to a ceiling that had been painted to look like a scene from an orgy, naked bodies entwined and intermeshed into each other. They were handed glasses of pink champagne by a near naked waiter, she almost choked as he turned away, his bottom was barely covered by a fig leaf.

"Isn't he gorgeous?" October squeaked in excitement, gazing lustfully after the waiter, whose body gleamed with the oil that he had slicked all over his skin. Stella nodded in agreement, hardly glancing at the young man. Somehow no one seemed to interest her any more, not even the gleaming, toned bodies of the waiter's all of the girls seemed to be gazing at in open admiration.

Stella began to wish that she had not come. She had spent so long wanting to belong to this kind of set, once she would have donated one of her limbs to have been invited to a party at one of the city's most exclusive night clubs, attended by some of the wealthiest people around. But it was not as much fun as she had thought that it would be. Having a quiet dinner in a small restaurant with Henry, tired and satisfied after a day at the races was far more fun. She had not realised how much she had enjoyed discussing the other horses and the trainers. She had always been longing for a different, better life. And now she had discovered that it was not as glamorous as she had anticipated.

"I was in Monte last week," the identikit blonde beside her was saying, "New York next week, I've got my name down for one of the new Marwari dresses, got to go for a fitting."

"Yah," droned an identical blonde, swishing her long hair back over her shoulder, "I've got my Marwari last week. Gorgeous. Amazing how each piece is hand woven by children in India.."

Stella wandered away, sipping her drink, half listening to bits of conversations as she mooched around, looking at the enormous lewd oil paintings on the walls, running her fingers along the cold stone carved faces of the marble statues.

"Dinner is served," a youth dressed in a toga blew a single note on a long gold horn.

Stella followed everyone into the dining room, long tables had been laid out with golden plates and cutlery, with huge bowls of fresh fruit in the middle of the table, huge bunches of grapes spilling out from amongst fresh peaches and oranges.

"The table plan is on the wall," Tamara repeated, standing in the doorway, guiding everyone to the seating arrangement.

Stella found herself sitting on the end of one of the tables, beside two of Xanthe's cousins, who had obviously been invited to smooth family feelings.

The two girls were definitely non-identikit blondes, both were very plump and very tanned and had no manners what so ever. Stella quickly gave up trying to talk to them after her attempts at conversation were met by grunts of agreement as the two girls shovelled the food into their mouths.

Stella was glad that she did not even want to try to eat; she would have stood no chance against these eating monsters, who clutched and grabbed at the food that was laid out on big platters in front of them as if they had not been fed for months.

Stella picked at a bread roll and a lettuce leaf, she still had no appetite. Halfway along the other side of the table Xanthe was holding court, ordering poor Tamara around as if she were a servant. Tamara, wearing a fixed smile, grimly fetched and carried, tending to Xanthe's every whim.

A movement in the shadows between the tall columns caught Stella's eye, she glanced up, horrified to see Derry walking across the room. He reached Xanthe, slid his arms around her from behind and seductively kissed the side of her neck.

"Derry," giggled Xanthe, rubbing her head against his where it nestled against her neck. "This is supposed to be a girls night. Ladies only,"

"Perfect," Derry said, standing up straight and surveying the girls who were looking at him open mouthed. "Hens should always have one good cock in with them."

"Can I offer you anything?" Xanthe said, huskily, turning to look at Derry over her shoulder.

"Yes, I think that you can," Derry said, ignoring the amazed stares of the rest of the girls. "But I'll let you eat now – you will need the energy," he said blatantly dropping a kiss onto Xanthe's bare shoulder. Derry moved away snapping his fingers in the air, one of the waiters darted forwards.

"Yes Mr Blake, Sir," Derry was obviously well known.

"Fetch me a whiskey," he walked away out of the dining area. A shocked silence fell over the party, Xanthe glanced around the table as if she had only just realised what a tart she had made of herself.

"Isn't he awful," Xanthe said, feigning shock, gazing up and down the table, "Tamara, how could you let him in."

"I'll get rid of him," Tamara said, between gritted teeth. She looked as if working for Xanthe was the worst experience of her whole life.

"Don't bother," snapped Xanthe, as if she blamed Tamara totally for spoiling her party, "I'll do it myself."

Once the dinner was over Xanthe got to her feet, her eyes glowed with mischief.

"You all head into the disco, I'll just go and get rid of our unwanted visitor," she said heading towards the bar, walking unsteadily on her high heels.

Stella followed everyone into the disco, loud music boomed from every corner of the room, making the floor and walls seem as if they flexed with the bass beat.

The near naked waiters slunk onto the dance floor as the girls began to dance, grinning as the drunken women groped at their slippery bodies.

Stella endured another hour of the booming music. Her head ached horribly and the thought of lying in her comfortable bed was very appealing.

October and Julia did not look as if they were too interested in leaving yet.

Stella grabbed her handbag, she would go home alone, leave them all to it. She headed out of the disco, her high heels clicking on the marble corridor as she headed out of the nightclub, then as the strap dug in to her toes Stella pulled off her shoes; they had been hurting all night.

She crossed the deserted reception area where they had originally had drink, her aching feet padding silently on the cool marble. Then she stopped, spinning around alerted by a soft murmur. Tucked away in a recessed alcove amongst the columns and statues, was a sofa, and lying on the sofa, entwined, oblivious to her presence, were Derry and Xanthe.

CHAPTER FORTY SEVEN

Stella itched to punch Xanthe.

She had betrayed Henry, dear sweet kind Henry, with someone as sl[
and rotten as Derry Blake. How the two of them suited each other, though
Stella glaring at Xanthe's immaculate mask of makeup and the body tha
was kept toned by the personal trainer she met at the gym every other day.

Everything about her was false. There was nothing real about her.

The real Xanthe, the one hiding behind the makeup and expensiv
clothes was rotten to the core, just like Derry. Neither of them cared a jo
about anyone else or their feelings as long as they were happy.

"You don't care about very much, do you?" Stella snapped, nastily, glarin
at Xanthe.

"I beg your pardon?" Xanthe stopped flicking through the magazine sh<
had been reading, looking for ideas for her wedding.

Tamara who had been sitting at the table behind her, jotting dowr
Xanthe's ideas stopped writing, her pen poised over the page while sh<
listened eagerly to the row that was brewing up.

"I said," Stella said coldly. "You don't care about anything very much."

"And just what is that supposed to mean?"

"You went off with Derry Blake." Xanthe shrugged her shoulders
opening her hands in a complacent gesture. Stella itched to launch hersel
the sofa and pound her fists into Xanthe's smug face.

"Oh Stella," Xanthe signed. "That was just a last little fling before I ge

334

married. My fiancée won't ever know. While the cat is away.....and all that"

Stella narrowed her eyes with hatred, unable to believe Xanthe's words, Stella shook her head. "But where does love come into it?" the hot anger that she had felt had vanished, to be replaced by a deep despair. Henry deserved something better for his life than someone who was just marrying him for who he was.

"I do love my fiancée," Xanthe said smugly, standing up, ending the argument and flounced out of the room, with Tamara trailing in her wake.

Stella slept badly, turning over and over in bed unable to get comfortable, or switch off from the myriad of thoughts that swirled around in her mind.

Teddy sickened, with the constant movement slunk miserably off the bed and finally curled in Stella's discarded clothes on the floor.

It was hard to bear the thought that Xanthe was marrying Henry purely for who he was, she did not give a damn about him, just that marrying him would give her some social standing while she carried on as if she were still single.

Henry would be devastated when he found out what an evil bitch he had married. He deserved better.

Twice she sat up and turned on the bedside light, ready to get up. But then she had turned off the light and lain back down. If she went to see Henry it would just look as if she wanted to damage his and Xanthe's relationship. It would look as if she wanted him back now that she had found out that he was rich.

And she did want him back, but not just because of his newfound wealth. She wanted him back because she loved him. She had loved him from the first moments that they had gone out together and had fought against that love because she did not think that he was right for her. Thought that he would never have made her happy, thought that she needed someone wealthy. And now she knew how wrong she had been.

Henry was the man for her, wealthy or not. And it was too late. He was going to marry someone else, someone who would never make him happy.

Stella seemed to have only just dropped off to sleep when her alarm clock buzzed signalling that it was time to get up.

There was no sign of the other girls when she went downstairs, none of them went off to a job like she did and so kept very different hours.

Xanthe had once laughed snidely that the only eight o'clock that she ever saw was the one when it was time to go out for the night.

She was glad to get to work; at least here she could find solace from the thoughts that swirled through her mind. She had to concentrate on her work, forget about Henry and Xanthe, she could not do anything about them.

"Morning darling," Peter Shaunnesy air kissed beside her head. "How are things with you? How is that new feature on stress free weekends coming along?"

"Great," Stella was glad to have something to focus on rather than the thoughts of Henry, "I've been contacting all the spa hotels that I could think of, Delphi, Inchydowney, to see…."

"Darling," her boss turned away abruptly, cutting her off in mid-sentence as the Head of Advertising, Hazel Brown walked down the corridor, "I wanted to talk to you about some new contracts."

Her boss walked away with his hand resting on Hazel's back, without even glancing back in Stella's direction. Stella signed bitterly; the moment that someone more important had come along her boss had not even wanted to know her. What a false, artificial world she worked in, where everyone was nice to each other to their faces and then stabbing each other in the back.

Stella walked up to her office, noticing as if for the first time the smarmy fake chumminess that everyone seemed to exhibit.

Ian McGowan, one of the designers cut his friend dead in mid conversation as Stella walked in, dashing to tell her about some photographs that he had been sent. Stella was more important than his friend in the hierarchy of the magazine. Suddenly she loathed every second that she was in the building.

She loved what she did for a job, she was brilliant at it, but all of the fake intimacy was awful. She did not want any part of it. If only people could just accept others for what they were. She had been part of that awful chain of artificial friends, wanting to be with people who were wealthy, looking down on those who were poor and humble. And now she could see the sham world for the fake that it was.

Just before lunch time she made a telephone call to another of the spas that she wanted to visit as part of the feature that she was writing.

At first the owner would not come to the telephone to talk to her, but then once Stella had explained to her secretary that she was an editor on one of the biggest social magazines in Ireland suddenly the owner was on the other end of the receiver, dripping sweetness.

Stella ended the call and put the receiver down. Slowly she got to her feet and walked out of her office, shutting the door quietly behind her.

"Can I come in," she knocked on Peter Shaunnessy's office door.

"Well, I..," he was on the telephone.

"This is important," Stella stood in the doorway.

"I'll call you back," he said, putting the receiver down and raising his eyebrows quizzically at Stella.

"I'm quitting," Stella surprised herself as the words tumbled from her mouth. She had intended to tell him that she was going to take some time off, but now it was done. She had ended her career.

"Why?" Peter asked simply, Stella crossed the floor and sat down on the leather sofa opposite his desk.

"I've just had enough of.........," Stella fumbled for the words. What had she had enough of? Everything. The whole circuit that she had become mixed up in, the whole game of striving to become someone, back stabbing and longing to be someone that she could never be.

Peter smiled suddenly, leaning forwards, meshing his fingers together and resting his chin on them.

"Take some time out," he said quietly. "Go home to the country for a bit. Recharge your batteries and then see how you feel. You can work freelance for me for a while and I'll keep your job open for a few months."

Stella headed back to the house; the drive was full of cars, so she parked out on the road and went inside. The lounge was full of wedding dress samples; they were draped over the sofa, on the table, all over the floor, spilling out of the boxes and suitcases that were stacked all over the room.

Amongst the masses of pale silk fabric and glitter sat October, Julia and Tamara, scribbling on her ubiquitous pad while Xanthe paraded through the room in a gorgeous cream silk halter neck dress, that clung to the contours of her body like a second skin.

"What do you think?" Xanthe asked, spinning around to give Stella the full benefit of her dress, her huge engagement ring catching the light as she turned, sending shafts of light across the room that reflected on the glittery dresses. Xanthe seemed to have completely forgotten their earlier argument, she was so thick skinned that nothing seemed to bother her.

"Lovely," Stella said, her voice filled with awe. Xanthe really did look stunning in the dress.

Suddenly Stella could not bear being in the house any longer.

She could not stand by and watch Henry marry Xanthe, it was a huge mistake and yet there was nothing that she could do about it.

"Don't you think that Xanthe's fiancée will just adore this dress?" October smiled at Stella.

"He is arriving soon, his plane lands at four o'clock," Xanthe grinned happily, holding her dress up at the sides and waltzing around the room.

Henry must have been to the sales in England or something, Stella thought fleetingly, aching with the pain of missing Henry and not being part of his life.

Then something inside Stella snapped, like flood gates giving way when the weight of water becomes too strong, the emotion within her surged out. "You don't give a damn about Henry. You shouldn't marry him, you will break his heart. You bitch!" Stella roared her face puce with emotion.

"His heart had already been broken by you," Xanthe stopped waltzing around the room and turned to face Stella. "If anyone is a bitch it is you."

Stella felt as if she had been hurled into a brick wall. Slowly she backed away. Everything that Xanthe said was true.

"I have to go," Stella said slowly, every word seemed to be an immense effort. She had to get away. It was impossible to stay here and watch Xanthe and Henry get married. Stella shot upstairs and threw some clothes into a bag and pounded back down the stairs

"Stella wait," October stood at the bottom of the stairs, "I need to tell you something."

But Stella slammed the front door in her face and ran down the drive to her car with Teddy hurtling after her as fast as his short legs would carry him.

October charged down the drive after Stella. "Don't go. Listen to me," she said, breathlessly.

"Just leave me alone," Stella snapped, throwing her bags into the back seat of the car she picked up Teddy and shoved him into the passenger seat and then scrambled into the driver's seat and slammed the door shut.

"You are making a mistake," October mouthed, hammering on the side window.

Stella turned on the car and drove away, the car tyres screeching in protest. Getting away from here was certainly no mistake.

A short time later Stella was heading out of the city, Teddy sat on the front passenger seat, looking eagerly out of the windscreen to see where they were going.

"Right then Teddy," Stella mused as she drove. "Where shall we go to?" she wanted to escape from the city, find somewhere where there was peace and quiet, somewhere where she could put all thoughts of Henry behind her and start her life afresh.

She steered through the traffic, not really driving with any purpose. "My boss said that I should go home, sort out my life," Stella gave a snort of derision.

Home was in Dublin, with those two faced bitches, who thought of nothing but money and social standing. Her life was….. had been, Stella corrected herself, the magazine, where she had worked so hard to prove herself. And at the day it had all been such an empty sham. All that had mattered to everyone around her was how important people where and how much money they had. The people that she knew would walk over you to get to someone who was better connected, or who they thought had more money.

It was all so empty and meaningless. And she had been part of it, wanting a rich man and all of the trappings of wealth.

She had despised Henry because she thought that he had not been wealthy and yet he had been the one man that she had really loved.

She had despised her parents because they had not been wealthy and had not been able to give her the life that she had thought that she had deserved, despised them while they struggled against poverty and her father's ill health.

She had fallen out with Amber because she had thought that her boyfriend was not good enough. Good enough for what, Stella sighed miserably.

Paul had made Amber happy, what right had Stella had to tell her who she should fall in love with.

"Oh Teddy," the tarmac blurred as tears began to flow. "What a mess I've made of everything." What a shallow, nasty bitch she had been, Stella could not see to drive any more. She stopped the car at the side of the road and laid her head against the steering wheel, weeping bitterly. "Home………?" Stella mused.

Teddy gazed solemnly at Stella as if he understood every word. "I have a lot of making up to do there."

Teddy cocked his head on one side, his small pink tongue lolling out of the side of the mouth as if he were grinning in agreement.

Stella sat up, searching for a tissue in her handbag to wipe her tear stained face.

For the first time in years Stella longed to be at home.

She had to see her parents to make amends for her behaviour, tell them how much she loved them. Stella turned on the car engine and eased her way out into the traffic. Teddy turned around on the front seat, curling himself up into a ball with a sigh as he settled down to sleep. "That's it," Stella smiled, stroking his soft fur. "Go to sleep just when I need you to navigate."

CHAPTER FORTY EIGHT

Stella put down her sketch pad and looked at the picture she had created. The seascape she had done in pastels was quite good.

"Not too bad, Teddy, what do you think?" Stella held up her sketch pad in Teddy's direction. The dog continued to dig in the sand, pulling at a half buried piece of drift wood.

"I think that it is lovely," Stella's mother reached across and picked up the picture. Stella smiled at her mother. "You have to say that,"

"Well it's true," her mother lay back on the tartan rug, shielding her eyes from the bright sunlight.

Stella sighed deeply. "This is lovely though," she said softly. "Spending time just doing nothing." Stella lay on her back and closed her eyes, letting the warmth of the sun soak into her body.

It was wonderful to be home. For the first time ever she felt truly relaxed here.

This was where she belonged, amongst people who loved her for herself.

"What are you going to do now?" her mother asked gently, for the first time since Stella had arrived on the doorstep. Stella sat up, hugging her knees to her chest, gazing out at the sea.

"I've spent my whole life hating this place," Stella said, quietly, biting her lip to stop the tears from falling, "I've spent years searching for something, pushing away the people that loved me because I thought that they weren't good enough." Stella stifled a sob. "All that glitters isn't gold, isn't that what they say?" She glanced across at her mother, who lay on her rug, looking at Stella, her eyes gentle.

"I've messed everything up," Stella said fretfully.

"You haven't," her mother said gently. "Give yourself a bit of time. Think about what you are going to do with your life now." Teddy dropped a small branch onto the rug beside Stella's mother. Irene threw it across the sand.

Stella rolled onto her belly and looked across at her mother, trailing her hand in the warm sand, digging her fingers down beneath the top layer until she reached the cool dampness beneath. Stella nodded slowly.

She did not have a clue what she wanted to do now that she had left Dublin.

Coming home had been the best thing that she had done for a long time.

Her heart, frozen with loathing for her childhood and her parents' humble life, finally thawed and at last she was able to return their love.

Stella had wanted to cling to her father with relief that they had another chance at a relationship. His treatment was working, the consultant had told her parents, they were, in the consultant's words, reasonably optimistic about Paddy being pain free and having a reasonable life span.

Paddy and Irene had persuaded Stella to stay at home while she rebuilt her life, maybe work freelance for a while. Stella felt calm and relaxed; here there was no striving for wealth, no relentless networking to build up more influential contacts.

Life in the countryside had a peace and gentleness to it that soothed her.

One thing played relentlessly on Stella's mind, though, she had rejected the one person that she had truly felt that she belonged with Henry. She could not put right the damage that she had done to their relationship, but she had to tell him about the bitch that he was going to marry. He might not believe her. But she could not let him go down the aisle without at least telling him the truth about Xanthe.

She had been such a fool, rejecting the two people who cared the most about her. Henry and Amber.

"Mammy," Stella got slowly to her feet, "I'll be back in a few days. There are a few things that I have to sort out."

There was no sign of anyone at the apartment. Stella pushed her finger onto the buzzer again, but no one came to answer it. Amber must have gone out.

"Shit," Stella sighed, she had been all fired up for apologising to Amber, had got all of her words organised in her mind and now she was not in.

On impulse Stella jogged across to the small corner shop opposite the apartment and brought a small card, with a picture of a dog on it that did not look unlike Teddy. Rummaging in her handbag Stella unearthed a pen, scrawled, 'I'm so sorry for everything. I'll call back later' on the card and shoved it into the envelope.

She went back to the apartment, there was no point in pushing the card into the letter box, Amber never checked her mail, she had always seemed to think that if she did not receive her credit card bills then they did not actually exist. Stella still had her key, she would go up and just shove the card under the door. That way she would be sure that Amber had received it.

Stella locked up her car, winding down an inch of the passenger seat window so that Teddy could get some fresh air.

As she walked away the small dog pressed his nose to the gap, whimpering crossly at being left. Stella opened the main door breathing in the familiar scent of the scented candles that one of their neighbours always burnt over laid with the faintly musty smell of the hallway. Everything was so familiar, as if she had never been away; even the bicycle that belonged to the man who lived in the bottom apartment was still resting against the wall.

Stella went upstairs feeling as if she were trespassing, expecting at any second that one of the residents would come rushing out and yell at her to clear off. But no one did.

She reached the door to her old apartment and crouched down to shove the envelope through the gap between the door and the carpet. A low moan of pain came from inside the apartment.

"Amber?" Stella gasped, There was a silence for a moment, followed by another moan and then Amber shrieked, "Stella, is that you? Come and fucking help me. Quickly."

"Amber," Stella could hear the panic rising in her own voice as she rummaged frenziedly in her handbag for the door key that she had thrown in as she opened the bottom door. "I'm coming. What's the matter? Are you hurt?" A thousand images flashed through Stella's mind, each one more horrific than the one before it, Amber being attacked by burglars, Amber suffering a heart attack, falling on a knife.

"For fuck's sake Stella," growled Amber, "I'm having the bloody baby."

Stella found the key and hastily fumbled to get it into the lock, frenziedly turning the key, unable to remember which way to turn it to open the door.

"Turn it to the fucking left," snarled Amber from inside the apartment.

"Yes, yes," gasped Stella, finally shoving the door open and exploding into the apartment.

Amber lay on the sofa, her back arched with pain. Stella felt her mouth drop open. Amber's belly was enormous, her sweatshirt straining across the huge mound.

"Help me will you!" Amber shrieked, distractedly wiping a sweat dampened strand of hair from her grey forehead.

"What do I do?" Stella turned around, took a stride towards the kitchen, memories of demands for hot water, soap and towels in the movies flooding back, she turned again, what did they do with them when they had them.

"What do I do?" Stella gasped again, turning to face Amber.

"Ring." Amber puffed, her face contorted with pain, "For. A. Fucking. Ambulance." "Right," Stella replied, turning around twice until her shock fuddled brain remembered where her telephone was.

Stella found her telephone and punched in the number for the emergency services. It seemed to take forever to direct her call to the ambulance service.

"I need an ambulance," Stella gasped, feeling as if she were some character in a television hospital drama.

"What is the problem," asked the super calm voice on the end of the telephone.

"My friend," Stella glanced across at Amber who arched her back, writhing with the pain. "She's in an awful lot of pain."

"Tell them I'm having a fucking baby you stupid cow," roared Amber, clutching at the back of the sofa, sweat pouring from her forehead.

"Oh," Stella could not get her brain to co-operate with her mouth.

This was not the scene that she had imagined. She had imagined herself and Amber meeting and quietly discussing their argument over a cup of coffee.

To find her so hugely pregnant and in such pain had taken her by surprise. She had known that Amber was pregnant, known that the baby had to be due around now, but still it had come as a surprise to see the changes that had been wrought on Amber's body and to see her in such a terrible amount of pain.

"Tell them I'm in fucking labour," Amber ordered, sinking back onto the sofa as the vicious wave of pain subsided.

"She's in labour," Stella yelled into the telephone. "She says how often are you getting contractions?" Stella put her hand over the receiver to ask Amber, as she clawed in agony at the back of the sofa.

"Just pain," Amber hissed, her legs writhing as she tried to escape from the dreadful agony that was trying to rip her body apart.

"Is she dilated?" asked the woman on the telephone.

"No, I think she is Catholic," Stella could feel the panic rising within herself. It was terrible to see Amber in such pain and to be able to do nothing about it.

"Right," said the woman patiently. "Listen, you have to try to keep her calm. We'll have an ambulance there as soon as possible. Give me the address."

Stella gave the woman the address, watching Amber fearfully. She was silent now, lying flat on the sofa, still, her eyes wide open, reflecting only pain and pure terror.

"She's dying," Stella shrieked into the mouthpiece.

"Calm down," snapped the operator. "You have to keep calm. Go and have a look at your friend then come back to me. Try to get her to breathe deeply."

Stella took a deep breath and walked over to the sofa, Amber turned her head fretfully, as if she had only just realised that Stella was there.

"Why didn't you get help before?" Stella said, gently, perching on the edge of the sofa and lifting a damp strand of hair off Amber's grey forehead.

"Paul's coming. He's just gone to see a house he wants to buy for us, out in the country." She flexed her legs, twisting in anticipation of another pain. "The pain started and I thought that he would be back in time to bring me to the hospital, but they got so bad, I couldn't move and then you came."

"Hold my hand, grip onto me when the pain starts," Stella slipped her hand into Amber's damp, hot one.

"Don't you dare say anything about him being unreliable," Amber gasped, tensing her body as another pain wracked through her, Stella felt every bone and fibre within her hand being crushed beyond endurance, she yelped as wave within wave of pain shot through her body.

"I wouldn't dare," Stella gingerly eased her hand out of Amber's grip, maybe the hold handing was not a good idea, it was just that they always seemed to do that on the television.

"I'm going to die," Amber wailed, fretfully, as she began to shiver, her body unable to cope with the pain.

"No you are not," Stella snapped. "You have to breathe, like they do on the television. Just breathe deeply. Like this," she puffed out her cheeks and blew deep breaths through her lips. Amber shook her head, a faint smile twisting her pale lips.

"I'm bloody well going to help you when you are in labour. See how easy it is to fucking breathe." She copied Stella's puffing, laughing and then yelping with pain at the same time.

Stella, remembering the telephone operator, got up. "Don't leave me," growled Amber, Stella hovered between Amber and the telephone and then dashed to pick up the receiver.

"She's breathing – puffing – you know."

"Brilliant, you are doing really well," said the operator, she sounded so calm that she could have been nonchalantly painting her nails or something on the other end of the telephone. "The ambulance will be there any minute now."

"It's coming," Amber writhed Again, puffing furiously, she half clambered and half fell off the sofa.

"Ha, ha," Stella felt her mouth open in panic. "Don't be silly. This is no time to joke."

Amber strained, her face screwing up with the effort. "No. Joke."

"She's having a baby," Stella roared into the telephone, she was quivering all over with panic and excitement.

"Can you see anything?" the operator said.

Stella glanced out of the window. "No, there's no sign of the ambulance," she said, hardly daring to look at Amber.

"Can you see the baby?" the operator said, her voice was calm, but there was an edge of tension in it suddenly. Stella shot a look around the room as if she expected to see the baby hidden in a corner somewhere. And then it dawned on her what the operator wanted.

"Ohhhhh," she put the telephone down and peeked.

"Oh fuck."

"Help me!" Amber whimpered.

"I can see something!" Stella hissed into the receiver.

"Stella!!" shrieked Amber. Stella threw down the receiver onto the work top and dashed to Amber.

A few moments later the door banged open. Paul, followed by two burley ambulance men shot into the room.

"You've got a little boy," Stella said, proudly, holding up the towelling bundle that she had in her arms, so that Paul could see the crumpled, angry looking red face of his son.

"We need to get you to hospital – get you both checked out," one of the ambulance men helped Amber into a wheelchair.

"Can I come and visit you again?" Stella asked, hugging Amber.

"Yes please," Amber grinned, lifting her hand to wipe a smear of blood off Stella's pale face. "Bring Teddy with you next time. I'll take him a walk and you can play with Junior." The ambulance man put the baby gently into Amber's arms.

"What did you want anyway?" Amber grinned at Stella over the top of the baby's head.

Stella grinned back. "Just to say that I was sorry."

CHAPTER FIFTY

Stella drove slowly up the hill, along a road bordered by trees, the sunlight shining through the canopy of leaves, made dappled patterns on the road.

At either side of the road the forest was a multitude of greens, the pale undersides of the bracken mingling with the waxy darkness of the rhododendrons and the glowing shades of the grasses.

Stella reached the top of the hill, slowed the car and pulled over to the lay-by where she had found Teddy, what seemed like a lifetime ago.

The little dog woke as the car bumped gently to a halt and stood with his front paws on the dashboard, his tail waving gently as if he recognised the place.

The leaden weight of nervousness that had settled in Stella's stomach had vanished as she had driven closer to Henry's home. Whatever lay ahead of her the beauty of this place could never fail to make her feel at peace.

One day, Stella thought, she would come back here and enjoy the beautiful view, without being torn apart by all of the painful memories and regrets that she presently lived with.

But for now she had to see Henry, so that she could make a fresh start on her life. But before that she needed to apologise for how she had treated him and to try to make him understand why he could not marry Xanthe.

Stella got out of the car, and looked through the canopy of the leaves, across the parkland to the beautiful Thornhill House. Henry's new home.

Soon to be the one that he would share with Xanthe.

The ancient house slumbered peacefully beneath its mantle of dark coloured ivy, surrounded by the gardens, a riot of colour sprawling in every direction. Stella took a deep breath, she had to see Henry and she was not looking forward to the meeting.

Stella clipped the lead onto Teddy's collar and started to walk back down the hill towards the tall stone pillars that marked the entrance to Thornhill House. She wanted to walk down the drive, just for once savour the house and the parkland.

Driving would have made it all happen too quickly, she wanted, just once to savour the gorgeous house, to try to imprint the memory of it deep within her, so that she could draw on it sometime in the future when the pain of losing Henry had receded.

The entrance to Thornhill House was at the bottom of the hill, the stone wall that marked the border of the parkland curved in to form an imposing entrance.

Stella felt her steps begin to falter, nervously. What if Henry told her to clear off? What if he would not listen to what she had to say to him? That was a chance that she had to take.

She could not let him marry Xanthe without telling Henry that Xanthe was totally wrong for him.

"Come on Teddy," Stella said in a voice that sounded a lot more positive than she actually felt and she strode past the towering iron gates and tall stone pillars towards Henry's home.

A long straight avenue stretched in front of her, running through grassland as smooth as a garden lawn.

Sheep grazed at either side of the avenue and lay beneath the shaded shelter of sprawling oak trees. Teddy strained at his lead, eager to be let off his lead to run free. Every stride brought Stella closer and closer to the house. And the closer that she got the more nervous Stella felt. It was so quiet, only the occasional bleating of a sheep and the nervous sound of her breathing broke the silence.

The avenue ended in a curved forecourt in front of the house. Stella felt tiny and very conspicuous as her footsteps crunched across the greys and creams of the gravel as she walked towards the house.

Close up the house was even more beautiful than it was from a distance. Henry's Jeep stood beside the stone steps that led up to the front door.

Stella smiled, shaking her head, Henry really did not care what anyone thought of him. He had no need to exchange his battered Jeep for something new and flashy, just because he was now the owner of a magnificent house and had just inherited a fortune.

Stella's footsteps scrunched across the gravel she ran up the stone steps. Beside the door was a huge recessed alcove where a chain with a fancy handle was hanging. Stella pulled the chain, turning back to look out at the magnificent view from the front door as the resounding note of a bell rang in the depths of the house.

A moment later Teddy whined, cocking his head to one side as footsteps that he recognised echoed within the house.

The enormous blue door swung back and Henry stood in front of her. Stella looked first at Henry and then gazed past him into the depths of the house.

A magnificent chandelier, at least five feet long hung from the ceiling behind him and beyond a vast hallway stretched so far ahead that she could not see where it ended. Teddy pulled at his lead, rearing on his back legs to jump up at Henry, whining for attention.

"Hi Teddy," Henry crouched down beside the little dog, rubbing his ears and his muzzle. "Great to see you." He stood up, slowly looked at Stella. "Hello Stella." His voice was cool, with none of the easy affection that he had greeted Teddy.

"You had better come in," he stood back to let Stella walk into the house. "Paul rang me and said that you delivered Amber's baby," he said, closing the enormous door behind her. "That was very brave of you. I'm glad that you two have made up."

Henry led the way along the hallway and through a door into a vast room. Light flooded in from the tall windows that looked out onto the gardens that Stella had seen when she and Henry had walked in the woods above his cottage.

"Sit down," Henry said, coolly.

Stella glanced around, there were three enormous sofas arranged around a huge fireplace and two more pushed back against the walls of the room. Henry perched himself on the edge of one of the sofas by the fire, Stella, following his cue took a place opposite him.

Teddy made straight for the rug in front of the empty fireplace and settled down as if he had lived there all of his life.

"How are you?" Henry asked, his voice politely cool as if she were a stranger that had just come to call at the house.

Stella quailed at the thought of talking to Henry, he was so cold, hard, hatred oozed from his every pore.

He did not want her here. He was always courteous when they met at the races, but this was his territory now, he was a different person to the one that she had once known. And he was making it very clear that he did not want Stella around.

"Henry, I...."Stella faltered, the words would not form on her lips.

She loved him so much that the pain of being close to him was too much to bear when he was making it so obvious how much he hated her.

The weight of her stupidity for dumping him when she had truly loved him was total agony. Stella wished that she had not come, she should have stayed away; let the pain of missing him gradually recede with the passing of time.

But she could not go away until she had said what she needed to. "Henry, you can't marry Xanthe," the words tumbled out of her mouth. Henry glared at Stella for a long time, silently. He lay back against the cushions on the sofa and folded his arms.

"What gives you the right to tell me that?" he asked, quizzically, snorting with sarcastic amusement.

Stella swallowed hard, this was the most awful thing that she had ever done.

Henry was furious. He loved Xanthe and he was furious that she had dared to come and tell him not to get married.

"I just don't think that she is right for you,"

"Why is that then?" Henry leant forwards, raising his eyebrows sardonically.

"Because she doesn't love you for who you are." Stella said, quietly, she could not tell Henry that Xanthe had betrayed him with Derry Blake. It would be too cruel, it would break his heart.

"And who will?" Henry said, coldly. "You certainly didn't."

"I did," Stella said, quietly, "I was just afraid of ...."

"Being with someone poor. A nobody," Henry finished the sentence for her.

351

Stella nodded bleakly. He really did hate her; he must despise her for being so shallow. She was as bad as Xanthe.

"And now you want me back because you think I'm rich."

Stella shook her head, violently. "No. No. I realised that I loved you before you got all ....this...." Stella gazed around the room. "And then when I heard that you had inherited the house I felt that I could not come because you would think that I just wanted you for what you were. Not who you were."

"And I did think that," Henry sneered, his eyes were icy cold when Stella looked up to meet them. "You are nasty and shallow and you did not love me because you thought that I was poor."

Stella nodded, feeling bitter tears trickle down her face. "And now you want me back because you think I'm rich," he repeated.

Stella shook her head again, unable to speak because of the huge lump that constricted her throat. "No," she whispered, "I knew that you wouldn't have me back because you would think that. I just wanted to say goodbye. I'm going away."

"I see," Henry said coldly. Stella buried her face in her hands, unable to bear Henry's impenetrable coldness.

There was a long silence, broken only by the sound of Teddy sighing as he turned around on the rug before settling back down to snooze.

"You can't marry Xanthe," Stella tried again.

"What the fuck makes you think that you have the right to tell me who I can or cannot marry?" Henry got up and paced in front of the fireplace as if he could barely control his anger.

"Because I love you," Stella whispered. Henry picked up one of the ornaments from above the fireplace and examined it as if he had never seen it before.

"Henry," Stella said gently, "I don't want you to make a mistake by marrying Xanthe."

The strength of Henry's hatred for her was like an impenetrable wall, he was lost to her forever. She had driven him away by her fear, but still she had to try to protect him from the chains of a marriage based on lies and infidelity.

"My only mistake was to fall in love with you," Henry crossed the room with three quick strides and pulled Stella to her feet. "You stupid, stupid woman," he entwined his fingers in the hair at the back of her head, tugging it downwards tilting her face up towards his. Henry's free hand moved to Stella's cheek, softly caressing the skin, his fingers moving softly over her lips. Stella closed her eyes, letting her lips trail over his skin, gently kissing the palm of his hand.

"Please don't marry Xanthe," Stella pleaded. "She could never make you happy."

Henry grinned suddenly, his eyes dancing with amusement. "I'm not marrying Xanthe," he smiled.

"Oh?" Xanthe breathed. Had Henry found out about Xanthe's fling with Derry Blake? Relief that Henry was not going to marry Xanthe mingled with concern that he could be devastated that she had been so cruel to him.

"I was never marrying Xanthe," Henry moved away from Stella and flung himself down on the settee, chuckling softly.

"What?" Stella frowned, her legs felt as if they could no longer bear her weight. Stella crossed the room unsteadily and sat down beside Henry. "What did you say?"

"I was never going to marry Xanthe," Henry grinned, his lips twisted as if he were barely able to suppress his laughter at Stella's confusion. "I've known Xanthe for years, her father keeps a few horses with me. The first time you saw us together her father had asked me to give her a lift to the Jockey of the Year award ceremony. He didn't want her drinking and driving."

"Oh God," Stella groaned, remembering how upset she had been when she had seen Henry going off with Xanthe.

"October had the idea that if you thought I was with Xanthe it would make you jealous and that you might come back to me." Henry shook his head at the memory.

"But the wedding...... Was that all a joke as well?" Stella could feel angry tears welling at the corners of her eyes, but her mouth twitched with laughter.

"Xanthe really is getting married," Henry said, quietly. "Her fiancée works abroad, he arrived back to Dublin for the wedding a few days ago."

Stella swallowed hard, remembering the pain of thinking that Henry had fallen in love with Xanthe. How devastated she had been when she had thought that they were getting married. October running after her when Stella had left Dublin, shouting, 'wait! Listen!' She must have been going to explain to Stella what was really going on.

"I came all the way here to try to stop you marrying Xanthe," Stella whispered. It was hard to speak.

The relief that he was not going to make the mistake of marrying Xanthe was immense, but over riding that was the pain that she had lost Henry forever because of her own stupidity.

Stella longed to touch Henry, to lay her body against his and feel the warmth of his skin against hers. But that was not possible, she had to go away from him, put her mistakes behind her and to start to rebuild her life.

"I have to go," Stella said in a flat voice, she needed to be away from Henry before she lost the fragile control of her emotions.

Stella walked away from him to one of the huge windows, trailing her fingers over the long silk curtains. She gazed out at the parkland beyond the gardens, the timeless scenery that had seen generations of Henry's ancestors live and die.

"I made such a mess of everything," Stella said, closing her eyes to fight back the tears that threatened to spill down her face. She had hoped for a moment when Henry had touched her that maybe he had still wanted her. Stella had been wrong, he was going to say goodbye to her.

"I hurt you. Amber. Everyone who was important to me." Stella whispered, "I spent my childhood hating my family for what they were. Now I can see how wrong I was. Love has nothing to do with money or possessions." Stella groped her way out of the house, half blinded by the tears that flowed down her cheeks. Teddy trotted obediently beside her, his warm body nudging at her calves as if he wanted to reassure her of his presence.

Stella walked slowly away from Henry's house, wiping her eyes on a crumpled tissue that she found the pocket of her jeans.

It was no use crying, it was all her own fault. Tilting her chin upwards she walked down the long drive and back up the road to her car.

As Stella opened the car door to let Teddy in a movement caught her eye, in the parkland at the front of the house, half hidden from view by the canopy of leaves, a horse was galloping, its rider crouched low in the saddle. Transfixed by the spectacle Stella stood to watch. The horse and rider came closer and then for a moment were lost from view. As she opened the car door to get in the horse and rider reappeared, clattering up the road towards her. Stella slowly closed the car door and moved to the front of the car as Henry vaulted from his horse.

"I don't want you to go," Henry said, gently.

Stella took a stride forwards into his arms, "I don't want to go either," she whispered, raising her face to kiss him.

As they came up for air the horse gave a snort of disgust at being ignored splattering Stella's tee shirt in the froth from his mouth. Stella looked down at her splattered tee shirt the marks spreading slowly as the moisture soaked into the fabric. One of the stains looked distinctly like a love heart.

THE END

.

About Louise Broderick

Louise Broderick was born in Derbyshire, England, but now lives on the west coast of Ireland. She has been involved with horses all of her life as an owner and competitor. While working as the editor of an equestrian magazine Louise published her first book. She has published books in a number of genres, using different pen names, but all feature horses and the people who love them. If you would like to join Louise's VIP Reader Club and be the first to hear about new releases and special VIP book prices please visit www.louisebroderick.com

More books by Louise Broderick
Trainers
Winners

A plea from Louise

Thank you for taking the time to read this book. I hope you enjoyed it, I certainly enjoyed writing it. Each time I sit down to write – and that is every day – I realise just how lucky I am this is my job. I can only keep this job because people like you enjoy my books and buy them. No words can express how grateful I am for that.

If you would like to find out more about my other books please visit my web site.
www.louisebroderick.com

I love to hear from readers so please feel free to contact me on via my Facebook page or email. The details of these are all on my web site.

I hope you enjoyed this book and would like to help me carry on living the dream, writing for a living. If you would like to help please take the time to leave a book review on Amazon. Positive reviews really do help to sell a book, so if you would do that for me you are helping me to continue creating my books and continuing as a full time writer.

Can I just say a huge thank you in advance to anyone who takes the time to do this for me. I know very well how precious time is and am hugely grateful for anyone who cares enough to spend some of their valuable time helping me. Thank you

40295924R00214

Printed in Poland
by Amazon Fulfillment
Poland Sp. z o.o., Wrocław